The Time in Between

The Time in Between

KRISTEN ASHLEY

The characters and events portrayed in this book are fictitious. Any similarity to real persons, living or dead, is coincidental and not intended by the author.

ISBN: 1545505489
ISBN 13: 9781545505489

Discover other titles by Kristen Ashley at:
www.kristenashley.net

Commune with Kristen at:
www.facebook.com/kristenashleybooks
Twitter: KristenAshley68

One

ONCE UPON A TIME

The gate wasn't very welcoming.

To one side it had a sign tacked on it, which declared in neon orange on black, PRIVATE PROPERTY. KEEP OUT!

To the other side the sign declared, ABSOLUTELY NO TRESPASSING!

And down the rickety white fence that led either side of the gate, these signs adorned the peeling painted wood at odd but frequent intervals.

"In the end, Magdalene's last lighthouse keeper was a little crotchety," the real estate agent murmured under his breath, sitting beside me in his Chevy SUV as he drove us through the opened gate.

I looked beyond the gate to the lighthouse in front of us.

Unlike from afar, up close the outbuildings of the lighthouse looked as dilapidated as the fence. Their white paint and black trim flaking and faded, some of the red shingles on the roofs askew or missing altogether.

The lighthouse, on the other hand, was a gleaming white (with glossy black trim) beacon of beauty rising five stories in the air. The top two stories all windows, other interesting windows dotted here and there down its circumference. And to end, there was startling green grass that fed into gray rock cliffs that led to the blue sea and blue sky with tufted clouds acting as the backdrop for its magnificence.

And suddenly, seeing it all that close, I was finally becoming excited about this adventure.

It's a sign, my darling. It couldn't be anything but. You're meant to be in Maine. And when I'm gone, when you write the end to this chapter of your life, that's where your next chapter starts. The one that leads to a happy ending.

That was what Patrick said to me two days before he died.

And one could read from the fact that Patrick died that that particular chapter did not have a happy ending.

Now, when he said it, he'd been significantly drugged up due to the pain caused by the cancer eating away at his body, most specifically his brain. But in weeks where his lucidity wasn't exactly something you could count on, when he'd said that to me, his voice was firm and his eyes were clear.

"It's automated now," the real estate agent said, taking me out of my thoughts.

I looked to him to see we were parked and he was opening his door and lugging his large body out of the car.

I opened my door, following suit, and slammed it, calling, "I'm sorry? What?"

He looked over the hood of the car to me. "The lighthouse. It's automated now."

"Oh," I mumbled, the breeze blowing my hair and my scarf all around, plastering my jacket to me, taking my barely there word and wisping it away on the wind.

"Was automated in 1992," he shared. "That's when the old owner started to get crotchety. Tending a lighthouse wasn't the easiest thing on the planet to do. But when it was automated, it was just about keeping it maintained and making sure the generators were fueled in case the power went out. After years of having something to do, something important, all of a sudden he didn't have that. Because of what happened to him, I tell my wife, I don't care if I'm organizing kitchen cupboards. Give me something to do every day until the day I die."

He delivered this wisdom and then started trudging up to the gleaming black painted wood door at the side of the house.

It had a fabulous, old, black gooseneck light over the door.

Heck, even if the place wasn't *absolutely glorious*, which it was, I'd buy the damned thing because of that light.

"So that said," the agent went on as he inserted a skeleton key (yes, *a skeleton key*) into the keyhole in the door, "you decide to take that on, it's not tough." He turned his attention to me before he opened the door. "It's taking on other stuff, in all honesty, not that you won't get the gist of it the second you walk in, that might be iffy."

He then opened the door and it was like he didn't. The gloom from inside slithered out and it was so intense, I actually leaned away from it.

He walked inside, the shadows completely engulfing him within seconds.

With no other choice, I followed him.

Gloomy it was.

And dirty.

And dank.

In fact it was dark, musty and smelled like wet brick and rot.

"Old guy died years ago," the real estate agent said as he moved through the murk. "All his kids had taken off years ago too. They lived with his wife anyway after the divorce. This is no place to raise a family. She knew that. He wouldn't leave it."

He made a motion, and I blinked as sunlight made a valiant effort to pour through a bank of grimy windows that followed half the curve of the lighthouse when he shoved aside what seemed like a long vinyl curtain. A curtain which totally disintegrated at his touch, falling with a *whoosh* and a poof of dust to the countertop underneath it.

"Whoops," he mumbled.

When I could focus again, first I saw an unadulterated (except for the filth) view of the sea that, even through filth, took my breath away.

Second I saw the agent's eyes resting speculatively on me.

As my family situation was none of his business, I said nothing to him in response to his unspoken query.

"Anyway," he continued, catching my hint of silence. "None of them wanted the place. But he'd let it go so bad," he swung an arm out, "no one else wanted it either. It's been on the market for nine years. There's also been a referendum for the town to buy it every year since he died, but the cost and upkeep, they couldn't absorb. Now the family's dumped the price so low it's almost criminal, what with two acres of coastal property coming with it. But there's a rider on the deed, considering this is a historic site. Current buildings can be renovated at the owner's discretion if they retain the look they already have on the outside, but nothing else can be built and the lighthouse must remain."

"So automation is very automated, considering no one has lived here for that long," I noted.

He shook his head. "We've had volunteer keepers since then. Not that they have to do much, but the old girl needs to keep lighting so it's gotta be looked after. In fact, it was getting so bad, the town paid for it to be repainted a couple of years ago. Other than that, as you can see…"

He didn't finish that but did since he swung his arm out again to indicate the mess of the large, circular room we were in.

I took in the mess of the large, circular room we were in and at first saw nothing but the mess—decaying furniture, a soot-covered stone fireplace, a kitchen that might have been put in in the forties but had not only not been touched the last nine years, it perhaps had not been touched the last nineteen (or more).

Then I saw more.

The extraordinarily carved railing to the sweeping wood staircase that ran the curved side of the house. The red brick walls. The plank wood floors.

"Once upon a time, long ago," the realtor was suddenly talking wistfully, "someone loved this place. Put that love into building it. Put that love into keeping it. Nine years and more when no one really gave a whit, and still you can see it once had a lot of love."

Oh yes.

You could see that.

"It's got a basement, more like a big crawl space," the agent declared, surprising me with his quick change in tone back to businesslike and informative. "The furnace is down there. You can get down there through a door in the floor. The furnace was put in a while back, and full disclosure, though an inspection will catch it, it probably needs to be replaced."

Through his words I stared at the fireplace, which scoured would be magnificent, and I noticed it didn't have a chimney as such, but the smoke probably went out a vent in the wall.

"This floor has a powder room under the stairs," the realtor kept on. "You can look at it if you want, but if you wanna save yourself that, I'll just tell you straight, it needs to be gutted."

I decided to take his word for it and told him that.

He looked relieved when I did before he stated, "Place has a garage, two car. Not in good condition, but think you saw that. Still, it's close to the house and there's a covered walkway to that door over there." He pointed at a door that was across from the door we'd walked in. "Means you might feel a chill but you won't get wet, unless it's raining sideways, which happens."

With a breeze that plastered my jacket to me on a sunny, early spring day, I did not doubt that.

"Garage has a loft space above it, which could be renovated as a studio rental if you've a mind to do that sort of thing. As for the property itself, it also has a building where the generators are stowed," the realtor carried on. "Hook up for a washer and dryer and good space in there. Lots of it for storage. Which is good because there's not a lot of storage in here for tools and Christmas decorations and whatnot."

I glanced around seeing he was right. There wasn't even enough cabinetry to house the things a decent cook would need in her kitchen. Though there was room for them. In fact, if you fought back the gloom, there was quite a bit of room.

"And there's a place outside, could call it a studio, could call it a mother-in-law house," he shared. "Whatever, it's got goodly space, two bedrooms, big kitchen. Could be renovated to be a guest house. Or like I said, a studio if you're artsy. Or you could rent it out like a B and B. I'll show you all of that after we have a look at the lighthouse."

"Thanks," I replied.

"Now, since I mentioned full disclosure, you have to know it all," the realtor continued.

Slowly, my eyes went to him.

When they did, he launched in. "Like I said, it's automated. And like I said, you won't really have to concern yourself with the functionality of that unless the electricity goes out, but then the generators automatically kick in. There are two. But you'll need to keep fuel on hand to keep them going in case a blackout lasts awhile. And just to say, this is coastal Maine. We get weather. Blackouts can last awhile."

When I nodded to share I took that in, he kept going.

"And if you're, say, away on vacation, you need to make sure someone is playing backup in such a case."

"Okay," I replied when he stopped talking, thinking this probably wasn't a good thing since I knew no one in Maine (or not anyone who wanted to know me) and thus couldn't call on anyone to do something like that.

I also didn't hold high hopes I'd make friends and win people. I hadn't had a lot of success in that in my life.

And last, although Patrick believed it completely, I held no hope that the reason I was out there was going to come to fruition.

That being me having a happy ending.

That being what Patrick thought would *be* my happy ending.

Which might mean I'd have someone, a certain someone, or actually two (at least), even though I knew I never would.

However, if I bought that place and wanted to go back to Denver to visit the family, I could pay someone to look after it.

The realtor nodded, unaware of my bleak thoughts, and went on, "Some folks don't put two and two together, but just to say, there's a big honkin' light on top of this building that flashes in a circle at night or during fog, going around every fifteen seconds. You'll need blackout blinds everywhere if you're like practically every other soul on this earth and will have trouble sleeping with a bright light flashing through the windows every fifteen seconds."

"Blackout blinds probably aren't hard to come by," I guessed, and they probably could be made to look nice, or at least I hoped.

"Probably not," he agreed. "But anyone who wants to live here and not go insane or end up a crotchety old curmudgeon with a bad attitude, and that may seem like I'm laying it on thick, but it's all warranted with our old keeper, they'll want to put in all new windows. This brick is solid. Nothing coming through."

He jerked his head toward a wall. "But if the foghorn needs to blow, it's gonna *blow*. So soundproof windows or sound-lock panels you can put in when you wanna drown out the noise will be the way to go to get some peace."

"That probably won't be hard either," I noted.

"It won't be, but they'll need to be custom so it won't be cheap."

I nodded.

Price was not an issue.

Thanks to Patrick, I had all the money in the world.

"Then there's the tourists," he told me. "Reason those signs are out there isn't only because the old guy was crotchety, it was because people think lighthouses are public places. They show and knock on the door wanting a tour, wanting to walk around, taking pictures. Doesn't help matters the coastal path is public land, but this lighthouse stands on private land. Walkers and bikers are supposed to go around the fence, but sometimes they aren't big on doing that. So you'll either need to be real patient, real friendly or you'll need to build a decent fence. My guess, though, is you're still gonna have to put up with some of the more persistent ones."

Now that…

That was going to be an issue.

People weren't my favorite things.

In fact, the last seventeen years of my life, I'd had precisely fourteen people (not all fourteen all seventeen years, and now one of them was dead so I only had thirteen) that I actually liked and wanted to spend time with.

The rest, I tolerated.

No.

That wasn't right.

The rest tolerated *me*.

"Your land, your fence," the agent stated. "That said, this is a historic site so if you're thinking of getting this place and then building a ten-foot wall around it topped with razor wire, the town council is gonna balk. They're a good bunch of folks with the best interests of Magdalene and its citizens in mind, so if you do something that will help you to have privacy but isn't unsightly, they won't have an issue."

"Do I have to get approval for any plans I might have from them?" I asked.

He shook his head. "Not if it isn't outlandish. Rider is relatively specific about a lot of stuff and mostly it's to keep this place in keeping with the seascape, the coast, the town and its history. So if you buy the old girl, you'll be legally bound by that rider to keep her within that purview. You build something outside of that scope, they'll be within their rights to demand you tear it down and build something else. You stay inside that scope, you'll be good."

I nodded but remarked, "That seems rather loose for a historical site."

"Like I said, town council is a good bunch of folks and they have been for a good while," he shared, walking toward me. He stopped within three feet. "But they're also pretty dogged about keeping Magdalene, Magdalene. Recently, the land west and south of this lighthouse was rezoned and is now unincorporated. But the coastal path leading up to it and the lighthouse remain under the town of Magdalene's purview. This is because the town mostly exists on tourist trade and the lighthouse is an attraction. So if you push them, they'll not hesitate to push back."

I was surprised about that land being rezoned and wondered distractedly why that had come about. Everything for quite some distance around the lighthouse was undeveloped, making the lighthouse an undisturbed beacon not only from sea, but from every direction by land.

However, I was not surprised Magdalene existed on tourist trade. I'd found the day before when I'd arrived that it was huge, coastal postcard from the minute you saw the town limit sign (which could be on a postcard itself, it was so pretty) all the way down it's meticulously preserved main street that traversed Magdalene Cove (containing wharf). Even the businesses and homes that dotted the sloping swell of land beyond fit the aesthetic.

"Wanna see the rest?" the realtor asked.

"Please," I answered.

He led the way and I followed him up the spiraling, wood stairs that didn't look rickety in the slightest.

Yes, this place had been built out of love.

We hit the second floor, which was one big room with one somewhat big window, another smaller fireplace and that was it. There was nothing else. Not a powder room. Nothing. Though there was an old, steel desk that whoever owned it surely bought it not actually wanting it.

Up we went to the third story and that was where things got interesting.

It was cut in half. There were two windows in what could only be the bedroom area (if the decaying mattresses and headboard where anything to go by), but these windows were half windows in a strange shape that looked like a shell and oddly set in the floor. Another window just like that in a dire bathroom that was rather small, no walk-in closet, no large bath big enough for two set in a platform. But the half circle space could be made pretty, and useful, should someone have the imagination to do it.

The bedroom part also had another, even smaller fireplace that, even in the current state of wreck of that room, was quaint.

After that, we walked up to the fourth floor.

And the instant I cleared it, I stopped dead.

Windows the entire circumference gave a panoramic view so stunning, it seemed like a miracle. Sea, cliffs, green forest and the picture-perfection of Magdalene were available to view unencumbered, and I knew that because I'd sorted myself enough to make a slow turn.

"This always gets 'em," the realtor murmured. "Can forget the mess downstairs the second you see this. Problem is, you gotta walk back downstairs to get out."

I didn't care about the other three stories.

I didn't care that I knew down to my soul Patrick was wrong, this was a fool's errand, coming out here to repair relationships that were irreparable, and live out the rest of my book of life.

There was one thing that room, that view, proved Patrick right about.

I was meant to be in Maine.

I was meant to be right there.

If I was meant to have no beauty in my life but the love of Patrick and his family, I was still meant to have this.

Because Patrick could give it to me.

And I knew in that second he was smiling down at me, happy as a danged clam and smug as heck, knowing he was right.

"The studio has a veranda so you got outside space if you're that kinda person who likes hanging outside," the agent carried on. "But I figure this is all the outside space anyone would need. Tell you, more than one showing, I thought it'd be worth the headache to put this place to rights just to have my morning cup of coffee sitting right up here and I wouldn't care I gotta climb three sets of stairs to get here."

He was not wrong about that.

And just then, I decided to have coffee up there every morning for the rest of my life.

"Whenever that notion overwhelms me, my wife disabuses me of it," he said.

I couldn't imagine.

She must never have been up there.

"'Cross the way, that's Lavender House," he stated.

I looked "'cross the way" as he was indicating, this being across the sun twinkling off the gentle waves rolling into the cove, to see a beautiful, rambling old home set back off a cliff. It was not nearly as magnificent as the lighthouse, but then again, I was standing where I was standing, so I'd think that.

"Almost as old as this place and just as pretty in its own way," the realtor declared. "That's private property too and always has been, like the lighthouse. And beyond that, that house you see that looks like it's floating on the cliff, that's Cliff Blue."

I trained my eyes where he instructed and saw a breathtaking home the likes I'd never seen before. It was the modern yin to Lavender House's yang, but even modern, it seemed somehow to fit perfectly where it was, like it had always been there.

"Prentice Cameron built that," the agent said. "And if you don't know who he is, Google him. Town council is choosy about what new plans they'll approve to be built on coastal land. Think they all drowned in their own drool when Cameron came in to design and build that. It's modern but pretty as a picture. Perfect."

After saying that, he turned from his perusal of the landscape to me with an expression on his face that captured my attention, all of it, as he continued speaking.

"And I'll just say, even in the state this is in, doing it with pride, this triumvirate of properties is what Magdalene is second most proud of, outside keeping the town as it should be. But they're all private properties and the folks in town, they're just as protective of them and their inhabitants as the owners, I figure. So, since this is open space and easily visible, not couched in trees like Lavender House, or in a private neighborhood like Cliff Blue, you might have your lookie-loos. But if anyone asks a citizen of Magdalene, all of us will do what we can to maintain your privacy."

"That's good to know," I said softly.

He looked me up and down, turned his gaze through the expanse then gave his serious expression back to me.

"Been doing this job a long time. I can see when a buyer is interested and I can see when they're interested in something that they know is gonna be a heck of a project, but that doesn't matter to them because they've fallen in love. And I see that last is happening with you. So I gave you full disclosure, now I'll give you full honesty."

"That would…" I hesitated because I wasn't sure my last wasn't a lie, "be appreciated."

He didn't hesitate.

"See, this is a lot of work and you got it in you to restore it, great. But there are buildings, land. Take an entire day even with a riding mower, probably, just to mow the lawn. And the townsfolk'd lose their minds, you mow over the tulips that coat the place come full-on spring. No one knows how those tulips got here, but Google 'Magdalene Lighthouse' and that's pretty much all the pictures you'll see."

God, I couldn't wait to see that and I was going to Google it the minute I got back to the inn.

"But you're a slip of a thing, apparently on your own, and this is gonna be a lot for you."

He lifted his hand and shook it at me even as he shook his head and kept speaking.

"I'm not being sexist. Like I said, I'm being honest. But more, it seems close to town, and it is, *ish*, you go the direct coastal path into town, which is just over two miles of walking. But by the roads, since it goes inland then eastward, it's over five miles to get out here and there isn't anything built within the first two, primarily because of that light and the horn I told you about. But also because Magdalene likes this view unencumbered, so a lot of that is parkland so it'd stay just that way. That means this is a lot more secluded than it looks from town."

This was not a deterrent.

This could be, in future, if things went awry (and they were probably going to go awry), a boon.

I'd need to be secluded, separate, *reclusive.*

But regardless, I was one of those people who could be good on my own. I hadn't had a lot of that in recent years, what with Patrick and his family, but when I had it, I could enjoy it.

And if I had this lighthouse all to myself, I had a feeling I could learn to love it.

"So, just to say, you should consider all that when you consider buying this," he advised. "But I'll also say I know you're from Denver. And I know New Englanders are considered unfriendly by folks out west. We're not. We're just different. We like what we know and *who* we know. We depend on tourists but, being honest, they can sometimes be a pain in the backside. But you move here, you'll be one of us. Simple as that. And to prove that's true, if you don't have someone who's coming here with you to help you take this on, then I'll be the first to share I'm happy to look after the old girl when you're away. You just call on me. And if I can't, I'll help you find someone who can. We in Magdalene been looking out for this lighthouse for years. But if she comes with you, we'll look out for you too."

I stood there, immobile, and stared at him.

And I did this suddenly needing to cry.

He didn't know me. He didn't know my past. He didn't know how stupid I'd been.

So unbelievably stupid.

He didn't know.

So he couldn't judge.

Maybe this *could* be a new chapter.

Maybe Patrick knew exactly what he was doing in a variety of ways.

I fought back the tears as he concluded, "And that's not a gambit to get you to buy. You can't know I'm telling you the truth until you put me to the test. But just to say, feel free to do that. You'll learn soon enough."

I tore my eyes from him and blinked at the landscape, taking in a deep breath through my nose, recalling his name.

Robert.

Robert Colley.

"You wanna see the outbuildings now or you wanna go up and look at the lens?" he asked.

I wanted to look at the lens.

Then I wanted to go look at the outbuildings.

But I didn't say either.

I looked again to him.

"I'll be needing the name of a good contractor."

His eyes lit as he studied me and one side of his lips quirked.

"You'll need to be looking at the outbuildings, gal," he advised gently.

"Yes, you're right," I told him. "But I'll also be needing the name of a good contractor."

He continued to study me and he did this until I smiled at him.

And when I did, the half lip quirk disappeared and Robert Colley smiled back.

Two

GOALS

Eighteen years earlier…

I saw him the minute he walked into the backyard.

He caught my eye because he was seriously good-looking.

But I kept watching, not only because of that, but because I liked the way he walked and I couldn't say why.

He was tall, kinda big but not huge, though the way he moved was lumbering. Like he was at a crowded party or club or concert and he was shouldering through the bodies to make his way to where he was going, even though he wasn't.

It was cool and it was strangely hot, like no one could get in his way no matter what way he was making.

And it communicated he was going to get there and nothing was going to stop him.

But where he was going right then was to Maria's boyfriend, my good friend, Lonnie.

Maria and Lonnie had been dating since high school and she and I had been best friends since grade school, so we'd been a pack for a long time.

Partners in crime, mostly.

We'd been pretty much inseparable since meeting, that was before Lonnie…and recently. And that attachment was because, for Maria, her mom and dad didn't give a crap, they were so busy fighting each other, they had no time for her.

For me, it was because my parents gave too much of a crap and had *a lot* of time to tell me what they thought of me, even though what they thought wasn't much.

I liked the idea that tall, dark-haired guy with his cool way of moving was a friend of Lonnie's.

That meant I might get an introduction.

I watched from where I sat in my folding lawn chair as Lonnie greeted him with an arm slap from one hand, a shake with the other and a huge smile, indicating he was happy to see him.

That was good.

Lonnie liked him.

Lonnie liked and was liked by just about everyone. This was because he was a great guy, up for anything, there when you needed him.

But the arm slap, hand shake and smile said he liked this guy more than most.

So I watched, thinking it was kinda weird that the guy somewhat smiled in return, but in a way it wasn't exactly a smile, and shook back.

But there was definitely something not right in that smile.

Lonnie was happy to see him.

This guy, however…

"Total drool-worthy," Maria muttered as she threw herself in a lawn chair next to mine, spilling some of the beer in her not-quite-as-full-now plastic cup.

It wasn't easy, but I pulled my gaze from the guy knowing exactly what she was talking about even before I saw her attention trained on her guy and *that guy*.

She'd never say it around Lonnie. Hell, around Lonnie she took pains not to give any indication she knew the other sex existed outside Lonnie (and she'd learned to do this in an extreme way), but around me, she'd look.

Not touch. Not talk, unless it was approved by Lonnie.

But look.

"Do you know him?" I asked.

"Yup," she answered, moving her eyes from the guy, I knew just in case Lonnie looked over and caught her staring, even if it was in his direction too, he'd know.

And he wouldn't like what he knew.

"Came over the other day. Name's Tony. He's buds with Lars," she told me.

That sent a shiver trilling up my back.

Lonnie had introduced us to Lars a few months ago.

I didn't like Lars.

Lars gave me the creeps.

I looked back at the guy with Lonnie thinking it was disappointing that he was buds with Lars.

"Girl, you need a refill," Maria told me, and I looked away from him, not only thinking it was disappointing Tony was buds with Lars, but the fact this was more disappointing because I even liked the way he stood.

He was paying attention, and a lot of it, to whatever Lonnie was saying. His intensity, the alert way he carried himself was awesome.

Crazy awesome.

But maybe understandable since he was friends with Lars, and I was suspecting Lars wasn't that good of a guy and the people he knew had to be alert for a variety of reasons.

I saw my plastic cup was mostly the dregs, backwash of beer not being my favorite thing.

Still.

"I drove here," I told Maria.

"So?" she asked.

I lifted my gaze to her but then turned it almost immediately away.

I loved her. *Loved her.* She was fun and she was funny. She was loyal as all hell. She was crazy and wild and I felt free around her. Free to be who I was (not who my parents expected me to be). Free to act how I wanted (not how my parents demanded I act). Free to do whatever I damn well wanted to do (which was not what my parents wanted me to do).

We'd had a lot of good times. She'd taken my back in a lot of bad times.

But sometimes, little things like that, like her thinking it was totally okay to get a buzz on then drive yourself home, bugged me.

She'd do it without blinking.

Lonnie'd do it, and he'd be high too and not give a crap.

But I kinda wanted to get home in one piece and not take anyone out along the way.

Maria had a way with peer pressure though, even if we were now twenty-three, so I knew how to play the game.

That was get up, get a beer and then sip at it or ignore it altogether, "spill" some in the grass, nurse it for an hour, and that way do my own thing without having to put up with her pushing.

Which meant I hefted myself out of the chair to head to the keg.

"Grab a coupla Jell-O shots while you're at it," she called as I moved away.

The real reason she wanted me to go get a beer.

But shit.

Jell-O shots were harder to put off.

My only choice was to take half an hour (at least) to get back to her. Another skill I'd honed in over a decade of friendship with Maria.

I hit the keg, poured out the dregs of my cup in the grass beside it and grabbed the nozzle.

I was just finishing pumping some into my cup when I heard a deep voice say, "I'll take that after you."

I raised my eyes and looked into hazel ones that, since the second my eyes hit his I arrested, I realized were more of a light brown with some green to make them so interesting, I couldn't move or speak.

"Hey," he said.

I stared.

"*Hey,*" he said more urgently and leaned into me.

When he did, it felt like a spasm hit my body, originating somewhere very private and snaking up my spine, the back of my neck and all over my scalp.

I felt his fingers brush mine, vaguely felt the spigot pulled away and heard him murmur, "Wastin' beer."

I jerked my head down, saw my over-full cup, beer having flooded over my fingers that I didn't even feel, then I jerked my head up to see him examining me.

He didn't do it long before he turned to the table next to the keg that had a variety of detritus—spent cups, spent bottles, spent cans, an overflowing ashtray, a huge red bong—and he nabbed a cup from an upside down stack of fresh ones.

I didn't have it in me to say anything before my beer sloshed all over my fingers again. This time because, all of a sudden, Lonnie had an arm tight around my neck and he was yanking me forcefully into his body, back (mine) to front (his).

"See you met my girl," he declared.

I wanted to scream.

I hated when Lonnie did this. It totally meant I never got asked out.

But this time?

I *hated* it.

"Or, my *other* girl," Lonnie clarified as the guy named Tony gave us his attention.

One of his brows went up in a way that was a shade too fascinating.

Then he asked, "You a threesome?" And I suddenly found nothing fascinating and further could think of nothing but the flames that I felt hit my cheeks.

Tony looked at them, and the instant he did, miraculously I wasn't thinking about the fact I had to be very obviously blushing and how completely embarrassing that was.

This was because his expression changed. In a there-and-gone I nevertheless caught, there was a hint of surprise and a definite softening of his features that was so beautiful, words had not been invented to describe its beauty.

"I wish, Cady's a prude," Lonnie shared jovially.

In a contradiction that I no longer found surprising, although Lonnie went ballistic if Maria even looked at another guy, Lonnie openly flirted… with me.

Only me.

It was a friends thing, teasing and sometimes sweet.

But even if I was used to it, I thought it was weird.

And I wasn't a prude. It was just, if Lonnie was around, he made it impossible for me to find any action.

"Right," Tony muttered, losing interest in us and turning his attention to the tap in order to pour himself his beer.

I pushed off Lonnie, this effort making more beer slosh on my hand (which was good, less of it I'd have to pretend to drink), and turned to him.

"Your *real* woman wants a Jell-O shot," I informed him.

"The bitch's got legs, she can get herself one."

This was not my favorite side of Lonnie, how he could be around other dudes. He was sweet as pie when it was just Maria (she told me, but I believed her because he was that way to her, and me, a lot of the time when I was around).

It was just when he had to be *a man*, this being when he thought there was someone who might size him up (and *this* being another man).

Like being sweet to your girlfriend made your dick shrink.

"Probably get yourself some if you got her one," I stated, mostly in an effort to make it known to someone who was within hearing distance that I was not a prude.

Lonnie grinned at me and it reminded me why Maria put up with him.

He wasn't as handsome and cool as this new guy, but he was all kinds of cute with his messy brown hair and sparkling blue eyes.

"I'll get myself some even if I don't get her one," he retorted.

He was probably right. I spent a lot of time with them, got toasted at their place, passed out on their couch so I wouldn't have to drive home. I'd heard it.

Often.

"Whatever," I said to him and his grin got bigger. I turned from him back toward Tony to see he'd filled his beer because he was lifting it to very fine looking lips and taking a sip as he gazed off in a different direction. "I'm Cady," I announced boldly.

Just his eyes slid to me, and I felt another spasm because that was cool and hot.

He took his sip, swallowed it and lowered his beer. "Tony."

I shot him a smile. "Nice to meet you."

He looked to my mouth and another expression chased across his face before he blanked it.

And I liked that one too.

"Best be gettin' Maria that shot," Lonnie chimed in.

"*I* don't want her to sleep with *me* when I get home," I quipped at the same time I tried to make a point.

Lonnie looked to Tony. "I wish on that too. Totally watch that. Sell tickets."

I felt the heat flame in my cheeks again, and in front of this guy, this tall, dark stranger with beautiful eyes and a way about him that was interesting and crazy appealing, I was fed up with Lonnie's shit.

"Don't be a dick," I snapped.

This was not a good move.

Lonnie's good nature flew out the window as he narrowed angry eyes at me and asked in a soft, disturbing voice, "What did you just say?"

I had a choice to make and had to make a split second decision.

Rub up against Lonnie in a not-good way and face consequences that could range from relatively benign (a freeze out or a verbal setting down) to him screaming his head off and even lunging, but only to give the thrill of danger.

He'd never hurt me physically, but he didn't mind threatening it.

My other choice was to have a backbone, just to have one for once with the added incentive of saving face in front of the gorgeous Tony.

I might never see Tony again (which would suck but I'd never seen him before, and even if evidence was suggesting he was part of the crew Lonnie was guiding us to, not seeing him again was still a possibility).

I practically lived with Lonnie and Maria (because my pad was crap and I hated being there, but I loved being with them…or I used to, this was sadly and weirdly fading).

Before I could make the decision that would make me look like a weak loser in front of Tony, Tony waded in.

"She said don't be a dick. And I'll add to that, *don't be a fuckin' dick*."

Lonnie's gaze flew to Tony.

Even if I felt a weird warmth steal over me that Tony had taken my back, I took a mini-step away.

Then I watched with a goodly amount of interest as Lonnie sent Tony a scowl that lasted all of half a second before he backed down.

God.

I couldn't believe it.

Lonnie was scared of this guy.

Though, I could see why.

He was a couple of inches taller, and although Lonnie was relatively built, he was on the lean side. This guy wasn't a powerhouse, but there didn't appear to be an ounce of fat on him, his shoulders were broad, his forearms brawny and veined, and his thighs were thick.

But in that moment when it came to my attention, it came speeding to my attention that it was more.

This was not a guy you messed with. He said that with his gait. He said it with the alert manner he held his body. He said it with the intensity of his gaze.

In a faceoff with him, you backed down or he'd mess you up.

He didn't need to act like a man in front of a man.

He was just *a man*.

And now I had to make another decision and this decision was how I was going to help my friend save face in this tense situation.

I did this by declaring, "Anyway, Maria's not my type seeing as she doesn't have a penis."

Lonnie looked to me and Tony looked to his boots.

Lonnie's attention went back to Tony and I felt him relax at the same time I noticed Tony was grinning at his boots.

It wasn't even aimed at me, and since this grin appeared genuine, it was still one of the most amazing things I'd ever seen.

"Now I'm going to move away from the testosterone before I start growing a beard," I announced, and immediately, even though it took me from Tony's sphere, I did just that.

I did it walking away from them, away from Maria and into the house.

I could pretend I needed to use the john and take that time to get my head together (and pour out a little more of my beer, not to mention, have an excuse for "forgetting" the Jell-O shots).

When I got to the bathroom, I used it because I was there (and wished I didn't have to because our new "friends" who lived at this house weren't fond of cleaning).

I then walked to the sink to wash my hands and pour out some beer.

While there, I looked in the mirror.

Auburn hair my mom gave me.

Freckles on my nose.

Green eyes I got from my grandmother, Dad's mom.

The hair was thick and could be unruly, but since I'd spent hours and hours over years and years learning how to tame it, I thought it was pretty awesome.

The freckles across my nose, although not prominent and fading the older I got, kinda stunk.

I wasn't short, as such, though I hit a shade under average height. And I'd always been curvy.

I could actually take or leave anything (except the hair, I'd miss my hair).

But I'd fall to my knees in gratitude in front of God for giving me my eyes.

They weren't a hazy green, a yellow green, a brownish green, a bluish green.

They were *green.*

A shock of emerald so pure, they were like jewels in my face (ringed, I'll admit, with a thin line of smoky blue but that only served to make the green stand out more).

I loved my eyes. I'd spent hours of my life praying to God that, if He let me give my eyes to my children, I'd be a good girl until the day I died (I often went back on this but did it knowing God was forgiving and I was never *that* bad).

But looking at my eyes in that mirror in that house with that man outside, I thought, just one of my kids, I'd let them have Tony's eyes if he was the man who helped me make that kid.

And truthfully, it wouldn't suck if we had a passel of kids and they all got Tony's eyes.

It was then I was freaking out in realizing I was totally falling in love with a guy I totally didn't know named Tony, who was a friend of Lars.

"Time to go home," I told my reflection.

I poured out the rest of the beer, threw the cup toward the bathroom bin without remorse, seeing as it was overflowing in a way that it'd clearly been doing that before the party, and I walked out.

I was heading down the hall toward the kitchen to go out back, thinking of excuses I could make to Maria that I had to leave, when Tony filled the mouth of the hall in front of me.

It wasn't a wide hall, and even if he wasn't a huge guy it was going to be a tight squeeze, so I stopped and stepped to the side, putting my back to the wall.

I skidded my eyes through him, suddenly shy, what with being alone with him in a hall, and I muttered, "Hey."

He kept coming at me but stopped too, still filling the hall, and he replied, "Hey."

When his shoulder (which was what I was focusing on) didn't move, I raised my eyes to his and shared, "Bathroom's free."

"Cool," he stated but still didn't move, and this would be explained when he asked, "You okay?"

This question was unexpected, so I answered, "Yeah. Why?"

"Lonnie's an open book, one that explodes, and what it spewed out just now spewed all over you."

I stared up at him, speechless, mostly because I didn't know what he was talking about.

I found my voice and said, "Sorry?"

"He's got a thing for you. Big. Figure he's into his girl and that's why he doesn't wanna hurt her, makin' a move on you to be his side piece or movin' from her to take on you. Still, even though he can't do shit about it, doesn't mean he wants anyone gettin' in there, and he makes that clear. It's gotta suck for you."

I could not believe what he was saying.

"Lonnie doesn't have a thing for me."

His attention was to me but I could feel it increase after I said those words.

"Right," he eventually grunted. "'Kay. Don't know the guy well. Maybe reading it wrong." He moved to pass, muttering, "Later."

But I caught his forearm.

He stopped and looked down at me.

"Do you…? Is that why he's always…?" I gave my head a little shake and then whispered, my gaze turning dazed. "Holy crap. Lonnie's got a thing for me."

"Probably shouldn't have pointed it out," he remarked, and I focused on him again.

"No. No. Absolutely no. You definitely should have pointed it out."

I let him go and lifted that hand to pull my hair away from my face, noting but freaking out so bad, not letting it filter through how his eyes watched my hand move.

And then my hair when my hand dropped.

"Now what do I do?" I hissed, wanting to be quiet but I did it loudly.

He turned fully toward me and took a step into me, something I absolutely let filter through me because I felt my eyes get wide and my heart start to race when he did it because that put him *close.*

"You're not into him. You don't give off any vibe except that he's your guy in the sense that he's your friend. He keeps getting that vibe, he'll get his shit together eventually."

I leaned in and up and whispered, weirded out, so it was also loud, "I've known him since high school."

He grinned.

I fell into it like it was the desired destination it absolutely was.

He then spoke.

"And how long's that been? What, you graduate last year?"

Ouch.

That stung.

I either looked young or acted it and neither was good when you were twenty-three, on your own, making your way in the world.

Sure, I was doing it poorly.

But I had a plan.

I didn't know how old he was but I did know he gave off the vibe of being older than Lonnie, who was twenty-five.

I'd put Tony at twenty-six, low end, thirty, high.

Which, at twenty-three, was the same as if I was fifteen and he was eighteen. Or I was seventeen and he was twenty.

In other words, it was miles apart.

I was still mostly a kid no matter that I was making my way (albeit poorly).

And he was past that.

When you hit the twenty-five zone, that was when you hit the adult zone and the age gap could be whatever it was.

But now, to him, I was still just a kid.

I rocked back to my heels and again looked at his shoulder. "No, like, five years ago."

"A whole five?"

It sounded like a tease so I chanced looking at him to see it absolutely was a tease if the twinkle in his eye was anything to go by.

That looked good on him. It was awesome.

I was still nursing the sting.

"I'm gonna work in retail," I told him, and his head jerked a bit with surprise at my change in subject. This did not deter me and I carried on, "I'm gonna work my way up to buyer."

"That's cool," he said slowly. "What are you doin' now?"

"I work at Sip and Save."

I said it proudly, because it was a job. I was gainfully employed. I had been (for once at the same place) for some time. I didn't show late. I didn't call off. I did my job as boring and menial as it was like it meant what it meant—rent paid and food on the table, both important.

But even so, I watched his eyes close down.

That was how my parents reacted to me working at a convenience store.

"The manager totally bailed last week so the assistant manager is gonna get promoted then I'm gonna get promoted to assistant manager and I've been there eight months. That's job loyalty. I stay awhile, get managerial experience, I can get a job at the mall and start my plan in action."

"It's good to have goals."

It wasn't said dismissively.

But I still thought it was dismissive.

"My second choice was being the president but politicians always wear red and I look crap in red," I shot back, preparing to slide away from him and give him a "later."

"Cady," he called, halting me before I even began, and I looked up at him again. "I was being serious. It *is* good to have goals."

I wanted to know what his goals were, being in this house, drinking beer from that keg, being someone Lonnie was excited to see, knowing Lars.

I didn't ask.

I said, "I need to get going."

And I did. Away from him and his association with Lars. Away from Lonnie and what Tony had told me about him. Away from Maria pressuring me to get shitfaced so I'd have no choice but to find someplace in that filthy house to pass out and sober up.

Away from all of this that was proving my parents right.

That Lonnie and Maria weren't the awesome-cool friends I thought they were, not anymore. That with this entry into a world that creeped me out at best, scared me at worst, Lonnie's goals were highly suspect and Maria *had* no goals except finding whatever good time or adventure and going gung ho into it.

It had all been fun and games when there wasn't rent to be paid and food to put on a table and that had been a blast.

But eventually, everyone had to grow up.

Even Lonnie and Maria.

And me.

So I didn't need to get caught up with a guy like Tony (not that he wanted me).

I needed to prove my parents wrong.

So I worked at a convenience store and lived in a crappy-ass studio apartment where I practically slept in the shower, it was so little (so little it didn't even have a tub)

It was mine. I worked to pay the rent. I volunteered for overtime whenever it was available (which was a lot) in order to have a little extra to sock away to get a nicer place, a nicer car, nicer things.

I had a plan.

I had *goals*.

And a guy like Tony would probably derail those goals, because I knew just looking into those eyes in that face on that body that I'd forget my determination to prove my parents wrong, and I'd slide even deeper into the denial I was living in with Maria and Lonnie just to stay tied to him.

It wasn't because he was hot.

It wasn't because I liked the way he moved and he was a guy you didn't mess with.

It was because, when I called Lonnie a dick, he'd backed that play.

I didn't see a lot of that with guys and chicks of my acquaintance.

And it was crazy awesome.

"Probably a good idea. The Jell-O shots started getting passed around while you were gone so I'm thinkin' it'll be about fifteen minutes before that backyard isn't a place a girl like you'd want to be."

I took a mental step away from common sense and self-awareness and slid closer to denial at knowing he thought I was a girl like that.

But I'd said I had to go and he was there probably to hit the bathroom, so I'd look like a moron if I didn't make a move.

"Right then, perfect timing," I replied.

"Yeah," he agreed.

"See you around?" I asked, pleased with myself that it sounded curious rather than hopeful.

"Not sure," he answered, making me even more hopeful than it was healthy to be and only because that "not sure" I decided to read as him not being sure he was part of this crew. "Maybe."

"Oh," I mumbled.

"Oh." He grinned then ordered, "Go, Cady. Get home safe. You good to drive?"

I was and for the first time that night wished I wasn't.

But I *totally* loved that he asked that.

I nodded.

"Good. 'Kay. Later," he said, turning from me, lifting a hand not very high at his side in a careless wave, and he trudged down the empty hall like he was clearing it for a celebrity.

"Later," I called to his back.

He turned the corner and disappeared without glancing back at me.

And suddenly I said a new prayer to God with a promise of being a good girl until I died (and this one I might keep).

That just seeing Tony disappear did not mean Tony had *disappeared.*

After I said that prayer, I went to the backyard and made my excuses to extricate myself from a party that had grown in my short absence, and grown an astonishing amount more rowdy.

Fortunately, Lonnie and Maria were engaged in making out so my effort was not as prolonged as normal.

I wanted to wait until Tony reappeared.

But with Lonnie and Maria all about each other, I figured it would seem to Tony when he came back that I was waiting for him to reappear.

So I took off.

And I did it repeating my prayer.

Even if I worried doing it actually made me the bad girl I promised I wasn't going to be.

Three

FORMER GLORY

Present day…

I sat on my bed at the Chickadee Inn in Magdalene with the lovely, elegant, large red wineglass the folks at the inn gave me to pour in the fabulous Malbec that I'd found at Wayfarer's Market in town.

I stared at the fire the young man had come up, laid and lit.

I was assured by their website that this wasn't preferential treatment considering I was in the White Pine Suite, the only suite in this small, spectacularly charming, ten-room inn. As the website proclaimed, most of the rooms had fireplaces, and if you put in the order in the morning that you'd be staying put in the evening to relax, they sent the young man up to lay and light your fire.

I'd been in Magdalene now for fourteen days, and I'd had a good many fires and a goodly amount of (exceptionally delicious) room service because I was laying low.

It wouldn't do for a certain someone to see me around while I was writing the outline to what would be the last chapter of my life.

I had taken a necessary trip up north, but just to get the lay of the land. I hadn't made contact.

That would come later.

It would all come later.

My eyes shifted to the papers strewn on the bed.

Now I was outlining.

The inspection on the lighthouse had been done.

It was, as suspected, a complete disaster. Every building (except the lighthouse itself) needed a roof-to-roots facelift—new shingles to re-stabilizing foundations. The lighthouse itself needed a new furnace, new plumbing, new electric, cable laid for TV and Internet, all new bathrooms and a new kitchen.

It was going to be a project of epic proportions, which was further fettered due to the fact the seemingly only local contractor had Yelp reviews that were so abysmal, I wondered why he was still in business. Even Rob (the real estate agent and my new friend) said he wouldn't recommend the guy.

So I had to go farther afield, find someone outside the county, and the three I'd contacted to look over the inspection report and property told me flat out they'd have to charge a travel fee.

That was not optimal.

But I wanted it perfect.

It would need to be.

It was where I was going to spend the rest of my life. It was where the family was going to stay when they visited me (or the studio and loft were).

It was going to be mine and Patrick had taught me not to accept anything but the best.

The family who owned the lighthouse had not been best pleased I'd deducted ten percent off the asking price when I'd made my initial offer, because even with that inspection the land alone was worth double what I'd offered.

But I felt they shouldn't get any hint of a reward for what they'd done. None of them had taken care of their father's legacy, shown it (or him) the least amount of respect, never mind love. They'd just left it to rot like it meant nothing when it was a beacon of safety (primarily) but mostly it was a memory of the man who had a hand in making them.

I'd learned in beautiful and hideous ways how important it was to respect someone who carries your blood, and do that no matter what.

No matter what stupid things they did, what toxic people they spent their time with, what drastic decisions they made.

We'd settled on five percent below the asking price and I was signing the papers in four days.

Then it would be done.

No going back.

No matter what, I was not going back.

I sipped my wine with one hand, gathered the house papers with the other, shoving them into a manila folder (except the inspection report, which was a whole *binder* worth of grim information).

I got up, set the folder and binder on the dresser and moved back to the bed, turning to the nightstand and setting down my wineglass in order to pick up a cheese knife (kindly provided by the inn) in order to slice into an extraordinary camembert (not provided by the inn, which made the knife another kind gesture) and slathering it on a hunk of fresh French bread (all this also from Wayfarer's).

I shoved it into my mouth and chewed, barely able to stop myself from closing my eyes to better enjoy its scrumptiousness.

It was all coming together.

I loved Wayfarer's.

I was being cautious about being seen, so I was careful how much time I spent in it, but regardless, I'd fallen in love with the town of Magdalene and couldn't wait to spend more time in the shops, not to mention experience the restaurants.

The contractors would be meeting me to go over the property and then they'd be getting back to me with their plans and bids very soon, so I'd need to make a decision and start that long process moving.

Now it was necessary I find an interior decorator. I was hopeless at that kind of thing.

What I wasn't hopeless at was knowing what I liked. I wasn't the kind of person who vacillated about making a decision.

Patrick had always loved that about me.

"You're a joy to go to dinner with, darling girl," he'd say at many a restaurant table after I'd open my menu, skim and make a decision within a minute.

Yes, I knew just scanning if I wanted seared tuna or steak Diane.

So I'd be able to pick between different comforter covers and wall hangings without taking six weeks to do it.

The outline was coming together. The framework was getting set.

It was going to be other things that would be difficult.

And as if the cosmos wished to remind me of what one of those things were (as if I'd forget), my cell on the nightstand rang.

When I saw who was calling, I not only grabbed the phone, I grabbed my wine because I figured I'd need it.

I took the call and put the phone to my ear.

"Hey, Pat."

"Hey, honey. How's things?"

It was not surprising to me that Patrick's eldest son, in four words, could communicate the depth of concern he had for me at the same time sharing how he wanted me so far away from Maine, if he could, he'd put me in a rocket ship and launch me to the moon.

I had not told Pat about the lighthouse.

I would also not tell Pat about the lighthouse until I'd actually bought it.

It was sneaky and thus wrong.

But he was Pat. His wife, Kathy, was my best friend. And he was my dead husband's oldest son, he was a lot like his father and he was definitely like my big brother.

In other words, if I let him, he could get to me.

"Things are great. Have you been to Maine?" I asked then went on immediately, "It's beautiful. Totally amazing."

"Yeah. Kathy and I did a whale watching thing before the hellions were born."

I knew that.

Kathy had told me.

And the hellions, officially my step grandchildren, Verity and Dexter, were not hellions at all.

They were now nineteen (nearly twenty) and seventeen, respectively. Verity was currently utilizing a full academic scholarship at Yale (which was close, another good thing about Maine, because Verity and I were super close—it was almost as traumatic for me when she went away to school as it was for her parents), and Dexter was considering Harvard, but only to annoy his big sister. He'd end up at Yale too.

"I should do a whale watching tour," I murmured, thinking that would be fabulous because it would just be fabulous but also because it was highly doubtful I'd run into a certain someone if I did it.

"Yeah, you should," Pat replied. "Listen, when are you coming home? The house is getting some interest and the realtor doesn't think it's going to stay on the market very long. We'll need you here for the sale."

I felt my back get straight as my eyes drifted to the fireplace because this shocked me.

A fifteen-thousand-square-foot house that had been on the market for less than a month was getting interest?

It was listed for six and a half million dollars.

How could it be getting interest? Or, I should say, the kind of interest that would lead to a quick sale?

"Cady, honey?" Pat called gently.

"I didn't…" I cleared my throat and looked at the lovely blue and white paisley of the comforter cover. "I didn't think it would go that fast."

"There are rich people who need houses too, Cady," Pat said on a careful tease.

"Right," I mumbled then spoke up. "Are you sure Kathy and you don't want it?"

"Soon-to-be empty-nesters bumbling around in fifteen-thousand square feet? I don't think so."

"What about Mike and Pam?" I asked after Patrick's second son and his wife (Pam being my other best friend). "Their kids are all home."

And they were, there were three of them and they were younger.

"We already had the family discussion, sweetheart," he said softly. "Mike and Pam and the kids hate to see it go but they don't want it. And Daly and Shannon don't want it either." There was a brief pause before he said, "Are you sure you don't want to stay there?"

"Patrick didn't give me that choice," I reminded him and took a sip of wine.

Not that I wanted to stay there. Me alone in that huge house with nothing but memories to keep me company?

Absolutely not.

"I know he put that in his will, Cady, but maybe we can talk to the attorneys. Find a way around that."

"Is it because you want the family home to stay in the family?" I asked carefully.

"I grew up there. I fought like crazy with my brothers there, even though I loved them like crazy too. We lost our mom there. Dad found you and we had good times there. Holidays. Those birthday parties you're so good at giving. Game nights. Your ridiculous slumber parties with our grown women that we guys definitely had to panty raid, so we did. But the family is the family. Dad and you, me and Kath and the kids, Mike and Pam and their kids, Daly and Shannon and their brood. *That's* the family. The house is just a house. But if you wanted to keep it, we'd find a way."

And find a way to keep me close to home so I wouldn't get my heart pulled out of my chest, twisted to mush and discarded like trash.

I drew in breath before I said, "Your father wanted me to move on, I need to move on, Pat."

"Yes, but how?"

I didn't answer that. I took a sip of wine.

"Cady." His voice was sharper.

Definitely like his father.

Or my big brother.

"That picture is coming clearer," I told him vaguely.

"You gonna show it to me?" he asked.

"When the time is right."

"Dammit, Cady," he bit off.

"Pat, he's been gone two months and six days. Give me time," I whispered.

Pat said nothing for a while.

Then he said, "I don't like this."

"You've made that clear, sweetheart," I said quietly.

He had. Kathy had. Mike. Pam. Daly. Shannon. Even Verity, Dexter, Riley, Ellie, Melanie, Corbin and Bea had, and Melanie was only seven years old.

They wanted me home.

In Denver.

"If you need to find your way, you should do it with your family."

They weren't my family.

They were Patrick's.

"You know I love you," I said softly.

"Yes, I know. And Kath knows. Verity. Dex. I could go on but I won't. What I'll do is say we love you too. Dad's gone and we all lost him. We all miss him. And trust me, because we're all *here* and you're *there*, I know it's easier to grieve when you're with family."

"To get back to our original discussion," I changed the subject badly, "Kath has my power of attorney. If the house sells—"

"If the house sells," Pat interrupted me, "then the stuff in it needs to be auctioned off."

"And I went through everything with Kath, Pam and Shannon before I left, so they know everything that I haven't put aside is good to go."

"I think with this break, you should come home and have another look. Kath tells me you barely put anything aside."

"None of it, as you know, is Patrick."

Again he said nothing but this time he stuck with that.

"I'm doing what your father wanted, Pat," I reminded him.

"I'm not sure he was in his right mind when he shared what he wanted, Cady," Pat returned.

"You know that isn't true," I chided gently. "You know he'd been planning this for years."

And again, Pat was silent.

"I need to do this, Pat. For your dad."

"If the place sells, you need to come home."

"Kath has my power—"

"When we say goodbye to that house, Cady, we'll want you home."

It was my turn to be silent.

"Are we agreed on that?" he asked.

"Yes," I whispered.

"Good," he said and it sounded almost like a grunt.

I nearly grinned.

Instead I took another sip of wine.

"I'll keep you informed with how the sale is going," he promised.

"Thanks, sweetheart," I replied.

"And Kath wouldn't mind hearing from you," he shared with me.

That surprised me.

"I called her just yesterday."

"She's used to talking to you every day, and seeing you nearly every day. So maybe think on that."

I closed my eyes.

We were thick as thieves, Kath and me. Pam and me. Heck, Shannon was my third best friend.

The rest of the family would miss me. But it would hit Kath, Pam and Shannon hard, and I knew this because if any of them went away, I'd be devastated.

And I was because I was going away.

I just couldn't think about that.

"I'll give her a call a bit later," I told him.

"Appreciated."

"Okay, then, I have a camembert bleeding here and—"

"I know you're going to see him."

I shut my mouth.

Pat didn't.

"I know you're going to try to see *them* and I'll just put my two cents in here to say neither of them is worth it, Cady. They both turned their backs on you. That one, that cop, what he did to you—"

I closed my eyes again and whispered, "Please."

"They don't deserve to know you, honey. They don't deserve to have your light in their lives. I don't know what Dad was thinking and I loved my father. The whole world feels strange without him in it because he was such a big part of mine. But he's wrong about this. I feel it in my bones."

"It's beautiful here," I said quietly, opening my eyes and staring into the fire.

"I know."

"Peaceful," I told him.

"I know that too."

"I need to do what he wanted me to do, Pat."

"And it annoys me, but I know that too. So now I'll say, we're here. We're always here. I don't care if we're most a continent away, we can be there or we can get you back here if you need us. All you need to do is call."

My heart was in my throat when I said, "Thank you, sweetheart."

I heard him clear his own throat when he replied, "Call Kath later. But don't tell her I browbeat you because she'll make me sleep on the couch."

Kath was a woman and a mother. Kath didn't browbeat and Kath wasn't a big fan of when Pat did (he still did it and thus sometimes found himself on the couch).

She had other weapons in her arsenal to get what she wanted.

And she was using them.

I had just so far been immune.

"I'll call her. And I'll also say thank you for being all you are and caring so much. But I'll be fine."

"We'll see."

We would.

We said our goodbyes and rang off.

I put the phone down, the glass beside it, prepared more cheese and bread and poured more wine while I chewed it.

I did this thinking about doing what I should absolutely not do.

But the conversation brought it all steaming full force into the present, into that lovely room in a lovely inn in New England.

So I went to the closet and opened the empty suitcase I'd stowed there after I'd unpacked (this something Patrick found amusing, if we were to stay somewhere for two days or more, I always unpacked).

The big envelope was in there.

I shouldn't have brought it. In my more fanciful imaginings, I considered a certain someone finding I was there, ordering a police raid and discovering it.

Of course, that wouldn't happen.

At least the last part of it.

I went back to the bed, pulled the two manila folders in the envelope out, and I set them on the bed.

I nabbed my wine and turned back to them.

I opened the thinner one.

There was an eight by ten picture paper-clipped to the inside, front left, of my brother leaving a lovely, shingle-sided home and walking to a blue Subaru parked in his drive.

The last time I'd seen him was at my mother's funeral. The last time I'd spoken to him was at my mother's funeral. Or, I said very little to him. What he'd said to me was that I wasn't welcome at the gathering at Mom and Dad's house, and I should feel my due respects were paid by attending her service graveside.

Patrick, who had been standing at my side, had been livid.

We did not go to the gathering.

Dad had died nearly two years before Mom did. Regardless of the fact he was a fitness fanatic, ran nearly daily and watched everything he ate, he'd had a bad heart that had led to a succession of strokes, the last one killing him.

Mom's death had been uglier.

She'd slipped, fallen and hurt herself badly in her greenhouse, cutting her arm on a pair of shears, nicking an artery and bleeding heavily. She'd dragged herself to the door and nearly through it before she'd passed out with the pain and blood loss. It was winter and it was during a cold snap.

And it was ghastly, my mother freezing to death (or bleeding to death, no one knew which came first).

I'd been in shock not only losing her, but losing her before I could make amends (or find some way to convince her to allow me to make amends, and I'd lost Dad the same way), but also her dying in such a distressing manner.

Patrick knew that, so because of that he was even less thrilled that Caylen, my brother, had been so awful to me.

But it was awful of me to think that it was pure Caylen when, not two months after Mom died, he'd divorced his wife (because Mom would have lost her mind, her brilliant, genius, perfect eldest child doing something like leaving his wife and legally severing ties with her), and he'd left.

He'd then done something else very Caylen, moving across the country, leaving not only his wife but his two kids behind.

He was a software designer and a good one. The company he worked for had headquarters outside of San Francisco. But he could work anywhere.

So he did, in a remote town in Maine one hundred miles north of Magdalene.

It would seem I wasn't the only Webster child who liked solitude.

His children flew out to visit him once a month. He flew to visit them once a month too. Apparently this was working for all of them and mostly, according to the PI, because my brother's children could just about stomach four days a month with their father. More was not as easily tolerated.

I skidded the papers out in a fan on the bed. Papers, which were the reports from the private investigator that Patrick had hired, that stated, as well as all of that, my brother hiked, he fished, he sailed, he biked, he worked.

He did whatever Caylen wanted to do.

I took a sip of wine, swallowed it, and then I took a very deep breath, my gaze going to the second, thicker folder.

Patrick had told me about his private investigator and what he'd done three weeks before he'd died. He'd given me the envelope with the folders in it then as well.

I hadn't touched it until over a month after he'd gone.

Now, the second folder, everything in it I'd read so many times, I'd lost count.

And I opened it again right then.

Paper-clipped to the inside, front left of that folder was an eight by ten picture of a tall, dark-haired, extraordinarily handsome man walking down a sidewalk I now recognized as being on Cross Street, the main street of Magdalene.

He had a child on his hip.

She had on a little cream hat that had little cat ears coming from the top sides of it, the insides of the ears pink, at the front of it at her forehead was a pink nose with little black yarn whiskers knitted to the sides. She had a little pink, puffy jacket on. And she had little cream mittens on her hands with little gray kitty faces on the outsides, pink noses and ears.

She had dark hair flowing from under her cute hat.

She had amazing hazel eyes.

Her name was Janie.

And in that picture, she had been two.

She was now four.

My eyes slid to the man.

Coert Yeager, the sheriff of Derby County Maine (said "darby," like the English pronounced it).

A man I knew almost all of our acquaintance as Tony.

Since the now-Sheriff Yeager had left Denver, or nearly since he'd left, Patrick had had him followed.

Not constantly. Patrick didn't set a PI to stalking him. But reports were expected every quarter.

And they were received.

Thus I knew Sheriff Yeager came to Derby County, to Magdalene, to accept a post as a deputy at the sheriff's department. A much different post in this small, picturesque tourist town on coastal Maine than the dangerous undercover police work he did in Denver.

I also knew he wasn't fond of his boss and he made this publicly known by running against him eight years into his tenure as a deputy. The campaign was acrimonious but apparently enough of Derby County's citizens didn't like the old sheriff that Coert had become the new one, beating his boss by a slim nine percent margin.

The second election against the same opponent he'd won by forty-one percent.

His last election he'd run unopposed.

He was known as good-natured, perceptive, dedicated, hard-working, sharp and just.

I further knew that he'd dated, lived with and become engaged to a beautiful woman named Darcy, who, after six years, the last two with his ring on her finger, he'd ended things with. She was hurt, bitter and moved to Marblehead, Massachusetts to escape him.

I understood that last part.

Boy, did I understand that.

He'd then dated, lived with but didn't become engaged to a beautiful woman named Kim, who, after four years, saw the writing on the wall after what had happened to the one before.

She was not wrong.

He ended things.

She, on the other hand, decided to make it so he wouldn't.

According to the townspeople, who were happy to talk about this juicy tidbit in particular, after four years without even a hint the couple didn't know how to protect themselves from an unplanned conception, the fact she turned up two months pregnant a month after he broke it off with her was widely considered her attempt at entrapment.

Sheriff Yeager didn't feel like being trapped.

Due to the risks involved, he waited to demand a DNA test until after the child was born.

What he did not do was reconcile with his ex in order to do "right" by the child, something that surprised many, for that was something folks commonly considered Sheriff Yeager would do (another reason many thought her getting pregnant was entrapment).

The DNA test was performed after the birth.

She was his.

They named her Jane but called her Janie.

I knew why.

I'll never saddle a kid with a crazy name. Somethin' he's gotta spell or repeat or correct someone who's sayin' it wrong. My kids are gonna be named names like John, Nick, Max, Mary, Jane, Beth. Solid names. Good names.

This, Tony had told me while we were in bed after we'd made love.

At the time, I thought this was an odd thing for him to say, especially the determination behind it. His name was Tony. His last name was Wilson. Neither were hard to say or spell.

I would understand why when I'd learned he was actually Coert, pronounced "Cort" and spelled in a way I'd never seen before.

Thus it was not surprising his daughter was called Janie.

The private investigator reported that after her birth, Coert stayed with his ex, sleeping on the couch in her apartment for three months in order to help her ease into having a child, be a part of their daughter's first months on this earth, but also in waiting for when Janie was able, and it was appropriate, that she be away from her mother in order to be only with her dad.

From that point on, he had her every other week and even dragged his ex into court when she threatened leaving Magdalene and taking their daughter with her.

He'd won.

Suffice it to say something the PI didn't have to report (but he still did), this ex not achieving her aim of trapping Sheriff Yeager but instead buying her ex-boyfriend sleeping on her couch for months and sharing a child with the man she loved enough (albeit clearly unhealthily) to do something that horrible to was not something she relished.

It didn't help matters that Coert also found time to date.

He was not a serial dater or a player. He asked out women he was interested in and not once, not even once since he'd left Denver, did he ever ask out a woman that he didn't see at least five times before he ended it.

Their relationship now was apparently a lot easier (if also clearly not everything it could be considering all she'd done) as she'd realized she had every other week free, so she was also dating.

Regardless that Janie's parents were getting along enough to co-parent, this situation could have been frustrating, upsetting or even infuriating.

If there wasn't a little girl with dark hair and beautiful hazel eyes that looked utterly adorable in a kitty cat hat.

I had no little girl or little boy, and in the years since I met Tony at that backyard party I'd had very limited opportunities to make one.

Patrick and I didn't sleep together. Not once. That wasn't who we were. Not at the start. Not ever. We even had separate bedrooms from the very beginning.

He was not my lover.

He was my savior.

He'd been sixty-five when we'd married.

I'd been twenty-four.

I did not marry him because of his fifteen-thousand-square-foot mansion. I did not marry him because he was the man behind Moreland Heating and Air, a company that had vans moving in sixteen states in the western part of the U.S.

I married him because he loved me, he wanted to protect me, he wanted to keep me safe and he wanted to give me a family.

Not of my own.

His.

It wasn't a road lined with roses we skipped down happily. It was rocky. Especially in the beginning when Patrick's children thought I was what everyone, including Coert Yeager, thought I was.

But he was Patrick Moreland. If he put his mind to something, he did it.

And he did it.

I took a very large sip of wine and shoved aside the stack of papers to get to the first of many eight by ten photographs at the back.

Janie, on her feet in a little pink corduroy pinafore dress with a little girl's long-sleeved thermal under it, which had big, bright pink, purple and aqua daisies on it and bright aqua tights under it, with little girl pink boots (that looked like Ugg) on her feet. She was arched back, smiling, her hand lifted and covering the smiling huge, beautiful lips of a beautiful, dark-haired man who was bent more than double to put his face in hers.

That was taken last October.

It was my favorite.

And it destroyed me.

I flipped the folder closed, hastily shoving all the papers back into it and doing the same with my brother's.

Coert and Caylen lived one hundred miles apart.

In what Patrick refused to believe was a coincidence (or say, a cruel twist of fate) my estranged brother and the only man I ever loved (that way) both had moved from Denver and now lived in coastal Maine, one hundred miles apart.

Patrick said it was a sign.

Patrick said it was time.

Patrick said he knew with everything that was him that I was meant to be here in Maine. That those two men were going to give me my happily ever after.

Patrick was absolutely sure of it.

He was also most likely very wrong.

But I owed him everything.

So I owed him this.

And from it, I'd have my lighthouse. I'd have my views of the sea. I'd have a fabulous place where the family could come, vacation and spend time with me.

And Caylen was one hundred miles away. After he delivered his last cut, I'd never see him again.

Now Coert…

Well, if he could handle living in the same town and co-parenting with a woman who tried to trap him by getting pregnant with his child without his knowledge…

He could put up with every once in a while (and less, if I could manage it), seeing me.

IT WAS AFTER I signed the papers.

After I'd made it impossible to turn back, but in an uncommon moment of indecision, I'd realized I'd made a horrible mistake.

After I'd decided to move forward with the renovations (because the old girl needed them), but I wouldn't go whole hog because I'd be creating three different spaces to rent out to tourists and not living there at all.

After I decided my best bet was to give up on Patrick's dream and go home to Denver.

It was after all that, I saw it.

I was returning to the lighthouse because first, it was mine and second, I had an appointment with one of the contractors to go over the site.

I'd been there three times since making an offer, and I'd seen them growing, the strong shoots of their shamrock-green stems and leaves startling against the greening (but not yet fully back from winter) spring grass all around them.

But it had been days since I'd been there.

And the last time I was there, they hadn't opened.

Now…

They were open.

You could see them from afar, but as I drove up the slope to the cliff where my lighthouse was, the spectacular beauty of them increased significantly.

I wasn't the only one who'd noticed.

There were three cars and even more bicycles all along the rickety fence surrounding the old girl with people out on foot, phones or cameras up, pointed at the spectacle.

And the spectacle was a bed of profuse magenta tulips that bled into lips of pure white coming from a sea of shamrock stalks and leaves. There were places where they were more sparse, places that they only trailed through the grass, but all around the lighthouse, the walkways, the outbuildings and much of the open area close to the buildings was a bed of deep pink and startling green.

With so much on my mind, I had not thought about Googling it to see the pictures.

Viewing it in all its glory for the first time in person, I was glad I had not.

I parked my rental by a medium-size SUV that had South Carolina plates and slowly got out of my car, wandering to the fence, staring at what lay before me.

No.

Absolutely *no.*

When Caylen cut me out and Coert tore me down, I wasn't going to turn tail and run back to Denver.

This, all of this, *was mine.*

And I was going to keep it.

I stopped, still in a tulip daze, staring at the display before me, wondering if it was a miracle. I knew a fair bit about gardening and would think that the wind and salty air would mean the plethora of this type of flora wouldn't grow easily.

Obviously I was very wrong.

"Your first time?"

I looked to the man beside me who had a camera up on a tripod.

"Yes," I replied.

He grinned. "Come up here from South Carolina every other year 'round 'bout this time because my wife likes the shops, I like the restaurants, we both love the sea, but this," he swung an arm out to my soon-to-be new home, "is what really calls me. Seen it maybe five times over ten years. Never get sick of it."

I looked back to my lighthouse.

He was correct. This was not something you'd ever get sick of.

"No, I can imagine one never would," I murmured.

"The lavender hits around now at Lavender House and the bluebells hit about now at Cliff Blue but it isn't easy to get to those places," he shared. "They're way more private. Still, I've driven by several times and they sure are beauties. But this is too beautiful to believe."

He was correct about that too (though I hadn't seen Lavender House or Cliff Blue, but I'd be doing drive-bys).

"Good news," he stated. I turned my attention back to him and he kept speaking. "Talk in town, someone's buying the place. It's been vacant since forever. Word is, new owner is gonna restore the whole thing to its former glory. Can't imagine what that's gonna do to their pocketbook, but I'll tell you what, if I ever thought I'd have that kind of money, I would drag the wife up here to do just that." He looked to my lighthouse, its tulips and the sea beyond. "Not sure I've ever seen anything this beautiful and I've been places. But this, this right here, this is it."

I trained my gaze where he was and thought he was again right.

This was it.

"So glad someone's finally gonna take care of the old place," he muttered.

"Me too," I whispered.

"Gonna set up over there so best be moving. Enjoy," he bid as he took up his camera and tripod and moved behind me to follow the fence north.

I kept my eyes on the beauty that was now all mine until I sensed movement at my side and looked right.

A man was out of a pickup that had a construction firm's information on its door and people were moving their bikes out of his way as he opened the closed gate (Rob and I had forced it closed and Rob had come back with some oil to lubricate the hinges so it'd be relatively useful until I had it replaced).

I watched him open the gate, walk back to his truck, climb in and drive through.

The onlookers watched too.

When he parked and got out to close the gate behind him was when I moved, walking toward him and calling out to forestall him.

We shook hands at the gate.

He then closed it and together we walked to the old girl to talk about restoring her to her former glory.

Four

USE THE GIRL

Eighteen years earlier…

It had been working for me. Working perfectly. Just what I needed to forget Mom being so mean and controlling. Just what I needed to forget Caylen was such an asshole. Just what I needed to forget how my life had turned on a letter into a disaster.

It was a tried and true method to get me past the shit of life so I could *deal* and it was working.

I was drunk, *trashed*, totally blotto.

And that was good.

Lonnie, Maria and I were also at Wild Bill's Rally.

This was mostly for bikers but other people could show, and we'd been showing for five years running. Pitching our tents. Dragging out our beer and vodka filled coolers. Making friends easily and hanging by their campfires at night downing shots, making out (or Maria and Lonnie did, Lonnie put a stop to such things for me and now I knew why). Forging through the hangovers by day only to perk back up with beer, shots, weed and the music Wild Bill provided on the big, makeshift stage in the middle of his just-worked fields, all of this providing a full weekend of fun.

I wasn't supposed to be there.

Not that year.

I was now responsible. I was now an assistant manager. I had goals. I was on the right path.

Okay, so the raise I got was only a couple dollars more an hour, but for me, that was a lot.

And the benefits were better. Better insurance. They even matched a little bit to a retirement account. And I got another week's vacation.

So I was giving it my all because people didn't stay long at the Sip and Save. The last manager had bolted after being there less time than me. The new manager would bolt eventually because this one was the third one we'd had since I'd been there.

If I showed loyalty, learned as much as I could, I might actually be manager before I'd given it what I thought it appropriate to give to show better forms of employment that I had job loyalty—this being a year and a half. If I made manager, I'd make that term two years, just to show gratitude (and more loyalty to prospective future employers).

So yeah, I had been on the right path.

I also didn't want to be at the rally because Lonnie and Maria were there.

After Tony pointed out some things that had not been sinking in, it sucked, but I was avoiding them. This wasn't hard seeing as I was now assistant manager and they knew I went for overtime as much as I could (and got it), so they were cool about me doing my all to achieve my goals.

And anyway, they were both getting into their own things. They just weren't, I feared, good things.

But they were there and I was there, and I didn't need to be there when I did need to be at work at seven o'clock the next morning.

I still needed it, though. I needed Wild Bill's Rally. I needed to get fucked up. I needed to let loose. And I didn't care I was probably going to call off (or not call in at all) because I was still fucked up or passed out or whatever.

Because really, I was learning it didn't matter how hard you worked, how loyal you were, how smart you were trying to be, life was just going to suck.

Life sucking for me in that moment was the fact that my car had broken down out of the blue the week before.

I needed my car, as people do, and even though I had some money in savings, it wasn't near enough to buy a new one (that being a new used one, even a junker). It was enough (just barely) to fix the old one. So I did.

But it left me broke. No savings, wiping out even the little I had in checking.

And then, two days ago, I got a letter from my landlord that they were evicting all the tenants. They'd sold the building, it was going to be razed and a parking garage or something put there, so we all had thirty days to vacate.

My apartment wasn't much but it wasn't in the worst neighborhood imaginable and the rent didn't cripple me (it just maimed me a little).

However, the listings I'd seen available at my rent *were* in the worst neighborhoods imaginable and they weren't as clean or relatively okay as the one I had. They were gross and totally *not* okay.

Furthermore, I didn't have any money for a security deposit. I'd used the money I got from graduation to get into the apartment I had, and to buy some yard sale stuff that I actually kinda liked to spruce it up, but they weren't returning security deposits for thirty days after we vacated.

This meant I either had to crash with Lonnie and Maria (not a good option for obvious reasons). Or I had to ask Mom and Dad if I could move in with them for a few weeks (also not a good option). Or I had to ask them to float me money for a security deposit so I could move to a new place (not a fun option).

As much as I didn't want to do it, what with Mom and Dad being clear about how they felt about Lonnie and Maria (since I first started hanging with Maria). And how they felt about me not going to college (I didn't get a scholarship like Caylen did and they told me I had to pay my way myself—with no job or savings, how was I going to do that?). Also how they felt about my lifestyle, and how I spent my time, the list went on. Still the only real option I had was to go to them.

Although Dad seemed kinda excited I was promoted to assistant manager and had held down a job at the same place for ten months, Mom wasn't all that impressed. And Caylen, home for a family dinner (this devised, I guessed, by Mom, who liked having her son around mostly because I thought she got off on how they could gang up on me), shared in his Caylen way he thought all this proved I was still a fuckup.

Even if *I* didn't make my car break down.

"It's called regular maintenance, Cady," he'd sneered. "You might look into it."

Like I didn't know about oil changes. I did and I got them even when it bit into my bank account to do it. My car didn't break down because of oil changes and switching out plugs and filters. My car broke down because it was old and mostly a piece of shit.

And even though *I* didn't kick myself out of my apartment.

"You live in a place like that, those things are gonna happen," Caylen had said.

Like he knew what happened when you lived in a dump. He'd bought his first condo, and it was a nice one, a year out of college.

I thought Dad was going to help out, but Mom put the kibosh on that right away, stating, "This is the life you chose, Cady. If you're on the outs with those friends of yours, it's bad manners to say I told you so, but I did, actually, tell you so. But when you choose a life like that you have to learn to handle it when things like this happen. So no, you can't have a loan. But you *can* come back home if you enroll at least in community college for *some* kind of advanced education. At this point I don't care if you become a nail technician. At least it'll be a skill. You can continue to have that job, pay us rent, and we'll be fair about that so you can use the rest of your salary, as it were, on your tuition and to save up so you can move out, *for good* the next time."

I didn't want to be a nail technician. I wanted to be a clothing buyer. I wanted to learn about fashion. I wanted to travel, go to trade shows and fashion shows and artist shows. I wanted to discover new trends. I wanted to beautify people (not just their nails). Find awesome shit for them that would make them feel they could take on the world.

I was willing to work at it. Learn it. Live it. Give it time. I didn't expect it to be handed to me, to walk into Neiman Marcus and have them yell, "Thank God you've finally arrived! What had we ever done without you?"

And I was twenty-three, not thirteen.

My mom telling me I could "continue to have that job" then telling me what I was going to do with the money I made in it *and* with my future was totally uncool.

Unfortunately as bad as I wanted to be an adult and prove to them I was, instead of taking a deep breath and communicating calmly, Caylen was his normal conceited, superior asshole and Mom was Mom and she tripped all my triggers, so I lost it.

Which meant I lost any support I might have had from Dad.

In fact, they'd kicked me out.

So now I had a car that might run for the next few days, weeks, months or I hoped years, but I had twenty-eight days to move out of my apartment and my only choice was Lonnie and Maria, who I hadn't talked to about any of this and they didn't have a huge place either. I'd have to sleep on the couch. And they might not even say yes.

To all this I did what I often would do because my brother was right.

I was a fuckup.

So I might as well embrace the fuckup that was me.

I decided to screw it all, so I *screwed it all.*

Therefore I was hammered and I was in The Trench at Wild Bill's Rally, the music loud, the crush of bodies undulating around me, the bottle of beer in my hand long forgotten as I swayed with the music and sang it at the top of my lungs.

It felt good.

No, it felt *great.* To be around people who didn't care I didn't have a college degree. To be around people who *lived* life, they didn't strategize every move in it. To be there and feel alive. To be there and not to be alone.

To be there and feel free.

That was, it felt great until they moved in.

They being two guys, who either knew each other and didn't mind crossing swords or who were silently vying to get the drunk chick out of The Trench and into a tent so they could have their way with her.

I wasn't in the mood to have anyone have their way with me so I decided to make that clear.

My first couple of maneuvers, letting the movement of the crowd suck me in and pull me away, didn't work.

They followed.

My second maneuver, saying, "Hey, uncool!" when one touched the side of my tit then I twisted around, saying, "Hey, stop that!" when the other one positioned behind me and started to grind into my ass also didn't work.

And pushing off, grabbing their wrists and pulling their hands away didn't work either.

"*Stop it, you assholes!*" I screamed, dropping my beer without a thought and moving more violently now that they had me fenced in, one at the front, one at the back, pressing closer, eyes to my body, hands to my body, *bodies* to my body, squeezing in.

My scream was swallowed by the music, the buzz, the flesh, lost in a haze of people gone on booze and drugs and the vibe.

No one was paying any attention to me.

Such was The Trench.

It could be awesome (but mostly only if you had a least a girlfriend taking your back, which stupidly I did not).

It could be *not* awesome *at all.*

Like now.

I tried to yank sideways but the guy behind me shoved me back between them.

They were working together.

Shit.

They wanted a gang bang, and as Wild Bill's Rally was an annual get-together for a lot of motorcycle clubs, this gang bang could be more than just three, they were just the ones sent in to find the prey.

That thought made the anger that had killed my buzz rocket straight to panic and suddenly it was a lot of hands, arms, shoving, pressing, grinding, grunts and shouts from me and low chuckles from them.

They were getting off on this.

One of them bit my shoulder and I cried out, turning around with effort in the small space they'd given me and cupping a hand under his chin to push him off.

He jerked away, and when his wild, bright, fucked-up eyes came back to me I realized he liked it like that.

Shit.

The other guy reached around and grabbed tight on my breast.

I whirled the other way, forcing both hands between us and pushing with everything I had, shrieking, "*Fuck off!*"

The guy now behind me was sliding a hand from my hip around to the front, down, almost there, and terror ran thick in my veins when suddenly I was slamming into the people beside me.

"Hey!" and "Watch it!" were shouted at me but all I could do was stand there, not looking at the stage, not struggling, not running, instead watching Tony land a fist solidly in the face of the guy who'd ended things behind me.

The guy didn't even get the chance to lift a hand. One punch and he was out, sinking down and hitting bodies who just shuffled away and let him fall to the turf.

The other guy tried to get the jump on him but Tony instantly readjusted, putting the guy in a headlock and squeezing, squeezing—the guy kicked and spat and tore at Tony's arm—but he kept squeezing until the guy lost consciousness and floated to the ground.

He barely hit before Tony turned to me, grabbed my hand in an iron-tight hold and started dragging me through the crowd. Using how he walked now in a practical way, he shouldered through people both stoned who didn't notice it or stoned who didn't like it but took one look at Tony and didn't say shit about it.

In no time, an almost impossible occurrence with The Trench—you went in understanding it spit you out when it was done with you and no sooner—we were at the edges, but Tony didn't stop there.

He dragged me through people, campfires, tents and pop-top campers to what seemed in the dark like a sky-blue with a thick stripe of baby-blue, old Chevy pickup.

He stopped me at the tail and turned while yanking me around and almost into his body.

He lifted up my hand beside us, shook it and gritted out, "Jesus, fuck, Cady. *Fuck*!"

I stared at him, not at a loss to what had just happened—not the part where he downed two dudes in probably two minutes, not the part where I was in a serious situation no woman wanted to find herself in—and I did it speechless.

He stared back and he did it seriously pissed.

He dropped my hand but only to jab his finger toward The Trench and clip, "That was *not* gonna end well."

"I know," I whispered.

"Where were your friends?" he demanded to know.

"I-I don't know," I stammered, swallowed and finished stupidly, "Lonnie and Maria are hanging with Chaos. A local MC. I went in alone."

I could feel the bite of his eyes at that admission before he growled, "All your signals contradicted each other, but guess my thought you were mostly clueless was the signal that held true. Not thinkin' that you had it goin' on, you just had shit friends."

I flinched at that, but suddenly he straightened up and lifted a hand to drag it through his hair, looking away and taking in a visible breath.

When he dropped his hand and looked back to me, he muttered, "None of my fuckin' business."

"My car broke down," I told him.

"Yeah?" he asked, like he didn't much care.

"And I was evicted. They're dozing my building. They're making it a parking garage."

His eyes narrowed on me.

"And?" he pushed.

"My parents want me to be a nail technician," I shared idiotically.

"So fuckin' what?" he bit. "You're tellin' me that's a reason to wander alone into the fuckin' *Trench* at fuckin' *Wild Bill's Rally* and nearly get yourself raped?"

That was what I was telling him but it was so lame it was humiliating, so I didn't answer.

Tony got closer and tipped his chin down so he could hold my eyes in the dark, lifted only by moonlight and not-very-close campfires.

I was still mesmerized.

"Not my job to look after you but I'm not walkin' away from you right now without tellin' you, girl, you gotta clue the fuck in real fuckin' fast. You gettin' me?"

Oh, I was "getting him."

About a variety of things.

And I felt them coming. I didn't want them to come but this was too excruciatingly mortifying to bear at the same time hold them back.

So I didn't and that was why the tears spilled over and my voice broke when I answered, "Yeah, To-tony. I'm g-g-gettin' you."

Then, to save face when they came full force, I turned, trying to fight back the sob but it burst forth anyway, and I started to run away.

But I got not a step before I was hooked around the belly and hauled back into a solid frame.

I shoved with both hands against his arm and demanded unevenly, "L-let go."

"Shh, Cady. Just…I don't know," he said like he really didn't know. "Let it out, I guess."

"I-I-I can do that so-so-somewhere else," I told him, still pushing at his arm.

"You can also do it here," he said in my ear, his other arm coming around me.

"Let me go, Tony."

"Just shut up and get it out, Cady."

I decided to do that, but as useless as it was, I did it letting my hands flop to my sides and turning my head away from his mouth at my ear like that was any form of escape from him.

He gave it a minute before he pulled us back. I heard the almighty loud squeak as he yanked the tailgate down and then he sat on it, hefting me up to sit beside him.

I made a move instantly to jump down but with an arm across my front, fingers digging into the side of my hip, he held me there at the same time ordering, "No. Sit your ass here, stay there and pull your shit together."

I supposed I owed it to him not to be more of a pain in the rear than I'd already been, so I kept my ass there but also kept my head turned away.

He let me go with his arm.

When the crying jag was just sniffles and deep abiding mortification, Tony murmured, "I don't have any Kleenex."

"That's okay," I murmured back, lifting the hem of my tee at the same time bending over to wipe my cheeks and my nose.

I straightened and kept my gaze to my knees.

"You all right now?" he asked.

No, I wasn't all right.

I had no money. I soon would have no place to live. It would take another ten months to save up what I'd saved to give myself something better (eventually) and in all likelihood, that would be eaten up by some other life shit that would come along and hit me. A hot guy I was attracted to just saved me from being gang raped. And he was right.

I was clueless.

My best friend's boyfriend was into me and had been since around the day we met.

I could work at the Sip and Save until I was forty and have stellar performance evaluations but still, Saks or Neimans or Nordstrom or Anthropologie were never going to hire me then set me on a career course to see me sitting beside Alexander McQueen's fashion show in London (or however they found their clothes).

I couldn't even hold my temper long enough to talk my parents into a loan.

I was probably going to end up hooked up with some dude who treated me like dirt, knocked me up, and I'd be working at Sip and Save for the rest of my life.

In truth, the world needed folks working at Sip and Save. If they didn't, how would they grab a cup of joe or snatch up that bag of Corn Nuts for their road trip or pick up that set of wipers they needed?

I just...I just...

Didn't want that person to be me (forever).

"Cady," Tony called.

I looked right at him. "I'm sorry. You're right. I'm being stupid. I have to be at work at seven and I don't even know what time it is now but—"

"It's past two thirty."

Great.

"Cady—" he started.

I cut him off. "I'm sorry. I had a bad day, a bad couple of weeks and I didn't handle it well and you had to…had to wade in and deal with it and I'm sorry. But I appreciate it. I really do. I'd make you cookies but I'm not going to have a kitchen for long and my car broke down and it took all my savings to fix it, and I don't have flour, or brown sugar, or butter, definitely not chocolate chips or vanilla extract. So—"

I was edging off the tailgate, but I stopped when Tony interrupted me and did it with his voice trembling with laughter. "Don't move."

I stared at him wondering how he could sound so amused when his lips were only curled up a little bit.

Though, his eyes were absolutely shining.

Even in the dark.

"No flour?" he asked.

I looked away.

"Teasing you, Cady," he said gently, still sounding amused, and both of those together were a double whammy of goodness.

Shit.

How could I forget how much I liked this guy?

"I'm kinda not really in the mood to be teased right now," I told the VW van parked next to his truck.

"Sounds like it," he muttered. Then not in a mutter, he demanded, "Talk to me."

"I really appreciate what you did but—"

I stopped speaking that time when his fingers closed around my chin, he turned me to catch his eyes and he repeated, more firmly this time, "Cady, talk to me."

I looked into eyes that were now very serious and it just happened.

It poured out of me.

Mom and Dad and how much they loved me, but how disappointed they were that I didn't fit in with their overachiever family. Dad who made big bucks as a bigwig at a big computer company. Mom the head of the occupational therapy department at her hospital. My brother getting an academic scholarship to Berkeley and ending his college career with three job offers, all of them making more than five times the money I made at Sip and Save, even when I did overtime.

I shared about my car breaking down and my soon-to-be homeless situation.

I told him I was worried about Maria, not only because her boyfriend had a thing for me and if she ever cottoned on to that, it wouldn't be Lonnie she told to take a hike. But that I worried about her because she seemed to have no direction, and I didn't want to sound like my mother (who was certain *I* had no direction), but it was coming time to find a direction.

I did not tell him about how I wasn't real sure about Lonnie continuing to burrow in with Lars and his crew, considering I might not have seen Tony since our first meeting a couple months before, but it seemed during our first meeting he was a part of Lars and his crew. I didn't know how he would take that and he'd just saved me from being raped. I didn't think it was cool to offend him.

But I did tell him that I was probably a loser for thinking a position at Sip and Save was going to get me wearing fancy shoes and scurrying with my expensive trench coat flying behind me while I jet-set between Paris, Milan, London and New York.

When I was done, he stated the obvious.

"That's a lot."

I nodded and drew in breath, now embarrassed about laying that all out.

It was then something strange happened because Tony looked for a second like he was undecided.

That was the second time I'd seen him in my life so I didn't know him well enough to know, but it seemed completely wrong on him not to know exactly who he was and what he was about.

He then curved an arm around my back and pulled me to his side, holding me there.

Holy crap!

"It'll get better," he murmured, again hesitating before he lifted the hand he had around me and patted me awkwardly on the arm before he dropped it again to curl his fingers around my waist, and that didn't feel awkward at all. For him, the way he held me, definitely not for me, being held by Tony.

Still, we sat in uncomfortable silence, both of us holding ourselves stiff, before I tried to break the feel by saying, "I'll figure something out. That's life, right? It socks it to you and you figure something out."

"Right."

"You're being really nice," I noted.

"Yeah, I'm nice."

He said that like it was absolutely not true, and a chill traced over my skin.

I turned within the circle of his arm and tipped my head back, powering through the forbidden feeling I felt having my face that close to his, and I did all this to say, "You can stop being nice. I'm all right now."

"I'll stop being nice when I know you're gettin' in your car, gettin' the fuck outta here and you're gonna drag your ass to work even if you drag around all day because you're on your path and you're not gonna blow it because your brother's a dick and your parents don't get you. Not sure the Sip and Save leads to Milan, but who cares? If you can lay your head down at night knowin' you put in a solid day's work and you're on a good path no matter where it leads, that's where it's at."

He was absolutely right.

It was then I wondered if he could lay his head down on his pillow at night and know he was on a good path.

I also wanted to lay my head down on the pillow beside his.

Lastly, I really wanted to kiss him.

But this would not be proving to him I'd learned my lesson from that night, had my blip and was going to find some way to pull myself together.

So I pulled slightly away and he let me by taking his arm from around me.

I didn't like losing it.

I didn't let myself think on that.

I promised, "I'm gonna get in my car and get outta here, get home, while I still have one, get as much sleep as I can get and then drag my ass to work."

He grinned. "'Atta girl."

I grinned back.

He jumped off the gate, taking my hand and pulling me off, saying, "Walk you to your car."

"'Kay."

He walked me to my car. Well, he walked beside me as I guided him to my car.

He stopped me at the driver's side door and turned into me, doing this (sadly) letting my hand go.

"You good to drive?"

Officially, probably not. But nothing sobers a girl up faster than narrowly escaping a gang bang she didn't want to participate in, being saved by a good-looking guy who was nice but (possibly) shady, who she totally wanted to bang and pouring her life out all over him, forcing him to awkwardly comfort her on the tailgate of an old Chevy pickup.

"I'm good."

He took a second to assess me before he nodded.

"Catch you later, Cady."

And with that, like before, he was done, turning and beginning to stroll away.

"Tony," I called.

He stopped and turned back.

"Thanks. I mean, *thanks*. A lot."

He gave me another grin. "Fortunately a man doesn't find himself in a place he has to play the knight in shining armor. Good I got that shot with a cute redhead."

A cute redhead?

What?

"Later, Cady."

"Later, Tony," I forced out.

He flicked a hand in a goodbye wave, turned again and walked away.

"YO."

I looked up from restocking the pork rinds to see Tony standing in the aisle of the Sip and Save.

It was the next day (well, essentially the same day, just later). I looked like hell. I was wearing my Sip and Save smock, which even Cindy Crawford couldn't make look good (unless it was unbuttoned all the way and she had a bikini on underneath).

And there he was.

He grinned again.

Gah!

"Hey," I greeted rather than running from the store (or running to my purse and hoping I had lipstick in it so at least my lips would look good). "Uh, are you looking for me?"

His grin stayed in place. "Not a coincidence last night happened and today I'm right here."

"Right," I muttered, then louder, asked, "How did you know which Sip and Save I worked at?"

This was a good question considering there were about five hundred thousand of them in Denver.

"Girl, we run in the same crew."

We did?

Did he think I "ran" in that crew?

And what did "running" in that crew mean, precisely?

Before I could ask any of that, even though I wasn't certain I would, he continued speaking.

"Talked to a bud," he stated, coming to stand close to me.

I didn't know why he was telling me that but the only thing I could think to say when those hazel eyes were on me was, "You did?"

More grinning and, "Yeah. I did. He's been out of town, gonna be out of town awhile. Three-month job he's on. Construction. I been looking out for his house, going over every coupla days to grab his mail and change timers on his lights so it looks like someone's home and they're not keeping the exact same schedule for three months. Asked him if he'd be cool with a free house sitter for a while, if she grabbed his mail, kept the place nice, and gave it a good clean when she left. Last job he was out on, got cleaned out, TV, DVD, his change jar, stereo, speakers, even took his blender. So he was all over it."

Oh my God!

He had a place for me to stay!

"Really?" I breathed.

He shot me a smile.

I nearly melted into a puddle of goo at his feet.

"Really." He dug into his jeans pocket, came out with what looked like a torn off corner of note paper. "My number. Call me when you wanna set up a time to go look it over. I'll show you around. If you like it, I'll get you a key."

I'd like it.

It wasn't sleeping on Maria and Lonnie's couch, listening to them have loud sex all the time, or tucking my tail between my legs and eating shit from my parents, so I'd definitely like it.

However.

"I…I haven't found a new place, Tony. And it's not easy to find, my budget doesn't exactly put me in the Ritz. It's probably gonna take a while."

"He's about three weeks into this assignment so you got a spell over two months. That be enough time?"

Living rent free at some dude's pad?

Totally!

I'd even have my security deposit back by then!

But…

"You don't, well… This is all nice and everything but you don't even know my last name," I said.

"What's your last name?" he asked.

"Webster," I answered.

"Now I know it," he stated, and I let out a little giggle. He smiled again and said, "Mine's Wilson. Nice to meet you. Now we got that down, you gonna call me?"

I was *so totally* going to call him.

He knew that so I shared, "I'm *so totally* gonna make you cookies."

"Pie, Cady."

"Pie?"

"Cookies don't suck but I'm a pie guy."

I was *so totally* making him about fifty pies.

I smiled at him and I smiled big. "You're on."

"Right. Great." He reached into me, grabbed a bag of pork rinds and held them up. "Lunch." And then with no further ado, bid his farewell. "Later."

And with that, as I was finding was Tony's way, he turned to walk away.

"Tony Wilson, you better get something more substantial for lunch!" I admonished to his back.

"Do it at dinner, Cady," he told the cash register, where he was heading.

"You better!"

He looked over his shoulder at me and it was *then* I nearly melted into a puddle of goo.

Tony bought his pork rinds.

I restocked the one he'd taken and then some.

He left.

I was dog tired.

But I walked on air the rest of the day.

TONY/COERT

"USE THE GIRL."

"What? Cap, are you serious?" Malcolm asked in disgust.

Coert sat back in his chair in Cap's office, ankle on his opposite knee, not breaking the stare he had aimed at his captain and trying real hard not to let it show as he swallowed back the bile that had filled his throat when his cap gave him that order.

"Nightingale, this Lonnie moron is into her, she's into Coert, Coert gets close to her, he's deeper in Lars's crew. A part of it. Hooked to one of their women," Cap told Malcolm.

"She wants out," Coert put in, having swallowed back the bile, now a pit was settling in his gut in a way it felt like it might stay there forever.

Cap looked at him. "She can get out after you use her to solidify your place in."

"If she wants out, Cap," Tom butted in, "this crew, we shouldn't do shit to keep her in."

"Savage, if she's stupid enough to even get her big toe in with that mess, not bein' a dick, but she gets what's comin' to her, and some undercover cop usin' her to solidify his cover is the least she'd have to worry about," Cap said to Tom and looked to Coert, who had straightened in his chair and put both feet to the floor when Cap had called Cady "stupid enough." "She's into you, use her."

"She's not feelin' the love for Lonnie anymore and she's breakin' away from his woman," Coert reported.

"So reel her back in," Cap returned.

"Cap—" Coert started.

"Coert," Cap bit off, "you got three months in with this shit and we got nothin'. You need to get cozy with Lars, which means you need to get cozy with his crew. Assholes like that consider themselves a family, until one acts out of line and gets a bullet in his brain. Best way to find your way into a family is to use one of their women. Not tellin' you to fuck her, that's your call. Shit happens when you're undercover. You want that, whatever. Not my business and don't wanna know how that goes either way. You just wanna playact with her, get creative about keepin' her hooked. But this girl is into you, so *use her*."

"And what about after it's done?" Malcolm asked.

Cap looked to him. "She's not indicted with the rest, she goes her own way and whatever."

"This is a twenty-three-year-old girl you're messing with, Cap," Tom reminded him.

"She's not a minor. She's an adult who needs to make adult decisions and face the consequences for those decisions. And all the intel we got is that Lars is flooding our streets with product, so we not only need to shut his crew down, we need to shut him down, but before we do that we need to understand who he's gettin' that shit from so we can shut *them* down. Lars hasn't bought into Coert, Lonnie has. But we need Lars's buy in. We need Coert deeper so we can nail the suppliers." Cap looked back to Coert. "So fuckin' *use the girl*."

Coert obviously couldn't let Cady be raped at Wild Bill's Rally.

He didn't have to call his bud Casey and see if Cady could crash at his place while she was figuring shit out, but he also did have to, because she was in a situation and it didn't seem she had anyone to help her out.

He also didn't have to tell Cap, Malcolm and Tom—his handlers on this assignment—about her.

And apparently that last, sharing about Cady, was his biggest screwup.

Fuck.

"We on the same page here, detective?" Cap asked, but it was an order.

Coert pushed out of his chair, replying, "We're on the same page, Cap."

"Good," Cap muttered dismissively.

In other words, they were all dismissed so they all filed out.

The door to Cap's office was closed behind them when Malcolm Nightingale, a man who had a bit over a decade longer on the force than Coert, a good guy, family guy, great wife, three kids— two of them hell-raisers but Malc would sort that out—and a brother's brother when it came to cops, asked, "Question now is, you into *her*?"

Coert stopped and looked to his colleague. "She's a short redhead with a great ass and rack."

She was more than that.

Too much more.

But he'd said enough. He wasn't going to dig that hole deeper. Not even with Malc and Tom.

Tom Savage, Malc's partner, a good guy, single dad since his wife passed years ago, his daughter was the definition of a hell-raiser, but that didn't mean she wasn't a great kid who loved her dad beyond reason, grinned big.

They both knew his type.

And Cady Webster was maybe a hint too young, just a handful of years older than Tom's daughter, and for that matter, Malc's (their two girls being best friends).

But she was absolutely his type.

And a whole lot more.

Malc looked worried.

"Wrangle that," Malc advised.

"Come again?" Coert asked.

"She part of this crew, I mean *really*?" Malc asked.

"Seen her three times. She tries to act tough and not sure she makes the right decisions but she seems like an outsider."

She was definitely an outsider. She had no business with that crew.

And she knew it.

So did Coert.

"Cap wants you to use her, use her, keep her removed and do it so when it's over she doesn't totally hate your guts," Malc replied.

The way she looked at him, Coert figured he could take her to the bank for a deposit and hold the place up after she did it and she'd not hate his guts.

And he loved that.

He loved the way Cady Webster looked at him.

And he'd loved it from the first moment she turned her head from the beer tap and met his eyes.

Shit.

Fuck.

"It's part of that life, Coert," Tom said quietly. "You leave here, put Tony's skin back on, your whole life is a lie and it isn't just the bad guys who get it."

This was his first undercover job, though he'd been laying the groundwork before he slid into that world so he'd had his taste of it. Now he'd been living it for three months.

He knew that.

But he'd never been ordered to make a twenty-three-year-old girl with the greenest eyes Coert had ever seen have feelings for him so he could use her to take down her friends.

"Lonnie's digging in deeper but Lars isn't stupid, and he knows Lonnie has a big mouth and is essentially a total fuckup. It's Maria who does the runs for them. She's pretty. Fast talker. Sly as hell. Lars is grooming her for bigger things, including warming his bed. Maria is Cady's girl. None of this is gonna end well," Coert told them something he'd already reported.

"Their decisions, their consequences. Cady's being loyal but staying removed, so you keep her in while keeping her out and use that to get in deeper," Malc advised.

"And you wanna share how to pull off that miracle?" Coert asked.

"Give her Coert but do it being Tony," Tom answered.

He'd already done that. Three times.

And she'd liked it, three times.

And Coert had liked doing it, three times (though he wasn't a big fan of watching her the five seconds it took him to get to her as she fought off two would-be rapists, he still liked that it was him who saved her).

Coert sighed.

"If you're Coert, man," Malc said low, "after it's done, if you wanna salvage it, it won't be hard to do."

He'd seen the girl . . . no, *woman* . . . three times and she even made hangover eyes and a Sip and Save smock cute.

She could be shy.

She could be bold.

She could be clueless.

She could be sweet.

She was growing up the hard way, needed someone solid in her life to make sure she did it the right way, and she didn't hide she was looking to let stuff she wasn't big on, but felt tied to due to loyalty, slide out of her sphere so she could focus on that.

He couldn't pretend to be in a drug dealer's crew and be that person for her.

But he'd been ordered to.

And he wanted to be.

So he was going to.

"Fuck," he muttered.

"Get out there, man," Tom encouraged.

Coert gave him a look, Malc a look, then he gave them a wave, turned and walked away.

Five

EVEN A SHADOW

Present day…

I drove up to the lighthouse, shocked that they'd been able to tear down and reinstall the fence in the period of time I'd been gone.

Sure, I'd been gone for five weeks, which was a long time, but it was a long fence.

And now it was all brand new.

After we'd agreed to accept an offer on Patrick's house, before I'd left to go back to Denver I'd been able to settle on a contractor as well as find an interior designer in Augusta.

In order to assist the workers to be free to do what they had to do without being disturbed (too much), not to mention perform a quick hit to assist in the overall look of the place, we'd decided the fence would be first. We also decided on a pretty white picket fence that didn't scream *go away* but did delineate the public space from private property.

Considering summer was coming on, my contractor had a bunch of jobs lined up, so he couldn't even start for a couple of weeks after I'd signed on with him and it was going to be skeleton crews until he could hire some more workers to see the old girl to rights.

But it was clear they hadn't messed about while I was away.

The single concave pickets rose from four feet up to five-foot, gothic pointed posts and was more solid than the old split rail, but it also seemed friendly and was amazingly attractive even if it clearly defined the boundary of the house versus the public tract.

And the post points were painted a glossy black that fit the color scheme of the buildings it outlined beautifully.

I loved it.

I loved the new gate even more.

Also a single, sweeping concave, even if it was a double-door gate, it was attached to substantial stone columns on either side and had huge black iron hinges with black iron spikes coming up through the wood rather than pickets.

Once I'd selected it, Walt, my contractor, said the gate probably wouldn't come in for six to eight weeks as it was a custom order. He'd obviously gotten on that right away, ordered it before I even left Maine, because there it was.

And it was *fabulous*.

I parked outside it (since it was closed), got out and walked to it, feeling a chill of anticipation slide up my back, and not because there were seven different trucks parked on my property, which meant a goodly amount of people inside doing things that would make it my home.

No, because what I had ordered also obviously had been completed and delivered, and since I'd had it sent to Walt he'd had it put up.

It was a large sign on the stone column beside the gate, brass with a black background, the words standing out in shiny relief.

I walked up to it and read it, even though I'd drafted it myself, with the help of Jackie, who ran the Magdalene Historical Society (needless to say, once I'd witnessed the tulips, I'd gotten inspired and thrown myself headfirst into a variety of projects in the three weeks between tulip witnessing and Patrick's house being sold).

The sign read:

Magdalene Lighthouse

Built 1832

Private Property

The lighthouse on Magdalene Point was designed and built by Abraham Thomson after the lighthouse that was built on this site in 1786 became unstable due to a fire. Mr. Thomson designed and constructed several lighthouses along the eastern seaboard of the United States, of which many still remain today.

Unlike many lighthouses, but a hallmark of Mr. Thomson's lighthouse architecture, Magdalene Lighthouse is wide, not narrow, designed for the keeper to live within the structure, rather than outside in a detached home or the beacon rising from a homestead.

Distinct from any of Mr. Thomson's other lighthouses, he included an extraordinary observation deck enclosed entirely by glass as the fourth story of Magdalene Lighthouse.

The lighthouse has always been manned but was automated in 1992.

This means the original structure prior to its demolition was the first lighthouse in Maine, however Magdalene Lighthouse was the last in Maine to be automated.

Magdalene's lighthouse has been privately owned and operated since it was built. Limited tours of the site are available by appointment only. You can find a history of the building and its keepers, as well as book tours, at the Magdalene Historical Society. Please do not disturb the owner to request a tour.

Outside of guided tours, although you are invited to take photos outside the gates and fence, the owner asks that you be respectful of privacy.

The owner further requests no photography after sundown unless previously arranged through the Historical Society. The police will be notified of violators.

Please do not block the road, gate or drive. Those who do will unfortunately be towed at the vehicle owner's expense.

I smiled to myself as I thought about the other signs I'd ordered, wondering if they'd arrived and were also put up.

Smaller, they'd be affixed (or perhaps already were) to the stone columns that supported the tall gates on either end of the property, where the coastal path led.

As drafted, they'd read:

Magdalene Lighthouse

Built 1832

Private Property

Please do not pass.

The owner asks with any photography that you're respectful of privacy.

Tours are limited and can be booked through the Magdalene Historical Society. Please do not disturb the owner to request a tour.

The owner requests no photography after sundown unless previously arranged through the Historical Society. The police will be notified of violators.

Much friendlier than the last owner, and suffice it to say, Jackie was beside herself with glee that I was going to allow ticketed tours of the lighthouse one Saturday and one Sunday (not the same weekend) a month, no matter the season. She was delighted not only that it was a draw for tourists, something they'd never had and something she was certain would be popular, but that I was going to allow the society to keep the cost of the tour tickets.

As for me, I could absent myself from the house two days a month, and due to space and in order to keep track of everyone so they wouldn't wander, tours would be no more than six people and only one guided tour would be in the house at a time.

Not to mention, if things turned out even half as beautifully as Walt and Paige (my interior designer) were planning, I'd be proud to show off just how much more magnificent it was going to be.

I noticed the wires coming out of the stone at the top of the sign where the sign (and gate) would be lit with gooseneck lights not only for curious tourists after dark but for me.

Studying the wires, I jumped as one side of the gate started to swing open and looked that way to see Walt was the person doing it.

"Elijah, one of my boys, clocked you, thought you were a tourist. Climbed up, saw it was you," he stated, finishing, "You're back."

"I am," I confirmed unnecessarily.

"How d'you like the gate?" he asked.

"I'd kiss it if I didn't think that would concern you about my mental health."

He laughed and gestured to the side he'd opened. "We got it wired but we haven't put the keypad or remote on yet. Now that you're back, I'll get a boy on that."

I shook my head and walked his way. "I won't be bothering you much, Walt. There's a lot to be done and you don't need a nosy woman stopping you or your men from doing it."

"Be obliged and be shocked," he returned. "To start with, it'd be a first. Clients are nosy but I get that. But also, I'd be curious as all hell to see how this place shapes up."

He was right. I was going to be curious.

But I preferred to get it done.

I looked beyond him to the buildings and saw the studio no longer had shingles on the roof.

The rest of it looked just like it had before.

"How are things going?" I asked.

"Doing the roofs now from worst to best," he told me, glancing behind him. He looked back at me. "That was a hard call so we kinda flipped a coin."

I smiled at him.

"Studio is being done now, as you can see. We'll move to the garage next then the generator building," he shared.

I nodded.

"Stuff you can't see from here, everything's gutted and it's been hauled away," he reported. "Clean slate now. So when we get the roofs on, we'll be able to dig in. As we decided before you left, we'll be doing the studio first since it won't take as much to get it sorted out so you'll have a place to stay while we work." He tipped his sun-bleached blond head and asked, "You wanna come up and see?"

I most assuredly wanted to come up and see.

"Sure," I replied.

His gaze turned to my rental car. "You wanna drive that up?"

I shook my head. "I'll walk."

"Suit yourself," he murmured, stepped out of the opening of the gate, and after I made my way through, he closed it right behind me.

I studied him curiously.

"To say we got interest in what we're doing is an understatement," he explained. "Good those signs came in. I couldn't get them up fast enough."

"So they're working," I remarked.

He nodded, starting to walk so I fell in step beside him.

"Still got folks taking photos, but they don't park in the way like they used to, so my boys and suppliers can get through. One of my men gets caught by someone while he's opening the gates, they might ask questions, but that's about all. Before, they just jumped the fence or pushed open the gate. So I'd say the fence works too."

"Do you think I need to have signs made to be put up along the perimeter?" I asked, hoping I wouldn't. They would muddle the clean look of the fence not to mention be unfriendly.

I didn't want people jumping the fence and knocking on my door, but I was of a mind a fence was a fence. The statement was made by its very existence. In other words, you didn't jump it. So I hoped it and the signs at all the entry points to the property would work.

"We'll keep an eye on things, see if we have any troubles. But so far, since the fence went up, no jumping, and since the signs went up, no one has pushed through the gate," Walt replied.

That was good.

We sallied forth with the tour and he had not lied. Everything was gutted in every building. No rotting furniture. No terrifying kitchens. No catastrophic bathrooms.

It wasn't clean but it wouldn't need to be. Not yet.

What it was, was *gutted.*

"Windows have been ordered, the ones on the outbuildings are standard and have been delivered, so those'll go in soon," he shared when we'd made it to our final destination, gone to the top and then retreated down the stairs and were on the bottom floor of the lighthouse. "Got men coming in to do the foundation work on the outbuildings starting next week. Paige says her people are good to send the stuff you guys decided on for the studio when we're ready. I'm thinking that'll be the week after. We're finding some rot under the shingles as I expected, but a goodly amount of it, something I didn't expect. So the roofs are gonna take longer than I thought. But only a couple of days."

"I imagine you run into a lot of that," I observed.

"We do, though don't run into a lot of clients who get it," he said, and I looked up at him.

"I want it done right, Walt, not in a hurry. If I could snap my fingers and have it all as I want it, I would have done that two months ago. Alas, that's not in my power."

He laughed again but sobered and said, "We're taking pictures, Cady. Not doing you dirty. We'll show you what we run into and if it gets hairy and things are gonna get outta hand or jack up cost, we'll share with you and get your go ahead."

"That's appreciated," I replied, looking around and fitting ideas Paige was sending me to the space in my head.

"Oh, almost forgot, the sheriff came by," Walt said casually.

My vision went blurry, the blood in my veins stopped moving and the functionality of my lungs ceased.

I could do nothing but stare at him, watching him pull out a wallet that, if I had any ability to think in that moment, I would have guessed his wife was in denial about its existence because it was stuffed full at the same time falling apart.

"He gave me his card to give to you," he muttered.

"The sheriff?" I couldn't help it. It came out as a squeak.

Walt stopped rifling through his wallet and looked at me.

"I know. I was surprised too. We don't get a lot of work in this county, contractor here underbids every job we quote on. We just have to come in sometimes to fix stuff he cuts corners on. You get what you pay for, but whatever. So I don't know the guy, never met him, never had any dealings with him. Or the sheriff in my county as a matter of fact. Not sure what the sheriff's business was but he seemed pretty laidback. Not like he had an issue. Just asked if you were around, and when I said you weren't, he asked me to give you his number."

"He asked for me," I cleared my throat, "by name?"

Walt nodded, going back to his wallet. "I figured you'd want to find out what that was about so I gave him your number. From your response to this news, he didn't call."

No.

Coert didn't call.

He had my number but he didn't call.

And it was worth it to repeat *he had my number.*

And he knew I was here.

So he'd come to the lighthouse to speak to me.

God, I wasn't ready for this. Not even close.

"Here it is," Walt said, pulling out a card and offering it to me.

I didn't want to take it. I didn't even want to look at it.

But so as not to give anything away, I took it.

I wanted to ask a million questions. Walt said he'd seemed "pretty laidback" but I wanted more on his demeanor, what he said, how long he was there, did he seem keen to see me in a good way or did he act like he might shoot me on sight.

The only thing I allowed myself to ask was, "Did he give you any idea why he was looking for me?"

"Nope, I asked though. He just gave me his card and told me to tell you to call him. That's it. He wasn't here but, say, five minutes, if that. Maybe he just gives his time to welcoming folks to town." He gave a tilt to his head to indicate the space we were in. "But I figure it isn't like this is just some house in a neighborhood. Maybe just wants to introduce himself, make sure you're good at the same time you got things covered."

That wasn't what he wanted.

"Maybe," I mumbled.

"And also, one of Boston Stone's people stopped by."

I hadn't come close to recovering from Coert visiting my new home, I couldn't move to a different subject.

"Of Stone Incorporated," Walt prompted when I said nothing.

"I, uh…don't know of that."

He shook his head. "Local developer. Big muckity-muck. Wasn't him that showed personally, one of his minions."

"I…" I shook my head too. "Why?"

Walt shrugged. "No clue. She said she'd come back but she hasn't yet. Though I don't do a lot of work in this county, I do know of that guy and he sticks his nose in with a lot of stuff. Especially if there are hammers, drills and money to be made."

"This is a family dwelling, he can't send a minion to every family dwelling that needs some updating."

Walt shot me a grin. "It is a *family dwelling*, maybe the coolest one I've ever worked on, though I wouldn't describe what we're doing as *some updating*." He stated that last like he thought it was hilarious, and in another frame of mind, I would have agreed. "But it's probably not about the property. He's tangled in a lot of stuff. We're gonna need a lot of supplies to set this place to rights. He probably wants to make sure your contractor is utilizing the right suppliers."

"And I can assume you aren't using suppliers he's tangled up in," I remarked.

"Never met the guy, only know his reputation, but to be honest with you, I do business with people who take pride in what they do and do it well, not people who just wanna make a buck. So no, we don't use his people."

I gave a short nod. "I approve of this philosophy."

He shot me another grin. "Thank God."

I could not exactly grin back. I didn't care about whoever Boston Stone was. I was still worried about what was happening with Coert.

But I gave it a shot, hoping it didn't come out as a grimace as I said, "If there's nothing else, I should leave you to it."

"Nothing else, Cady. But if there is, I'll give you a call and we can do some regular meets to go over progress. You back at the inn?"

This was an issue I'd had prior to returning.

Magdalene was a tourist town with all-year tourist trade, though part of the year due to weather was not as fruitful as other parts.

We were heading into summer, one of the fruitful parts. So I'd actually had to delay my return because the suite had been booked at the inn and now it was open for two and a half weeks. Somewhere to lay my head when I didn't have to pack up and move to another room after a day or two.

But finding accommodation wasn't easy considering most places had had bookings for months. Walt gave me his estimates of when the studio would be done, but with the roof, window and foundation work having to happen before he got into anything on the inside, that estimate was two months away. If they were delayed, and they would be delayed, it would be more.

So now I had bookings at the inn for two and a half weeks, moving to an Airbnb for two weeks, then moving to a bed and breakfast with an open cottage at the back for a week and a half, after that, back to the suite at the inn for a week. I was working on where to go after that and it would seem to be a safe bet that I'd need to tack on at least another week or two.

It would not be fun packing up and moving around so much only to end that going somewhere that would still be a construction zone for months.

But in the end, it would be worth it.

And if worse came to worse, I could just go home to Denver for a visit.

"Yes, back at the inn," I told him. "But I'll be moving around. It was hard to find space for a long period of time with the season almost on us."

"I hear of anything semi-permanent that comes up, I'll let you know," he shared.

"That'd be nice."

We shook and I walked out, not taking in the view or the workers or my fabulous new fence and gate.

I walked right to the gate, opened it, went through, closed it and got in my rental.

I sat in it thinking that I needed a car, this being my ploy to stop myself from thinking about something else.

To say the renovation of the lighthouse was going to dig deeply into what Patrick had left me was an understatement (not that it would dig that deeply, that was just how solid Patrick had left me).

Just the fence would give many people heart palpitations.

When Pat heard about the state of the place (and I'd showed around pictures), he'd lost his mind (on top of losing his mind that I was moving across the country at all, much less doing it to live close to, "those two fucking, fucking *assholes*," this said loudly and Pat didn't talk loud…or curse, not very often).

I stared unseeing at my beautiful new gate thinking that it had been good I'd been unable to obtain the suite at the inn in order to return, making my visit home a long one. It lessened the impact of the blow (somewhat) of the news I'd delivered.

Kath and Shannon, particularly, behaved like my move was a betrayal.

Mike had practically been apoplectic and used much harsher words when referring to Coert and Caylen and my future proximity to them.

I didn't blame them for these reactions.

At the very least I should have been open about the decisions I was making. That said, even explaining to them why I'd done it the way I had, they didn't realize that their heated and inflexible belief that I was doing the wrong thing made my sharing moot. We would never have agreed and it would have made the process even more painful than it already was.

In the end, it was the lighthouse that did the work.

Like it was the magic it was, even with the state of it, the photos (especially with the tulips) couldn't help but win everyone around.

The kids came first, the younger ones beside themselves that visiting Auntie Cady meant going *there.* And Verity had been thrilled, considering Magdalene was only about a six-hour drive from New Haven. It meant she had family close. It meant she had *me* close. It wasn't easy going home for the weekend from Connecticut to Colorado. But it would be to hop a flight up to see me (and me to do the same to see her).

The adults eventually followed suit, but only when I told the men I'd keep them abreast of everything that had anything to do with the renovation and when I told the women they could help me decorate.

On this thought, to keep my mind off Coert, I tossed Coert's card into my bag, grabbed my phone and got out of the car to take pictures of the fence on both sides as well as the gate.

I texted the photos to the guys and gals and got back in my car.

I'd just turned around outside the gates and was about to drive down the lane when I pulled off to the side and idled in order to take a call.

Kath.

"Hey there," I greeted.

"Oh my God! That fence is *sublime.*"

Kath.

My sweet Kath.

Coert had come to the lighthouse looking for me, knowing I was *there*, getting my *phone number*, and just her voice made me feel better.

Her excitement helped that feeling even more.

"You have to see it in person," I told her. "Sublime doesn't cover it."

"Totally. And guess what?"

"What?" I asked, feeling my lips curve up.

"After you left yesterday, we had a family discussion, and with you and Verity both out there, we thought it'd be awesome to come for Christmas. So we're all coming. *All of us.* We're trying to figure out who's going to sleep where and finding some space so you aren't covered in thirteen people, but everyone's excited. We can't *wait.*"

They couldn't wait?

"Oh my God, Kath, that would be amazing!" I cried.

"I know!" she cried back.

I immediately started strategizing.

"Okay, well, some of the kids can sleep in the family room on the second floor, but we'll have to be creative about getting showers in because there'll be only one in the house. And two couples could definitely do the studio. That's quite a big space. And Daly and Shannon and the kids could be in the loft over the garage. It'll be a close fit but we can get air mattresses. And if Verity and Bea are good with it, they can take the downstairs living room. I'll make sure the couch is a pullout. I don't know, but I think we can make it work so everyone can be together."

"We'll book some rooms somewhere close, just in case," Kath replied.

"Good plan," I agreed.

"And just to say, definitely that soft green blend of tile for your bathroom. It's utter *perfection*," she told me.

I was not surprised at this abrupt subject change. I'd been sending her ideas that Paige had sent me and all the women were excited to help, but Kath was throwing herself into it with unadulterated glee.

"I totally agree. I fell in love with it and tried to see if I'd fall out, but I just couldn't."

"That shield mirror she found is inspired too. All those fancy edges. *Fabulous.*"

I grinned. "It's like we have one mind."

"Get her to order it," she commanded. "And I cannot *wait* to see it all come together and then see it *in person*."

"Me either, sweets."

And suddenly I felt like crying.

They were coming out for Christmas.

They didn't like what I was doing. They were worried about me. But just like Patrick's kids, they were supporting me regardless in every way they could do it.

"He came to the lighthouse," I blurted, my voice hoarse, the words seeming yanked from me.

I didn't want to share but I'd already moved forward with life-altering plans that altered everyone's life, not just my own, doing this very soon after we all lost Patrick. I knew I'd hurt them, Kath especially, so I shouldn't do it again.

But more, I couldn't do this on my own.

I didn't have her near but the way we were, she was never far.

"I'm sorry?" she asked.

"Somehow he knows I'm here. While I was in Denver, he came to the lighthouse looking for me."

"Which one?" she asked quietly.

"Coert," I told her.

"Not the one I'd pick," she muttered.

I pulled in a deep breath because he was not the one I'd pick either.

Caylen would be difficult, but I'd had a lifetime of him being an ass. Mom and Dad both loved me, but they were hard on me. They had expectations of me that hurt when I couldn't fulfill them and they didn't back down (or Mom didn't).

But Caylen had always been just an ass.

Coert, however…

"It's not like you're not out there for just that, babe," she said.

"I know but I'm not ready."

"You know the right way, Cady," she replied.

I did.

My parents had taught me. Patrick had taught me the same. And I'd watched Pat, Kath, Mike, Pam, Daly and Shannon teaching it to their kids.

Don't procrastinate, especially on the things that were the hardest.

Get them done and out of the way.

"Regardless of what happens, you both need to establish the lay of the land," she decreed.

This was true.

"So he knows you're there. Seek him out, share you want to talk, ask him out to lunch…or whatever," she suggested.

Ask him out to lunch.

The very thought terrified me.

"Okay, you're right, I…he knows I'm here, I shouldn't hide. I should let him know that I know he knows I'm here and that I'd like to have the chance to explain things so maybe we could get a coffee or something," I planned.

"Like you have anything to explain," she grumbled.

"Kath," I warned, not wanting to go there.

She hadn't been there. She'd only heard the stories.

She didn't know.

They thought Coert was the two-faced villain in that tale of woe.

But he was just doing his job.

And I was just being the me that I used to be.

He'd done his best to do right by me.

There was just no "right" in the way all that went down.

"Okay, right, it's a good plan. Time has passed. Wounds hopefully healed. You've both grown up. Life is life and what happened, happened, and you've both matured, moved on. Go ask him to coffee," she encouraged.

"I'll let you know how it goes."

"Girl, I'll be on a plane by nightfall if you don't."

That was Kath and she wasn't being dramatic.

It still surprised me, at the same time it warmed me down to my bones, all that Patrick had given me. The girl in a Sip and Save where he got his coffee on his way to work that he was always kind to. The girl he found wailing like a lunatic at the side of the building and sat with her on the dirty sidewalk next to stinking dumpsters and listened.

And then did something about it.

I had been a damsel in distress often back then, the distress part being all my own doing.

He'd also pulled me out of my bent to be just that.

Oh yes, he'd given me a lot.

"Since I'd love for you to come for a girlie weekend when things start shaping up, let's not waste the frequent flier miles right now," I returned. "I'll call."

"You better."

"I'll *call*."

"You *better*."

"I'm hanging up now," I warned her.

"So am I. Order the tile and mirror. And if he's a jerk, then he's a jerk, Cady. It's just proving what your family already knows. Let him be a jerk and then move on and make that lighthouse a masterpiece, and he's what he's actually been for nearly two decades. History. If he's not then...well then, we'll see."

We'd see.

We'd see...*what*, exactly?

What did I want?

Forgiveness?

A second chance (that thought gave me a shiver)?

And what might Coert want (except the biggest probability, nothing to do with me)?

I didn't ask any of that.

I said, "Right."

"Love you," she replied.

"Love you more."

"Love you most."

"Love you more than most," I parried.

"Shut up and go deal with the sheriff."

God.

Deal with the sheriff.

"Okay, Kath. Speak soon."

"Yeah, babe. 'Bye."

"'Bye."

We hung up and I stared at the lane in front of me, any courage I had coming through my bond with Kath starting to dissipate immediately now that the connection was lost.

I hit the button to slide down the window, stuck my head out and looked back at my lighthouse.

Only then did I have it in me to put the car back in drive and head to town.

UNFORTUNATELY BY THE time I made it into town and found a parking spot outside the sheriff station, all the nerve had totally left me.

Therefore I found myself sitting in my rental, staring at the building, trying to pump myself up to do something, anything. Get out of the car, walk in and ask to speak with Sheriff Yeager. Or just grab my phone, his card, punch in his number and tell him I'd heard he'd come out to the lighthouse and I'd like him to meet me somewhere for coffee.

At the very least, if he knew I was there and this showdown was behind me, I could finally go to a shop or restaurant without worrying about him seeing me.

The problem was, that didn't seem like very good motivation to endure the showdown.

No, there seemed about five million better reasons to indefinitely delay the showdown.

It was on this thought that I jumped in my seat and swallowed a scream when knuckles rapped on my side window.

I turned my head to see an attractive male hand disappear only to be replaced by the attractive face of Coert Yeager.

It was a sad fact that many men aged well.

And it was an absolutely dismal fact that Coert aged better than any man I'd ever known. Even Patrick, who was handsome at sixty-five and retained vestiges of that even into his eighties, giving that to all of his sons, didn't have the staying power of handsomeness that Coert had.

I'd seen it in the pictures the private investigator took.

But having it right there beside me blew my breath clean away.

"Roll down the window, Cady," he clipped, his angry voice also making me jump and alerting me to the fact his face was not only still beautiful, it was furious.

This was not starting well.

I should leave.

I should start the car, pull out and *leave.*

I turned the key enough to give the car power and hit the button to roll down the window.

"Not a good idea, casing a sheriff station," he declared before the window was fully down.

I took my finger off the button leaving it a third of the way up.

Casing a sheriff station?

What was he talking about?

"I—" I began but I barely got that out.

"Figured when your PI disappeared that somethin' was up, looked into it, saw your sugar daddy bit it. Shoulda known you'd make your move after the old coot was out of the way, but Christ, didn't think after all this time even *you* could be that screwed up."

I struggled to breathe, my chest moving cumbersomely in an effort to force down oxygen.

Your sugar daddy bit it.

Sugar daddy.

Bit it.

Make your move.

God, *old coot.*

And he knew about Patrick's PI.

Of course he would.

Of course, of course, of course.

He was a police officer. This would not go unnoticed.

Damn!

"He wasn't my—" I started to tell him that first, it wasn't my PI and second, Patrick wasn't my sugar daddy and last, as old as he'd become, he'd never been an *old coot.*

I didn't get any further with that either.

"Have no clue what's in your head, you movin' out here. Then again, I never had any clue how your messed-up mind worked. But for the record, I don't like it. And on that record, I'll state plain I don't wanna see you. I don't wanna hear from you. I don't want anything to do with you. I can't imagine what would give you even that first hint that I'd ever wanna have you even a shadow in my life again, but just to make absolutely certain you're with me on this, I don't want even a shadow of you in my life again. If that means you abandon the lighthouse, folks'll deal. We have before. And that would be my choice, you getting the hell out of town, as far as you can go, and staying there. But if you stick around, Cady, you do it avoiding me. All that needed to be said was said. There's no going back even if I wanted to. But just to make certain we're clear, I irrevocably *do not.*"

I stared through the window at him wondering if he could see me bleeding.

"Confirm we're clear," he ground out.

He could not see me bleeding.

Then again, the last time he'd shredded me, he didn't see it either.

"We're clear," I whispered.

And with that, just like Coert, he didn't nod, he didn't say farewell. He straightened and sauntered in his hulking way (even if, still, his frame was far from a hulk) to the steps to the sheriff station and in.

Not looking back.

I started the car.

I took pains to check my mirrors then turn my head to make certain that, backing out onto busy Cross Street, I wouldn't hit anyone.

I then drove the three blocks to the inn.

I parked in their lot at the back. I got out. I went up to the lovely White Pine Suite with its fireplace and delicious soaking tub and scrumptious gray sheets under its crisp blue and white paisley comforter with its shock-of-color red toss pillows and let myself in.

I went right to that bed and fought picking up the phone to call the front desk and ask them to send up two bottles of their very good Syrah.

Instead, I called Kath.

"How'd it go?" was how she greeted me.

I didn't tell her.

I burst into tears.

Six

STICK WITH ME

Eighteen years earlier…

"So what do you think?"

I did a slow turn, taking in the condo.

Tony's friend obviously made good money in construction because the place was nice.

But Tony's friend wasn't exactly tidy, and even though he wasn't filthy, he didn't clean every week (or every month) and he'd clearly not given the place a scrub down before he'd left.

Although it wouldn't be my first choice to clean up the house (and bathroom) of some guy I didn't know, I'd had to clean the bathrooms at Sip and Save so the bathrooms here would be a walk in the park.

And it was free. A *way* nicer place than what I'd had before, and bigger, multi-level, two bedrooms, two baths and a basement with washer and dryer.

A *washer and dryer.*

Practically luxury!

This meant no laundromats.

I hadn't been home to do my laundry since the last time my mother watched me fold my undies in their huge utility room, weighing me down with her disillusionment that I'd broken all of the dreams she'd had for her daughter.

Mom and Dad's utility room was the worst but laundromats sucked (almost) as much.

Now it was like my whole life had changed. A little cleaning, pick up the mail, plenty of time to find a good place, to save up money and get my security deposit back.

I didn't know what to do with all this good fortune.

"Their job is gonna run long," Tony said when I didn't reply. "'Least two weeks and the boss wants my bud to stay and do some finishing work. So you can move in when you want and you got nearly three months to find a new crib."

More good fortune.

I stared up at him and took in those hazel eyes.

Totally more good fortune.

"So it good for you?" he prompted.

"Totally."

He grinned. "Awesome. When do you wanna move in?"

"My landlords said they'd give anyone a bonus of seventy-five bucks if they moved out by the end of next week."

"Then we're movin' you out on your first day off."

We were moving me out?

"Uh...you don't have to help," I shared.

Though I didn't know who would. I didn't want to ask Lonnie. Maria was not immune to working diligently at a fabulous hairstyle but not so much lugging furniture around, but to help me out she wouldn't say no, she just wouldn't like it. But with her came Lonnie and that was out.

I had a daybed that was my couch and bed, a dresser, an end table, some kitchen and bathroom stuff and clothes, so it wasn't going to take a mammoth U-Haul and an entire day of dragging crap around.

But I couldn't move myself.

When I said what I said, Tony looked guarded. "Lonnie helping you?"

I shook my head. "No...I haven't even told them I have to move yet."

"So who's gonna help you?" Tony pushed.

I bit my lip and looked anywhere but him.

"Cady," he called.

I forced myself to look at him.

His eyes were shining. "Not like you got a mansion of shit to move, am I right? You said you live in a studio?"

"All my stuff could probably fit in the back of your truck," I admitted.

"Then your next day off, we're putting it in the back of the truck. Casey's extra bedroom is empty, and if you need more space, we'll use the basement. And you're all good."

"You've already done so much," I noted.

"And I wouldn't offer if I had a problem with doin' more," he returned.

"Tony—"

"Cady."

He cut me off saying my name but said no more.

He really didn't have to say any more.

It wasn't like Lonnie and Maria were my only friends (just my closest ones, and to be honest all the rest had grown distant—mostly because of Lonnie and Maria) but I had to work the next two weekends, my days off that week were Monday and Thursday, it was Tuesday. My other friends had real jobs and worked during the week. So unless I wanted to lose my shot at seventy-five bucks or ask for an extra day off, I had no choice but to lean again on Tony.

"Pies," I said. "Lots of 'em."

He reached out and touched my cheek, not a stroke, just touched the tip of his finger under the apple for not even a scant second. It was gone so quickly, it was like I imagined it.

It still felt *amazing*.

"So your next day off?" he asked.

"Thursday," I answered.

He went into the kitchen, opened and closed some drawers and came out of one with a pad of paper and pen.

He tossed them on the counter my way and said, "Address, Cady."

I moved to the counter and wrote down my address.

"YOU ARE NOT gonna pay for that," I declared what I thought was firmly.

This I did before Tony handed twenty-five bucks to the pizza delivery guy and said to him, "Keep it."

"Thanks," the guy muttered, didn't even look at me and took off.

Tony was holding the pizza and he was also closing the door.

"Let me pay you back," I said, wondering where my purse went.

I didn't have a lot of stuff but somewhere along the line my purse got lost in the shuffle of me getting moved in.

That being me getting moved in with Tony's help (this being me getting moved in with Tony doing most of the moving because he was bigger, stronger and super bossy, and part of that bossy was the clear indication he gave that he didn't think women could do manual labor outside of standing around, pointing and saying, "I want that there").

"Don't worry about it," Tony replied as he moved the pizza box into the kitchen.

"That's your thank you for helping me move," I told his back, following him. "So you can't pay for it."

"Already did," he told the kitchen, not looking back at me.

"So let me pay you back."

"You paid me back by ordering it. I'm hungry and I hate calling to order. They put you on hold, like you got a year to order a pizza. We're good," he shared as he dumped the pizza on his friend's kitchen table.

"It's not paying someone back to *order* a pizza, Tony."

His hazel eyes hit me. "It is when the person you're paying back says it is."

With one look into those eyes I knew I was going to get nowhere with this argument.

So I just whispered, "Tony."

"Cady," he replied, giving me a crooked grin that stated plainly he liked winning and it made big, bad, possibly felonious Tony Wilson look boyish and cute, something that made me, pathological fuckup Cady Webster, an even bigger moron because I could live just for the promise of another of those grins.

"I don't even have beer," I sniffed huffily, deciding to glare at him rather than think about how much I'd like to jump him (this an endeavor I'd been working at all day, we could just say Tony carting boxes and furniture was not hard to watch).

"You got Coke in any of that shit I lugged around today?" he asked.

I didn't.

Damn!

He knew my answer without me having to verbalize it, grabbed the pizza to toss it in the oven and muttered while snatching up my hand (*snatching up my hand*), "Let's go get some beer."

"I'm buying the beer," I proclaimed, and on doing so he stopped dragging me to the door and looked down at me.

"Which part about this aren't you getting?" he asked.

"Uh…what?" I asked back, apparently not getting any part of it.

"Cady, I'm doin' you a solid," he shared. "Shit goes bad for you, you end up soused and alone in the Trench at Wild Bill's fightin' off two assholes then sittin' on my tailgate bawlin' your eyes out, and *then* layin' a load of shit on me that life saw fit to land on you. First, guys don't like to see women fighting off assholes. Second, guys do not like it when life lands a load of shit on sweet girls who are just tryin' to make a go of things. And last, and this one might be almost as important as the fighting off assholes thing, guys do not like women crying. Gonna share somethin' about the brotherhood that might get me a demerit since I'm breaking the code and blabbing one of our secrets, but guys have no fuckin' clue what to do when women cry even a little bit. They're completely lost when a woman loses it and bawls herself sick. So if I gotta buy a pizza and a six-pack so you can stay on the right path and no other shit will hit where I gotta consider carrying a handkerchief, please, God, let me."

I wanted to kiss him.

He was being funny to hide how sweet he was actually being and I liked both enough to lay a hot and heavy one right on him.

But I couldn't kiss him.

So I glared at him again. "I'm not a crier."

His brows shot up over amused eyes. "Are you seriously laying that bull on me?"

"Things were extreme," I explained.

"Yeah, I know, split the skin on one of my knuckles landing my fist in that guy's face. So that didn't really escape me," he retorted.

Again with the funny but also mingled with me feeling bad he split the skin of one of his knuckles for me.

I did not remark on that.

I stated, "And I didn't bawl myself sick."

"It was close."

I arched a brow and put my free hand on my hip. "Are we getting beer or what?"

That got me the crooked grin (yep, that grin made the world turn), a tug on my hand, and when he was dragging me to the front door, he answered, "We're definitely getting beer."

I shouldn't go get beer with Tony Wilson.

I should serve him tap water with the pizza he bought, and as soon as he looked done with eating, shuffle him out the door and do my best never to see him again.

But I went to get beer with Tony Wilson.

I did this because it was coming clearer with each moment I spent with him that my life would never be the same if I never saw Tony Wilson again.

I was not ready for that to happen.

And something else far more alarming was coming clearer too.

This being the feeling that I probably never would be.

"SO I'LL PICK you up at nine."

It was after pizza and beer and get-to-know-you talk with a lot of banter and Tony's teasing.

Tony and I were standing at the door to my temporary new condo when he said that, confusing me.

"Sorry?" I asked.

"Saturday. Lars's party. Pick you up here at nine."

I stared up at him.

Was he asking me on a date?

Tony stared back but his confusion was not the same as mine, I knew, when he asked, "Didn't Maria tell you about it?"

She'd called, left a message, but what with packing and avoiding her and all, I hadn't had time to call her back. And she'd certainly call to invite me to a party.

"Well…no," I answered.

"Right," Tony stated. "Lars is havin' a party. Saturday night. You said you worked seven to three thirty Saturday, three thirty to midnight Sunday. So you're good to hit it and I'll pick you up at nine so we can do that."

I tipped my head to the side, deciding to explore this concept but do it carefully. "So in your quest to make certain I don't burst into tears again, you're not only acting as a house hunter, mover and pizza buyer, you're also my self-appointed chauffer?"

To that, he had no response but to give me a lazy smile, lift a hand, touch the tip of his finger under the apple of my cheek, take his finger away nearly before he touched me and turn to open the door.

He walked out of it, caught my eyes over his shoulder and said, "Saturday. Nine."

I guess that was that.

And I honestly didn't have any problem with that (outside of Lars and maybe seeing Lonnie and Maria, and there was of course the problem of Tony perhaps not being a guy I should allow myself to fall for).

"Can I thank you for helping me move?" I asked as he started to turn and walk away.

My question didn't stop him from turning and walking away, but he responded, "Yup."

"Then thank you. Now can I thank you for finding this awesome pad for me?" I called to his departing back.

"You can do that too," he returned, not even glancing over his shoulder.

"Then thank you again. Now can I warn you that I'm totally gonna find a way to give payback?" Now I had to kinda shout.

He lifted his hand and flicked it out at the side.

I didn't know what to make of that and I had no chance to make anything of it.

The evening shadows beyond his friend's little courtyard swallowed Tony up and I lost sight of him.

I still stood in the door, staring into the night after Tony, trying to talk some sense into myself and I did this for so long, the motion sensor light that illuminated the courtyard went out.

I closed the door thinking of nothing but the fact I did none of the heavy lifting that day, I didn't pay for the pizza *or* the beer, Tony was picking me up on Saturday at nine and I could still feel the touch of his finger on my cheek.

In other words, I didn't talk any sense into myself.

Instead, I wondered how important it was in life to be sensible.

And with Tony on my mind, I was coming to the conclusion the answer was…not much.

"SO WHAT'S UP with that?"

I turned from openly watching Tony from my place planted in a spot in Lars's living room, where I could see him standing talking to Lars in the kitchen, and I looked at Maria.

"What's up with what?" I asked but I knew.

She hadn't missed that Tony and I showed together and she *really* hadn't missed that he was holding my hand when we walked in the front door.

Now she was watching me closely in a way that didn't say girlfriend-ticked-her-best-friend-didn't-share-about-a-hot-guy. Instead, the way she was watching me made me feel funny, not with guilt that I hadn't shared, in a way that was strangely scary.

"When did you two become an item? And while we're at it, *how* did you two become an item?" she pressed. "You've been living in a world of Sip and Save ambition, not around long enough to say hello much less find time to flirt with shady characters."

I found it odd that Maria would describe Tony as a "shady character" when, okay, he kinda was with the company he kept, but he was a super nice guy outside of that. And anyway, it seemed she dug hanging out with Lars and if there was a shady character to beat all shady characters, Lars was that.

I lifted a shoulder, trying to shake the feeling I was getting from her. "We had a thing and I think he feels sorry for me."

"What kind of thing?" she asked.

I licked my lips and rubbed them together, sliding my glance away.

I hadn't shared about Tony, which meant I hadn't shared about The Trench either.

"Cady," she prompted impatiently.

I looked back at her. "I got in a situation in The Trench when you guys were hanging with the Chaos guys. It wasn't good. Tony showed and helped me out. I kinda lost it on him because my parents were being my parents, my landlord evicted me, my car was acting up, then that happened in The Trench and I was just done. I needed to unload and he was the closest one so he got it dumped on him. And now…well now…" I glanced back down the hall. "Well, now I think he's worried I'll fall off the deep end if he doesn't look out for me."

"He wants in your pants."

My eyes shot back to her and I felt my heart start racing. "He doesn't want in my pants. He's just a nice guy."

"He's not a nice guy, Cady. I don't know what he is but he's not a nice guy," she stated. "But first, *you got evicted*?"

I gave her a stretched-mouth *eek* look, which pretty much was my way of putting my hands up and saying *caught* in the best-friend-not-sharing gig.

"Babe, what the fuck?" she snapped.

"I need to look out for myself," I defended. "Shit is always going wrong for me. You and Lonnie have been there loads but I have to learn that I can't lean on other people all the time."

"Wait, let me get this straight," she started sarcastically. "You lookin' out for yourself and not telling your best girl you got fuckin' *evicted* is you leanin' on some dude you don't even know?"

I moved closer to her and lowered my voice. "Maria, in The Trench he dropped two guys who were being seriously uncool with me."

"Good," she shot back. "I'm glad. I'll buy him a beer some day for helpin' my girl out, a girl I'll say right now didn't share any of that shit with *me*. Her *best friend*. But just because he shows he *might* be one of the few decent ones who has a dick doesn't mean you should trust some dude you barely know."

"He found me a place to stay while I'm sorting out my home situation."

She rolled her eyes to the ceiling, mumbling, "Totally wants in your pants."

"I don't know what kind of guy he is really," I admitted, and her eyes rolled back to me. "I just know he's nice to me and it isn't like what you think. He hasn't made a move. He may hold my hand and a couple of times he's touched my cheek but he's not into me. He just, I think he's just one of those guys who's protective of chicks. Maybe he has a little sister or something and I remind him of her."

Though I was a little sister and my brother never held my hand and not only because he was an arrogant ass.

"You know, you really need to clue in," she returned, a flash in her eyes that seemed catty but it looked like it was chased with some kind of pain and that made my stomach lurch. "He wants to fuck you. Period. Dot. The end. And if you want that, then cool. Go for it. I bet he's good. But, babe, you need to get with the program. I don't know where your head is at half the time, but shit is happening all around you and if you don't start lookin' out for yourself better, Cady, I don't see good things."

Once she'd landed all of that on me, she took her beer and weaved through the crowd.

I lost sight of her only to feel the back of my neck tingling, so I looked again down the hall to see Tony's eyes on me. When his caught mine, he lifted his chin and shot me a small grin before he returned his attention to Lars.

My gaze drifted from him because my attention was on what Maria had said, and not just the fact that I'd missed Lonnie was into me and she was pointing out that maybe I was missing Tony was into me too, but mostly the other stuff she said.

She warned me to start looking out for myself better but it wasn't me who wanted to be here. I came with Tony. If he hadn't said he was picking me up to bring me here, I would have found an excuse not to come at all. And she was there and it seemed she liked being there, more it seemed like she liked all of these people just as much as Lonnie did.

But maybe she didn't. Maybe she had worries and doubts about who Lonnie was hanging with too.

And that catty, pained look? Did that mean she'd already noticed Lonnie had a thing for me and she was blaming me?

I had no opportunity to sort through all of this or weave through the crowd to get to Maria to have a clearly much-needed chat with my friend.

I was in a headlock, which made it fortunate I was sipping from a bottle of beer, because if I'd taken a cup from the keg in the kitchen rather than the beer Tony pointedly handed me from a case he'd pointedly brought and promptly hidden in the back of Lars's fridge after he gave me one, with the headlock, I'd have beer all over my hand.

"Where you been?" Lonnie asked, curling me around so I was forced into a full frontal headlock.

I lifted my eyes to him. "Jeez, Lonnie. I might want to drink a full beer one day."

His arm tightened and I noticed he wasn't being good-natured Lonnie, playful in a pretend-like-she's-your-little-sister way to hide you dig her.

His regard was serious and maybe even ticked.

"I asked you a question, Cady. You've like, totally disappeared. You get that big job then you say you gotta work all the time but you show up here with Wilson? What's up with that?"

Assistant manager at Sip and Save was hardly a "big job."

Then again, Lonnie didn't have a job that I knew of, how he and Maria got their money I had no clue, and in that very moment I realized I didn't have a clue not because I was clueless.

It was because I didn't *want* to clue in.

"Lonnie," I pushed at his hold on me with my neck as well as with my hand in his chest, "loosen up."

He didn't loosen, he tightened, and between my pushing and him tightening, I felt pain at my neck.

"Cady, I asked you a *fuckin' question.*"

"You're kinda hurting me," I told him. "Please, loosen up."

"I will when you answer my fuckin' question," Lonnie returned.

I opened my mouth but I didn't have the chance to get anything out.

"She said loosen up."

Oh boy.

That came from Tony and I could see Lonnie wasn't happy, but now I could *hear* Tony wasn't.

Shit!

Lonnie's gaze slid to the side right before mine did and we saw Tony standing close.

Eyes locked on Lonnie and yes…

Totally not happy.

"You're not in this," Lonnie declared.

"She said loosen up," Tony repeated.

"And, man, *I* said *you're not in this*," Lonnie reiterated, his hold on me getting tighter.

He may have backed down in that backyard months ago, but me walking in holding hands with Tony, drinking the beer Tony brought, Lonnie wasn't backing down now. Lonnie was making a statement it wasn't his to make ever, but especially not at a party where Maria was.

"Lonnie," I whispered calmingly.

"Let her go," Tony demanded.

"Take off, Wilson. Me and Cady are havin' a chat."

"Won't say it again," Tony warned.

"Don't give a fuck what you wo—" Lonnie started.

He didn't finish because Tony moved and suddenly I wasn't in Lonnie's hold.

Lonnie's arm was ripped from around my neck, Tony was shoving me clear at the same time twisting Lonnie's arm behind him and he didn't stop there.

Lonnie grunted with pain in a way I felt that pain before his knees buckled and he went down, flat on his belly, cheek in the carpet, arm thrust up his back. Tony was standing with a foot planted either side but bent over him and using his leverage to continue to put the hurt on Lonnie.

And putting the hurt on Lonnie he was doing to the point I worried he'd dislocate Lonnie's shoulder or actually break something.

I didn't get the chance to shake myself out of the shock all of this caused and tell Tony to back off because Tony was speaking.

"I walk into the house holdin' a woman's hand, *you* don't put your hands on her. You're stupid enough to do that, I tell you to stop, *you fuckin' stop*. But backin' that shit up, *she* tells you to stop, you…fuckin'…*stop*."

"Got it, man, fuck, got it. Now get off me!" Lonnie grunted, the pain he was feeling not hidden in his words.

He'd gotten his other hand under him and was pushing up but with the contortions of his face, I didn't think that was helping matters *at all*.

"No," Tony returned. "Since I got your attention I'll share you got yourself some and it isn't red. Mine's red. Yours is dark. Advice, *man*, take care of what you got or you're gonna lose it."

"Fuck off!" Lonnie bit out.

"You gonna leave Cady alone?" Tony pushed.

"Yeah, *fuck*! Now fuckin' *get off*!"

"Good," Tony clipped, and it looked like he twisted Lonnie's wrist for no other reason than to underline a point that was already boldface and italicized before he shoved him deeper into the floor and straightened from him.

He walked over him, grabbed my hand but didn't look at me.

He was looking beyond me, and when I hazily followed his eyes, I saw Lars was watching him closely.

"If this is your crew, bud, straight up, maybe it's me who doesn't want to move forward," Tony declared, and with that he tugged my hand so I was closer to him.

I tipped my head back to look up at him and saw his attention now focused on me.

"Where's your purse?" he asked.

"I—"

"Get it," he ordered.

It didn't occur to me to do anything other than hightail it to the couch where I'd tucked my purse and jacket behind an end table.

I nabbed them, shrugged on the jacket, returned to Tony, his fingers closed around mine again and he hauled me out the door, down the walk and to his truck. He unlocked and opened the passenger side door and I wouldn't have been surprised if he lifted me up and dropped me in the seat.

He fortunately didn't do that but I could feel the impatience wafting off of him as I climbed in, even if I did it hurriedly.

The door creaked loudly as he slammed it shut behind me and stalked around the hood.

He got in, started up and we chugged out into the road.

I sat silent and not because he was not hiding he was still pissed, and he was kinda scary when he was pissed.

I sat silent because he'd dropped Lonnie, who was my friend. Perhaps not a smart choice on my part but that didn't negate the fact he still was, and Tony hurt and humiliated him in front of a house full of people, who might not be good people but they were people Lonnie wanted to get tight with.

Not to mention, with great skill and not a second thought, Tony had taken care of the two guys who were on me in The Trench.

This said to me that Tony was not a stranger to violence. He not only didn't shy away from it, with very little ado, he instigated it to make his point and get what he wanted.

My mind was so taken up with all this, Tony was parking outside the courtyard to the condo before I realized he had also not spoken the whole ride home.

He got out, and I quickly did the same, but when I was out, he was right there, slamming my door shut with another loud shriek of the hinges.

As we walked to the front door, he didn't hold my hand.

No.

He lifted the hem of my jacket at the back and with a firm hand at its small, guided me to the door.

That was not a brotherly thing to do. That wasn't even a friendly thing to do.

That was what a girl's guy would do.

I was fighting shaking for a variety of reasons while trying to get my keys out of my purse, but when I managed it, I didn't even get the house key separated from the rest before Tony took them from my hand, found the right key and unlocked the door.

He pushed it open, turned to me, pressed me in and came in after me before I could open my mouth to speak in order to say something like, maybe I might need a few days (or a year or forever) to think about where my life was heading and who I was spending it with so I might need a little bit of space.

He slammed the door behind him and I jumped at the violence of the sound.

Freaked out now because I was alone in the house with an angry Tony who was kinda scary, I stood immobile right inside the door and watched his shadow move to a lamp on a table by his friend's couch.

He switched it on, tossed my keys irately on the end table and turned on me.

"A guy's up in your shit, Cady, you don't want him there, you never, not fuckin' *ever* say *please*," he ground out.

I blinked up at his face, realizing he might be pissed at Lonnie.

But he was also pissed *at me*.

"To—" I didn't quite start.

"Twice, I've seen that guy's hands on you. Twice, I've seen it clear you don't like it. And twice, you didn't do dick about it."

"I did."

"You didn't."

"I said—"

"You don't *say* shit. A man's got his hands on you, hands you don't want on you, you punch him in the fuckin' throat or knee him in the goddamned balls."

"He's my friend," I said quietly.

"He's not your friend," he shot back. "He's your girlfriend's boyfriend who wants to tag your ass. That's not a friend."

One could say he had a point with that.

"He's also a moron, and not just because of that," Tony carried on. "You need to distance yourself from him. You don't, when he fucks up…and he's gonna fuck up, Cady, that's the kind of guy he is, it's just waiting to see how huge that fuckup is gonna be…he's gonna drag everyone in his wake right down with him."

And here we were.

The crux of the matter.

So when I spoke again, I was whispering. "You hang with his people."

One could say I'd been more than a little bit clueless, maybe my whole life.

But right then I didn't miss the shutters slamming down over Tony's eyes.

"You do," I pushed carefully.

"I got my reasons," he returned.

"Okay, well…okay," I said, still not quite able to explore that mostly because I didn't want to, maybe not ever. "But that…that…" I looked to the door even as I threw my whole arm in that direction in a vague way before I looked again to him. "We haven't known each other very long but I've been with you maybe five times, Tony, and twice in those times you've gone straight to violence in front of me."

His chin jerked back in his neck as his brows shot up and he bit out, "Are you being serious here?"

I stood my ground. "You did."

"You wanted me to tap one of those guys who was grindin' up on you in The Trench on the shoulder and say, "Scuse me, you mind not bein' a motherfuckin' dick?'"

Another valid point.

"Okay, well, maybe the guys in The Trench don't count," I muttered.

"Ya think?" he asked sarcastically.

I decided to move us beyond that. "But you could have handled Lonnie differently, or you know, maybe let me handle him."

And, say, let me open the lock of my own front door.

"You weren't handling it."

"I've known Lonnie longer than you."

"And in that time you haven't been *handling it.*"

Shit.

Yet another valid point.

"Tony—"

I got no further.

He demanded to know, "Do you get what's happening here?"

I was beginning to.

I just didn't get where I was with all of that.

That wasn't true.

What was true was that I didn't want to go to the place that was smart and sensible and responsible, which would take me away from the place where Tony held my hand, handed me a beer, stating without words he didn't trust the assholes we were with not to date rape drug me and that was not gonna happen on his watch, and he touched my cheek in that sweet way of his.

I also didn't want to be in a place without Lonnie and Maria and the history we had, the memories we shared, bringing an end to good times, lots of laughs, the freedom to be crazy and stupid because we were young and that was the only time you could do that.

But I had to go to that place. The time was now to make that decision. And that time was now because if it wasn't made now…

"That can't happen," I told him quietly.

He shook his head once. "It's already happened, Cady."

I shook my head too, more than once. "I…this is me saying now, after what happened tonight, that I'm seeing the way things are and it can't happen."

"Something like this starts, you can't stop it," he told me.

That was exactly what it felt like.

He was like…like…a magnet and I was metal and all the laws of nature said there was nothing for it. But it wasn't like I was drawn to him. It was like I was connected to him and nothing could shake me loose unless all my molecules were jumbled up and I became a different me.

But *this* was where I had to pull my shit together.

This was where I had to decide I was going to be manager at the Sip and Save and who cared what my parents or anyone thought of that, it was good work, honest, and I could do it, and do it well and lay my head down on any pillow at night and know that.

And I was going to find an apartment in a nice part of town, it could still be a studio, but I wasn't going to slum it anymore, and even if I had to take babysitting jobs or whatever to make the extra I'd need, I was going to do it.

And when I made manager and I made okay money, I was going to start taking classes at a community college in management and marketing and shit like that.

I had no idea where that was going to take me. I just knew that was where I should go.

And I was going to do all of this because I was going to be someone I liked, someone worthwhile. I was going to make my way on the right path no matter how hard it was.

I was not in the right place. I was not around good people. It sucked to admit, but Mom had always been right. It wasn't so simple as to say they weren't good people, but Lonnie and Maria didn't make good choices and I had to separate myself from that.

And all that came with it.

Which meant separate myself from a man who saved me from being raped, silently listened as I poured all my shit out then he helped me deal with it, found me a place to live, moved me, bought me pizza, beer, held my hand and could make it seem like the world turned on his crooked smile.

"You scare me," I whispered.

The air in the room went heavy as his cheeks flushed and his eyes burned and he stood still and silent.

But I could actually *feel* the inner battle he was waging.

I just didn't know what the fight was about.

"People…they don't…people don't do that, Tony," I explained hesitantly. "They don't nearly twist a man's arm out of his shoulder for touching a girl they like. I can't…they all…" I shook my head. "All of them, even you, the people with Lars, they scare me. It's not right. They're not right. And I just…I…I just *can't*."

"Stick with me."

His words were so low, I almost didn't hear them.

But I heard them.

"Please don't ask me that," I whispered.

"Stick with me."

"Tony."

"Stick with me. Believe in me, Cady. Even if you don't know what I'm asking, I'm still gonna ask it. Don't give up no matter what."

He was asking something huge. Something I didn't understand but I knew it was too much. Too much to ask of me, Cady Webster, as the girl I was. Hell, maybe too much to ask of anybody.

"There's nothing to give up on. There's nothing at all," I told him, maybe trying to make myself believe my own words.

"There's something," he returned.

"Pizza and beer, that's all we had. And I'll make you a pie, Tony. Five of them. Payback. You don't get without giving. And then I'll find a place and I'll clean this one before I leave, and I'll ask my mom and dad to help me move out and you and me are square and we're done, and that's where I need to be. That's what's safe for me. That's what's right."

I realized I was breathing heavily watching him do the same, his eyes never leaving mine, the battle within him still warring on and it seemed he had to force it out when he repeated, "It's not pizza and beer. You know what it is. And no matter what, don't give up on it."

I didn't understand even though I totally did.

But I held on to the not understanding part so I wouldn't give in and race right over the start line of the very wrong path in the hopes of catching up with Tony.

"Right now, there's nothing to give up, Tony. We shouldn't make it so there is."

I was just able to get that out before he wasn't four feet away, he was right in front of me, his hands on either side of my face, his face bent to mine.

"You get it already, you just don't understand what you get," he whispered.

He made no sense at all and I understood him exactly.

I shook my head in his hands. "Please don't do this."

"You get it. You look at me and you get it. Believe in that, Cady. Believe in what you see. Believe in *me*."

"Stop it." My voice was now trembling as was my body. "There's nothing to get. There's nothing to believe."

"There's something."

I wrapped my fingers around his wrists and put pressure on to pull them away, but his hands didn't move.

"You've been so nice, so sweet, so cool about everything, but you told me yourself I need to stay on the right—"

"Look in my eyes and tell me you don't believe."

I looked in his beautiful eyes, right there, so close, the breath of his words rushing across my lips. And looking into those eyes I remembered thinking about giving our kids those eyes the first night I met him, and the trembling increased.

"You're scaring me," I whispered.

"You'll never be safer with anyone than you are with me."

I could oh so totally, easily fall into believing in him.

But that was hard to believe.

"But, Tony," I gave his wrists a shake and they didn't budge an inch, "you *scare me.*"

That was when, from inches away, I watched the shutters fly up on his eyes, brilliant, bright light beamed out, blinding me so bad, I blinked.

Then his mouth was on mine.

I was going to be manager at the store.

I was going to take classes at a community college.

I was going to *be somebody.*

I tried to pull away but his fingers slid back to curl into my scalp and his mouth opened over mine, his tongue touching my lips.

What happened next, maybe it was reflex.

Maybe it was instinct.

Maybe it was recklessness overwhelming me again, telling me I had this one chance, this one shot at this one beautiful adventure and I should take it.

Maybe it was because he was Tony and I was Cady and he was not wrong.

There was something.

Whatever the reason that made me do it, I opened my mouth, his tongue slid gently inside and it happened.

I tasted him.

He tasted of beer and old trucks and dark nights and bright days and holding hands and playful teases and crooked grins and shining eyes and man and musk and sex and a million, billion other things that made Tony that I hadn't yet discovered, and I couldn't have stopped my tongue from touching his in my need, my hunger, my *yearning* to have more.

To have *it all.*

My fingers tightened on his wrists not to push him away but to hold him right there, and he felt it. Making a rough noise in my mouth, he slanted his head, took the kiss deeper and gave me more.

And with his kiss, he filled me. He warmed me. My breasts swelled, my nipples hardened, my toes curled, my skin tingled, between my legs thrummed, my heart beat wild in my chest, and it wasn't all about sex.

It was about that moment. Me being fully present *in that moment.* The only one of its kind we'd ever have.

Our first kiss. Our beginning. The beginning of us which was the beginning of everything.

He broke the kiss and I made an involuntary mew at the loss of his tongue, his taste, *that moment*, but he kept his lips where they were, light and beautiful.

My eyes fluttered open and his were so close, our noses resting along each other's, our eyelashes actually brushed.

And I looked into his eyes and I knew what he knew I knew. I knew what I got but I still didn't understand, even after that kiss.

I knew I would walk to the ends of the earth with Tony Wilson. I'd jump off a cliff holding his hand. I'd cut for him. I'd bleed for him.

And I suspected one day I'd probably be willing to die for him.

But after that kiss, this didn't scare me.

With him right there, nothing else mattered, nothing else even existed.

This was simply where I was supposed to be.

No matter what.

He blinked and our lashes brushed again, bringing my focus to his gaze that was not boring into mine, not burning, but resting there, holding mine because there was nothing in the world I'd want more than to look into his eyes, and I saw right then he felt the same way.

"There's something," he whispered.

Yes.

There was something.

And that something felt like everything.

"Promise, Cady," he continued whispering. "Stick with me, no matter what."

There was no other answer to give him than the one I gave.

"I promise, Tony."

Something flickered in his eyes that was uneasy when I said his name, but before it could make me feel the same, the pads of his fingers dug into my scalp, his mouth took mine, his tongue slid inside and I was all in.

No matter what.

Seven

HE DIDN'T

Present day…

"Okay…okay…okay…holy *cah-rap*, that's way more beautiful than the pictures."

There was nothing I could do but smile as I drove Kath up to the lighthouse.

It was August. The sun was shining. Fluffy white clouds dotted the bright blue sky. My pristine white fence ringed the sloping green grass with the intermittent gray rocks poking through along my property. And the outbuildings had all been painted so their dazzling white and glossy black trim matched the perfection of the lighthouse with only their warm red roofs being disparate.

Months ago, after the altercation with Coert and after Kath had calmed me down, we'd made a plan.

I had bookings in inns and B&Bs and I had a mission.

Restore the lighthouse. Live there, if not happily ever after, then contentedly ever after.

Coert had been out of my life for a very long time and frankly, the time he'd been in it had *not* been long (it had just been eventful).

He wanted me to avoid him?

That I could do.

What I wasn't going to do was let him break me.

Not again.

So I honored my bookings and I watched the roofs go on and the windows go in and the studio begin to be transformed.

I did this finally enjoying Magdalene.

I went shopping in town and at what I learned were new shops at the jetty. I found a shack on the wharf that made such good coffee I went back and learned the man in the shadowed interior also made excellent seafood omelets. I had lunch at the Lobster Market in town. I had dinner at a place that was recommended by a cashier at Wayfarer's that was a town over called Breeze Point. I got salads or sandwiches on more than one occasion at Weatherby's Diner.

I also went on a whale watching tour (we didn't see any whales but I was loaded and I lived in Maine, I could try again a hundred times until I saw one).

I went down to Portland to explore. I went up to Bar Harbor because I heard it was beautiful and artsy, and it was, so I bought a bunch of stuff for the lighthouse, the studio and the apartment over the garage.

I went to Augusta to meet Paige and decide all things interior decorating.

I even went down to Boston, because in all the traveling I'd done with Patrick, we'd never been there and I'd always wanted to see Old Ironsides and eat real clam chowder. Not to mention walk the Freedom Trail, see the Old North Church, go to Lexington and Concord and be where the shot was fired that was heard round the world. And as sad as it would be, I wanted to visit Salem and soak in that history. I had even more reason to go in order to hit Harvard, take selfies and send them to Verity and Dex in aid of Dex harassing his sister.

But once my bookings ran out, even though I saw Coert nowhere (thank God), I turned tail and ran home, giving myself the excuse I needed to get my stuff because I'd be able to move in at least to the studio in just weeks, and Mike said we were going car shopping in Denver or he was flying out to Maine to help me find a vehicle, no ifs, ands or buts.

The real reason was that I needed the family to prop me up, help heal the wounds Coert had reopened and prepare to settle in, because I couldn't act like a tourist on a daily basis (actually I could, I just didn't want to, it was exhausting).

And now the time was right to come back. I didn't have to stay at the inn or find anywhere else because the studio was done. They'd begun work on the lighthouse so in a few weeks I could *move in*, move in and they would finish with the apartment over the garage after I was in my real new home.

Kath had come with me, citing that she just could not *wait* to see it all, but I knew she did it to make sure I was all good there before she'd be leaving and not seeing me for months.

Walt had shared that Paige had "set the place." He'd also mailed me a remote to the gate so right then, as I drove up the lane, I hit the button on the remote on the visor of my new Jaguar SUV and watched the gate start to swing open.

"Oh my God, Cady, this place is *perfection*," Kath breathed.

She was right.

This I could do, I thought as we rolled in when the gates opened.

This beauty that Patrick gave me. Verity (and then Dex) coming up some weekends. The family out for Christmas. Spring breaks. Summer holidays.

And when they weren't around, I could help at the Historical Society.

I could volunteer at an animal shelter.

I could garden.

I could cook.

I could read.

I was forty-one years old and had forty years (I hoped) ahead of me of, essentially, retirement where I could just sit back, enjoy "the kids" and do whatever pleased me.

Most people would kill for that opportunity.

So Coert was in town, and Kath wanted me to go up north to visit my brother when she was here so she could be close when he treated me like dirt.

I'd lived through worse.

Much worse.

My mother had frozen to death, for God's sake.

And I'd had to watch Patrick waste away.

If Coert wanted me to avoid him, fine. This wouldn't be hard. It was a small town but my lighthouse was miles away.

It would be fine.

It would all be fine.

Because I had that.

I stopped in front of the garage and Kath and I got out. I saw her head was tilted back, her attention focused on the beauty of the lighthouse.

I looked to the left, beyond the garage to where the studio was.

There was nothing happening there. No men walking in or out. The activity was at the lighthouse.

But the new windows were shining in the sun in a way the whole structure looked like a beacon, summoning me to safety.

"Nice ride."

At these words I turned my head and saw Walt strolling toward the car.

"It all looks fabulous," I called.

"You haven't seen nothing yet," he replied, looking to Kath and dipping his chin to her.

"Walt, this is my sister, Kathy. Kath, this is my contractor, Walt," I introduced when Walt stopped at Kath.

"Pleased to meet you," she said.

"Same," he responded then asked, "Your first time?"

"Yup," she answered. "I live in Denver."

"Bet you just rearranged your vacation schedule," he guessed.

She gave him a big smile. "Yup."

"Wanna see your home that's about fifty yards away from home?" Walt asked me.

"Yup," I replied.

He chuckled then threw out an arm. "Lead the way."

I led the way, trying not to run. I knew all that was in it, obviously, since I'd chosen it, but I'd eventually asked Walt to stop sending pictures because it was looking so amazing, I didn't want the surprise reveal of it all together to be spoiled.

When we walked in, I found that was the right call.

Downstairs was bright whites (walls, slouchy furniture and cupboards in the kitchen), gray carpet (living room), parquet floors (everywhere else), bold blue toss pillows, lush but trimmed plants in white pots giving a dose of healthy green, the common areas seemed big, open, breezy and amazing.

The bedrooms and bath upstairs couldn't be more different.

One bedroom had busy pink, old fashioned wallpaper with a recurring pastoral scene against cream and heavy colonial furniture, gingham and ruffled bedclothes, all of this screaming *New England.* The other was calm, light grays, taupes, blues and greens with a padded headboard upholstered in a heavy damask of delicate colors, matelassé covers on the bed. The pink bedroom had a chintz armchair and ottoman with a reading light over it and side table stuffed in a corner, the other bedroom had a white loveseat with gray trim and toss pillows in damask matching the headboard against one wall. And the bathroom had a boxed tub jutting out perpendicular to the painted white wood walls and its original cabinetry that was updated with fresh paint in a dusty cornflower blue and white marble countertops with veins of gray.

The downstairs was spacious and contemporary but cheerful and inviting while the upstairs seemed cozy, busy, overfull and warm.

I loved it. Every inch.

Including the veranda with its curvy, ornate wicker furniture painted cerulean blue with crisp seafoam-green pads and matching side tables and ottomans.

Definitely a place you could sit and enjoy a coffee in the morning or sip a wine of an evening, watch the sea and just…*be.*

Oh yes, I could avoid Coert Yeager here.

I could absolutely avoid him here.

I could love every minute of it.

"So?" Walt prompted as I stood on the veranda and stared at the sea.

Slowly, my eyes turned to him.

"It's perfection," I whispered.

His face changed after the words came out and he studied my expression.

He was probably my age, maybe a bit older, looked it, weathered and tan, not unattractive, but he was a durable man, a hardworking man, and he showed it, which made him more attractive.

He'd been friendly and entirely professional in every encounter I'd had with him.

But right then, I watched his face soften and his eyes grow warm with pleasure at my approval and concern at what was not his to know, he just knew it was there.

"I…our…the…" Kath stammered, cleared her throat and said quietly, "We lost the patriarch of our family not too long ago. Cady was particularly close to him."

"Right," Walt murmured, looking away in a manner I knew he was giving me privacy.

"We'll just, uh…let you get on with it while we get the boxes in," Kath said.

"You wanna see where we are with the lighthouse?" Walt asked.

"Maybe tomorrow," Kath answered for me.

"You want me to send some boys down to help with those boxes?" Walt queried.

I finally piped up. "I…yes, that'd be nice. It shouldn't take long."

"Okay. I'll get a couple of the boys and I'll help myself. If you wanna drive your car closer to the studio, I'll be back with the guys," Walt said.

"I'll do that," I replied.

He jogged off.

I turned to Kath. "We'll get the things in then go to Wayfarer's and get something lovely for dinner tonight."

"Cheese, bread, pâté and lots of wine. You are not cooking tonight and neither am I. We're enjoying that." She jerked her head to the view. "Tomorrow, we can break in that kitchen. You said Paige outfitted it with plates and knives and pots and pans and stuff?"

I nodded.

She grinned. "Then we're set."

I wanted to see the pots and pans "and stuff" I'd picked for this space.

But I needed to drive the car around so we could move in the boxes and suitcases, which were almost entirely filled with clothes, shoes, books, DVDs, CDs and photo albums and not much else.

"I'll get the car and we'll get started," I declared.

"And I'll prepare to ogle cute construction guys and I'm calling the pink room."

She was calling the pink room because she knew I'd go for the damask room.

God, I just loved her.

"Let's get cracking," I said.

She clapped her hands and rubbed them together.

I shot her a smile and walked with a spring in my step to my car.

And we got cracking.

THE AIR HAD a nip to it, a light breeze was flirting through the sky, I had a belly full of cheese, pâté, bread, wine and too many of the selections of mini-cakes the bakery counter at Wayfarer's sold individually or, in our case, by the dozen.

The boxes were inside.

The construction workers were long gone.

And I was sitting holding a stylish wineglass filled with an exceptional sauvignon blanc, my behind on a crisp, seafoam-green pad in a fabulous wicker chair on my veranda in Maine next to the best friend I'd ever had and the finest woman I'd ever met in my life.

"I talked to Pat about it."

I looked from the buttercreams and pinks of the sky painted by the setting sun on the horizon behind us to Kath when she spoke.

"About what?" I asked.

She turned her gaze to me. "About this place. He looked into it."

I was perplexed. "Looked into what?"

"He says you got it for a song. The renovation is steep but would be worth it any way you cut it. He said it would take years to make it profitable, but as luxury rentals, it'd be hugely popular, so that would eventually happen."

I was no less perplexed.

"Are you saying you want me to rent out the extra spaces so I'll have company or something?" I asked.

"I'm saying I saw you in town, and you were good here at the lighthouse, great, actually, happy, nearly skipping. But there you were stressed out, tense and looking over your shoulder a lot."

I drew in breath, turned my eyes back to the sea and sky and took a sip of wine.

"You're gonna see him," she said gently.

"I know," I told the sea.

"And it's gonna hurt."

"I know," I repeated and looked back to her. "But then it'll hurt less and less and it won't happen often anyway. And in the end, I'll have all of this." I gestured around me with my wineglass.

"What I'm saying is, if you want to come home, we can keep this in the family. We can make a go of it. Once we earn back the investment in a few years, it'll even turn a profit. The kids absolutely love the place, all of them, and they haven't even seen it yet. Maybe one day, when they're making their own way, one of them will—"

"This is my home, Kath," I stated firmly.

"He had no right to speak to you that way," she stated far more firmly than me.

My back straightened and I turned toward her in my chair. "Kath, I've had a lot of time to think about this and it's not a surprise he's this angry."

Her brows shot high. "How is that not a surprise? How, in all that happened, does he have even the ittiest *bit* of right to be angry, much less *that* angry? *Still?*"

"I promised him I'd stick with him," I explained something I'd told her before. "No matter what. I didn't stick with him, Kath." I lifted a shoulder. "Sure, when I thought he was a drug dealer or the lackey of a drug dealer or whatever I thought he was, which by the way I never asked, I was completely okay with it and our life and how I fell into having one with him. When I found out he was an undercover cop, though…" I let that hang because she knew the end of that sentence too.

"He lied to you."

"It was his job."

"He lied to you and he slept with you and he listened to you making plans for your future together all while he was *lying to you.* You didn't even know his real name."

"It was his *job*, Kathy," I repeated.

"When he knew who you were, *how* you were, he couldn't tell you that?"

"Our connection came strong and fast, and it was there but it wouldn't be very wise of him to share with some girl he didn't really know that he was working undercover in the dangerous pursuit of bringing down drug dealers, possibly increasing that danger enormously if he did."

"He thought it was wise enough to sleep with you in order to use you to make others think he was what he was not," she parried.

"He slept with me for more than that," I whispered.

"Cady," she whispered back.

I shook that hurt off because I knew she didn't mean to deliver it and stated, "I knew who he was. I knew *how* he was. It was a shock when I found out what exactly he was, but when I had time to calm down and think about it, it wasn't a surprise and that's what it was all about. When we began. When he practically begged me to believe in him, stick with him, not give up on us. Because I saw it in his eyes. I knew he was good down to his soul. I knew in some part of me he was not the man he was pretending to be. And when it all happened, I let it all get to me and I stopped believing when I'd promised him I would never do that."

"And through all of that he couldn't know who *you* were enough to trust you?"

This was the part I hadn't been able to come to terms with.

However.

"I was a twenty-three-year-old girl perfectly okay with starting an emotionally and physically intense relationship with a man I suspected of being a not very good one, in those terms. And then, even if I'd promised to stick with him, weeks after my world collapsed around me, when he came back to me to put us back together, he found I was engaged to a very wealthy, sixty-five-year-old man. He didn't know why. He jumped to conclusions. But honestly, Kath, could you blame him?"

She turned to the sea.

She couldn't blame him. She, too, had not been my biggest fan when Patrick essentially decided to adopt me and do it the only way he could—as bizarre as it was, it made sense in a time when everything happening was bizarre—adopting me by marrying me.

"It was weird, what Patrick and I did, even you thought that," I reminded her carefully.

"I got it in the end," she muttered.

She did.

"Coert thought it was a betrayal," I told her.

She turned screwed up eyes to me. "Yeah, he did, and he made sure you weren't in any question about that, didn't he? He didn't even listen. And if he'd *shut up* and *listened*, maybe you would have never married Patrick. Maybe that baby of his would be a fifteen-year-old baby of *both of yours* and you'd have a couple others besides."

"Then I wouldn't have had Patrick, and Pat, and *you*, and you know I could go on."

"Do you think Patrick would have given up on you? Let you out of his life?" she scoffed. "Hardly. He always wanted a daughter and you know the lengths he went to for that years before he'd even met you."

I tried not to wince at the memory of learning that knowledge but Kath was on a tear, so she didn't notice my struggle, she just carried on.

"He'd always wanted his sons to have a little sister. If that came with her boyfriend, he'd take it. He wanted you to have his last name because he didn't think those two jerks deserved you carrying theirs. But if you took this sheriff guy's name, he wouldn't have cared. He'd have done anything to give you what you wanted, including getting back that cop for you. Why do you think he had him followed all these years?"

"I know that and that's why this is all on me," I returned.

And it was all on me like everything was all on me.

"You know, this is beautiful and it's peaceful and I'm so glad this place rocks, and I'm okay leaving you here because half of me wants to drag Pat out here just to live in this studio. Not to mention this is our first night here and all. But I'm gonna shatter all of that right now by saying I'm sick of that shit."

I blinked at her.

She kept talking.

"You were twenty-three years old, barely more than a girl, and hurting. Your family had totally turned their backs on you. Your best friend hated your guts, and I say that part since I don't wanna get into all the other insanity she perpetrated. It turned out the man you were desperately in love with lied to you from the second you met and *used you* to hurt people who were, let's face it, not that great but they were *yours*. Your *friends*. People you *cared about*. So your head was screwed up and some old guy with a kind heart and a gentle way with words offers you love and support and an end to all that garbage, and you took him up on it. So what? You know, if all that happened to me and I met Patrick knowing how he can be and he said, 'Let me help you leave this all behind.' I'd say yes too. In a second. So give yourself a break with all that for once, would you?"

"I don't even—"

She shook her hand at me. "No. And no again with you cutting this sheriff some slack when you won't cut yourself some. You've forgiven him for *using you* and *lying to you* and *putting you in danger too* but you can't forgive yourself for trusting the *right* man who pulled out all the stops to take care of you. And furthermore, you have no problems with that sheriff holding a grudge after all these years when he never gave you the opportunity to explain where you were with all that."

It was then she shook her head and turned back to the sea.

"No," she continued. "He doesn't get my forgiveness that easily. You can do that, okay. But he doesn't get that from me."

I didn't share with her Coert wouldn't care because he didn't know her, and furthermore, he wasn't like that. I knew Tony, not Coert, but I figured both were one and the same (at least the Tony he gave to me, mostly) and he never cared what anyone thought.

Which meant Coert didn't even care how I felt about these things.

However, the bottom line was it was a long time ago. So he was still beautiful. So he was still single. So he had the most adorable little girl I'd ever seen (outside of Verity, Ellie, Melanie and Bea).

It was a long time ago.

So it was time to move on.

I'd come out here not even knowing what I'd wanted to come of it (exactly).

But what I got was my lighthouse. A place of peace that wasn't full of memories of Patrick but was still another something beautiful he gave me.

And that was a good place to be.

"It was almost two decades ago, Kathy," I reminded her. "It's time everyone moved on."

She turned again to me. "And you tense and looking over your shoulder at the gol'darned market? Is that moving on?"

"That will stop too. We just got here today. I'll settle in. I promise."

"He should have told you he was a cop," she spat.

"He didn't."

"He should have listened to you when he came back to you."

"He didn't."

She glared at me for a long time before she puffed out air, turned to the sea and mumbled, "I need more cake."

"I'll go get them," I replied and got out of my seat.

I was nearly to the door when I heard her trembling voice come at me.

"It breaks me."

I turned back to her and it took a great deal, too much, to stare into her beautiful brown eyes shining with tears and not allow my own to come.

"What you could have had," she finished. "What you two could have built together. When I think about it, it breaks me."

It broke me too.

A long time ago.

Now I needed to fix me.

"You didn't date," she said.

"I did, Kath, honey," I replied gently.

"On the sly because you refused to divorce Patrick," she shot back. "He didn't care, he wanted you to, but those society bitches would have torn you to shreds."

This was all too true.

"If I divorced him, the times he got sick, I wouldn't have been able to be at the hospital with him the way I needed to be, make decisions he wanted made," I reminded her.

"Pat had those papers drawn up."

"They weren't what a wife is offered…" my voice dropped low, "or a daughter."

She looked to the table where our wine bottle was sweating.

Pat could have had a million papers drawn up, but when you hit the hospital, none of that mattered.

"Are you his daughter?" they asked because at my age, that was what was assumed. I had his last name. So I said yes. I looked nothing like him. Like any of his sons. But that was all that mattered.

If they'd pushed it, they'd have found I was legally tied to him.

That would have been all that mattered.

And I needed that. I needed it to be in the position to take care of the first man on this earth who loved me unreservedly just for me being me.

He'd had cancer when I'd met him. He had not shared that. His boys didn't even know that at the time. It had taken a while for all of us to learn that.

And when I learned it, the deal we'd made changed.

He took care of me.

And then after we found out, for twelve years, as it came and went, ravaging him then giving him time to recover only to ravage him again, I took care of him.

"I don't regret it," I declared.

Her eyes lifted to me.

"Not a minute," I whispered.

"You need to find a man," she whispered back.

"I know Pat is awesome and you love him more than anything, but a man isn't everything, Kathy," I told her.

"You've got time. You need to make babies and a man is kinda essential to that."

I gave her a soft smile. "I had seven babies I could help look after, honey. I'm good."

Her lips trembled before she said, "I want you to be happy."

"I'll be happy," I assured her.

"You came here because you're still in love with him."

It was my turn to look away because I didn't want to admit that out loud.

But she was right.

"I want you to be happy, Cady."

I looked back to her. "I'll be happy, Kath." I swallowed and finished, "Eventually."

"I'm sorry I was a bitch to you when we first met."

And there we were.

All of this was bringing up feelings of guilt she had no reason to feel.

"It was understandable and it led to this, so do you think I care?"

"I love you, Cady. I only have brothers so Patrick gave me a sister too, and I cannot tell you how many times I thanked God that He led Patrick to doing that."

I smiled at her. "And I love you back, Kathy. Totally more than you love me."

She straightened her shoulders. "No way, I love you totally more than you love me."

"Who's up getting cakes?" I teased. "That's love when I have to leave that view."

"I carried a whole, single box into your house earlier before the boys showed up, now *that's* love."

"Shut up."

"*You* shut up."

"Do you want cake or do you want me to stand here bickering with you?"

She pretended to think about it and then answered, "Cake."

I grinned at her and saw her mouth twitch before I felt my grin die.

"This, right here," I stated. "Seriously, my beautiful Kathy, I don't regret a thing."

I didn't let her reply.

She knew I'd made my point and done it grandly.

I just walked in and got the cakes.

Eight

THE WORLD WOULD STOP SPINNING

Present day…

"I knew. I heard the stories. But *oh my God.* You are *so totally a* dick."

"Kathy," I snapped under my breath.

She lifted a hand and jerked a thumb at my brother Caylen. "He's totally a dick."

"I see you haven't changed the company you keep," Caylen drawled.

We were standing at his door. He hadn't invited us in.

This was not a surprise.

He looked fit and spry and perhaps ten years younger than he was.

This was also not a surprise. If every minute of your life you lived precisely as you wanted to, I would imagine anyone would look fabulous.

He also had not been kind.

Or even polite.

Also not a surprise.

A disappointment, but not a surprise.

In his (limited) defense, we had not shared we were going to surprise *him* by showing on his doorstep. This was a tactical maneuver on my part considering, if I'd given him advanced notice, he would probably have booked a vacation in Siberia or rented a pair of Rottweilers to chase us off his property.

Even so, his reaction to our unexpected visit was not only not kind, or polite, or even unwelcoming…

It had been scathing.

"You're not helping, Kath," I told her.

"Why do I need to help? You came. You saw. He acted like a dick. Let's go. I want to hit those shops in that town we drove through on the way back."

"Enjoy your shopping," Caylen murmured, and I caught his movement so I turned swiftly, lifting a hand to the door he was closing.

I also lifted my eyes to his.

"Please, you're my brother, our parents are gone. We're all we've got left of that family."

"I'm good the way things stand," he replied.

"Caylen, do you honestly think Mom and Dad would want us to leave it like this?" I asked.

"What I think is Dad had a soft spot for you I never got because you were a waste of space from the beginning. Mom always thought you'd turn yourself around but the minute that girlfriend of yours murdered her boyfriend and then got sent to prison for doing it, and the icing on the cake of *that* monstrousness was that she was also sentenced for dealing drugs, she knew you were a lost cause. You only proved it to her by gold digging that poor old guy who put up with it to have a trophy wife."

"Now wait a fucking—" Kath started growling.

I whirled to her. "Kath! Stop. You are *not* helping."

"He has no idea what he's talking about!" Kath retorted hotly.

"Nice mouth on that one," Caylen put in. "Is she a drug dealer or a drug dealer's whore, or one of your gold digging buddies?"

I turned to Caylen. "She's—"

"Forget I asked. I don't care," he cut me off to proclaim. "I see the company you keep hasn't changed nor your manners. Usually you phone before you come calling. But just to say, Cady, don't phone because, please, I beg you, I don't want you ever again to come calling."

He started to put pressure on the door to close it but I settled my weight in my arm to stop him.

"I made some poor decisions…" I began.

Kath swore under her breath.

Caylen narrowed eyes at her then at my hand then they came back to me as I kept talking.

"…and I understand that. But that was a long time ago and there's a lot that's happened since, including us losing both our parents. I know you don't believe me now but the truth is that I grew up. And I'd like to introduce you to the woman I've become, and I'd like to have the chance to get to know my brother. To meet your children. To start fresh and get what's left of our family back together."

"Do you honestly think I want my children to meet you?" he asked scornfully.

"*My* children know her and they love her, and *they* call her Auntie Cady and they're old enough to call her Cady. Cady's told them to call her Cady, but they refuse to call her anything but Auntie Cady because it shows her the *respect* she *deserves*."

"Well, bravo for your children," Caylen sneered.

Kath opened her mouth but I stopped her from speaking when I asked, "Do you need to go sit in the car?"

"Do you think I'm leaving you alone with *this fool*?" she asked back.

"All right, I've had enough. I don't need to stand in my own front door and be insulted," Caylen declared.

I turned back to him. "Caylen, seriously, *please* just give me ten minutes. Kath will sit in the car."

"Cady, seriously, *no*, not ten minutes, not ten more seconds. I don't know why you're here out of the blue but I don't want to spend ten minutes listening to you talk circles, when in the end you're going to ask for money or tell me you and your friend need a place to stay or whatever it is you think you can get out of me," Caylen retorted then ordered, "Take your hand from my door."

"Uh, dude, do you *not* see her bodacious Jag?" Kath asked under her breath.

Caylen shot her a scowl.

I stayed on target.

"Mom loved me," I told him softly.

He looked back to me. "She birthed you, she had no choice."

"Dad—" I kept trying.

He pushed hard on the door. "We're not doing this."

I wasn't going to let another important man in my life shut me out until I'd given it my all, so I put my weight in my hand.

"They would want us to try—"

"Get your hand off my door."

"Caylen, okay, just five minutes," I haggled.

"Get your hand off my door, Cady, or I swear to God, I'm phoning the police."

"But you're my brother and I'm *your sister.*"

"You can think that, but just so you know, you're nothing to me. I haven't thought of you in years. I wish I didn't have to think of you now. And when I close this door, I won't think of you again, I hope, until the day I die."

Hearing that, I took my hand off the door. Caylen wasn't ready for it so I caught the flash of surprise in his face before it slammed hard into its frame.

Though even if he was ready for it, he'd probably have done the same.

"Oh my God, he isn't a dick, he's a total—" Kath started to fume.

I turned to her and she took one look at my face and clamped her mouth shut.

She then took my arm and guided me back to the Jag. She led me to the passenger seat. She took my keys. She got into the driver's side and adjusted the seat (Kath was tall—tall, blonde, brown-eyed, sporty and willowy—a California girl raised in the Mile High City), reversed out of Caylen's drive and set us on the road to home.

I stared out the side window.

After some time, she said softly, "Your mom did that."

I drew breath in through my nose and said nothing.

"You were the black sheep. Didn't fit. Instead of celebrating your differences and opening their eyes to see how kind and caring and generous you are, or any of the many wonderful things that make you, they only saw the part about you being different. Your dad would have gotten there. But your mom was controlling and she wanted to carve you into the model that fit in with the little world she'd decided you were all going to live in, and her behavior toward you gave your brother permission to be that way, treat you that way, feel superior the way he feels. He grew up with that. He doesn't know anything else."

I didn't have a reply so I didn't say anything.

"Though, now I'm thinking it also has a lot to do with him just being born mostly an asshole," she muttered.

I had no reply to that either.

"You want him to be your father," she continued gently. "You want a chance to relive the time before you lost your dad so you have another shot of winning at least your father back. But he's not your father, Cady. He's not your mother. He's that guy and that was going to happen no matter if you got down on your knees and begged him to give you a chance."

I looked forward. "You're probably right and I love you, but I have to say I'm not sure you helped very much."

"I'm Patrick Moreland's daughter-in-law and I have been for twenty-five years, and in that honored position *and* as your friend it's my job not to let anyone shit on you, Cady. You have all the patience in the world for that kind of thing because your parents and brother taught you that. Patrick, Pat, Mike, Pam, Daly, Shannon, me…not so much."

She was right.

We both fell silent.

She broke it, asking hesitantly, "Did you have hope it would go another way?"

"Not even a little bit."

I felt her relief hit the car that she hadn't messed things up.

I looked out the side window and murmured, "But it would have been a lovely surprise."

She reached out and squeezed my knee.

I sighed.

She drove.

I rode.

I encouraged her to stop in the town with the cute shops.

We had dinner there too.

So we got back to the studio late.

IT WAS THE next morning and I had no idea how he got in. The gate was closed. The workers were careful to do that.

But he got in.

And he got in while I was sitting on my veranda with my mug of coffee. I had on a pair of heather-gray jersey men's-style pajamas with a bright-pink drawstring on the bottoms. And in such an outfit, and with Kath still asleep enjoying a holiday with me in Maine, away from mom and wife duties and determined not to get too far out of her time zone sleep-wise, I wasn't ready and I had no backup.

Truth be told, I'd probably never be ready.

And what I wasn't ready for was Sheriff Coert Yeager strolling around the side of my studio in his sheriff shirt and his impeccable jeans, wearing smoky-lensed aviator sunglasses looking tall and beautiful and in command.

Even through his glasses I could feel his eyes on me as he walked across the front of the studio, stopped at the bottom of the steps and put his hands to his narrow hips.

I sat frozen, one leg curled under me, one leg bent with my bare foot in the seat, my coffee cup held aloft in both hands in front of me, my eyes glued to him.

His deep voice growled across the ten feet between us.

"Got a call from the boys up in Waldo County."

"I'm sorry?" I whispered, wondering if he could even hear it.

I didn't know if he did or not with what he said next.

"They reported that Caylen Webster contacted them to share two foul-mouthed women came to his door and harassed him, refused to leave when asked repeatedly, and barred the door when he tried to close it against them."

My God.

Did Caylen hate me that much?

"I'm gonna have to ask you not to return to your brother's, Cady," Coert stated. "And whatever," he jerked his chin up toward the house, "*friend* you got in there with you, I'm gonna have to ask you to make sure she does the same."

"I was attempting—"

"Don't need an explanation."

He didn't need one seventeen years ago either.

"Of course you don't," I murmured.

"Pardon?"

"Nothing, Sheriff," I said louder. "Rest assured, we won't be returning to Caylen's."

He tipped his chin this time like a man would do if he was touching his hand to the brim of a hat then he said outrageously, "I'm gonna have to ask you not to make trouble in town either."

I stared at him with my lips parted.

I parted them farther to state, "I don't have a brother who hates me so much he reports a visit from his sister who was attempting to reconcile with him to the police living in Magdalene, so you can rest even further assured that there'll be no problems from me in town. Unless the folks at the Lobster Market take issue with people eating too much seafood, that is."

He looked to his side, off into the distance, and I wished it was not with the complete and utter fascination it actually was that I watched a muscle jerk up his jaw into his cheek.

He'd always had such a beautiful jaw, strong and square.

His cheek was far from unattractive too.

When he didn't move, I called, "Are there any other warnings you wish to issue, Sheriff?"

His gaze cut back to me. "You know my name, Cady."

"Are you here as Coert?" I asked.

"No."

"Then let's keep this official visit official, shall we?"

"Did the society ladies teach you how to talk proper, or was it your sugar daddy?" he retorted.

I had muscles in my cheeks too but none of them jumped because I didn't grit my teeth like I should have done.

No, regrettably, I did not.

"It might be ill-advised to say this directly to an officer of the law, but if you call Patrick my sugar daddy one more time to my face, I might be moved to violence."

"Memory serves, you aren't a big fan of violence."

"No and especially not when it's being used to demonstrate to a drug peddler that someone is a tough guy and deserves to have his place on his crew when it isn't part of their nature at all."

"Considering Lonnie got his face blown off by your best friend, gotta admit, gives me a shudder to think I took his ass down and humiliated him just months before he stared into his girlfriend's eyes as she pulled the trigger that ended his life."

"I think we all learned the hard way that Maria was far more troubled than we knew."

"Than you knew, Cady. I had her ticket."

"Yes, of course you did, Coert. Though, among many other things, you didn't share that with me until it was way too late."

Another muscle leaping in his jaw and then, "You knew the things you needed to know."

I raised a brow. "Like the fact my best friend was running drugs and capable of murder?" I then shook my head. "I must beg to differ. Only you knew that."

"First part, yeah. Second part shocked the crap outta me."

"Then we both experienced that emotion."

"You visit her?" he asked.

That question surprised me so much I sat up in my chair.

"Why would I do that?"

"You were tight with her."

"She murdered her boyfriend and ran drugs, Coert," I returned.

"You thought your boyfriend ran drugs and you didn't have a problem with that."

It was a wonder my head didn't jerk to the side considering his words felt like a slap in the face.

"Just a second ago you said I knew the things I needed to know," I snapped. "And I thought I did."

"I thought so too."

Another blow.

"Is this a part of your official visit?" I asked cuttingly.

"Nope," he replied easily. "This is indication of why your ass should not be in that chair or anywhere near the entire state of Maine."

"So you get *all* of Maine?"

That was snide.

"If I had my choice, yes. And when it comes to you, I'd add and then some. But your ass is in that chair so it's apparent I don't have my choice. So how about you don't give me another reason to come out here?"

"You're very aware my brother is an ass," I reminded him.

"I'm very aware of a lot of things," he retorted. "Like the fact trouble dogs you like a shadow."

"Not that you care, but I've lived a trouble-free life since my best friend went down for life without parole for first degree murder with five years unnecessarily tacked on to that for her drug dabbling. Though I don't need to tell you that since you were the arresting officer. In fact, with a few hiccups," not how I'd normally describe helping a man I adored battle cancer for twelve years but I was on a roll, "it's been positively jolly."

"Money buys a lot of shit."

I knew this to be true but I didn't get the chance to confirm that knowledge.

Coert wasn't quite finished.

"Guess in all I thought you were, I never imagined it'd buy you."

I felt my face get tight. "If you're quite finished with insulting me, I'd like to go back to enjoying my coffee, the view and my *solitude*."

"Whoever that friend of yours is in there, Cady, keep her reined in."

Kath was hell on wheels with a credit card and the ability to online shop and fortunately her husband was loaded, but that didn't mean on occasion she didn't take things to extremes.

Other than that and her recently revealed rabid bent to protect me, it was laughable that Coert assumed she needed to be "reined in."

"She's the mother of two," I informed him.

"She swore at a man repeatedly on his own doorstep and he didn't even know her name."

"She was upset on my behalf," I defended.

"It's not an excuse."

He somewhat had me there but then again, he hadn't been present when Caylen was being…well, *Caylen.*

"I'll endeavor to make certain Kath doesn't cause heartache and mayhem in Magdalene," I assured.

"Cady, I'm not takin' this as a joke."

I pressed my lips together.

Coert did not press his together.

"It's not like nothing ever happens in this county, but we don't have South American drug cartels making deals with assholes who're perfectly willing to flood our streets with dope and girlfriends blowing holes through their boyfriends' faces as their way of killing three birds with one stone. Breaking up with him, solidifying their position in a bad guy's crew and clearing the way to take their place in that guy's bed."

"Coert, that happened *seventeen years ago.* I hardly got caught up with another Maria in the time in between."

"I don't know what you got caught up in but you haven't been here long and I already got a sheriff of another county callin' me to have a chat with you to tell you to back off, so what am I supposed to think?"

I was seeing Kath's behavior yesterday as less supportive than I felt it was at the time and more a pain in the behind.

"Kath will be leaving next week," I shared with him.

"Good," he muttered.

It wasn't but I wasn't going to dwell on that.

"And all will be quiet again at the lighthouse," I went on.

"Good," he said louder.

"Now, can this tender trip down memory lane be done?"

He wore his shades through our entire discussion and I couldn't see his eyes.

I still knew that his regard had changed and I knew it with the heat that suddenly seemed to be burning my skin.

Even his voice had changed in a way that I didn't quite understand. It was lower, rougher, almost thick when he said, "Yes, this trip down memory lane can absolutely be done."

And then it absolutely was because he dropped his hands from his hips, turned and sauntered away.

I watched him go and only then realized how fast my heart was beating and how it made my skin feel tingly under the burn he'd left behind.

Long after he'd gone from sight, I turned to the sea and took a sip of my coffee.

I couldn't keep it up, though, and since I couldn't, I gave up, set the coffee aside, put my feet on the veranda, bent double so my belly and chest were to my thighs, and I wrapped my arms around the back of my head.

I deep breathed because I was not going to cry. I was *not* going to cry. I'd vowed to myself after I hung up with Kath months ago that Coert was never going to make me cry again.

It took a long time.

But by the time I sat up straight, grabbed my cup and went in to warm it up, I'd won that battle at least.

I had not cried.

KATH

WELL AFTER THE sheriff strolled off, Kath backed slowly and silently away from her place eavesdropping at the side of Cady's open front door.

She tore her eyes away from Cady slumped over in her chair with her arms wrapped around the back of her head and dashed on bare feet up the stairs.

She closed the door to her room.

She grabbed her phone.

She made her call.

And she sat on the side of the bed, listening to it ring.

"Sweetheart, it's early. Everything okay?" Pat asked, sleep still in his voice.

"Sheriff Coert Yeager is totally and completely head over heels in love with Cady."

Pat treated her to a long moment of silence before he growled, "What?"

Quickly, eyes on the door, voice lowered, she told him about the scene she'd just spied on through the screen at Cady's front door.

"Bring her home," Pat ordered.

"Pat, did you hear all I just said?"

"I heard you tell me this guy is an asshole and we knew that already but he doesn't need to be driving up to Cady's house and being *more* of an asshole. Especially when she's alone. So bring her home."

"Pat, *did you hear all I just said?*" Kath asked.

"I heard every word."

"Did you understand the meaning behind any of them?"

"Kath—"

"No way, all this time in between, he's got this shot with her alone, he's gonna take that shot to drag past history through the gulf between them if he does not *love her like a crazy man.*"

"And I should listen to this because clearly I love a crazy woman," Pat muttered.

"Pat!" she snapped, trying not to be loud.

"Kathy, honey, do not get all gushy and romantic. Not about this."

"He didn't even have to come out himself. I'm sure he's got deputies. This isn't exactly a small town. I mean, it is, but it isn't. And everywhere is populated around here and he's sheriff of *the whole county.*"

"Kath—"

"And he instigated it, went right in there, saying stuff just so, I don't know…so he wouldn't have to leave. His business here, which I'll repeat he could have sent a deputy to do, or really, ignored it all together, could have taken about two minutes. But he launched in and that was it."

"What did Cady do?"

"She launched right in too!"

Her voice was rising so she got up and raced to the window to see if she could see the veranda from there, and since she couldn't she started to pace so she could take her agitation out on her feet, not express it with her mouth.

"Do not say any of this stuff to Cady," Pat demanded through her movements.

"Of course I'm not going to say any of this to Cady. That'd take the fun out of it."

Pat's, "What?" sounded alarmed.

"This is gonna be *epic.*"

"Kath—"

"And he's *cute.*"

"Oh boy," Pat mumbled.

"I mean, not cute-cute. He's manly. Like, very manly. All tall, dark, aviator glasses, sheriff *manly.*"

"Do you need a cold shower, sweetheart?" Pat asked half-teasing, half-annoyed.

Kath stopped pacing, stared at her pink toes and whispered, "He's perfect for her, honey."

"Shit," Pat whispered back.

"You should have seen them go at it. I kid you not, if he'd taken one step up, she would have flown out of that chair and thrown herself in his arms and they'd have done it on the veranda. Or if she'd gotten out of that chair, he'd have been on her in a flash, and *they'd have done it on the veranda.*"

"I'm seeing you *do* need a cold shower."

"After all the frustrated sex vibes I just absorbed, I need my husband not to be most a continent away."

"Okay, I gotta make breakfast for our son and daughter this morning, baby. No turning me on unless you intend to do something about it and fast."

For once, Kath was not in the mood for sex (or in this case, phone sex).

"They're gonna get back together," she informed her husband.

"We'll see," he murmured.

"She made some joke in the beginning, because you know Cady can be so funny, but she was being sarcastic, though still funny. He didn't hear the sarcasm. He just heard Cady being funny and, Pat, honey, swear to *God,* it looked like she'd sunk a knife in his heart, it hurt him so much to be reminded of that part of Cady."

Pat made no reply.

"He's not gonna last long."

Pat still said nothing.

"Did I lose you?" Kath called.

"Dad said."

"What?"

She heard her husband clear his throat and he repeated, "Dad said."

"Your dad said what?"

"He said there'd come a time when Coert Yeager realized he'd been a fool and then the world would stop spinning, that's how fast he'd run back to her."

Kath felt tears prick her eyes and she whispered, "He was right."

"You think it's safe to leave her alone?" Pat asked.

"I think it'll delay things if I don't."

"Yeah," Pat mumbled.

"You're worried," Kath surmised.

"She's my little sister."

"Yeah," she said gently. "She'll be okay."

"You sure?"

"I think the road there will be bumpy, but I also think when they look back at it they'll love every minute of it."

"Just as long as that road's not long."

"What I saw, it won't be long."

"Good," Pat replied.

"Miss you," Kath said.

"Miss you too. Call later so you can talk to Dex and Verity."

"I will, babe. Love you."

"Love you more."

"Love you the mostest, most most."

Pat chuckled and ordered, "Go to Cady, make sure she's all right."

"Okay, honey. Talk to you later."

"Yeah, sweetheart. Later."

They hung up.

Kath set the phone aside.

And then she ambled downstairs to make sure Cady was all right.

Nine

WHAT WAS HE WAITING FOR?

Present day…

"As you can see, it's all comin' together."

I turned from taking in the view from the observation deck of the lighthouse and looked to Walt who was coming up the stairs.

"No offense, Walt, but what I can see with my unprofessional eyes is that it looks like a disaster."

He shot me a smile and stopped a few feet away. "The windows have been replaced. The new furnace is in and functioning. The plumbing got done three days ago. The electrical will be done tomorrow. That means we're able to get into the good stuff. In other words, from a professional standpoint, it's all comin' together and you might wanna start your self-imposed absence because if you thought the studio was perfect, this place is gonna knock your socks off."

I smiled back. "Then you won't see me for a while even if I'm fifty yards away."

He nodded, looked beyond me toward the studio and back to me. "Your sister still here?"

I shook my head and endeavored not to look sad. "She left a few days ago."

"Right, my wife wants to see this place."

I blinked up at him. "I'm sorry?"

"Been telling her about it, she's dyin' to come have a look. And she doesn't need the reveal, she likes to watch the whole thing come together, but she'd love a shot at lookin' at the studio. If you don't have a problem with me bringing her around, maybe you two can have a coffee in town after or something."

I stood still, and for a second speechless, as I realized I might or might not have hidden my sad look moments before about Kath leaving, but that didn't matter.

Walt knew I was from out of town. He could guess I knew no one or mostly no one. He knew I'd lost someone. And he liked me enough to introduce me to his wife and a possible future friend so I wouldn't be so alone.

"I'd love to meet your wife and she's welcome at the lighthouse any time," I said quietly.

"Great," he muttered, looking uncomfortable.

"We'll sort a time," I offered.

"Great," he repeated.

"Now I'll let you get to work."

"Right. Got any questions, you know where to find me."

I nodded.

He jerked up his chin and moved to the stairs.

I watched him disappear down them and then turned to my view.

From start on the lighthouse to finish, Walt assessed the work would take six to eight weeks. They were three weeks in. I was thinking it'd be closer to eight, which meant I'd be in by October.

This meant I could contact Kath and have her ship the rest of my stuff in a couple of weeks. If it came early, I could store it in the generator building. There wasn't much: more clothes, winter stuff we didn't need to take up room in the car to pack when we drove out there, some keepsakes.

I'd have it and I'd be in and that would be it.

I'd be back home.

Turning to a fresh chapter with blank pages for me to write.

And as long as I had no more clashes with my brother (and I'd have no more clashes with my brother), I could just enjoy and draw strength from all I'd wrought (well, Walt, Paige and Patrick's money had wrought, but I'd picked the fixtures and fittings). And if I ran into Coert occasionally, considering he'd proved he was a man who could carry an unnecessary and mean grudge, so be it.

This was me.

Cady Moreland.

I did things that were perhaps unwise, like make friends with Maria and Lonnie, get drunk and nearly raped, which put me in the path of an undercover police officer who would use me to (rightly) stop my friends from their illegal pursuits, marry a man old enough to be my grandfather, and finally, pull up stakes to live in the town where the only man I ever loved (that way) also lived, and did it hating me.

But I was right here.

My decisions meant I'd replaced a family who didn't understand me, and one of them detested me, with a family who adored me. They meant I'd been given the honor of making the last years of a good man's life as comfortable as they could be as he battled pain and wasted away before my eyes. And they meant I had the opportunity to take hold of a historical legacy and was breathing new life into it, showing it the love it deserved.

So my decisions might be unwise but they were a part of me, and in the end, they'd put me right there.

So I should embrace them.

Because they were me.

And on that thought, I wandered down the stairs, through the disaster that was now my lighthouse, doing this what would be the last time for weeks because the next time I walked through the front door, I'd be coming home.

IT WAS SATURDAY, four days later, when it happened.

I was walking down Cross Street in Magdalene. There was a used bookstore there that I had not taken time to fully peruse and I needed a new book (or five), and if memory served, they had a small espresso counter and I fancied a coffee.

I was marveling at how lovely the streetlamps were so I wasn't really paying attention to where I was going.

Therefore, the door to the ice cream parlor in front of me had opened and the little girl had danced out, but I didn't see her.

Or the man who came out after her.

But I ran into him as well as my shoulder slamming into the still-opened door.

I cried out in surprise, not pain, took a small step away and opened my mouth to offer my apologies for not paying attention when I tipped my head back and looked from close into hazel eyes that were more light brown with some green in them to make them interesting.

And my lungs squeezed.

"You al'right?" a little girl's voice asked.

I stared into hazel eyes I'd seen that close time and again before a kiss, after a kiss, lying on a pillow across from them.

"Hey lady, you al'right?"

The voice came again and I tore my gaze from Coert's and looked down into an identical pair of hazel eyes, and when I saw them, my lungs didn't squeeze.

Every inch of skin on my body opened up, causing pain even with the life I'd lived I couldn't believe.

"Hi," she said brightly.

"Hi," I forced out, the one syllable sounding strangled.

She tilted her adorable little head to the side. "You al'right?"

"Sorry?" I whispered.

"You ran into Daddy an' the door."

Daddy.

It happened then.

God.

God.

It happened and I couldn't stop it. I wanted to. I should have been able to. I'd seen her pictures. I knew she existed. I should have been able to stop it.

But I couldn't.

I couldn't stop the tears from filling my eyes as I stared down at the most beautiful child in history.

"You aren't al'right," she whispered, her eyes getting big as she stared up at me.

"Cady," Coert murmured.

I took a quick step away.

Jerking my head to look at his shoulder, I mumbled. "Fine. Fine. I'm fine. So sorry."

"Cady," Coert said again.

It seemed he was reaching to me so I lurched away, feeling the wet fall over and course down my cheeks.

"I'm…I…" I looked down at Coert's girl. "You should eat that, honey," I pushed out, clumsily angling my head to the cone she was holding. "It's melting."

And with that and a choked back sob, I let my eyes list through Coert's and I turned and rushed away.

I got into my car and I had the presence of mind to sit in it, stare at my steering wheel and take deep breaths before I switched it on, dashed my hands across my cheeks, carefully backed into the street and went home.

It seemed to take a year for the gates to open, and my phone started ringing while I was waiting.

I left it to ring, and when the gates opened I drove around the garage to park beside the studio.

I got out, grabbing my purse, and let myself into the house.

I didn't know what to do then. All the words I said in my head telling myself it was all right, I could do this, I'd done the right thing, I was in the place I was meant to be were gone, vanished, with just one look at Coert's daughter's face.

I'd made a fool of myself. I'd alarmed his daughter.

God.

God.

Why hadn't I handled that better?

It wasn't like I didn't know it would happen (eventually).

It was just that I didn't think it would happen that soon.

My phone rang again and for something to think about that was not the humiliation I'd just perpetrated on myself, I pulled it out of my purse and stared at the screen.

No name, just a number. A local one so it probably had something to do with the construction or the Historical Society, or it was someone from Stone Incorporated calling for reasons unknown (since they only said "Mr. Stone wishes to make an appointment with you," something I always refused) for the fiftieth time or I didn't know.

And I didn't care.

It wouldn't have anything to do with what just happened so I took the call like it was a lifeline, putting the phone to my ear.

"Hello," I answered.

"Where are you?" Coert growled.

My body froze solid.

He had my number.

I forgot he had my number!

"Goddamn it, Cady, where are you?" Coert bit out when I didn't answer.

"I'm home," I whispered.

"Do not leave," he clipped, and I heard a beep that said the call was disconnected.

I took my phone from my ear and stared at it.

Okay, I needed wine.

No, I needed whiskey.

No, I didn't drink whiskey so I didn't have any whiskey (but Pat and Daly drank it so I'd have to get some in, mental note).

Vodka was out, that wasn't my thing either.

I'd never even tasted gin.

I only drank rum on vacation on a beach.

And I only drank tequila in a margarita and I didn't have margarita mix (another mental note).

In fact, I actually only had wine in the house.

"*Why can't I drink spirits?*" I shrieked like a lunatic.

I needed to go to a liquor store and break my rule about rum only on a beach.

But Coert said not to leave and frankly I was in no state to drive.

"*Shit*," I hissed, breaking another rule and that was to curse as sparingly as possible, because Patrick was a gentleman and he'd made me a member of his family so I felt it was my duty to be a gentlewoman.

And anyway, it was only two o'clock in the afternoon.

I would allow myself to have a glass of wine (or a bottle of it) in two hours.

Until then…

Until then…

Until then I was going to clean the bathroom.

Shoving everything out of my head except cleaning supplies and getting on with a chore I'd actually done only two days before, so I didn't need to do it again, I was just starting to do that when there came a hammering on my door.

The boys worked on Saturdays, not the whole crew of them, but a few here and there, picking up overtime or finishing up a certain job.

I knew that hammering was not one of the boys or Walt.

"*Shit*," I hissed again and threw the sponge into the sink, rinsing my hands and drying them but hurrying to the door when the hammering didn't stop.

Really, what was the point of a gate when it didn't keep anyone *out*?

There were three small squares of windows at the top of the door and most people were tall enough to be seen through them.

Coert was definitely tall enough.

He also saw me through them and only when he did, did the hammering stop.

He scowled at me through the windows, and witnessing his scowl, I considered running and hiding in a closet or perhaps attempting the impossible and trying to vaporize.

But I didn't do either when he saw me stutter step and slow, making him order irately through the door, "Open this, Cady."

I moved the rest of the way to it, opened it and stepped back mostly because he stepped right in, the screen door he'd opened in order to give him free access to hammer on the front door whooshing closed behind him.

"Are you all right?" he ground out.

"I…yes, sorry, that was—"

"Scared the shit outta me."

I clamped my mouth shut and stared up at him in shock.

I scared him?

How?

Why?

Why would anything I did scare him?

"Freaked my daughter out totally," he continued.

Oh no. I'd upset his little girl.

"I'm sorry," I whispered.

"Got behind a wheel and drove home in the state you were in, are you flipping *crazy*?"

"I took a few deep breaths before I—" I began to assure.

"Could you *see*?"

"Um…what?"

"Your eyes were filled with tears, Cady."

God.

Could this *get* any more *humiliating*?

"I'm so sorry, Coert," I said feebly.

"What was that?" he clipped.

God, God, *God*.

"I just…well, it seems I wasn't prepared for—"

"You had someone follow me. You gotta know I have a girl."

I pressed my lips together, unprepared for all of this, definitely not prepared to get into the subject of the fact my husband-not-husband had him followed on and off for nearly two decades.

"I gotta deal with you, on top of that I don't need you runnin' into my baby on the street and fallin' apart, freaking her out."

His baby.

It might not be able to get more humiliating but it clearly could get more painful.

"I'm really sorry, Coert." I didn't look beyond him even though it seemed she was somehow no longer with him when I asked, "Is she okay?"

"She's in dispatch talkin' to my deputies on the radio, her favorite pastime when she's not makin' a mess of my kitchen bakin' cupcakes, her current obsession."

Oh my *God.*

How adorable.

"So she's fine," he stated curtly. "Apparently she gets over a freakout when some strange lady loses it on the street if she's got a mic wrapped around her head and she can babble at my men."

Completely adorable.

I swallowed.

"I hope you…you, uh…oversee the cupcake making business," I said lamely since he'd stopped talking, but he didn't make a move to end this or leave and I desperately needed to fill the silence.

It was a mistake.

His eyes narrowed dangerously and he asked incredulously, "You think I let my daughter near an oven when she's *five years old?*"

"Of course not," I replied quickly.

He lifted a hand and dragged it through his hair, looking beyond me, all this with a muscle jerking up his cheek.

His gaze came back to me.

"That shit can't happen again," he demanded.

"You're right. Definitely right. I won't…it was just bad luck. I was looking at the streetlights. I wasn't paying attention. I was taken off guard. Next time I'll…well, there really isn't likely to be too many next times but if there is, I'll hold it together."

"I'm talkin' about you getting behind the wheel of a vehicle and driving in the state you were in," he bit out impatiently.

He was?

He was more worried about me getting behind the wheel of a car while I was upset?

Really?

I didn't ask for confirmation of that.

"I won't do that again either," I offered quietly.

"Good," he rapped at me. "Make sure you don't."

I nodded swiftly.

He glowered at me.

I stood there taking it.

He continued doing it.

I continued taking it.

He didn't end it and he didn't leave.

And for some reason, I didn't end it either nor did I ask him to leave.

Instead, I stupidly blurted, "She has your eyes."

"She'd have yours if shit didn't get fucked," he fired at me.

I took a step back, winded, like he'd punched me in the stomach.

He watched and I saw him flinch, the color draining from his handsome face.

"Cady—" he started softly.

I interrupted him. "I think all that needed to be said here has been said."

"Too much seein' as I shouldn't have said that last."

I accepted that version of an apology with a terse lifting of my chin.

"Honestly, I just came to see you were all right," he told me.

"I'm fine," I lied.

He stared into my eyes and was back to talking soft when he shared, "She's a good kid."

"She's adorable," I replied.

"She makes terrible cupcakes."

It almost made me smile but instead I turned my head away and fought back new tears because in that moment I wanted with everything I had to taste his daughter's cupcakes, and deeper, somewhere I could never go, I wished I'd had the opportunity to taste *our* daughter's cupcakes.

"Cady—" he started again.

I looked back to him, sniffing through my nose before I guessed, "I bet you eat them anyway."

"Yeah," he murmured.

"You shouldn't come back here," I told him.

"Don't give me a reason to," he retorted.

"If I get home safe or not is not your responsibility," I shot back.

"Normal case, no. But I'm the sheriff, Cady," he returned.

This was true. It was also a stretch. He probably didn't make house calls to every upset woman to berate them for driving while upset.

It was still true.

Stymied.

It was then curiosity got the better of me.

Curiosity, and if I was honest with myself (something I would not be until much later, when I had a glass of wine in my hand), an effort to keep him standing right there inside my door, I asked, "*How* do you get in here anyway? I've got a gate."

"And your gate is the gate to the town's lighthouse so it has a keypad and the emergency code to it is sent to local agencies in case fire and rescue or the police need access to your property."

"Oh," I mumbled, thinking that was probably good should the unlikely and awful event happen that I had a heart attack or something caught on fire or the lens stopped revolving, they wouldn't have to barrel through my beautiful gates.

"Your friend leave?"

I stopped thinking about heart attacks and fires and focused on Coert again.

"Yes."

"Right."

He stood there.

I stood there.

He didn't leave.

I didn't ask him to leave.

I opened my mouth to say something (and it was not to ask him to leave) when he glanced around and queried, "You got a dog?"

I shook my head. "No pets."

He looked again at me. "You should get a dog, Cady."

"Well, I'm not exactly all settled in yet, Coert. The lighthouse won't be done for several more weeks. After that, I'll think about getting a pup."

"You're out here all alone, lotsa land around you, you should have an animal. Best early warning system you can have."

"I'll look into that."

"A shepherd or a rottie, retrievers and labs are too friendly," he advised (though it sounded more like a boss).

"Good advice."

"None of those accessory dogs. They won't help for shit."

Definitely a boss.

"They're cute and they *are* able to bark, Coert," I informed him.

"They wouldn't put the fear of God into even my daughter."

"This is probably true," I murmured.

He looked out the screen door then back at me.

"I need to get back to my girl," he declared.

I nodded. "Of course."

"Get a dog," he ordered.

I nodded again but said nothing.

In a low voice, but not a nasty one, he said, "You made the decision to be here, Cady, you know the lay of the land. I've been clear on that. You need to keep it together."

"You're right," I whispered in agreement. "It was…" I gave my head a slight shake. "You're right."

He hesitated, it looked like he was going to say something but instead he just gave a single nod of his head and turned to the door, saying, "Take care of yourself, Cady."

"You too, Coert."

He had the screen door open, his hand on it, and I thought he'd do what Coert always did, just walk away.

But he stopped in the door, looked to his feet then twisted at the waist and looked at me.

"You shouldn't have done this to us."

I stood where I was and just stared into his eyes.

"I can't begin to fathom what was in your head when you came out here and did this to us."

"Coert—"

"I was good. You were good. It was a memory."

I clenched my teeth.

"What you're feelin', on that sidewalk, what you showed me when you looked into my eyes with tears in yours, what do you think I feel?"

Oh God.

"I—"

"Please, for the love of God, steer clear."

I didn't exactly plan to run into him and his daughter at the ice cream parlor and then fall apart.

But I did move to his town and buy the lighthouse, not some sweet cottage hidden in a forest twenty miles away, but instead a beacon that couldn't be missed from practically everywhere in town.

As these thoughts ran through my head, I noted he still hadn't done what Coert always did and resumed walking away.

He was standing there, mostly out of my door but not *completely* out of my door, torso twisted, eyes locked to mine, waiting.

Waiting.

For what?

What was he waiting for?

"I'll steer clear," I said quietly, thinking I was giving him what he was waiting for.

An expression passed his face I couldn't exactly read (but I thought I could) before he closed his eyes a scant second, opened them and nodded.

And it was then Coert turned and walked away.

"SO WHAT DO you think he was waiting for?" I asked Kath several hours later after my bathroom was cleaned, I'd gone back to town on the errand of creating a very large liquor cupboard, put a chicken in the oven and was sitting on my veranda with a glass of wine in my hand.

"Hmm?" she asked back.

"Coert, when he stood there, what do you think he was waiting for me to say? Because, Kath, what I said, I mean, I can't say, I don't know, it's been years and honestly, I barely knew him when I actually knew him, obviously. But he looked…he looked…" I couldn't believe I was going to say what I was going to say but it was what it was so I said it. "Well, he looked disappointed."

"Babe, I'm sorry, I know you want an answer to that but I've never met the guy. I really can't say."

"I should come home," I muttered.

"No!" Kath nearly shouted, and this was such a surprise, I jerked in my chair.

"What?" I asked.

"No, uh…no, you know, I mean, that place is gorgeous, right?" she said very fast, strangely like she was backpedaling.

"It is but I'm thinking what happened today, I didn't make the right decision. For him. For his little girl. For me. If I can't keep it together like I didn't keep it together on that sidewalk today, I shouldn't be anywhere near either of them. I fell apart, upset her. It was terrible, Kath. I mean," here it was and this was the biggie, "*what am I doing*?"

"You're restoring a lighthouse."

"I didn't move across the country to restore a lighthouse, Kath."

"Well, that's what happened in the end."

"To what cost?" I asked. "I think I'm actually…actually…" Could what I was going to say next be right? "Hurting him."

"Well, you know, whatever. He'll get over it. Time heals all wounds."

"Kath, *seventeen years have passed*."

"Some wounds take longer," she mumbled.

I stared at the view wondering who I was talking to.

Before, she was finding ways to get me to come home.

Now, she was finding ways to keep me here.

She'd been here, of course, she saw how lovely it was.

But I had the sneaking suspicion that wasn't it.

"Right, I think it's safe to say out loud that you went back there because you're still in love with him and you wanted to see if that could be salvaged," Kath said baldly.

I drew in a sharp breath and kept staring at the view.

"Right?" she pushed. "Is that safe to say?"

"Yes," I whispered my admission.

"And that didn't work out. In the meantime, you found that lighthouse and you feel right there, yeah?"

"Yes," I answered.

"And those two don't fit together. I get that. I get how that'd be super confusing. It's still the way it is. I also get that today really had to stink. I feel for you, honey. That sucks. But you're right. It was a coincidence, an ugly coincidence, but better to get something like that out of the way fast than have it blindside you further on down the line. Am I right?"

She was, actually.

"You are."

"And, I mean, maybe he isn't *totally* a jerk, you know, coming out to check you were okay, doing it being kind of a jerk but still doing it. So, you know, he's a jerk. But only *mostly* a jerk so that's good to know, right?"

"I guess," I murmured, though he was somewhat of a jerk, the bottom line was he came all the way out here, admitted he was worried about me and told me to get a dog.

What did I do with all of that?

"What he said, he's clearly a good dad and a good dad doesn't take his daughter to the ice cream parlor every day. And anyway, fall is coming so she'll be wanting hot chocolate or something, not ice cream. So you can go buy a book whenever because it's unlikely you'll slam into them after they grab a cone."

She was just as lovely as she was irritating, at the same time.

"Stop making me want to laugh when I'm undecided about the entirety of my future and all the money I'm investing in a place I might pack up and leave tomorrow," I demanded.

"Something's holding you there."

Her change in tone made me brace, which was good because she wasn't done.

"Whatever it is, something drew you there, something made you make the decision to buy that place, and something is holding you there. You've had every opportunity to change your mind and leave. You know you can come home at any time. We'll deal with the lighthouse. But you told me that was home. When you did that, you meant it. You went all in, Cady. That's you. You know what you like. You know what you want. You want to be there. So you went there for him and he made it clear that's not an option. But after that, you also went *back*. There's a reason you did. Don't let something like today, as difficult as today has been, make you make a decision that you're going to regret. Ride this out. There's a reason you're there. Stick with it. Don't give up so easily."

Stick with it.

I wished she hadn't put it like that.

And part of me was glad she did.

"You're right," I told her.

"I know," she replied.

"You're also annoying," I told her.

"I know," she replied.

I felt my lips curve up.

Then I felt them stop doing that.

"What was he waiting for me to say, Kath?"

"I don't know, honey," she answered gently.

"I need to steer clear of him," I told her distractedly, my eyes unfocused on the view, thinking I needed to do just that, for him, for his little girl.

For me.

"Mm," she replied noncommittally, my distraction not taking in the mumble or vague way she uttered it.

I came back to the moment and said, "I need to check my chicken."

"And I need to check my daughter is packing or she'll go back to Yale without underwear and the Victoria Secret line item on her credit card will give her father an aneurysm."

I grinned.

"Okay, honey, I'll let you go," I said.

"And I'll let you go."

"Right. Speak tomorrow?" I asked.

"Absolutely," she answered.

I got up and started toward the door. "Thanks for listening."

"Always."

Yes, that was Kath.

Always wise, always sweet, always loving, always funny, always loyal.

Always there.

"'Bye, Kathy."

"'Bye, babe."

We rang off.

I checked my chicken.

I ate it and some peas and wild rice in front of the television then put on a cardigan and went back out to the veranda with a cup of herbal tea.

When I did, I had my answer for what was holding me there as the light from the lighthouse rounded around, again and again—not annoying, not distracting—the steadiness of it, the sure rhythm was relaxing as I watched it tirelessly share its warning and keep the untold, unknown, unseen safe.

Alone and doing nothing, I sat with my lighthouse until a gentle lethargy overtook me.

And then I went in and went to bed.

Ten

LONG LIVE MAGDALENE LIGHTHOUSE

CADY

Present day…

The door opened to the studio and we all turned to it.

Paige had her head stuck through and she was smiling madly.

"Ready," she announced.

"Oh my God, this is *so* exciting," Amanda, Walt's wife, breathed excitedly.

"I so agree," Jackie, the head of the Historical Society, replied.

"I got these, let's get going," Rob, my real estate agent/new friend, declared, holding two bottles of chilled Perrier Jouët, one in each hand.

I drew in breath, looked around and saw they were all waiting expectantly for me to make a move.

I made that move, going to an armchair to grab my cardigan because autumn had settled heavily on Maine, and now October, it barely got over fifty degrees during the day and it wasn't a dry fifty degrees. It was wet. Not nippy. *Chilly.*

But now it wasn't during the day and it would be downright *cold.*

In my boots and with my cardigan on, I headed out and walked the fifty yards through the dark to the lighthouse.

I saw a big delivery van trundling down the lane toward the gates but I only glanced at its movement.

Mostly, my eyes were to the lighthouse, the light rotating around, illuminating the space rhythmically, all the windows having warm light pouring out of them.

I hit the covered walkway from garage to house, put my hand on the handle of the door and turned to see Walt, Amanda, Jackie, Rob, Paige and Rob's wife, Trish, behind me.

I gave them an excited smile, faced the door, turned the handle and pushed inside.

A fire was crackling in the fireplace, which was the first thing I saw.

The rest…

Oh…

The rest…

I wandered the floor and then the next and the next and saw how beautifully Paige fit the circular rooms and brick walls and unusual windows and maritime history into an overall welcoming, warm, cozy space. It was all things classic and contemporary, feminine but with masculine appeal, nautical but not kitschy, charming without being precious, all of this in every nook and cranny.

And I couldn't believe the mastery with which she'd separated the bedroom space, both sides tiny, but she'd fit a queen size bed in (not a lot of floor space, but who cared) and a bathroom with small shower *and* small, round soaking tub, which would mean I couldn't stretch out but I could luxuriate in the bath. She and Walt had also fashioned amazing cabinetry all around the bathroom that had some mirrored panels in it, with the creamy, eggshell-painted horizontal wainscoting from floor to ceiling, making the space seem much larger than it was and afforded a lot of storage space.

I stopped in the observation deck, at first seeing the built-in curved seating around the edge, a couple of wicker pieces facing it in front of the railing to the stairwell.

And I saw Magdalene spread along the cove, lights dotting the sweeping hills beyond, and the inky dark of the sea that stretched for eternity, the rounding of the light just above us sending out its signal steady and true, again and again and again.

"Cady?"

I heard Walt's voice call me but I was stuck on the ink of the sea and the rounding of the beam and the understanding, finally, of why this was where I needed to be.

Patrick had been my beam. Patrick had come into my life, and for the first time, at twenty-three, given me something steady and true.

And now Patrick had given me a new beam that would see me through.

"Cady, are you good?" Walt asked from right beside me.

Abruptly, I turned my head his way and tilted it back.

"Yes, Walt. I'm better than good. I'm home."

His face split into a huge smile two seconds before I heard a cork pop and Trish shouted, "*Hurrah!*"

I turned to them, people I barely knew, all of them I very much liked, and watched Paige hand out champagne glasses she'd obviously grabbed on our way up.

Walt took up the other bottle of champagne from where Rob put it down on a low wicker table in order to open the one he had and then Walt popped its cork.

The men filled the glasses, and when everyone's was charged, I lifted mine.

"To new chapters and new friends," I said.

"Hear, hear!" Rob called.

Amanda bumped her shoulder against mine.

"New chapters and new friends!" Paige cried.

We all drank.

When I took my glass from my lips, I lifted it again and said, "And long live Magdalene Lighthouse."

"Long live Magdalene Lighthouse!" Jackie called.

I looked to Walt and lifted my glass up one more time to him and waited for his smile and the dip of his chin before I sipped.

"I've got some munchies downstairs in the kitchen. Since we shouldn't move *an inch* from right here, I'll go down and get them," Paige declared.

"I'll help," Trish offered.

"Me too," Jackie said.

The three women descended the stairs.

I turned back to the view.

Walt turned with me.

Rob came to stand at my other side.

"You did it," I said to Walt.

"We did it," he replied.

He was a very lovely man.

"Never thought I'd see the day. And if I did, never would have dreamed it'd be this perfect," Rob put in, and I looked to him. "Glad I got this shot."

"Thank you for not talking me out of it," I said.

"I tried," he replied. "You just weren't listening."

When my face scrunched up in a smile, I actually *felt* my eyes twinkling.

Walt put his glass in front of me and murmured, "Long live Magdalene Lighthouse and God bless Cady Moreland for preserving a legacy."

"Please don't, I picked toss pillows," I murmured with embarrassment.

"Shut up," Walt returned teasingly.

Rob reached out with his glass and clinked Walt's. "God bless Cady and her legacy."

I rolled my eyes.

The two men drank.

Then Walt put his rough hand on the bottom of my glass and pushed it inexorably toward my lips.

I started giggling but stopped enough to sip.

"If you three are done congratulating each other, I'm going to go check out every *inch* of that bathroom. Cady, wanna come with me?" Amanda asked.

Did I want to come with her?

"Absolutely," I answered.

We moved down the stairs and it wasn't just every inch of the bathroom Amanda and I checked out.

It was every inch of the old girl made new.

Only after we'd done that did we join the party.

COERT

COERT LEANED AGAINST the side of his truck, head tipped back, eyes on the observation deck that was lit up and filled with people who looked like they were having a party.

They were far away but he could still see Cady's auburn hair in the mix.

It was only in his mind he could see her green eyes.

Then again, he hadn't been able to get those eyes out of his head for years.

Her anywhere near him, for weeks, he had not seen.

She was steering clear, as she'd promised.

And there he was, on public land but not far from her house, at night, in the cold dark, staring up at her like a brooding romance novel hero or worse, a creepy stalker.

But there was no way in hell that woman after all these years had hauled her ass across the country and set herself up in the middle of nowhere in Maine, that middle of nowhere being right where he was, unless something was going down.

Something she intended to drag him into.

Or something she hoped he'd protect her from.

He just had no freaking clue what that was.

If she wanted to reconcile with her brother, she could have set herself up in Waldo County where that asshole lived.

If she wanted another go with him, she'd be in his space, in his face, *something.*

But there was nothing.

All he knew was her husband was dead, her investigator had disappeared, but she'd appeared.

Other than that, nothing.

But something was up with Cady Moreland, Coert could feel it in his bones.

He just had no idea what it was.

He wanted to let it be.

He wanted to forget her and move on.

But he hadn't been able to do that for years either.

And now she was here and there was a reason she was here. People didn't up stakes and move from where they grew up and lived their whole lives, in her case forty-one years, and plant roots somewhere else for nothing.

And women sure as hell didn't do that where a man from her past, who made no bones then or now about the fact he wanted her no part of any present lived.

He just could not get a lock on why she'd done what she'd done. Why she'd shown out of the blue and reopened the gaping wound she'd delivered them both that obviously neither of them had found a way to permanently close.

And it was driving him crazy.

Eleven

YOU NEVER DESERVED IT

Present day…

I paced the observation deck, but even pacing, my eyes were glued to the jetty. I had my phone in my hand and my heart in my throat.

Because the shops on the jetty were on fire.

I could see the inferno from there. The blaze burning high, billowing smoke shrouding city lights and streetlights.

If there was a fire, police would be called, I was sure.

Yes. If there was a fire, especially in a small town, police would be called to help, to keep people back.

Would they be called to go in and help get people out?

I mean, exactly how large could Magdalene's fire department be? It *was* a small town. With a fire that big, surely it was all hands on deck.

Now I couldn't go to town and loiter on the outskirts of a fire to see if I could catch a glimpse to ascertain if Coert was okay. They didn't need a bunch of people hanging around when property was burning to ash.

I also couldn't go into town and loiter outside the sheriff station because that was weird (and Coert had already caught me doing that once and that hadn't been pretty).

And I couldn't call him because the last thing he needed was to have his phone ring if he was carrying a small child to safety at the same time hopefully not singeing his lungs from smoke inhalation.

But *there was a fire in town.*

And Coert was the sheriff.

That required him enforcing the law all over the county, but *Magdalene was part of that county.* The sheriff's station was situated right on Cross Street, for goodness sakes, just blocks from the jetty.

Okay, so it was quite a number of blocks from the jetty.

But it wasn't fifty *miles* from the jetty.

"*Fuck it,*" I whispered harshly, deciding to go back to not swearing tomorrow, and I stomped down my stairs through my fabulous, snug, gorgeous bedroom, down to my fabulous, snug, gorgeous family room with its extraordinary and comfortable circular sectional and curved TV. And finally I stomped down to and through my fabulous, warm, inviting living room to my fabulous kitchen with its window that looked like the semi-circular window at the bridge of some big, awesome ship.

I had obviously transferred my liquor cupboard from the studio to my new kitchen, and there I found one of my new brandy snifters in which I put two pieces of ice from my new fridge and over it I poured some smooth but fiery tequila (this description offered to me by the liquor store owner, not that I'd had any of this smooth and fiery tequila myself...yet).

That done, I stomped back up to the observation deck and fretfully watched a fire while I ridiculously tried to settle my nerves with (exceptional, it must be said, but highly ineffective at that moment, no matter how smooth and fiery) tequila.

In the end, I went to get the bottle.

And in the end, after I'd woken from a doze with my head on the back of the built-in couch, I saw some smoke still shading the dark sky but the fire was out. Thus I snatched up my phone and stabbed it with my finger, hitting a number I'd programmed in even if I'd done it tremendously foolishly, my actions at that moment proving that thought irrevocably true.

I put it to my ear and it rang once before Coert's voice came over the line.

"Cady, are you okay?"

"Are *you* okay?" I somewhat slurred.

Bad tequila.

Bad. Bad. Bad.

And bad ex-undercover-cop boyfriend who lied to me but made me fall head over heels in love with him and ruined me for all other men.

Bad. Bad. Bad.

"Why are you asking if I'm okay?" he asked.

"*There was a fire!*" I screeched.

"I'm a cop, not a fireman, Cady," he stated like he was Dr. McCoy and I was James Tiberius Kirk.

"So you didn't save any small children tonight while suffering smoke inhalation?" I asked.

A moment's silence before, "Are you drunk?"

"*There was a fire, Coert!*" I shrieked. "*A big one!*"

"Calm down, Cady," he said in a voice I hadn't heard in years.

Years.

Millennium.

(Not really, but it felt like it.)

Soft and sweet and playful and amused, but he still meant to be obeyed.

My toes curled.

Bad, bad, *bad* ex-boyfriend.

"Now answer me, are you drunk?" he pressed.

"No," I lied.

"She's drunk," he muttered.

"Is everyone okay?" I asked.

"Why are you asking?" he asked back.

"Because there was a fire that engulfed the jetty, Coert," I stated like he was a dim bulb.

"How do you know?" he queried.

"I have a panoramic view of, I don't know…*everything*," I responded.

To that, he inquired, "Are you alone?"

"If your question is, have I gotten a dog yet, the answer is no. But I'm in search of one. A Newfoundland because we're close to Newfoundland. I mean, not really, but I'm a heckuva lot closer to it than I was in Denver. But I think that might be goofy and I've always *loved* Hagrid's dog in the *Harry Potter* movies. I had to look it up. It's a Neapolitan mastiff. I haven't gotten around to Googling breeders because I also think I want a French bulldog, so I can't make up my mind. But I don't want a dog that slobbers so I'm not sure I'm on the right trail."

"You aren't on the right trail," he muttered.

"That's what I thought. But how bad *is* dog slobber?" I asked. "If you love something, they could slobber everywhere for all you care."

"Did half the jetty go up in flames tonight and I'm sittin' here talkin' with a drunk woman about dog slobber?" he asked.

I shut up and rethought the wisdom of phoning Coert to make sure he wasn't suffering smoke inhalation.

"My question wasn't about a dog, Cady," he stated.

"Oh," I mumbled.

"Are you alone?" he asked.

Oh my God.

"Do you…think I…I would phone you if I had a man—"

"Don't need details," he interrupted me curtly, "but do need an answer."

Suddenly, I was sobering.

"Why do you need an answer?" I inquired.

"Half the jetty went up in flames tonight."

I stared at my lap then I looked over the back of the couch at the town.

"Are you…?" He couldn't be. Could he? "Are you asking me if I have an alibi?"

"I'm asking if you're alone."

He could!

"You're asking me for an alibi."

"I haven't seen you in weeks, Cady, and you're callin' me to see if I'm all right after a bad fire sweeps the jetty. I'm not a fireman. I'm a cop. I'm pissed half my town's new jetty went up in flames but I'm all right. Now what I want to know is why you're calling me out of the blue about something that has shit to do with me."

This was a question I couldn't answer verbally because first, answering it verbally would be admitting verbally that I'd made myself drunk with worry (literally) about a man I was supposed to leave alone and move on from. And second, I was too angry to enunciate words since I'd worried myself drunk about a man who was asking me for an alibi for a fire I had nothing to do with.

"We're done talking," I stated stiffly.

"Cady—"

"And don't you come out here using your secret emergency code on my gate and hammer on my door in order to be mean to me, Coert Yeager. Forget I called. I didn't call. This conversation didn't happen. I'm back to steering clear. But warning, when I get my Newfoundland or mastiff or bulldog, I'm teaching him to bite tall, dark-haired, handsome men in aviator glasses."

Uh-oh.

Did I say the word handsome?

"Ca—"

"Goodbye, Coert."

I disconnected, and then I turned the ringer off and finally I just shut the phone down altogether.

I mean, *really*.

He asked for my alibi?

I glared at my phone not wishing it would explode but wishing my glare could transfer through it and scorch Coert Yeager.

I then turned it back on for the sole purpose of erasing Coert "Mr. Judgmental and Grudge Holding Champion of the Universe" Yeager's number from my phone.

It rang in my hand.

It was Coert.

I took the call for the sole purpose of saying what I said in my greeting, "Do not ever call this number again."

"Do not ever hang up on me again," he growled back.

"I can hang up on who I want," I retorted. "And anyway, it won't matter because we're never *speaking* again."

"Cady, why are you getting drunk by yourself at the lighthouse?"

"Because I *live* at the lighthouse. I mean, how crass, going to some bar to drink yourself drunk. Especially while the jetty is burning down. That would be terrible manners. And anyway, you know I *detest* drunk driving."

"Yeah, I know that," he said softly, reminiscently.

Since I was allowing myself to swear that night, *fuck him* and his soft reminiscence.

I mean, *really*?

"Am I done with my interrogation, Sheriff?"

"I asked you one question," he retorted.

"Perhaps *this* conversation, but just to say, the heavy, judgmental burden of *shame* is leaking through, Coert. Next thing you know, you'll have me walking through the streets naked while people throw garbage at me."

"What the fuck?" he whispered.

"Don't you watch *Game of Thrones*?"

"No."

I stared at my knees in complete and utter shock.

"Who doesn't watch *Game of Thrones*?" I asked incredulously.

"Me," he said impatiently. "Listen, Cady, try to focus on what I'm saying and how I'm saying it. Okay? You with me?"

He seemed earnest now and not jerky so I said, "I'm with you."

"Are you in trouble?"

I stopped thinking he wasn't being jerky.

Instead, I was just plain *hurt*.

"She had nothing to do with me," I whispered.

"What?" he asked.

"I wanted to pull away. It was you that kept me in."

He finally grew silent.

"You knew I did. I told you I did. From the start, Coert. You knew. Or at least Tony knew."

"Cady."

I didn't know if he intended to say more but it didn't matter.

I didn't let him.

"You can't make me pay for what she did. I had no idea she had that in her but it didn't matter. She was my friend but I wanted to be on the right path. I wanted to pull away. It was *you* who kept me in. So you can't make me pay for something that had nothing to do with me. I didn't pull the trigger on Lonnie. I didn't sell drugs to high school kids. I worked at Sip and Save and prayed every night my boyfriend would break free."

"Cady—"

"I earned it, you know. I earned what you thought of me. I earned you being mad at me. I earned you walking away from me," I told him. "I know that. I *know*. But I didn't earn this."

"Cady," he whispered.

"Goodbye, Coert, and please, God, do not phone again."

With that, I hung up, erased him from my phone and then turned it off.

"Newfoundland," I declared, staring at the dark sea.

Then I got up and left my snifter and the tequila right where it was, my phone too, not that it mattered since it was off, and I went through my house and turned out lights on three stories before I hit my snug bed and climbed in.

"No, a mastiff," I said to the dark.

By the time I went to sleep, I'd changed my mind to bulldog then Newfoundland and back to mastiff about fifty times.

What I didn't do before I fell asleep was cry.

I WAS SITTING outside my lovely, curved, butcher-block topped island with the raised outer counter so it had an inset area on the inside where I could tuck canisters (and I did). It also had double spice pullout shelves in the middle where I could keep spices handy (something I did). This island, something that Paige had designed and Walt had had built for me, was one of the seventy-five thousand, six hundred and twenty-two things I *adored* about my lighthouse.

There wasn't a lot of room but they went to pains to make every inch not only gorgeous, but functional.

It was the day after the fire and Magdalene's newspaper website was speculating about what happened, but not speculating about the fact that four shops had burned down, because they had, and fortunately no one was hurt.

I'd gone on from researching the meager details to be had about the fire to searching for Newfoundland breeders (and mastiff and French bulldog, and by the way, pedigree dogs were not inexpensive) when there was a knock on my door, not the one by the garage, the other one at the foot of the stairs.

I stared at it, and even though it had no window, the gate was closed so I knew who was behind it.

I wanted to ignore it and as I turned my head to look out my kitchen windows at the blustery, gray day, I tried to talk myself into ignoring it.

Then a louder knock came and on its heels the dulcet chimes of the doorbell that Walt had installed, which rang on the bottom and second floors just in case I wouldn't hear it farther up in the house from the main floor. I had this as well as an intercom system that was tucked discretely on the stone column by the gate should I get an unexpected visitor or a delivery or something.

It was just that the person outside my door didn't feel the need to use my intercom system.

I got off my stool leaving my laptop behind and moved to the door.

I opened it and looked up at Coert.

He was frowning.

So was I.

"You need a peephole."

"What I need is a local sheriff who's unconcerned about his citizens' safety."

"I hope to God that such a thing doesn't exist."

I ignored that and went on, "I also need a dog trained to bite all strangers, even ones with badges."

He ignored that and declared, "Cady, we need to talk."

"No, Coert, we need to go back to our strategy of avoiding each other. You were right. That was a good call. Let's head back there."

"You said some things last night—"

"I introduced myself to drinking tequila on the rocks last night. It was an experiment that failed so I won't be repeating it."

His jaw clenched before he asked, "Why are you here?"

"Why are *you* here?" I parried.

"I asked first," he bit out.

"It's *my* house you're inexplicably standing at the door of, so I get dibs."

"We aren't at recess, Cady."

"Good, because school was awful, my grades were terrible, it drove my mother insane and gave my brother something *else* to bully me about."

Coert fell silent.

I did too.

He broke it by repeating, "We need to talk."

"Has evidence been uncovered that a short, red-haired woman careening uncontrollably through middle age was sneaking around the jetty last night with her bottle of wildly expensive but completely worth it tequila, dousing buildings and setting them on fire?"

"That isn't a joke."

I stared up at him and asked in shock, "Was it arson?"

"The report isn't in but that isn't funny, Cady."

"I'm not trying to be funny, Coert. I'm trying to communicate to you how ridiculous, and I'll add *offensive* your inferences are of me having something to do with said fire."

"You were in Denver. Now you're here," he declared.

"Yeeeeeees," I said slowly and unwisely carried on, "It's clear you haven't lost any of your keen observational skills."

His jaw clenched again.

I was losing patience and frankly I was losing a lot of other things.

Like the battle to beat back a fresh broken heart.

"You were in Denver," he said quietly. "Now you're here."

"Coert—"

"Why?"

I looked over his shoulder.

"Cady, look at me," he demanded.

I looked at him.

"Why?"

I said nothing.

He changed tactics.

"Why the investigator?"

Okay, I could stop swearing tomorrow.

Because…

Damn.

"Why, Cady?" he pushed. "Why the investigator?"

"Please leave," I whispered.

"You've been intruding in my life for years. *Years.* I ignored it because it was a nuisance and you were there, I was here. Now you're here so I think I deserve to know why you've been intruding in my life, don't you?"

"He wasn't my investigator," I told him.

"God, please," he shook his head, "please do not stand there and lie to me. Not about something like this."

"He was Patrick's."

His entire body went still except his brows went up. "So…what? He was worried I'd come back to you or something?"

"No."

"He was worried you'd come back to me and he wanted to know how to find you if you did," Coert guessed.

"No."

"Cady, for fuck's sake, your dead husband had a man reporting to him about me since I left Denver. You can't be so far gone in whatever it is you got going here not to think I don't have the right to know why."

"He knew you meant the world to me, and I meant the world to him, so if I ever worried about you, wondered about you, he wanted to have the answers available for me the instant I did."

Yes.

That was what I said.

Right there.

To Coert.

In the door of my fabulous lighthouse.

The truth.

Or most of it.

And Coert heard it, and after my words visibly pummeled his tall, strong, motionless body, only his lips moved for him to say, "I meant the world to you."

"You meant the world to me," I whispered.

"I meant the world to you," he repeated.

It was now me clenching my teeth.

"I meant the world to you so after it all went down, you couldn't wait two weeks for me to come to you and explain why I did what I did. Instead, I found you making plans to marry a man old enough to be your grandfather."

"Coert—"

"I was in love with you."

I took a step back.

He took a step into my house.

"Oh no," he growled. "You don't get to do that shit. You don't get to look used and abused and beat down, Cady. I don't give a fuck it was the name Tony you whispered when I was inside you, *you knew me.* You knew how I felt *about you.* You made a promise to me that you broke the instant the going got tough, you cut loose and you let go and you found another way to make the path easy for you."

"Don't," I begged.

"*Don't?*" he spat. "Don't? You said it yourself, you *earned* this. So you know you earned exactly *this.*"

"You wouldn't listen to me explain."

He leaned toward me and bellowed, "*You had another man's ring on your finger! Two weeks, Cady!* Two weeks after the last I saw of you was when I left our bed with you in it smiling at me and *you were with another man*!"

"Okay, let me explain now," I said hurriedly.

"Explain what I want you to explain," he demanded, throwing both arms wide. "Explain *this.* Explain why you're back. Explain why you *just couldn't leave well enough alone.* I got a kid I love, a job I like doing in a town I like bein' in with friends I like being with. What *the fuck* would motivate you to shake *any* of that goodness that *I*," he thumped his chest, "earned. That *I* worked for. That *I* carved out of the rubble *you* left of me."

My heart was thumping in a chest that was moving rapidly as I tried again desperately.

"To explain that, I need to go back and explain the rest."

"I don't give a shit about that."

"If you want an explanation, Coert, it has to start there."

"You shared the bed of a man nearly three times your age for seventeen years, Cady," he sneered with his lip curled. "Do you think I wanna understand any of *that*? Do you think that doesn't turn my goddamned stomach to think *that* body," he tossed a hand my way, "*my* body, the one *you* gave me, you shared with *that* guy? It might have been okay with you considering the mansion and the Jaguars and whatever the fuck. But it was a kick in the balls for me."

"Coert, *please*, if you'd just listen—"

"No," he bit off. "You don't get to come here and be wounded, bleeding Cady making me feel like a dick because the woman I loved jumped ship faster than I could blink, has finally got a healthy bank account and a dead husband and is free to do whatever the hell she thinks she's free to do and lands on my doorstep. Fuck that."

"You're on my doorstep, Coert," I pointed out quietly and not entirely accurately, though he was just in from it.

"Not anymore," he retorted, turned and walked right out.

I stared at the space where he'd been, the open door, hearing the wind whistling against the jamb and seeing Coert again *gone*.

And then I ran out.

Coert was at the door to a Ford Explorer with sheriff stuff emblazoned all over it when I shouted, "You don't know me!"

Hand on the handle, wind whipping his dark hair, he scowled at me.

"You *never* knew me!" I yelled.

"I knew you," he bit back.

I stopped well away from him and shared, "No, you didn't. You absolutely did not. And the worst part about it for me was, you never even tried."

"You're so full of shit," he clipped.

"All that, in there," I jabbed a finger back toward the lighthouse, "proves it. And you don't have a clue. You don't have that first clue, Coert. And you know what? All these years I wished I'd had the opportunity to explain. But now I'm glad. I'm glad I never had the chance. Because now I know you never deserved it."

With that, I stormed right back to my house, slammed the door, threw the bolt home and stood glaring at it, breathing heavy and fighting back the urge to scream.

Instead, I ran up the stairs and the next set and the next until I was in my observation deck.

And from there I watched a sheriff Explorer drive away.

Twelve

HOLDING HER HAND

COERT

Present day…

"Daddy!"

Coert bent low to sweep his baby girl up in his arms.

He barely got her steady when she had her little arms wrapped around his neck and planted a kiss on his jaw.

When she caught his eyes, he asked, "How you doin', cupcake?"

"Good, Daddy," she replied.

"You ready to go?" he asked.

"Yup," she answered with a firm nod of her head.

He lifted his brows. "You sure about that?"

She looked confused.

"Shnookie, sweetheart," he whispered, knowing she could sometimes forget the worn-out, bedraggled teddy bear she had to sleep with at night, but he couldn't because when she got in bed and remembered she didn't have him, he'd have to strap her in his truck and take her back to her mother's to pick it up.

His Janie's only vice.

A bear called Shnookie.

"Oh," she mumbled.

"Oh." He grinned and set her down. "Go get him then we'll go."

"Okay, Daddy," she agreed and dashed off, tossing a bright smile to her mother along the way.

Kim, his ex, Janie's mom, stood looking after her until she disappeared then she turned her head to Coert.

"I really appreciate you doing this," she said.

"Said it before." And he had, about ten thousand times, not that he had to, he'd jump at the chance to have his daughter every day if that was a chance offered to him. "Not a problem."

"It's a bachelorette party, I can't miss it. If it wasn't important, I wouldn't switch days."

He'd been living with Kim kissing his ass and acting apprehensive since he'd dragged her to court after she tried to move herself and their daughter to Portland.

Half of it, he knew, was him sending the unmistakable message she shouldn't pull that kind of shit again in order to yank his chain and bring him to heel, something she'd tried to master the art of while they were together. This the reason why she never got his ring on her finger, regardless of the fact that most other times she was sweet and could be outrageously funny.

She hadn't ever brought him to heel and he got tired of attempting to break her of the habit of trying.

The other half of it, he knew, was Kim finally cottoning on to the fact that she'd redirected both their lives with her play to "win him back." It turned out beautifully in the end because they got Janie, but it had been a seriously whacked play and brought her diapers and bottles, and attorney's fees when he pulled her into court to share he wasn't messing around with his daughter's life and he was taking his responsibilities as her father deadly serious.

"Again, it's fine," he said impatiently. "I'll take her to preschool tomorrow then you got her back tomorrow night."

"Okay," she mumbled, studying him trying not to look like she was before she asked, "You okay?"

No, he was not.

Preliminary reports from the fire inspector stated that the fire on the jetty was arson and that was absolutely not good.

And Cady Moreland lived in his town, in the damned lighthouse, something he couldn't avoid because he saw it fifty times a day, which meant he was reminded of her the hundred times a day his mind decided to do that plus the fifty he saw the lighthouse.

You're on my doorstep, Coert, she'd said.

And that's where he'd been.

In fact, except for when he caught her sitting in her rental outside the sheriff station, it had not been Cady who had approached him. Not once. And she didn't even do it when she was sitting outside the station. He'd gone to her.

Every time, he'd gone to her.

Those tears, that breakdown on the sidewalk, that had not been planned. She'd been blindsided running into Janie and Coert.

Blindsided and gutted.

So bad, he couldn't even think about it because he felt her pain straight down to his soul.

But the fact she had not approached once made her being there at all an even bigger mystery than it already was.

And Christ, it had been Coert's job for years to solve mysteries. He got off on that but he wasn't much on having that shit a part of his life.

However, the fact remained she wouldn't move there, buy property there, especially the property she'd bought which anchored her there, if she did not have reconciliation on her mind. But it was Coert finding every excuse he could to haul his ass out to her, not the other way around.

The Cady he knew had been confused, struggling with learning how to be an adult because she had no firm foundation to keep her steady or help guide her, and trying to teach herself not to act out by doing stupid shit when she was frustrated or felt trapped by life.

What the Cady he knew had not been was a woman who'd played head games.

And for the life of him, all the times he thought of it, and he thought about it too damned much, he couldn't see where she was playing head games now.

So the prevailing question on his mind when he didn't have to think about his job or his daughter or her mother or the fact they might have arsonists in their town was...what was the woman doing?

And he had to admit, outside his daughter, that prevailing question was *prevailing.*

So he was not okay because Cady and her lighthouse and her proximity and her green eyes and thick hair and round ass were practically all he could think about.

"I'm fine," he answered Kim.

"You sure?" she pressed.

He leveled his gaze at her. "I'm sure."

"Coert, if you..." she trailed off, looking like she was considering the wisdom of her next, and then she shared that she didn't consider it long enough by saying, "Everyone's heard about the fire, and I know you get wrapped up when bad stuff goes down so if you ever need to talk, I just want you to know, I'm here."

"I got folks I can talk to, Kim, but thanks," he dismissed.

She looked hesitant again before she said softly, "We could try to be friends, you know."

"Think when you stuck a pin through all my condoms that option was taken off the table."

She blanched even as she winced because during one of their many unhappy discussions after she'd told him she was pregnant with his kid, she'd also admitted to doing that, sharing at the same time that was "just how much I love you, Coert."

He'd had his fill of women making drastic decisions that altered the course of his life. He wasn't a big fan of it seventeen years ago, he wasn't a big fan of it five years ago, he'd never be a big fan of it.

"All right, I just...thought I'd offer," she muttered uncomfortably.

He just got a nod in to share the offer was heard but not accepted before Janie tore into the room, waving Shnookie and shouting, "Got 'im!"

"Come here, you. Let me get your jacket on," Kim called.

"Okay, Mommy," Janie replied, going to her mother but keeping hold of Shnookie, transferring the bear from one hand to the other as her mother put her jacket on and zipped her up.

And Coert watched his beautiful little girl, thinking Kim's play had been whacked but now he couldn't imagine the world without Janie in it, which sucked because he couldn't quite get over being pissed at her mother, but he was still grateful to her.

So Coert was also not a big fan of women who dredged up conflicting emotions that messed with his head.

He'd had his fill of that too.

Especially very recently.

"Mittens," Kim said as Coert moved to the couch to grab Janie's hat that was laying there.

Kim put on the mittens and Janie held Shnookie close to her chest while Coert pulled her hat on her head and made sure it was over her ears.

"Ready?" he asked.

"Yeah, Daddy." She beamed up at him, moving to take his hand.

"Hug for your mom," he ordered.

She instantly turned and threw herself in her mother's open arms.

Janie kept hers around Kim even as she pulled slightly away and asked, "See you tomorrow, Mommy?"

"Yeah, sweetie," Kim replied, giving their daughter a smile.

Janie danced to Coert and took his hand. He led her out to the truck, muttering his goodbyes to her mother, and strapped her in her seat in the back when they got there.

He angled in behind the wheel and reversed out of Kim's drive.

"We gonna go have dinner at Weatherby's?" his girl asked when they were on the road.

"Nope. Makin' my baby dinner at home," Coert answered.

"Hamburglers?" she asked.

"You want hamburgers?" he asked back through a grin.

"Yes!" she yelled.

He kept grinning at the windshield. "Then I'm making hamburgers."

"And curly fries," she ordered.

"And curly fries," he agreed.

"And after we clean up, we can make cupcakes."

Coert chuckled but said, "Maybe the next weekend I have you we can make cupcakes, Janie."

"But it'll be fun to make them tonight."

Only she thought it was fun. Coert having to clean up after the cupcake-making bomb exploded in his kitchen was not fun.

"Weekend, baby," he said quietly.

"Al'right, Daddy."

Damn, she was a good kid.

She'd always been a good kid.

This was obviously awesome and always had been, but right then, something about that rattled him.

He got them home. They made hamburgers and they ate them. His Janie "helped" him through the making and the cleaning up after. She then grabbed one of her coloring books and sat on the floor by the coffee table, and with her tongue sticking out, colored with her book by his stocking feet up on the table while he watched TV.

When she started to get tired, she crawled up next to her dad and burrowed in, cuddling and not really watching what was on the television.

And when it was time, without a word after he said she had to go to bed, she went up with him and did what she did every night he had her with him. She brushed her teeth and got in her pajamas and she picked the book she wanted him to read to her. She then climbed into bed, snuggled into her dad and listened while he read until she fell asleep.

That night, however, after Coert closed the book, unease stole over him as he stared down at her dark head and he thought about his sweet Jane.

She was the perfect kid.

This was not a proud father thinking that.

She just was the *perfect kid.*

Even her terrible twos had been more like mildly annoying twos. She didn't throw tantrums. She didn't get moody. She didn't talk back. She did what she was told. She was bright and cheerful and sunny. She skipped and danced. She didn't pout when she heard no.

And stretched in her bed with his sleeping girl tucked into his side, Coert wondered if somewhere in her little girl psyche she got how she was made, and she got how her mom screwed that up and she got how it pissed off her dad, and they—most importantly *he*—were making her feel that she had to be perfect in order to smooth all that over.

To make all of that worth it.

Kim had stuck holes in the condoms he was obsessive about using even though they were in an exclusive relationship, precisely because he did not want to get her pregnant and that was one gravely messed-up move.

But the bottom line was, he got Janie out of it.

So why the fuck was he still pissed and taking that out on his daughter's mother?

This being a mental road Coert knew he needed to travel not only for his daughter and his relationship with her mother, but also another woman who was suddenly back in his life. It was also a road he couldn't travel right then with his girl fast asleep beside him in her little bed.

So he carefully extricated himself, tucked her in, kissed her temple, made sure Shnookie was close, turned on her nightlight, turned out the bedside light, and he walked down his stairs.

THE FULL REPORT on the arson his deputy gave to him four hours ago sat on his desk next to Coert's open, beat-up leather folder with the legal pad inserted.

His notes scribbled everywhere on the pad, pages flipped up, others torn off, Coert looked from computer to his notes, pen in his fingers, flicking pages, touching keys on the keypad, back and forth.

They'd found fires fitting the same MO in Nevada, Wyoming, Minnesota, one each in those states, four in Colorado.

Minnesota and four in Colorado.

And Maine.

Could seem random. Could be a firebug for hire. Could be copycats admiring the work of the man out west and trying their hand. Could be the man out west had apprentices in the North and East.

But the instant Coert read his deputy's report on the fires, he felt his stomach sink because Colorado, Minnesota and Maine were not coincidences.

It took four hours but he found it. He found the link. He knew why those shops had been burned down. And after he checked and double checked and the facts did not change, every molecule of his body prickled with adrenaline.

The first thing he did was get up, grab his jacket, and he had to stop himself from jogging to his county Explorer.

Or sprinting.

He got in and drove directly to Janie's preschool.

He punched in the code to get in the front door and walked right into the administrator's office.

She was fortunately at her desk and looked up at him, surprise hitting her features.

"Hey, Coert. Is everything okay?" she asked.

He shut the door behind him, walked to the front of her desk and did not sit down.

"When Kim and I enrolled Janie here, we had a chat about vigilance due to my position. I'm regrettably in a place where I need to remind you of that chat, Linette. I also need to request you speak to your teachers and staff and make sure they're consistently aware of the grounds, outside the fences in the playground, and you do not buzz anyone in or give the code out to anyone that is not known to you, not expressly related to one of the children or on a parent's official list."

"Oh my goodness, Coert, is everything okay?"

No.

Everything was far from okay.

"A reminder of vigilance is good as a matter of course. Though I apologize if this alarms you but there's a reason I need to make that reminder. Now just to say, starting very soon, there will be regular drive-bys of sheriff cruisers and at times there will be a manned cruiser parked close to this property. This is simply a precaution. Frankly, a father with the means doing what he can to be absolutely certain his daughter is safe. Cruisers or not, I don't care if you or one of your staff feel you may be acting rashly, but if you're even mildly concerned about someone you see, you call the station and me or one of my men will come and check it out."

"Of course, Coert, but I have to know if Janie, which means the other children, is in danger."

He shook his head. "My hunch, no. But I'm not in the job of taking chances with people's safety. So I need you concerned enough to be alert but not so concerned you're frightened."

That was what he said.

What he didn't add was that if something happened, it would likely happen to him.

Or Cady.

"Oh, Coert, I'm so sorry," she said, sitting there with a pale face, staring up at him.

"An important part of your job has always been to keep my daughter safe, Linette. I don't want Janie scared or worried so her mother and I won't be changing her routine. But I do want the adults around her to be notified and act accordingly."

"We will. I'll call a quick staff meeting tonight after the kids are gone and see to it. And you should know I'll need to share with the other parents."

"It's your job to keep them all safe so you do what you have to do. And if you have any questions at all, or they do, tell them to feel free to phone me directly."

She nodded.

"Thank you, Linette," Coert ended it, turning toward the door because he had a lot to do and he needed to do it.

"Stay safe, Coert," she called as he walked through the door.

"Will do," he returned, not looking back.

He didn't go see his girl because he rarely popped in to see his baby and it wouldn't be good to do it now with where his head was at.

And he didn't have time.

So he got in his truck and drove to his next destination, doing it calling Kim.

"Hey, Coert. What's up?" she answered.

"I'd like to do this in person but I don't have time to do it in person right now so I need to do it over the phone."

"Oh God," she muttered.

"We talked a long time ago, Kim, about things I've had to do in my job and the fact there are people who won't like it. One of those people got out of prison not long ago and he's been active since then. I'm going to be calling an alarm company later today to have them install an alarm in your house. If you can't be off work to be there when they install it, you tell me and I'll be there. Once it's in, you keep it active at all times, when you're in or out of the house, with Janie or not. And I'll pay the bills. That said, my men will be driving by and sometimes even sitting outside your house when you're there. Don't alert Janie to it and don't concern yourself with it. When the threat is gone, I'll let you know. It's important to point out I'm uncertain there is a threat to either of you. But I'm not taking any chances."

"Shit, Coert, what's going on?"

"We talked about this, Kim. Just be smart, be aware of your surroundings, and if you think something is fishy, you phone me immediately."

"Is Janie in danger?" she asked fearfully.

"My gut says no but she's our daughter, Kim, so like I said, I'm not taking any changes."

There was a hesitation before, "Are *you* in danger?"

He gentled his voice when he replied, "There's always that and you know that too."

"Okay, I…okay, I…" She didn't finish that.

"You got this, Kim. Yeah?"

"I can…I can…pay for the alarm, Coert."

"I'm not discussing that now. If we need to chat about it later, we will. But now just let me do what needs to get done. I'll be around later to give you a picture of the man who got out so you can be aware. Again, I doubt you'll see him. But if you do, you don't call me. You call 911 immediately."

Kim hesitated again before she asked, "Are you gonna handle this?"

"Yes," he said low. "I am absolutely going to handle this."

"Okay," she said.

He heard her relief and he had to admit it felt good he could give her that, not to mention she gave such easy indication she believed he could do what he said.

But he couldn't focus on that now.

"Gotta go," he told her.

"Of course," she replied quickly. "Be safe. Stay safe, Coert. Okay?"

"Right, Kim. Later."

He cut her off while she was saying goodbye, and he made more phone calls that needed to be made that also had to do with the safety of people in his life but more about bringing that about in a permanent way.

He did this as he drove to the lighthouse.

He ended the call he was on with one of his deputies when he stopped outside the gate.

He got out and punched in the code. He returned to the truck and was driving in when he saw Cady walking up from the direction of the coastal path.

She was wearing a light down jacket with horizontal stitching in a green olive color, jeans, lace-up Storm Chaser boots with a patterned wool hat pulled down over her ears, making her mass of dark red hair bunch out the sides.

She looked like she was born in Maine.

Then again, transplant her to a mountain, she looked born for the Rockies.

She also looked ticked and her gait changed from wandering to irritated when she saw his truck. This meaning she advanced toward it quickly while he drove to the side of the lighthouse.

He parked, got out, and she was almost on him when she called out irately, "I'm really going to have to ask that you—"

"Did you get a dog?" he asked over the whipping wind.

"Really, Coert, it's not—" she started, still advancing fast.

"*Did you get a fucking dog?*" he barked and watched her stutter step and stop.

So it was him that took the last four strides to get to her.

"Asked a question, Cady," he prompted tightly.

"No," she said softly, staring up at him.

"Get your purse. We're going to the pound."

She blinked, her head jolting and she opened her mouth.

He didn't let her get anything out. He turned his back on her, walked directly to the door and turned the knob.

Fortunately, it was locked.

"I've got the key," she said, still soft.

Using her shoulder to push him out of the way, she unlocked the door and went in.

He went in with her.

She moved to the island where her purse was, nabbed it, but turned around and stayed right where she was.

"Talk to me," she urged gently.

"In the truck," he said.

She looked a little panicked before she tried, "Maybe we should—"

"In the *goddamned truck*, Cady," he growled.

She took him in with big eyes, nodded and scurried to the door.

He closed it and took the keys out of her hand to lock it mostly because he was too unsettled to stand there doing nothing. He handed them back to her when he was done, and she moved double time to keep up with his long strides as he walked to the passenger side door.

He opened it and closed the door when she was up and in.

He knifed up into the other side, rounded the truck in her huge yard and headed back to the gate.

He hadn't closed it so he could drive them right through. It was annoying to have to get out and hit the keypad to close it but no way in fuck he was leaving it open.

He got back in and started driving.

She was silent beside him and he could feel her unease.

Finally, she got up the nerve to start, "Coert—"

"Lars got out of prison. Two years ago. He did his whole stint. Since then, fires have been started in Wyoming, Nevada and Minnesota with four more in Colorado. Lots of destruction. No deaths."

"Okay," she whispered shakily.

"The deaths occurred from five days to three weeks after the fires were set. The lighting of huge fires with a good deal of damage caused by arson being a focus, the murders of every member of Lars's crew would not go unnoticed, but they would go unlinked."

"Oh my God," she breathed, fear wrapped around each word.

He didn't like hearing that, he hated being the cause of it, but she had to know it.

And know it all.

"Lars thought you were a snitch. You were with me, and I turned out to be who I was so he thought you were a snitch. Maria knew that you knew dick, but Maria is a whacked-out bitch. As far as I know she did not disabuse him of this notion. They knew Lonnie was stupid, and Lars calling for his hit was about him being stupid, not being stupid in giving all he gave to me, because at the time Lars didn't know it was very bad for him that anyone gave anything to me. But it wasn't only Lonnie who spilled shit all over the place. I got close to two of Lars's other crew, and Lars was a wannabe big man but he was not dumb. When he went down, with the scope of evidence we had against him, he knew his boys were not as smart as him. So he's out and he's pissed and he wants vengeance, and knowing that man like I do, he doesn't care none of them ratted him out. He's working his way through all of them to make them pay for his dream dying and his ass rotting in jail for fifteen years."

"And you think he'll come after me?" she asked.

"I think there's a possibility he'll come after both of us."

"Oh my God," she breathed.

"You need a dog. You need an alarm. You need a peephole. And we're getting you a gun."

He knew she'd turned her head his way when she whispered, "Coert—"

"Not arguing about it, Cady. You get all that or you move in with me."

"I'll get a gun," she stated immediately.

Coert clenched his jaw.

He unclenched it to say, "We get you one, I'll teach you to use it. It'll be all good, Cady."

"Okay."

She said it but she totally didn't believe it and he didn't blame her.

"We get this done at the pound, I'll get on the phone with my boys back in Denver. I've already got men at the station on calls with the folks in Nevada, Wyoming and Minnesota, sharing the link with them, others on the job of alerting local law enforcement what we're on the lookout for. We all work together, one way or another, we'll get him."

"So you think he's here now?"

"I think he's here now."

"You think he's watching us?"

"I think he's watching us."

"Oh my God."

He knew it was a tall order but he had to give it.

"Keep it together, Cady."

She grew silent.

Coert did too.

She broke it.

"How did he find us? I mean, is it that easy to find people?"

Shit.

Shit.

"Coert?"

Shit.

His name came more urgent now because she felt his mood. "Coert!"

"Your investi…I mean, Moreland's investigator."

"I'm sorry?" she asked.

"He didn't just keep tabs on me."

"Oh my God."

"That I got," Coert told her. "He wanted to keep you safe so he kept tabs on all of them."

"How do you know this?" she asked.

"Several years back, I broke into his hotel room and read the shit he was handing over about me. When I did, I found he had a lot of shit on that whole crew."

"And…what? He worked for Lars on the sly?" she asked.

"I've no idea. And this might be jumping to conclusions. I just know I clocked him because I'm a cop. We notice when people are following us. Lars is a felon. He'd notice the same. And when Lars got out, my guess is Moreland would be sure to put that guy on him. And Lars is probably a whole lot better at breaking and entering than me."

Cady said nothing.

"It might not be that," he told her. "There aren't a lot of Coert Yeagers in the world. Cady Morelands either. We wouldn't be hard to find. That said, the rest of that crew would make it so they aren't easy to find and only someone with investigative skills could find them. So it's a stretch to put that two and two together, but maybe not that long of one."

"I still don't understand the fires," she said unsteadily.

"I don't know his state of mind, but I knew it back then. He was setting up to be the kingpin of Denver. He had schemes of taking out much bigger players than him to take over their operations. He was even making plans to build his army so he could take down actual gangs in order to get their turf.

He was like a drug dealing Napoleon. He had delusions of grandeur. He had the charisma, and he was smart, but he didn't have the kind of intelligence he'd need to see those kinds of plans through. He was not happy for more reasons than getting arrested and thrown in prison. He had big dreams and he was enraged when I killed those dreams. After he went down, he was paranoid that his crew had turned against him. The only one he trusted was Maria because he put her to the ultimate test and she passed. So now, I don't know if he doesn't give a shit if he's caught again, but my hunch, he knows he will be caught but he'll only give a shit if he's caught before the job is completely done."

"And the fires?"

"Distractions. Cover so he can get the job completely done. This was his MO. Back then it wasn't fires, but to throw cops and enemies off the scent, Lars connived to have shit happen to turn attention away from the real shit he was doing that would put a focus on him and his operation. Now, you just got the deaths, one after another, easy to link individual murders in that crew with known associates in past felonies and pinpoint the perpetrator. But if you take your time, which he is, and the cops' attention is turned to investigating an arson and not turned to investigating what appears to be a random murder, their focus on the fire, the fact it's arson, the fact there were others before it with the same MO, doesn't translate to linking that with what would appear to be random murders days or weeks later. And Lars is not a firebug. He's a dope peddler. A good choice to go outside his norm giving him more of a smokescreen to put investigators off the scent. But just to say, in the mess of crime that can happen in places like Reno, Denver and Cheyenne, thin links like that can get lost. That slim link beefs up when Mills jetty goes up in flame and something happens to you or me."

"Saved those for last," she murmured.

Coert said nothing.

But he didn't think that was where it was at.

The Minnesota fire and the ensuing murder had happened only three months ago.

So his guess was, he and Cady were just the farthest away and Lars simply worked his way east, and now, at the end of the road, he didn't care what links were made.

Actually, his guess was Lars had no intention to go after Cady but she'd moved into Coert's town, so she could end up being icing on his mindfuck of a cake.

"It still seems thin, Coert," she noted. "How did you put it together?"

"Arsons with the same MO in those different places, I wouldn't have if it didn't happen in Colorado, Minnesota and here. Minnesota being the change of location to report for parole that one of the crew requested so he could go there and look after his sick mother. Add those together, run the other names, find them all dead, it fit together."

"Are they all gone?" she asked.

"No. But there are only three of us left. You, me and Maria."

"He can't get to Maria," she murmured.

"He won't get to Maria. No way he'd take down his Josephine."

"I never caught that," she said like it was to herself. "You told me to watch for it, be careful around them but I never caught it."

No she didn't. She knew her friend was making exceptionally poor decisions, but she'd never caught how bad it was getting. Part loyalty. Part history. But mostly she'd been wrapped up in Coert.

"You weren't watching as closely as I was, Cady," he said gently.

"Yes," she whispered then asked, "Do you think she knows he's doing this?"

"She can't have any contact with him, so unless he's being clever, I doubt it."

"He could write to her under another name that maybe she'd know but the prison people wouldn't."

Prison people.

He'd laugh if he wasn't entirely freaked out.

"He didn't strike me as a letter writing guy," he shared.

"Right," she murmured. He knew he had her gaze again when she asked, "Um...why are we going to the pound?"

"To get you a dog."

"I know but...well, shouldn't you be looking for him?"

"You need a dog."

Again with the silence but this silence was weighty.

She broke it this time too.

"Five days to three weeks, Coert. It's been five days since that fire."

"He'll come after me."

"Your little girl."

"Cady, he'll come after me."

"How do you know?"

He didn't.

He just didn't want her scared out of her mind.

"Dog, peephole and we'll order you an alarm installed."

It was then he knew she'd turned to look out the side window when she said, "When will all that stuff be over? It feels like we've lived it for eternity."

Those words hit him in the gut because she was absolutely fucking right, it did.

But it never occurred to him she shared that with him.

He thought she'd gone on to live her life with her sugar daddy, and he was not unaware that she kept tabs on him, but he refused to allow himself to think on that or why she'd do something like that, telling himself she was screwed in the head and that was all the reason anyone like that needed to do anything.

But far more recently, he'd also been refusing to see that she'd been just as haunted by all of this since things ended between them as he had.

And she hadn't kept tabs on him, her husband had.

But she'd absolutely lived those years just like him, being haunted by all the shit that had gone down that led to the end of them.

He didn't comment on any of that. He couldn't even take the headspace to process it.

Not then.

He said, "When people like that infest your life, sometimes it's never over."

"Yes, I'm sure that's how Lonnie's parents feel."

She said that and fell quiet again.

That time, Coert broke it.

"You really never went to visit her?"

"I do believe your colleagues probably shared that we had a rather dramatic altercation when I visited her in the police station."

He couldn't help it, he grinned at that because that was not only shared, it was on tape and he'd watched it.

She'd gone apeshit on Maria.

And even with a glass partition separating them, Maria had gone apeshit right back.

"He was messed up but he was a good guy," she said pensively. "He was funny and sweet and he'd do anything for you. He had a crush on me and that wasn't right but you can't control who you like. I know that wasn't his worst transgression but he didn't deserve that." She took a moment and finished quietly, "He didn't deserve that."

"No, Cady, he didn't deserve that."

They drove the rest of the way to the pound in silence and he knew they both had their heads in the same place, and that place was all over the place, none of it good.

When they got inside the shelter, Coert took the lead.

Without preamble or greeting, he declared, "She needs an adult dog, not too old, well-behaved, large, protective, loyal, unfriendly to strangers with a loud bark."

The shelter worker stared up at him with her mouth open.

Coert was about to prompt her to get her ass moving and show them some dogs when he felt Cady sidle up next to him, and then he felt her knuckles graze his before her fingers closed around his own.

And for the first time since he put it together, he was not thinking of Lars or his daughter's safety or Cady being in danger.

He was thinking about a memory that had remained vivid since the event happened when he was twelve and he was teasing his father about holding hands with his mother.

His father had been smiling but his voice was stern in a way that captured Coert's full attention, and that and what he'd said created an unforgettable memory when he'd replied, "Trust me, when you find her, the woman you'll wanna spend the rest of your life with will always be the girl you wanna hold her hand."

He'd held hands with a lot of girls and his fair share of women.

But he and Cady didn't move anywhere if they were in close proximity without his fingers curled around hers.

He'd missed her smell. He'd missed those green eyes. He'd missed the feel of her hair. He'd missed his hands on her ass. He'd missed her sense of humor. He'd missed how she might not have had a lot of experience in bed, but she was the best he'd ever had not (only) because of her enthusiasm, but because she was so fucking into him, she'd loved him so fucking much, that spilled out—especially when he had his hands and mouth on her, his cock inside her.

But there had been more times than any of those since he'd lost her that he'd missed just holding her hand.

Moving slowly like he was forcing his way through molasses, he looked down at her to see she was sending a gentle smile up to him.

"You can't custom order them, honey," she whispered.

He had no fucking clue what she was talking about.

He just knew he never wanted to move from that spot in that position staring down in those green eyes with her fingers wrapped around his for the rest of his life.

She was not caught in the same spell, he knew, when she turned to the shelter worker and said, "Can you just show us to the pups?"

At her last word, Coert forced himself to pull it together and squeezed her fingers.

"You're not getting a puppy, Cady," he told her when she looked at him.

"They're all pups, Coert," she replied.

"That's very true," the shelter worker finally spoke.

Cady shot her a grin before she turned into Coert and tipped her head way back.

"We're here, we're safe," she said under her breath. "I'll go look at dogs and you probably have some calls you want to make."

He did and she was right.

She could look at dogs and he could make sure shit was in motion to find Lars.

He nodded.

Her face got soft, her fingers closed tighter around his and then she let him go and walked away with the shelter worker.

COERT SPENT FORTY-FIVE minutes getting briefed from his senior deputy then calling Denver to give Malc and Tom a heads up about what was happening and getting them started on their end of the chase.

He'd find it was forty-four and a half minutes too long when he followed where Cady had disappeared and saw her in the middle of a wide hall in a large room filled with big cages on either side, most having dogs in them.

He tried not to look.

If he looked, Janie would also be getting a dog (or three) and he needed to take care of a dog as well as his daughter and a whole county like he needed someone to drill a hole in his head.

Cady was on her ass on the floor and she had a dog out of its cage. The dog was sitting between her legs, letting her pet it and looking like it was enjoying the attention if the amount of licking of her face the dog was attempting was anything to go by.

At first glance, it appeared she'd chosen well. The dog was large, formidable (not counting the licking) and looked like it had a lot of German shepherd in it.

Then he got closer, the dog went on alert, awkwardly getting on all fours, and the shelter worker moved cautiously toward the pair.

"Cady, no," he said before he even arrived at them. "That dog's lame."

And it was, its left rear leg was holding some of its weight but not much, it was misshapen, having been injured so badly it clearly was unable to heal properly.

"She's beautiful," Cady murmured, hands in the dog's ruff trying to get her to turn her attention back to Cady.

"Cady—"

Her head tipped back and Coert shut his mouth at the look on her face.

"Her name is Gorgeous Midnight Magic," she whispered reverently. "Isn't that *perfect*?"

Shit.

"Cady—"

"She's purebred German shepherd, black," the shelter worker said. "We were given her history and an elderly gentleman answered an ad for her in the paper. Her owners said her back leg was caught in a trap, but the gentleman was suspicious of this information and regardless that she was lame and exhibiting some behavior he found concerning, took her on. A vet confirmed his suspicions that the injury wasn't due to a trap, but to abuse and the fact the injury received no medical attention, so it never healed as it should have."

Shit.

The worker continued, "The gentleman unfortunately passed not long after and as his daughter and son both had a number of pets, they had to bring her here. She's been with us for a while, and so we find her the right home, I have to disclose she has issues when it storms. She displays those mostly just trembling and hiding, usually in closets."

Fucking shit.

"Cady, just to say, it storms a lot in Maine," he pointed out.

The shelter worker wasn't finished. "She also is perhaps a little on the *over*protective side and has been known to corner humans that are strangers to her, and it's been reported to us she can seem quite vicious, though to anyone's knowledge she's done no harm. However, she can only be called off by someone that's known to her. And it's important you know she's a one-owner animal, and although friendly and affectionate to people that she knows or that she senses are okay from her owner, it's been noted that her loyalty is focused almost solely on her owner."

Coert looked to the worker. "We'll take her."

The worker's lips quirked and she said, "We have an application process that takes just a few days to get approval."

"We're circumventing the application process," Coert announced.

"Coert," Cady murmured soothingly as he sensed her getting to her feet.

"I can see you're the authority, sir," the worker began, eyes tipping to his sheriff's shirt and jacket. "But the procedures we have in place are for our animals' protection and we take them seriously. The application process only takes three days since we also obviously want our animals to find their way to the warmth and comfort of home."

"Ms. Moreland will apply but she's taking the dog right now and if you have any issues with her application, you can inform her and we'll deal with it then. Since you won't, it'll all be good."

"Sir—"

He wasn't one to throw his weight around.

Unless something like that was necessary.

Like now.

"Sheriff," he corrected.

The worker sought help from Cady by looking her way.

And Cady did her best, saying to him, "I can wait three days for this beauty."

The dog was sitting next to her, Cady's hand in the fur between her ears, her tongue lolling, her eyes on Coert.

Coert looked to the worker. "How long has the dog been here?"

"About four months."

Cady made a distressed noise Coert did not like *at all.*

Right.

"We're circumventing the procedure," he declared.

"Sir…I mean, Sheriff—"

"Do you seriously want this dog to stay in one of these cages for three more days?" Coert asked.

She looked to Cady, the dog, Coert and then she sighed before she said to Cady, "I'll get you the forms."

She took off and Cady got close.

The dog came with her like she was born to walk at Cady's side.

Brilliant.

"Coert, I don't have a lead or collar or any food or—"

"We'll stop by the pet store."

Her brows shot up. "Don't you have a fire-starting, murdering, ex-drug peddler to catch?"

"Fortunately, I have sharp deputies that kinda like me and are fully briefed about the fact their boss is a likely target of a fire-starting, murdering, ex-drug peddler so they can get shit started while I take you and your new dog to the pet store."

"I think you're kinda crazy," she whispered.

"I think I kinda already won't sleep jack shit until I know Lars is caught, so maybe you can help me out by letting me set you up with a freaking dog so I might get a whole hour's sleep at night instead of, say, *none.*"

She stared at him with big eyes for several very long beats before she said, "Okay."

"Okay, now let's fill out this application and get this girl outta here."

To that she gave him a smile.

"Okay."

She filled out the application.

They went to the pet store.

And finally he took her back to the lighthouse, burying the look Cady gave him when he refused to allow her to carry the huge bag of dog food into the house (like he'd refused to allow her to load it into the cart in the store *or* in the truck and the same looks she'd given him those times as well).

The dog did not explore her new home.

She jumped right up on Cady's couch and lay down with a groan like she'd lived there since she was a pup, they'd just been on a tiring outing and she needed some shuteye.

When Cady witnessed that, she shot him a beam.

A goddamned *beam*.

Okay, yeah.

He missed holding hands with her, definitely, and all the rest, for certain.

He'd also missed her smile.

He responded to that emotion by clipping out, "I'll be back later to put in your peephole."

The beam died and she said, "I can get Walt to do that."

He didn't know who Walt was, and right then he didn't have the mental capacity to think on that without maybe roaring his demand to know precisely who the fuck this Walt guy was and maybe freaking her out more than being the possible target of vengeance already was.

This meaning he'd also have to process his way to understanding why he felt such an overwhelming urge to demand precisely who the fuck this Walt guy was.

Even though, fuck him, he knew why he had that urge.

Instead, keeping tight control, he asked, "Can Walt drop everything and do it tonight?"

She bit her lip before she said, "Maybe, if I terrify him with the knowledge that someone may want me dead. But then he'll only come to kidnap me because he's that kind of guy, but even if he wasn't, his wife is that kind of woman. So maybe I should just say I'm feeling a little weird about not having one and ask him to get around to it as soon as he can. He's still here with his guys doing up the apartment over the garage, though this afternoon they're off because they laid floors this morning and they can't walk on them until they're set. But I'll only have to wait until tomorrow at most."

Walt had a wife.

And they weren't done working on the property so Cady would only be alone at night and the rest of the time a team of men would be on the premises.

Coert relaxed.

"How about we just say you'll have one tonight because I'm installing one tonight?"

"Coert."

"Cady."

He said not another word, and for some reason her body locked.

He didn't have time for that.

She had a dog. A dog that was reportedly vicious in protection of its owner. And Coert had no idea if the dog understood the concept of Cady at that juncture but he had a hunch the dog understood the bag of food and the couch, so if she wasn't there yet, she was closing in.

So he could rest on that for an hour or two.

He had to get to the station and see how far his men had gotten with his orders. He had to order an alarm installed at Kim's place. And he had to get to the hardware store to get a peephole. Then he had to get to Kim and give her a photo of Lars Pedersen.

"I'll text before I show," he told her.

"Right."

"Locked doors, always, Cady."

She nodded. "Right."

He looked to her still in her cap with her hair bunched out around her cheeks and neck.

He looked to her dog that appeared fast asleep.

Then he walked right out the door.

Thirteen

GUTS AND BALLS

CADY

Present day…

"Okay, normally I'd call Kath with all this but I can't call Kath and tell her that the drug dealer my ex-undercover-cop boyfriend brought down is firing a swath of vengeance, literally, across the United States, headed toward me. She'll lose her mind. Pat will lose his mind. Then the Moreland dominoes will fall and I'll be shunted back to Colorado, maybe never to see my lighthouse again. So I have to tell you."

Midnight lay on her belly on the couch, ears perked, eyes alert and on me as I paced in front of the fire.

"So, girl, it's going to be you who I share that I think I may be a little touched in the head, that I'm far less concerned about the fact Lars is literally firing a swath of vengeance with Coert and I as his final targets than I am about Coert showing up here in a few minutes to put in my peephole."

When I stopped talking, Midnight wagged her tail.

"No, no." I shook my head, moving to her, squatting by the couch and giving her head a rubdown.

She licked my wrist.

I admonished, "It isn't exciting. It *feels* exciting because we spent a whole two hours together without any shouting or alternate verbal devastation. But we must remember," I held her face in both hands and looked in her brown eyes, "Coert *does not like us.*"

Midnight whined and shuffled a little toward me on her belly.

"Okay, you're right. He likes you. Very much. You were a very good girl when he put your collar and lead on and you just sat right down at his feet at the pet store. That was very smart of you to show what a good girl you could be. That's why he's the sheriff, and still he stole that doggie treat right there from that canister and gave it to you. But it wasn't really stealing since he told them at the cash register he did it then he paid for it."

Midnight panted.

She remembered the doggie treat.

Or maybe she remembered Coert giving it to her before he bent over her to give her a full body rubdown, murmuring in his deep voice, "That's a very good girl."

It was a long time ago but I remembered when he gave me a full body rubdown, and he might not have said I was a good girl but he *showed* he felt that way and I liked it a whole lot.

"It's not good I'm having these thoughts five minutes after he texted to say he's coming over to install my peephole," I muttered.

Midnight kept panting.

I looked into her intelligent eyes and decided to change the subject.

"Tomorrow, we'll go for a walk around the fence so you'll get to know your new home. And after Coert brings down the bad guy...*again*...we'll take walks on the coastal path. Does that sound good?"

Midnight just kept panting.

So I raised my voice an octave and asked, "Does that sound good, girl?"

She gave a soft, "Ruff."

"Yes," I said. "That sounds good."

I straightened, moved to the fire and then grew worried about the fire.

Patrick had several fireplaces in his house in Denver as well as several in his cabin outside Vail. He loved having fires and he'd taught me how to build them. Thus, since I moved into the lighthouse, I had fires every night. It made the space seem even more warm and cheery, not to mention it provided heat, which was needed in Maine for certain.

But looking around the room with its big, plush, chocolate couch that dominated the space, the club chair and ottoman squeezed to the side, the thick throw rugs over wood floors, the heavy iron light fixture that hung in the middle of the room, the curved, dramatic iron candleholders, the décor in warm earthy tones with deep blues intermingled, that fire burning made it look like a seduction scene.

All I had to do was light some candles and put on Barry White, and Coert would walk through the door and then he'd walk right back out of it.

I looked to Midnight. "I shouldn't have started a fire."

She tipped her head to the side.

"I mean, we got along for two full hours and maybe even longer but only because both our lives are in danger."

Midnight just stared at me.

"He'll go back to hating me once he catches Lars."

Midnight got up, jumped off the couch and made her mostly graceful, part lumbering way toward me.

Watching her, I refused to think about her back leg. This was because I was rich. I could hire my own investigator. I could find the owners she'd had who'd hurt her. And I could shoot them with the gun Coert was going to give to me.

But if I did, Coert being a good policeman would catch me and I'd go to jail and then who'd take care of Midnight?

She snuffled my thigh with her nose and I bent over her to give her head another rubdown. "Okay, I won't go shoot your ex-owners. But I'm not saying I won't dabble in voodoo curses."

She licked my wrist again.

Approval.

Voodoo curses it was.

She then went on alert, her head jerking to stare at the wall, and I jumped when she then made an almighty racket, barking ferociously at the wall.

Coert was there.

Or somebody was.

Best early warning, indeed.

Midnight made her way to the door, still barking but doing it louder, faster, more ominous.

A knock came on the door and she stopped barking and started growling, teeth bared, as I followed her there, cautious, cooing to her and telling her it was all right.

She tried to shuffle me away from the door so I took hold of her collar and whispered, "Good dog. Good Midnight. You're such a good girl. But it's okay. We're okay." Before I called out, "Who's there?"

"Coert!" Coert shouted.

Midnight started barking again but I kept a firm hold on her collar, gently pushing her back as I reached long to the bolt and kept shushing her with, "It's just Coert. You know him. He's okay."

I turned the knob, and with my hand still on Midnight's collar, I held tight as the door opened. Coert looked to me, to my barking and growling dog, and then he immediately crouched low.

"See. It's Coert. He's friendly. You know him. He's nice. We like him," I said to Midnight.

"Good girl," Coert murmured, slowly lifting his hand toward the dog. "Takin' care of Cady. Good girl."

"He's nice," I said. "See?" I shuffled to him but held on to her collar. "He's friendly. He's here to look out for us."

Midnight made a growling, cautious approach toward Coert with me. The growls started intermingling with whines before she did a few sniffs of his fingers, more, got closer then bumped his hand with her nose.

He scratched behind her ears, still murmuring, "That's it, Midnight. Make sure it's all good for Cady."

I let her collar go when Coert engaged his other hand, they got to know each other again and finally Coert said to the dog, "Now get back, girl. Gotta get my tools and get this door shut on the cold."

He straightened slowly and moved her back a bit before he turned toward the door, grabbed a big toolbox and a plastic bag he'd set on my front step, brought them in and closed the door.

It was then, his eyes came to me.

"Hey," he greeted.

"Hey," I replied.

God.

It came out breathy.

I tried to mask that by stating while indicating Midnight with a hand, "Obviously, she works."

He glanced at the dog before looking back to me and saying, "Yeah."

We stood there staring at each other.

Okay, now what did we do?

Coert knew the answer to that because he lifted the bag and toolbox and said, "Best get on this."

"Right," I mumbled.

"I got peepholes, Cady, but I also got the stuff to give you a speakeasy."

"Sorry?" I asked.

"A speakeasy," he repeated. "I'll cut a box, make a door, weatherproof the edges and put it on hinges with an inside bolt so you can open it and look out. Better range of vision than a peephole, and you get your guy to put something decorative on the outside, looks nice and'll fit this place better than a peephole."

I knew what he was talking about and he was right. Peepholes were for hotels. Those little doors were much nicer and you'd expect one at a lighthouse.

But I also considered this with some surprise.

Back in the day, Coert hadn't given any indication he was a man who had a toolbox the size of the toolbox he had right then. He was not that fixer-upper, dig-in-and-sort-problems kind of guy. The truth was, we hadn't been together long enough for anything to get fixed up, and the entire time we'd been together, we'd lived together in his friend's place so it wasn't exactly ours to change anything. But still, he just didn't seem like that sort.

Years had passed, I knew. You lived and learned how to deal with things that came along, I knew that too.

But it still surprised me he could cut speakeasies into doors.

And this knowledge settled on me like a weight. A weight that drew out the lightness I'd felt earlier when we'd talked (for once without it being ugly) about what we'd been through that long time ago.

Obviously I'd told Patrick all about it. I'd also told Kath and all the girls. I knew Pat and Mike and Daly knew too.

But talking to them about it wasn't the same as talking about it with Coert.

He'd been there. He knew Maria and Lonnie and Lars. He knew how intense and ugly that situation was, like only someone who'd been involved could know.

He didn't just commiserate that I was dragged into something so ugly.

He *got it.*

I'd never had that.

And there had been something that felt nice about talking with him about it earlier. Like we were a two-person support group, the only two people who could belong.

But now I was being confronted with all the time that had happened in between. Confronted with the fact Coert had lived a life where he got a toolbox, the tools in it and had learned how to do things because experience and years and life had taught him how.

Experience and years and life I had not been a part of.

"So, what do you want? Peephole or speakeasy?" Coert prompted.

"Speakeasy," I answered.

He nodded and immediately turned to the door, set down the box and muttered, "Gotta go out and grab my saw."

And with that, he opened the door and walked through it.

Midnight woofed.

I instantly felt even more uncomfortable and at a loss of what to do.

I knew he wasn't there to share a drink or do a chore and then be paid back by staying and having dinner.

But his matter-of-fact, get-on-with-it attitude told me he simply was there to do what he needed to do and then leave.

I moved to the kitchen to find something for myself to do.

I decided to pour wine. I had no beer for him because I no longer drank beer. But he probably wouldn't accept one anyway.

Feeling deflated and then feeling more deflated because I knew I had no reason to feel deflated in the first place, I opened a bottle of red and poured myself some wine. I kept my eye on Midnight when she woofed again, dashing to the door as Coert came through it carefully, eyes on the dog, murmuring to her as she gave Coert another sniff then started to wag her tail and crowd around him as he got down to work.

"I don't have beer but would you like something to drink?" I asked to be polite.

But drat it all, for other reasons besides.

"I'm good. This'll take a bit but not too long," he replied, not looking at me, looking for a socket in which to plug his electric saw with its thin blade.

Apparently he was very much a fixer-upper kind of guy if he had one of those. I couldn't fathom what anyone would need to cut enough of to have a tool with a plug to cut that much of it. And I felt relatively certain that he didn't offer the service of giving every single woman in his county a speakeasy so she could make sure she knew who was behind her door before she opened it.

Coert went to work on the door at the same time he went to work ignoring me (but not Midnight, who he talked to a lot as he worked, mostly because she was excited about his activity and getting in his way, his handling of her something that was sweet and I found it highly attractive, something *I* had to go to work on ignoring).

I also went to work answering meager emails, mostly replying to Verity about a possible visit that I'd been looking forward to planning with her but now I regrettably had to find a vague way to postpone, because I didn't want her around when Lars was on the loose.

Then I started randomly online shopping, this being random because I was a woman who needed nothing so I had nothing to look for.

But no woman actually needed *nothing*, and I proved that true when I found a fabulous, quilted microfiber, memory foam dog bed that had personalization and cost a veritable fortune (for a dog bed) that Midnight *had to have.*

I was ordering it when Coert said, "Got a Dustbuster?"

I looked to him then down to the floor where the shavings were, back up, and I saw the little door with the little hinges and little bolt and tiny knob that was very attractive, and my stomach sank that he was done.

"I'll take care of it, Coert," I told him.

He nodded and moved to the other door and my stomach flipped that he was going to stay to do both.

The stomach flip was not good.

None of this was good—guard dogs, guns, speakeasies, men firing swaths of vengeance—but insanely I felt that stomach flip was the worst of all.

Midnight moved to help him and I moved to the small utility cupboard Walt had put in at the end of the kitchen where I kept cleaning supplies and plugged in my Dyson handheld.

Midnight was as enthralled with my noises and movements as she was with Coert's, dividing her attention between us as I vacuumed up the shavings. Then she went back to Coert when my paltry chore was done.

I went back to my laptop.

Coert came to me twenty minutes later when he was finished.

"My boys know you're a possible target so they're gonna be driving out here regular to check on things," he stated.

I looked up at him from my stool and nodded, wondering how he explained to "his boys" that I, too, was a possible target. That being a possible target along with their boss.

"You order an alarm to be put in?" he asked.

I nodded again and told him, "Midnight and I researched that and made an appointment while you were gone."

This time he nodded. "I got a piece, a little .22. Got a friend, handin' it off to him. He's gonna meet you at the range in Blakely. I'll text you the address, you text me some times you can meet him and I'll set it up."

So Coert wasn't going to show me how to use his gun. His friend was.

Definitely done with spending time with me.

Definitely deflated.

"Okay, Coert."

"He'll show you how to handle it, load it, fire it, give you safety lessons. You won't use it. Just backup security. In the unlikely event you do use it, it's a .22. The damage it can cause when it comes to guns is not as much as other calibers. So unless you got great aim, that kind of gun is about slowing him down, not killing him. Does that make sense?"

"Yes," I repeated.

"You comfortable with that?" he pushed.

I was really not.

I nodded.

"You go somewhere, be sharp and keep eyes on mirrors to spot if someone is following you. And don't walk the coastal paths unless you have your phone and dog with you, or preferably not at all until I get this guy caught."

"Okay," I said again.

"You hear something, get tweaked, I don't care, Cady, you call 911. Okay?"

Call 911.

Not him.

More official and possibly a faster response time.

Still, my stomach sunk deeper.

But I nodded.

"We got a BOLO on him. Every law enforcement agency in this county and the surrounding ones know we're lookin' for him and have his picture and what we know about the vehicle he may be driving. He's targeting a cop, they're motivated. You understand?"

"Yes. I understand."

"Good," he muttered. "Be alert and you can't be too cautious. You tell the guys workin' for you about this so they can keep an eye out too. I'll have a deputy come out and put a picture of Lars in your mailbox so you can show that around. It might freak 'em but better they're freaked and got their eyes peeled than they just think Lars is some other tourist who wants to take pictures of a Maine lighthouse. Yeah?"

"Yes, Coert."

"Right," he muttered. "Gotta go."

And he did indeed have to go because after he gave Midnight some neck scratches, he grabbed his stuff and moved to the door.

I trailed him. "I really must thank you. You didn't have to—"

He stopped at the door, turned to me and cut me off.

"I did have to. You were right. I kept you in when you wanted out. Now, all these years, you're still in. This is my responsibility."

This mention of what happened didn't feel like a support group in the slightest.

And his taking that responsibility made me feel awful because I'd made him think he held it.

However, there was something deeper in this admission. I could feel it, sense it, actually *see it* in the set of his face.

It was just that we weren't anywhere near a place I could explore it.

But *it* was so present I felt I needed to try.

"Coert—" I began.

"It is and I'll keep you as safe as I can keep you. You help with that, this gets done and then that's it. It's finally over. For the both of us."

That's it.

It's over.

For both of us.

No Coert using his gentle voice. No Coert understanding how something that happened so long ago could reverberate through our lives to this day. No Coert with his fingers wrapped around mine looking down at me like he still belonged at my side, holding my hand.

That would just be…

It.

"Thank you anyway," I said quietly.

"My job," he muttered, looked down to Midnight, gave her another head scratch and then turned to the door. "Later, Cady."

"Goodbye, Coert."

His eyes moved through mine.

And then he and his saw and his toolbox disappeared through the door.

TONY SAT UP *as I moved on him, both his hands racing up the sides of my spine, into my hair, but I didn't need the invitation.*

I'd already bent my neck, was grasping his thick hair at the sides of his head and my mouth was on his, open, my tongue plundering.

I couldn't get enough of the taste of him. Never could. No matter how often we kissed and we kissed often.

I couldn't get enough of the feel of his hard cock deep inside me either. I wanted to grind into it but I needed *to move, feel the friction, slam my clit into the base.*

He tore his mouth from mine.

"Cady," he growled, his fists in my hair tugging back, the pain at my scalp searing down my spine, over my bottom, between my legs, buzzing my clit.

My back arched, his mouth closed over a nipple…

"Tony," I moaned.

In the memory.

"*Coert*," I moaned in my bed with my vibrator held to my clit, my back off the bed, my heels digging into it.

The orgasm flowed through me so deeply, I had to snatch the toy from my flesh because it was too much, too beautiful, too perfect.

I whimpered and panted and let it happen then I breathed deeply and opened my eyes to the dark of my bedroom. Total dark with the blackout blinds over the windows closing out the rotating beam of my lighthouse.

As if she knew it was over, Midnight moved from the floor to the bed and settled beside me as I stared into the dark, setting aside my toy and pulling an arm outside the covers to dive my fingers into her fur.

She adjusted her head so it was on my hip.

I kept staring into the dark, feeling the wet hit my eyes as the memory of one of the many times Coert and I had connected overwhelmed me in a different way.

Since him, I'd only ever fantasized about him, mostly using memories, like that one.

Since him, I'd never climaxed again with a man, though there were very few men I'd allowed myself to share that intimacy with.

And before him, I never even got close.

So really, it had only ever been him.

Tony.

Coert.

Him.

Midnight whined and burrowed closer.

In the few days I'd had her, I'd begun to learn she was not only a one-person dog, she was an exceptionally sensitive one.

"I'm okay, baby," I whispered, stroking her fur.

I was not.

I was in love with Coert Yeager in a way that it just simply would never die.

Never.

I'd denied it long enough. Hid from it. Buried it.

But the fact was, I was out there not (just) for Patrick.

I was out there for me.

I was out there for Coert.

I was out there to get him back.

And I'd been out there for months.

But I hadn't even tried.

IT WAS RISKY for more than one reason, but risks had to be taken, especially when something this important was at stake.

And opportunities could no longer be missed.

I'd had opportunities since I got to Maine, small ones, huge ones, opportunities so colossal, they shouted at me in my own living room.

But I'd allowed emotion and history to guide me to squandering them.

Not anymore.

Eighteen years ago Coert and I fell together against all odds.

Then it ended.

And neither of us got over it.

No more missed opportunities.

It was time to risk everything.

Since Coert had shared that Lars was a threat lurking out there possibly intent on killing one or both of us, he'd set me up with my dog, my speakeasy, and he'd held true on getting me a gun and getting me somewhere where someone could show me how to use it.

But outside a woman from the sheriff station who identified herself as "Monica, Sheriff Yeager's assistant," phoning with some frequency to share (not always the same words but always the same message), "The sheriff is still devoting all the resources he can to the matter of finding Lars Pedersen. However he wishes you to know that you still need to be cautious, stay alert and report anything troubling because Mr. Pedersen is still at large," there had been nothing from Coert.

So he wasn't giving me any opportunities.

Thus I had to make one.

And the one I decided to make was, considering he was the sheriff and there'd been a fire in town and the town website provided the news they'd be discussing a referendum about whether or not to devote more resources to Magdalene's fire department, I thought it highly likely Coert would attend the town council meeting.

He probably attended them all.

So I would attend as well.

I had cover.

I mean, there *was* a man out there who might want me dead.

The problem was, I had to go and there *was* a man out there who might want me dead.

Since I'd learned this news, Midnight and I might go out during the day, but we stayed in at night.

As Coert had instructed, I'd told Walt what was happening.

As I had suspected, Walt lost his mind and tried to get me (and Midnight) to move in with him and Amanda (and it should be noted, their three young children).

I had gently refused (I didn't need Walt, Amanda *and* three young children in the path of a man bent on vengeance).

However, I did not gently refuse him planting one of his guys in my studio. It was, Walt told me in an effort to convince me to say yes, a win-win since his guy was on the outs with his girl and she'd demanded he leave the home they shared so he was sleeping on a buddy's couch.

I didn't really need him to convince me.

So Elijah moved into the studio, but Walt really only lost his bad mood about all of this when he saw the alarm company install my alarm.

I had met Elijah in passing. He was large. He seemed friendly.

I found later he loved dogs and he also could put away a great deal of food, and I knew this because I cooked for him every night (it was nice to have company, and anyway, I liked Elijah a lot). And Midnight, he and I watched TV in my second floor family room every night as well, after he helped me clean up, and while watching, Elijah snacked unreservedly (yes, even after a large dinner).

So like everything in my life, bad (even very bad) turned to good, because I got Midnight out of it. I got Elijah out of it. And Midnight might be (somewhat) lame and *really* did not like strangers (thus would be a little scary if I didn't know she was a cuddle monster), and Elijah might be twenty-six and from our conversations entirely clueless about women.

But they were now mine.

And I was keeping them.

Even with all that, the town council meeting was at night and I couldn't exactly bring Elijah with me (though he'd come if I'd asked because he was clueless about women but still very sweet and protective) when I was planning to attempt to make inroads with Coert.

And although I'd learned to load and shoot a .22 caliber pistol, I wasn't really feeling comfortable carrying it in my purse.

So my line of defense was going to be Midnight (when we loaded up, though, I put the gun in the glove compartment as one couldn't be too careful when someone might want them dead).

And as beautiful as she was, I couldn't take Midnight into the council meeting.

Therefore I decided to hang outside with Midnight in the car in hopes of catching Coert outside, and when I did, I'd make my move.

I was right. Coert showed at the town council meeting.

But he showed and walked right in.

Which was not helpful.

Fortune bloomed when some time after (and it was so long, both Midnight and I were having second thoughts, her because this was boring, me because quite some time meant plenty of it to lose courage), Coert walked out alone with his phone to his ear.

I watched as he walked to the side of his sheriff's truck but stopped there between his truck and another car and kept talking.

I ignored my head screaming, *No! He hates you! Just go to your lighthouse, light a fire and plan a cross country road trip with Midnight for a long visit back to Denver, one that'll last until everyone comes out for Christmas, meaning Coert will have Lars again behind bars and you can go back to avoiding one another.*

Instead, I took hold of Midnight's lead, opened my door, climbed out, she climbed out with me, and we started across the street, moving toward Coert.

I saw what appeared to be a family walking down the sidewalk but I paid no mind to them as I heard Coert saying curtly in his phone, "Trouble follow you from Denver?" And without giving who he was talking to even a second to reply, he demanded, "Answer me!"

I bit my lip and wondered if approaching him in this mood was a good idea.

However, Midnight had clearly caught our direction and she hadn't forgotten Coert this time, so she had another idea. This being she started straining to get to him.

I knew immediately when Coert noted our approach, feeling the heat of his eyes as they cut to me.

But when Midnight made it to him, dragging me right along with her, Coert showed he was not a man to take a bad mood out on a dog. He did this by bending to her and giving her some scratches at the same time getting some puppy kisses.

And talking.

"Your notes are thorough, but your intuition and ethics are shit. You led him right to her…and me."

Uh-oh.

I stopped.

In the streetlights I saw Coert's eyes skewer mine before they dropped to my dog.

"Sit," he ordered.

Midnight sat and I considered doing the same thing.

"My dog," he said into the phone.

His dog?

"If Moreland was alive, he'd wring your neck," he snarled.

Uh-oh.

I felt dread fill my veins.

Coert just kept speaking.

"Since I'm still alive, here's a warning and you should listen to it. Don't get close to my town again." He paused then he said, "I know that. But the fact remains, you not only made it easy, you had an opportunity to stop it altogether."

With that, he took the phone from his ear, beeped it off and scowled at me.

"You got great timing," he declared.

"What?" I whispered.

"We closed in on Lars this morning."

"That's good, isn't it?" I asked hesitantly, because it not only seemed good, it seemed fantastic, but he didn't seem to think the same.

"It would have been, if he hadn't cleared out before we got there. By the state of the place where he was crashing, *right* before we got there. Didn't get the chance to take anything with him. Left clothes behind. Even ammo. And lots of other shit I spent the afternoon combing through that was interesting."

I didn't like the idea of Lars having ammo, even if he left it behind.

"Why do I get the feeling that you're using the word interesting but you mean annoying?" I queried.

"Because I just got a return call from your husband's investigator and he admitted that, on Moreland's orders, he started tailing Lars the second he was released from prison. He also stated he *thought* Lars made him but he couldn't be sure. But he backed off. Lars then vanished. My buddy Malc in Denver has a son, who's a PI, who Malc's got lookin' into shit. Part of that is Malc's boy Lee helping himself to this investigator's notes and reports. And what Lee found was this guy never picked up Lars's trail again, definite indication that Lars made him and this guy knew it. Problem was, this was a screw up of massive proportions and this guy knew that too. So in his reports to your husband, he made up shit about keeping tabs on Lars when what we found in Lars's hideout was that Lars followed that jackass, that jackass clearly never made him and so that jackass led him to every member of his old crew." A weighty pause and then he finished, "And us."

"Oh no," I whispered.

"Oh yeah," Coert returned. "So he's been unwittingly aiding and abetting an arson and murder spree, and on top of that, for two years, your husband didn't know the man he'd hired to keep tabs on people who could make you unsafe made you fuckin' *unsafe*."

"And you," I said, my voice shaky.

"What?" Coert asked.

"And he made you unsafe."

"You lived in a mansion, Cady. I'm the sheriff for Derby County. He'd find me, no sweat. You with a husband who goes to those lengths to keep informed on anything that might harm you, nothing would harm you. This investigator should have been the first to catch on to what was happening. Not go to lengths to hide his screw up at the same time not link together that he'd lost Lars and his old crew was dropping like flies."

I pressed my lips together because I had nothing to say since it would be useless to confirm to Coert something he knew was true.

Midnight shifted to the side so she was leaning on my legs.

Coert looked into the night then looked at me.

"What are you doin' here?"

"It's the town council meeting and I thought you'd be here, so I thought I'd come so I could get updated on what was happening with Lars."

"Isn't Monica calling you?" he asked.

"Well, yes."

"And don't you have my number?"

I didn't and I did. I'd erased it from my contacts but I could easily resurrect it from his texts.

"I erased it," I admitted.

He seemed to grow in size, this making Midnight go to all fours, as he asked irately, "Why would you do a fool thing like that?"

"I was drunk at the time."

His brows snapped together. "What are you talking about?"

"It was the night of the fire when you were accusing me of having something to do with the fire when I actually did but I didn't know I did at the time."

"You don't have anything to do with that fire," he clipped tersely.

"Lars is here to hurt me or you, so I do."

"Don't shoulder blame that isn't yours."

"It's hard not to when four business owners are suffering for me making poor decisions nearly two decades ago."

"Stop that shit," he growled. "It's a waste of energy because what another person does is *not on you*. And think it's important to point out, I didn't think you had anything to do with the fire."

He didn't?

"You made it sound that way."

"I thought you were with someone or knew something about someone who might know something about the fire."

"That, Coert, is saying you thought I had something to do with the fire."

"It is not."

"It very much is."

"It very much fuckin' isn't."

How could he not see that it was?

"If I knew something about the fire, I wouldn't call you and then not tell you I knew something, *anything* about the fire. Especially not inebriated. I'm chatty when I'm inebriated, as you well know. And furthermore, it was incredibly insulting you'd assume that."

"Cady, history and you parking your ass in Magdalene then goin' off and pissin' off your brother with some unknown but reportedly unpleasant friend is hard to ignore."

"Only because you won't let history go," I retorted hotly, this not being where I'd hoped the opportunity I was creating and the risk I was taking was going to go.

But in my defense he was *such* a grudge holder!

"You're right."

I blinked.

"I'm…right?" I asked for confirmation.

"You wanna know the truth…"

I wasn't sure I did but it wasn't a question because he kept talking.

"It felt nice that you were worried about me. Worried enough to get drunk and then call me and express that worry. That felt good. On top of that, you were being cute and funny. I remembered you could be cute and funny a lot and I also remembered how much I liked it. But at the time I didn't like any of that, so I was probably lookin' for shit to fight that feeling and in the end acted like a dick."

I stared at him and I was afraid I did it with my mouth hanging open.

Coert's mouth, however, continued moving.

"I been thinkin' a lot about things lately, with my kid, her mother…you, and what I've come up with is I gotta get my head straight about a lot of crap that I've let stay twisted for a long time. Problem with that is, I got some guy out there who wants at least me dead, probably you too, so that kinda takes precedence."

He quit speaking and this went on some time before I got myself together enough to say, "Yes, I agree. That probably takes precedence."

But only probably since the rest was *earthshattering* and I sort of wanted him to focus on that.

"Unless I'm scared outta my mind something is gonna harm you or my kid or me, taking me away from my kid, we don't seem to be able to communicate without both of us lashing out, so I decided maybe giving you a wide berth while I sort shit out was a good call."

"I…yes…maybe—"

"No maybe, Cady," he said quietly. "I can imagine I'm not giving you indication of this but it isn't fun getting up in your face when you haven't done anything to deserve it."

Oh my God.

That was very nice.

However.

"I moved here," I reminded him carefully.

"You did and I get there's a reason behind that but we'll have to talk about it when I sort shit out."

This was probably smart.

But what if his sorting went in a direction that was not good at all?

Or at least not good for me.

I proceeded cautiously and more than a little fearfully when I asked, "You have things happening with your daughter and her mom?"

"If you're worried I'm getting back together with her, don't. That's not gonna happen."

That was a big relief except the part he jumped to the thought that was what I was worried about.

Even if that was what I was worried about.

"I don't think that—"

"Don't," he whispered, and I stopped speaking instantly. "We got so much between us, Cady, don't add a stupid lie to it that'll make all the rest explode in our faces. We don't seem to need much to ignite that mess, no reason to throw a flaming torch in it."

I shut my mouth and I felt my blood start going way too fast in my veins, making me feel hot all over.

"You came here for me," he stated.

Oh God, this was it.

Oh God, no matter how totally obvious it was, out loud, right now, I had to admit this was it.

"Yes," I said.

"So you want something from me," he again stated.

Oh God.

This was it!

"Yes," I repeated.

"And I know what you want."

I stared up at him, frozen to the spot.

"And I gotta know where I'm at before we have that discussion, because I've known where you were at and I wasn't there and instead of handling it in a way I didn't cause further harm, I did the opposite."

"I haven't been handling things all that well either, Coert," I shared a truth he knew but he deserved to hear from me.

"So maybe we should be smart about what's goin' on for once and wait it out while I hunt down a psychopath bent on revenge with us in his cross-hairs, and then maybe we can figure some things out."

I'd waited seventeen years to pull it together to make this trek to Coert, emotionally and physically. I loathed the idea of waiting another day.

Especially with the way he was being now.

I did not share these thoughts.

I said, "That sounds like a wise plan."

He stared at me, and he did it so hard it made me uncomfortable and weighed down the budding hope that maybe I was getting somewhere.

To stop him from continuing to do that, I asked, "Is everything okay with your daughter?"

"She's perfect."

"Well, that's good," I murmured.

"No, that's the problem."

"I…" I shook my head. "Sorry?"

"She's perfect. And the stuff that's been going on between you and me I've been seeing I've been doing the same to her mom. We'd split before she found out she was pregnant. It wasn't good news at first because I'd never met Janie and I couldn't know how beautiful she'd be to have a part of my life."

And it was oh so beautiful how he said that.

"Of course," I whispered.

"I just got ticked at her mom for doin' something that was indisputably whacked, and even though we shared a kid, a good kid, a perfect one, I never let that go."

I couldn't believe he was saying this to me.

I couldn't believe he was *sharing this with me.*

"I still don't understand how a perfect child can be a problem," I prompted hesitantly.

"Because kids absorb everything. Your words. Your facial expressions. Your moods. The way a room feels. Stuff that goes unsaid, especially between two people they care about. They feel the vibes and take that shit inside themselves. So I'm pissed at her mom, what's Janie doing?"

"I don't know," I said softly. "What do you think she's doing?"

"Being perfect so maybe I won't be mad at her mom anymore or have any reason to be mad at her, or to prove to me she deserves to be on this earth when the way that started I didn't take to real great."

"She's very young, Coert. Do you really think she's processing and acting on stuff this advanced?"

"Consciously, no. Unconsciously, absolutely."

He was sadly probably right.

"I can see where you'd think this."

"Yeah, so now not only do I need to get with the program of co-parenting my daughter with a woman who broke my trust in a bad way, but I gotta find my way there. I also gotta worry if I did lasting damage to my daughter."

"If there's something amiss, which there might not be, kids do bounce back," I shared.

"You confronted your brother for a reconciliation, and that ass was always an ass to you. He hated you. He was a huge dick to me. Fortunately I only had to be around him a couple of times, but both of those times I wanted to land a fist in his face for the way he behaved toward you. But here you are, forty-one, trying to hold on to him when he never deserved a second of your time. My guess, this is because, from the time I knew you until the time you hit his house this past summer, you never gave up hope you could fix your place in a family that never wanted you."

He took in my stricken expression and got closer.

Midnight got excited and snuffled him but Coert only had eyes for me.

"I don't say that to hurt you, Cady. I never got why you held on to those people. Your mom never looked past who she was sure I was simply to see who I was to you. But it wasn't about me. It was about the fact she didn't hide she barely tolerated you and the decisions you made in your life, even the good ones, and I say that knowin' she'd have to dig deep with me, but she didn't even try not only to see me but to see what *you* had in me. Your dad was always solid and he was cool with me but he was weak. He let her guide things when he should have looked out for his daughter. What I'm sayin' is, I need to stop being weak and look after my daughter."

"You're not weak, Coert," I said firmly.

"It takes a lot more guts and balls to forgive and move on than it takes to hold on to resentment and nurse it to bitterness, which is just a way to twist the emotion of regret into something you can stomach."

I had nothing to say to that.

Because I had everything to say to it and my head was filling with words, my heart was filling with hope but my mouth needed to stay quiet and give him time to get where he was going.

Although quiet on that matter, I couldn't stay quiet altogether.

"There was something missing with my brother and parents, Coert, that your daughter has. I know they loved me, maybe not my brother, but my mom and dad did. They just didn't love me enough. And just you thinking about all of this, worried about it, taking the time to process through it says you love her more than enough. So it's just a guess, but I think your daughter will probably be just fine."

"For a dad, 'probably' doesn't cut it."

I stared up in his face remembering precisely why I'd fallen so deeply in love with him.

He held my hand.

He was an amazing lover.

He laughed at my jokes.

He got me when no one else did.

And he was the kind of man who would say things like that.

"For a *good* dad, 'probably' doesn't cut it," I returned. "So considering that's the God's honest truth, in the end, I know she'll be fine because you're intent to make it that way."

He looked over my head.

I stared at his face.

He drew in a deep breath.

I watched.

He seemed to be having some inner battle.

I let him fight it and hoped to God he won and landed on the right side.

He looked down at me.

"Think I'm the only dad on the planet who wants their kid to whine or throw a tantrum when I say no."

I smiled at him. "Has it occurred to you that she's just a good kid?"

"What hasn't occurred to me until recently is that might be true but only because she's got a dad who loves her and a mom who loves her the same so I need to give Kim credit because she screwed up and then kept doing that. But since all that went down she's gotten herself together, and through it all, she's been a great mom."

Kim.

The ex.

The ex I'd seen pictures of who had brown hair, brown eyes, very large breasts, an envious behind and an exceptionally pretty smile.

I tried not to allow my expression to change.

I knew I failed in this when he said quietly, "Maybe we should stop talkin' about this."

"In all I regret," I whispered, "and it's not bitterness, Coert, just regret, it would be impossible to cope if I was standing here with you and you hadn't had people love you along the way. If you hadn't had your daughter. You're not the only one sorting through things. And I think I've made it plain even if I've done it in a convoluted way that I wished things had gone differently. But it's not in my power to change that. So at least I have those things to hold on to. In the time in between, you were loved and made something beautiful. So it might be difficult, but I know you had those things. So I can cope."

As I spoke, his handsome face had changed, gone stunned, even staggered, and I decided that was all the risk I was willing to take that night.

Therefore, I murmured, "Goodnight, Coert. I really hope you find Lars soon and not just because I want to introduce Midnight to the coastal path."

I then pulled on Midnight's leash, turned and hurried away, careful to look both ways before we crossed the street because it wouldn't do to be splatted to oblivion in front of Coert, or worse, get my dog hit when she'd finally found a loving home.

Fortune was shining on me that no one was coming.

But I'd used up all my courage and had no reserves so I started out walking briskly.

And ended up running away.

Fourteen

GAVE IT TO HER GOOD

COERT

Present day…

Lars kept in shape in prison, and when he got out, Coert could tell as they chased him through the forest outside Shepherd.

Coert might be in better shape but it didn't matter because the Shepherd cops and Coert's deputies, who were in foot pursuit with him, were younger than both of them, faster, and pissed since Lars had shot at them.

As he ran, all the officers' flashlights bobbed and weaved through the dark night, keeping Lars in their sights. So they saw when Lars turned and squeezed off two rounds blind.

But in the direction of Coert.

Coert kept running but did it jagging behind a tree as those around him kept shouting for Lars to freeze. Coert kept with the pursuit, gun in hand but only his flashlight in his other hand was raised.

He'd been counting and he might be off a round or two, but since they'd run Lars off the road and he'd taken off on foot, he hadn't had time to reload. So by Coert's count, he was either out of ammo, or he only had a round or two left.

This was important but within seconds it wouldn't matter.

When Lars twisted again to raise his weapon toward Coert, he wasn't looking where he was going and ran smack into a tree.

He careened around it, losing balance, firing off a shot straight up in the air, probably more reaction than desperation, and with no aim.

Lars hit the dirt and Coert saw the gun fly to the side. He was barely down a second before one of the Shepherd officers was on him, kicking the gun through the leaves.

One of Coert's deputies got to him next. Rolling him to his stomach, he twisted his arm, knee in his back, other hand going for his cuffs.

Coert and the four others in pursuit stopped, fanned around, guns at the ready, but it was only Coert that was breathing heavily.

Time to carve some of it out to start running regularly again.

"You wanna read him, boss?" Clarke, Coert's deputy who was cuffing him asked.

"I don't even wanna look at him," Coert muttered.

Clarke gave a terse nod, finished cuffing Lars while he read him his rights then got off him and yanked him up to his feet.

Coert had holstered his weapon, and as Clarke turned him around, he caught Lars's eyes.

"Fuckin' *pig*," Lars spat, literally, aiming saliva Coert's way after he said it.

Unfortunately for him, at that exact time, Clarke started pushing him and Lars ended up spitting on himself.

Coert didn't smile.

He just watched Clarke guide Lars back through the forest, the other officers moving in behind.

Then he followed them.

COERT WAITED UNTIL after he'd called Kim to let her know they got him and it was all okay. He waited until he'd called Malcolm and Tom in

Denver to let them know it was all good. And he waited until he'd told Monica to call Cady and share that she was again safe.

The last being what Coert did first.

Only after he'd done all that and Lars had long since been processed and was sitting cuffed to a table, ankles in shackles in one of Coert's interrogation rooms, did Coert go in.

It was a blow, being alone in that room with that man after all these years.

But the blow was not about Lars.

It was about all he brought back in regards to what Coert had done to Cady.

"Man, *fuck*," Lars bit out on seeing him. "Just fuckin' fuck off, you fuckin' pig."

Coert moved opposite the table to him but didn't sit.

He stayed standing, looked into his eyes and spoke.

"We have your notes, receipts and other detritus, the stuff you left at your pad in Blakely. We have the Denver investigator's travel notes and reports, all of these linking to information we found in Blakely and we're likely to find in that mess of a car you left us. We have your gun and the ammo you left behind. Different guns used in seven murders in five states, but the ammo you left behind matches four of those murders. We have clothing with residue on it of the accelerant used in fires set in Magdalene, Denver, Reno, Cheyenne and Litchfield, Minnesota. We can place you in all of those locations at the time of the murders. You've been processed here but we're extraditing you tomorrow to Colorado. You'll be tried and convicted there for four fires, four murders. From there, I don't know. We'll see how much travel you'll be doing. But since you'll get life, and you gotta hope you get a decent attorney or you might face the injection, it might end for you in a lotta ways in Denver."

"You like this don't you, standin' there, thinkin' you're the shit, big man sheriff, shiny badge?" Lars asked snidely. "But you're a piece of shit."

"We have very different definitions of that, Lars."

"Pretty red pussy feels that way, I can tell," he sneered, and Coert had to fight his body tightening. "You lied your ass off to her, to me, to all of us. Now *that* defines a piece of *shit*. You sure must know how to use your dick, she's still panting after it after all this time. After you totally fuckin' played her, *buddy*. My good *buddy*. Not a word outta your mouth was anything but *shit*. We all got buried under it but she was *fuckin' it*. You were good with that mouth in a lotta ways, I can tell. Bet you talked your shit real pretty to her. Gave it to her good with that mouth. The man she was so fuckin' addicted to, she couldn't tear her eyes off you anytime you were anywhere near. Such a great guy. Such a big dick. *Tony*."

Coert felt his scalp prickle but he just stared down at Lars.

"Goodbye, Lars," he muttered, turning to leave.

"You didn't have to get her a dog," Lars called, and that prickle got worse at this proof that Lars had been watching Cady. Him and Cady.

But Coert didn't stop moving to the door.

"I wouldn't have hurt sweet Cady. No, *buddy*. The way I'd fuck sweet, stupid Cady right up the ass is makin' her live a life in a world without *you*. She'd end herself that happened. And I wouldn't have to do *dick*."

The door closed on the word "dick," and through Lars's last Coert didn't even turn around.

But that didn't mean he didn't taste the bile that had risen up his throat.

HE WAS ON his way home after Lars Pedersen was cozy in his cell and Coert had confirmed all the arrangements to get his ass out of it and on his way to Colorado the next day.

He looked down at his phone and saw it said CADY CALLING.

The prickling came back to his scalp.

He didn't answer his phone.

THE NEXT DAY, Coert was sitting at his desk dealing with Lars Pedersen paperwork, when his cell chimed.

He looked down at it.

It was a text from Cady.

Can we talk?

He let it lie and only answered hours later.

Busy. Sorry. Lots to do.

She texted back.

OK. That's understandable. Maybe later. Hope you're OK.

Coert did not reply to her text.

TWO DAYS AFTER that, Coert was moving to his truck after work and his phone went with a text.

He pulled it out and looked at it.

It was from Cady.

Do you have time to get a drink?

He waited until he'd driven to Kim's house before he answered.

Got Janie starting tonight.

He turned off the ringer and pulled himself out of his truck.

"DADDY!"

Coert crouched and smiled as Janie came at him. When she got there, he swung her up in his arms and smiled at her after she gave his jaw a big kiss.

"Hey, cupcake."

"Hey, Daddy. I'm ready!" she cried.

"Good." His eyes slid to Kim then back to his girl. "But can you do me a big favor? I gotta talk with your mom real quick. Can you run up to your room and color for a while? We'll call when we're done. Okay?"

She looked at him, to her mother, back to him and nodded.

He put her down and said, "Go, baby. But when you come back, be sure you got Shnookie."

"I'll be sure!" she said, tossed him a nothing-ever-fazes-me smile, threw it her mother's way and then dashed out of the room.

Coert looked to Kim who was looking freaked.

"Is everything okay with that guy you caught?" she asked.

"Everything's cool with that, Kim. We just need to talk."

Now she was looking sick.

He did that to her.

Arguably, she'd bought it, but that didn't mean he had to do it to her.

"Do you have time?" he asked.

"I…well," she visibly swallowed, "sure."

He moved in from the door and got closer to her, but not too close.

"I wanted to thank you for keeping it together while that whole thing with Pedersen went down. You didn't freak. You didn't freak Janie. I know you were worried and scared, but you kept it together and didn't give me anything else to worry about and you gotta know, I appreciate it."

She stared at him like she'd never seen him before.

"It was cool of you, Kim. Says a lot. About you, about how you get it that your kid's dad is the sheriff and about how good a mom you are."

"I, um…wow, Coert," she whispered. "Thanks."

"Don't thank me for you having it together."

"Okay, right," she murmured, no longer looking sick, but still looking freaked and now also embarrassed.

"There's more we gotta talk about."

She shuffled her feet, realized she was doing it, stopped and replied slowly, "Okay."

He launched in.

"Not long ago, you were trying to be cool with me and I threw that in your face. That was totally uncool. However it happened, it happened and even if how it happened wasn't right, we got Janie out of it and she *is* right. So I've had a think about a lot of things and what's done is done. I gotta put it behind me and be a good dad. And being a good dad means getting along with my kid's mom."

"Right," she whispered, her eyes glued to him and they were wide.

"So Thanksgiving is comin' up and we have all that stuff doled out with Janie. But I think, since I get her in the morning and you're takin' her to your family in the afternoon, instead, you should come to my place in the morning. I'll make breakfast. We'll eat it together and watch the parade. I'll ask but I'm sure they'll be cool with it, but after that, since I'm having Thanksgiving with them, we'll all go to Jake and Josie's and hang together and watch football. Then when it's time, you can take her to your Mom's."

"I...I...that would be great, Coert," she agreed swiftly.

"If we do this we gotta do it so Janie doesn't get confused," he warned. "Not Mom and Dad getting back together. Mom and Dad getting along and being Mom and Dad for her at all times, important ones and the not important ones. So we'll keep things separate but we'll still give her together, especially during the important times."

He'd been watching her closely, and although her face fell when he noted they weren't getting back together, she hid it quick and squared her shoulders slightly, indicating she was keeping her shit tight.

"This would be good for Janie," she stated.

"It would. We can do Christmas the same. You get her in the morning, me the afternoon. I'll come over in the morning for presents and breakfast and then leave you to it. You can bring her to me in the afternoon."

"You can stay Christmas Eve," she said quickly. "Sleep on the couch." Her voice lowered. "You know Janie gets up early but it'd help a lot, you around to help me play Santa."

It also might give Janie the wrong impression, couch or not. She was too young to get that and never had a man and woman do that with her around and old enough to put two thoughts together. She'd just think Mom and Dad were together and might take that in the wrong direction.

But it'd still be freaking fantastic to be there when his baby girl got up on Christmas morning. Since she understood Christmas, that was the best few hours of the year and it sucked, missing every other one.

"I'll think about it," he replied.

She looked like she was going to move toward him but stopped and told him, "I think this is good, Coert. Really good. And I think it's gonna work."

"I think we need to make it work, Kim, but I also think you're right. We can do this. We can give this to Janie. If life changes, you get a man, we'll discuss how we'll need to alter things. But at least she'll have it for now."

She nodded and said, "And if you get, you know...a woman."

"Right," he grunted.

She gave him a tentative smile. "Okay...I...okay, Coert. I really think this is gonna be awesome and I'm really glad you had a think about things because I think it's gonna make Janie real happy."

"That's the goal."

She kept smiling at him.

He tried it out and it worked so he smiled back.

She took it in, looked like she was going to cry for a second then she looked at the door, drew breath in her nose, and again caught his eyes.

"It's time for her dinner so you should probably go."

"We should."

"But…Coert…" she said these two words fast but didn't say any more.

"Yeah?"

She took a few seconds, they were long ones, then she went for it.

"It was messed up."

"Kim—" he started, bracing.

She lifted a hand and shook her head. "I know it was messed up. I didn't know it then. You were…" She paused and when she began again her voice started to get thick.

Shit.

She pushed through it.

"You thought I was funny. It felt so good when I made you laugh. You… you just always seemed like you were sad. Not up front, but deep down, like you were trying to hide it. So it felt good to make you laugh. You always made me feel pretty. You made me feel safe. You fixed things in the house and never complained and it was nice to have someone take care of stuff like that. Take care of *me*. You were so sweet and so protective," an awkward smile cracked her face, "and not hard to look at. I fell, got deep, knew from things that happened with you and Darcy that I wasn't gonna…I wasn't gonna—"

"Kim—"

"Make it," she forced out. "I panicked and did something stupid and—"

"And we got Janie."

"I know but—"

"Kim," he cut her off, "that's the focus. It wasn't right but we got Janie. And that's our only focus. It wasn't right but if we both keep focused on that I'll stay pissed and you'll keep feelin' guilty and where's Janie in all that?" He didn't wait for her answer. "Not in a good place. So it wasn't right but in the end it was the rightest thing in the world and that's all. Done. Over. Moving on. Yeah?"

"Yeah, Coert, but I still want you to know I'm sorry."

Shit.

That felt good.

"That means a lot, Kim. Know that," he told her.

She pressed trembling lips together and nodded.

"I gotta get our girl fed," he reminded her.

She unpressed her lips to whisper, "Yeah."

"Janie, baby!" he shouted. "Your mom and me are done talking!"

"Okay!" he heard shouted back.

"Don't forget Shnookie!" he yelled.

"Shoot!" he heard his girl cry, then footfalls he heard coming their way changed direction.

At that, Coert smiled at Kim.

Kim smiled back.

"YOU OKAY, DADDY?"

"I'm totally okay, baby."

They were in his truck heading to his house.

And he was lying to his kid.

"What do you want for dinner?" he asked.

"I love you, Daddy," she answered.

Coert's fingers tightened on the steering wheel and he turned his eyes to the rearview mirror to get a look at his daughter in the dark.

She was looking out the side window.

Yeah.

She absorbed everything.

"I love you too, Janie. You know that?" he replied.

"Yeah, Daddy."

"A whole lot, you know that too?"

"I know. I love you a whole lot too," she said and added, "A whole lotta lotta lot."

He felt his face get soft.

"And I love you a whole lotta lotta lot and then a whole lot more. But you can't eat love, cupcake," he teased, glancing back to the mirror.

He saw her face forward and smile his way.

Coert looked back out the windshield.

"I bet if you could, it'd taste good," she declared.

She'd be right.

Because Coert knew what love tasted like.

It tasted like sunshine and balloons and sloppy kisses with lollipop residue from his little girl.

And it tasted like cinnamon and moonlight and toffee from redheads with emerald eyes, that coming from lips and tongues and between her legs.

"I think I know what love tastes like, Daddy," Janie stated.

He had to clear his throat before he asked, "What does love taste like, Janie?"

"Cupcakes!" she proclaimed.

Coert chuckled at the windshield.

Then he said, "You're probably right."

"So we can go to Wayfarer's and get a bunch so we can eat a whole lotta love."

"How about we do that? But you gotta have something else so what's it gonna be?"

"Grilled cheese and chicken noodle soup," she decided.

"That's a deal," he told her.

"Hurrah!" she cried.

Coert chuckled at the windshield again, and at the end of the street he made a right toward town and Wayfarer's instead of a left, toward home.

IT WASN'T UNTIL much later when Coert got out his phone, turned on the ringer and looked at the screen.

OK. Maybe we can set something up next week. Have fun with your girl.

This was from Cady.

It tore him up.

But Coert didn't reply.

Fifteen

CLEAN IT UP

COERT

Present day…

It was right before Christmas when it happened.

And no matter the shitload of headspace he'd given it, Coert wasn't ready for it to happen.

He should have made himself ready. He shouldn't have delayed. He shouldn't have put her off.

He shouldn't have been weak.

If he hadn't been, he wouldn't have destroyed her.

But this happened when Cady caught him on the sidewalk.

He didn't know if she was just done and maneuvered a time to face him or if it was a chance meeting.

It was just that he was about to learn she was done with waiting.

And he was inadvertently and very unfortunately about to make her done with a lot of other things.

"Coert!"

He heard her call, felt his gut clench and turned to see her rushing up to him.

She was a forty-one-year old woman and still cute.

And that sucked.

She looked like she'd been absorbed by Maine.

She had a wide wool headband pulling back her thick hair and keeping her ears warm. A turtleneck that looked light but was probably made of some expensive yarn that was warm as hell. One of those puffy vests. Jeans. And high-heeled boots that classed up the casual.

Even if she'd looked like shit, he wasn't ready for this so this wasn't going to be easy.

But Cady had proved back in the day and more recently she was immune to looking shit. Even in a Sip and Save smock or sitting on her front porch first thing in the morning with her mane of hair messy, wearing a pair of pajamas.

"Cady," he greeted when she made it to him.

"I…you…uh…are you busy?" she asked.

"Kinda," he answered, indicating his shirt. "On the job," he explained.

This was an excuse. But at least the last part was true.

She looked down to his shirt then to his eyes. "Oh, right. Of course."

"I know you've been texting and I've been putting you off," he began.

"Yes," she agreed.

"But I been concentrating on my kid."

"Oh, right," she repeated, her shoulders falling. "Of course."

"So maybe we can get through Christmas and then we'll sit down and…" Fuck. What were the right words to use? "Handle things."

Her head jerked almost like he'd slapped her.

He didn't find the right words.

Yeah.

Fuck.

"Handle things?" she asked.

It was lame but, unprepared for this, it was all he had.

"Yeah," he confirmed.

"After Christmas?" she asked.

"Yeah," he said.

"Christmas," she whispered, the way she was looking at him suddenly changing.

Coert felt his stomach turn sour and did his best to ignore it.

"Christmas," he again confirmed.

"You…um…you—"

He interrupted her stammering. "So I'll text you sometime after. Yeah?"

"You won't."

That was when he felt his body lock and he stared into her eyes.

"Let's not do this now," he suggested gently.

"You won't. You won't text."

"Can we not do this now, Cady?" he asked, still trying to go gentle.

"You won't do it at all. You don't want to do it at all."

"Cady—"

"You can't forgive me."

He moved into her but she stepped back and the way she did, the look on her face, it burned through him.

"After Christmas." His voice was beginning to sound rough.

"Why make me wait?" Her voice was getting high.

"So I can get my head together," he told her.

"It's already together," she shot back, but he could see it.

She was unravelling and pushing herself to getting pissed instead of falling apart.

He'd seen that happen before, mostly when she was dealing with her parents, and it was never pretty.

So he leaned into her and warned, "Cady, keep your shit together."

"Why?" she demanded. "Why do you care if I have it together?"

"We'll talk…*later*," he ground out.

"About what? About how there's nothing to talk about?" she asked.

"Cady—"

"It's done already, isn't it? You've made up your mind, haven't you? It never was even close to changing in the first place, was it? You never were going to forgive me, were you?"

Now as contradictory as he knew it was, she was shoving him in a corner, a corner he'd felt trapped in for seventeen years, and he was getting pissed she was not giving him time.

"Don't push this. Not now."

She didn't heed his warning and pushed it further.

"So…what? You can break my heart later?"

And he got pissed.

"I see you don't get this but a man does not get replaced like you replaced me and just gets over it, Cady. Maybe women can do that kinda shit, but he can dig as deep as there is to go and he just won't *get over it*. But you gotta back off and let me try to dig deep just so I can actually *talk about it*."

"And what I'm saying is, if it's a foregone conclusion, what's the point?" she fired back.

"You haven't changed," he bit out.

"You wouldn't know since you didn't even know me before," she retorted.

"That was bullshit when you tried to feed that to me at the lighthouse and it's bullshit now. I know you. I knew you then. With this crap, I know you now. If someone told me this would go down," he pointed to the sidewalk, "I'd lay money on exactly this happening," he hurled at her.

He saw her eyes start to get wet before her cheeks got very pink and she turned to storm off.

"Cady," he hissed.

She kept storming.

"Goddamn it, Cady," he clipped, starting to follow her.

She whirled on him, her face no less pretty twisted in anger.

She then lifted a finger and shouted, "You no longer know me, Coert!"

He moved toward her, stopped, put his hands to his hips and growled low, "This is the same shit you'd pull without even a thought. Not a surprise you never grew up enough to grow outta it. So yeah. Fuck yeah. I know you, Cady."

She lost it then, the shroud of a rich man's wife she'd been wearing since he saw her again sliding away, but he saw it in her eyes, the emotion that she was hiding behind anger so she could deal.

And holding on to the anger, she yelled, "Kiss my ass!"

After delivering that, she whirled around so fast, her hair flew out behind her and she stomped away.

Coert stared after her, feeling a muscle tick in his cheek, wondering if there was any way he could have played that where it would have gone better, and doing that trying not to think of the emotion he saw behind her eyes before his Cady came back and told him to kiss her ass.

He then turned and prowled the other way.

It wasn't a long walk to his office but he didn't get back to it before he yanked out his phone, pulled her up, hit go and put it to his ear.

Surprisingly, she answered right away, saying only, "Coert."

"Where are you?" he bit out.

"I'm sorry."

That was another surprise, but he could tell the emotion he'd seen had taken over so he couldn't dwell on it.

Now he had more concerning things to dwell on.

"Where are you?" he demanded, turning to the steps of the sheriff's station and jogging up.

"I'm fine."

"You're in your car."

"I'm not."

She was in her car.

"And you're crying," he stated, pushing through the front doors.

"I'm not."

She totally was crying.

"What'd I say about that?" he bit out, walking toward the stairs that would take him up to his office.

"I'm sorry. You didn't want to talk and I promised no dramatics, and I forced you to talk and then made a scene on the sidewalk."

Shit.

Shit.

Totally crying. Hardly keeping it together. Her voice was so rough it was hoarse.

"Cady—"

"You're the sheriff. You can't have some crazy woman making a scene on the sidewalk."

"Damnit, Cady—"

"I promised and I broke my promise. Guess I'm good at that."

At that, he stopped dead and turned his eyes to his boots.

"Cady," he whispered.

"I get it and I shouldn't have pushed it. It was…it was…it was *cruel.* All of it. All I've done coming back. It was cruel."

"Listen to me," he said urgently.

"You don't have to talk to me. I won't make you do that. I get it. I understand. I really do, Coert."

"Please be quiet and listen to me," he begged.

"No, that's okay. Don't worry. I get it and it's done. I should have known. I shouldn't have…"

She made a noise.

Coert made a noise too but his was a growl.

And she kept going.

"I shouldn't have done this to us. I should have left well enough alone."

He changed directions, going back where he came from, toward the front doors. "I need you to stop talking now, Cady. Pull off the road. And listen to me."

"I'm going home."

"Okay, I'll meet you there."

"I mean Denver."

Fuck!

"Cady, please, God, listen to me," he said fast.

"I shouldn't have come here. I've hurt you. You have a good life. You're happy here with your adorable little girl and your job and your…your…well, your life, I guess."

Now out of the station, he pulled his keys from the pocket of his jeans and beeped the locks on his cruiser.

"I'm coming to you," he told her.

"You don't have to. I'm good."

She wasn't *good.*

Fuck, she sounded like she was being strangled.

"Cady—"

"I'll leave and you can get back to your life."

"Ca—"

"I just want you to know, Coert, really, not to make you hurt, or not to make it worse and not to cause any harm, but you should know, it's really important you know, whatever happened after, I loved you. I really did love you. And I know that because I still do."

His throat closed.

He thought he heard a disconnect.

"Cady, goddamn it!" he shouted after he'd angled up into his truck.

But he said it to dead air.

She was gone.

He started the truck, checked, backed out when it was clear and only called her back when he was on the road.

She didn't answer.

He considered putting on his police lights but that was highly, and in that moment frustratingly unethical, so he didn't.

But he did drive like a bat out of hell.

There were no cars or trucks inside the fence or out of it when he got to the lighthouse, which meant construction was done on her property, which meant they'd be alone.

That was good.

What was bad was that after he got through the gate and drove up, got out and approached the house, there was no sound of barking coming from inside the house.

He moved to the window at the kitchen facing the sea and looked in.

No Cady, no Midnight, no movement.

He walked to the garage and looked in the side window.

No Jag.

She'd made it home, got her dog and took off.

Fuck.

He pulled out his phone, called her, got voicemail and left a message.

"You get this, you call me and you tell me where you are, Cady."

Coert then went back to his office.

He did his best to keep his mind on work.

His best failed so he went through the motions.

And when it was time, he went to go get his girl from preschool.

They had dinner.

They cleaned up.

They snuggled in front of the TV.

He read her to sleep.

He left her with Shnookie in her bed with her nightlight on.

And he went downstairs and called Cady.

She didn't pick up.

He felt his stomach sink.

But his mouth moved.

"Call me," he growled into the phone.

And then he hung up.

THE NEXT MORNING after dropping Janie off at preschool, hearing nothing from Cady, Coert drove back out to the lighthouse.

When he did, he saw what he wasn't in the state to see the day before.

A long, wide path of snow had been cleared from gate to garage, all along the front of the garage with narrow paths around the lighthouse.

No shovel did that, unless she spent six hours doing it. She had to at least have a mower with a snow plow.

A good one.

He also saw Cady decorated for Christmas.

But as he drove up to the gate, he wondered how she managed it.

There were large, evergreen wreaths on each side of the double gate and heavy evergreen boughs draping along six sections of the fence on either side. More boughs scalloped all around the circumference of the lighthouse, about eight feet up the sides, with even more swathed around the lighthouse door, along the covered walk between the garage and house, and around the garage. She also had wreaths on the house door he could see with big ones like the ones on the gates on the garage doors. The finishing touch was potted spiral pines on either side of the house doors with bigger ones on either side of the garage.

He suspected they were all lit at night and when they were, that would be a show of festive cheer that was classy as all hell. In fact, it was classy as all hell now.

These were distracted thoughts, mostly centered around wondering how she'd managed to do all that by herself, thoughts that were an effort not to think of what lie ahead in talking to her.

Coert stopped outside the gate, got out and moved to the keypad.

He saw he was right. The boughs and wreaths were lit

And when they were, they were sure to be a showstopper.

He had two digits punched in the keypad when he sensed movement, so he took two steps back to look through the iron bars in a gate that dipped low in the middle.

He didn't see Cady.

He saw a large man jogging his way. Young, in his twenties, he was Coert's height but probably had thirty to forty pounds on him, some of this muscle and broadness of shoulders, some of it at his gut.

"Hey!" the guy shouted, still jogging toward him.

Coert looked to the house. He didn't see any trucks or machinery but maybe the renovation wasn't done.

"I'm here to see Ms. Moreland," he told the guy.

"No you're not."

Coert's back snapped straight.

"Pardon?" he asked when the man stopped on the other side of the gate.

The guy looked to his sheriff jacket, to him, but stood solid at the dip in the gate. "Sorry, don't want any trouble, but gotta say, no you're not."

"Can I ask who you are?" Coert queried.

"Last night, the basket case Cady was and hearin' your name when she talked to her sister on the phone, knowin' you were the cause of it, feel like sayin' no. You can't ask. But seein' as I gotta make some things clear to you, I'll tell you I'm Elijah. I rent the apartment over the garage. And I'm Cady's friend."

There were things there that hit Coert hard but he focused on only one.

"Cady doesn't have a sister."

Elijah's face screwed up before he replied, "See you didn't get to know her real good when whatever went down between you two went down since she doesn't only have a sister, she's got three."

Three?

"No, she doesn't."

"Dude…I mean, Sheriff, she does. I know 'em. I've met 'em. Okay, I did that over Skype but it still counts."

This was interesting, all of it, primarily this guy being close enough to Cady to Skype with her "sisters."

It was also a waste of time.

"I need to see Cady," he stated.

"That might be true but she doesn't need to see you," Elijah retorted.

Coert opened his mouth but Elijah kept talking.

"Doesn't matter anyway. She took off this morning to go down to Connecticut. The family is spending Christmas here, but she's goin' to meet her niece down there and her sister's flyin' out. They're gonna do some girlie Christmas road trip on the way back up here to try and take Cady's mind off whatever you did to her yesterday."

Goddamn it.

"I don't want trouble from you," Elijah went on, "but seriously, Cady's good people. She's been, like, super cool with me. Actin' like me hangin' in her pimped-out studio was a lifesaver when it was me who needed a place to crash after my chick kicked me to the curb. Didn't have the cabbage to put down a deposit anywhere, sleeping on my bud's couch seriously sucked. I liked her, she liked me, when things got safe for her, she asked me to stay. That apartment might not be as pimp as the studio but it's still the freakin' bomb and she gives it to me for a song, sayin' it's worth it. I plow snow and help with Christmas stuff and in the summer I can mow her grass. She knows I'm gettin' myself together after my girl tore me up and I needed a break. But it hits a guy where it hurts, feelin' like he's takin' advantage of a little thing like that. She doesn't make me feel like that. Still, it's there and so I gotta give back where I can."

He held Coert's eyes as Coert stared in his, all of this knowledge sluicing through him in good ways and bad, and Elijah's voice lowered when he continued.

"She was a mess last night, man. Like, Midnight was *fah-reeked.* I was too. Took forever for Kath to calm her down. And so, I don't know why you're here but I know from what I heard you're not good for her, so if you give a shit about her, do me a solid, no...do Cady a solid and just vanish. Yeah?"

Coert's voice had dipped too when he asked, "When's she coming back?"

Elijah looked like he was starting to get ticked.

"Man, you are not listening to me."

"I see you care about Cady and it's a relief she's had someone looking out for her, but even with that I still have to tell you this is none of your business."

"Dude, you are not right 'cause it wasn't *you* who had to stop her tossin' stuff in her suitcase when she got home last night, doin' that by clampin' down on her, she was in such a state. And it wasn't *you* who had to call Kath and tell her Cady was fallin' apart. It was *me.* What was *you* is who did that to her."

"There's a lot happening here I suspect you don't know," Coert forced out.

"I got that," Elijah bit back.

"I need to make sure she's all right," Coert made himself share.

"I see that might work for you but what you are not gettin' is that's not gonna work for her. Whatever it is, she's convinced herself she's the one done wrong and I don't know what went down but I know Cady and I know that shit's not right. But you got that twisted in her head and I'm not thinkin' it's good you got more chance to twist shit in her head."

It was after he suffered those blows that it belatedly occurred to Coert that, as illuminating as this was, it was a waste of time.

Therefore he turned from Elijah, saying, "Good to meet you," and walked to his truck.

"Man, you give even the littlest shit about her," Elijah called as Coert opened the door on his truck, "you'll let her family do their work."

If he gave the littlest shit about her, he wouldn't let her family anywhere near her.

He didn't know who this sister was, but he was wondering even if Caylen continued to be estranged, maybe some unfortunate female had married him and it wouldn't be a surprise Cady got close to her.

The two other sisters, he didn't know and at that time, he didn't care.

"Have a good holiday," Coert called back, swung up into his truck and did a three-pointer in Cady's lane to turn around and head back to town.

When he was on his way, he called her.

She didn't pick up.

He left a message.

"Went to the lighthouse this morning and Elijah says you're heading down to Connecticut. I get that. But I need to know you're okay, Cady. You don't have to call and talk to me but when you stop for a break, just text that you're okay. Please, honey. Just text me you're okay."

He disconnected, shoved most of what Elijah said in the back of his mind and concentrated on the fact she'd be back.

The problem was, she'd be back and "the family" was spending Christmas with her.

He didn't know if her mother or father (it would be the mother) got hold of Caylen and sorted him out, but he couldn't imagine any visit from them, including and especially a holiday, would be good for Cady.

She'd want it.

They'd ruin it.

So now he needed to see her, *really* needed to see her when she got back.

For more than one reason.

HER TEXT CAME half an hour after he sat down at his desk at the station.

I'm fine. Thank you for checking.

He didn't hesitate to text back.

Call me when you get home.

His reply was immediate.

Her reply took fifteen minutes.

I appreciate your concern and you're being very nice. But you don't need to be concerned. I'll be OK.

He didn't make her wait fifteen minutes for his reply.

Please just phone when you get home. We need to talk.

Her reply came quicker that time, only a few minutes.

You're off the hook, Coert. This is very sweet but truly, I'm taken care of. It's done now for the both of us. Be happy and have a Merry Christmas.

His reply was again instant.

Just call when you get home.

And her reply that time was instant too.

Goodbye, Coert.

He returned, *See you when you get back.*

She didn't respond.

Coert looked at the wall of his office, that beyond it was the lighthouse.

Not a word outta your mouth was anything but shit. *We all got buried under it but she was* fuckin' it. *You were good with that mouth in a lotta ways, I can tell. Bet you talked your shit real pretty to her. Gave it to her good with that mouth. The man she was so fuckin' addicted to, she couldn't tear her eyes off you anytime you were anywhere near.*

He'd needed to take care of his daughter. He'd needed to sort things with her mother.

And he'd done that. Thanksgiving worked well. Janie didn't seem to change but that didn't mean she didn't like having her mom and dad around, getting along. He knew she was feeling it, the way they were when they changed hands with Janie. Kim calling because that outlet was loose in her bathroom and she wanted him to come and tighten it up. And he did when he had Janie, bringing her back to her mom's house. Doing that for her mom. Sitting down to dinner after.

Janie was still just Janie. Sweet. Cute. Smart. A good kid.

It had only been weeks. Maybe she wouldn't change, turn into a terror because she knew her parents would still love her anyway, and he definitely wouldn't mind that just as long as he knew the other stuff was how it needed to be for his little girl.

The bottom line of that was that it was important he and Kim were working on giving her better parents.

And it had only been weeks but he'd had time. He'd had time to face his past and the fact that Cady was in his present and find his way to deal with all that had happened.

He just couldn't find it in himself to face it.

To face her.

So he'd screwed it up.

Royally.

Again.

She was a mess last night, man.

Shit, he'd made a mess.

He'd made a mess of Cady.

Again.

And he was scared as hell, just like he didn't last time, that he wouldn't find a way to clean it up.

TWO DAYS BEFORE Christmas Eve, Coert stood in his living room with the Christmas tree lights on, a lamp by the couch, these the only things illuminating the room.

It should be cheery, especially since Janie liked colored lights on the tree and from the time she was two he'd taken her on a special outing and let her pick a bunch of ornaments, every one on the tree her choice. So the entire tree was of her design, childlike, unsophisticated, nothing matched, it was just bright and unpredictable and gorgeous.

Even with the coolest Christmas tree in Magdalene, Coert was not feeling in a festive mood.

He was staring down at his phone seeing a one-sided text conversation that he'd had with Cady the three days since she'd left.

You get to Connecticut OK?

You good?

Cady, is everything good?

You home?

Cady, phone me.

She didn't phone or text back and Coert felt like a fucking stalker.

Which was something he latched onto because it was better than focusing on the fact he *was* just a fucking asshole.

He needed to go back to the lighthouse. That Elijah guy was there and that probably wouldn't go well. And Midnight might no longer be his biggest fan if Elijah and Cady gave off that vibe, which they would. Not to mention her parents and Caylen might be there and he had no idea how they took the news she was with an undercover cop she didn't know was an undercover cop but he didn't like them (and he'd hated Caylen's guts) as Tony, and since he *was* Tony, just Coert playing Tony, and a cop and who he was to Cady, he didn't figure that was going to change.

But she'd had her time.

And her time was up.

He was just about to pocket his phone and haul his ass into his truck when a knock came on the door.

He looked that way and was going to ignore it when another knock came, louder and it didn't stop for some time.

He could still ignore it but he was the sheriff. It wasn't frequent people showed at his doorstep—mostly neighbors thinking he was not only the sheriff but a one-man neighborhood watch that would drop everything and help look for lost dogs or get in his car and cruise the streets to find teenage girls who'd stormed off in a fit of teenage dramatics—but it happened.

When the knocking stopped and started again immediately, Coert went to his front door, a door made out of windows, to see man he'd never seen in his life.

He unlocked it, stepped to the side and opened it enough to put his body in it.

"Sorry, don't got a lot of time," he declared.

"Please don't close the door," the guy replied immediately and Coert's shoulders grew tight when he went on, "I know this is not right. Totally not right. I want you to understand that I know that and I wouldn't be here if I didn't feel it was urgent that I come. But I'm Pat Moreland, Cady's brother, and I need to speak to you."

Coert stood staring at Cady's stepson, a man who was maybe a decade older than her, a man who said he was her brother.

"Please," the guy said, eyes locked to Coert's. "I'll try not to take up much of your time, but something's wrong with Cady, something bad, we're concerned and we're desperate so I need to find out what it is. I need to find out so I can fix it."

And with that, Coert stepped back and fully opened the door.

Sixteen

BELONGED TO YOU

COERT

Present day…

Pat Moreland looked surprised when Coert nonverbally invited him in. And then he walked right in.

Coert closed the door behind him, passed him to guide him into the living room and stopped. He turned and stood there, crossing his arms on his chest, studying a good-looking man who he now saw had a lot of his father in him.

A man who looked worried out of his brain.

This kept Coert quiet.

Because this man being there was enough of a surprise.

This man worried out of his brain for Cady gnawed at his gut so much, he had to keep his mouth shut or he'd vomit.

"Thank you for letting me in," Moreland said.

Coert nodded.

"I know that you probably don't want to be disturbed with this at all, much less this close to the holiday," he declared.

Coert's voice was not his own when he spoke, brusque, harsh and deeper than normal as he pushed out, "No offense, but you don't know anything about me."

There was a tightening of his mouth and the shift of a little worry to let annoyance in when Moreland muttered a curt, "Right."

Coert stared at him, feeling hot and cold and sick with his palms itching and his heart thundering in his chest.

He was about to expend the effort to tell him to get on with it when the man got on with it.

"Mom died when I was twelve."

Already braced, with that opening, from head to toe Coert grew solid.

This was not where he thought this would start.

"She and Dad, they liked kids. Best parents you could have. Loved us. I remember her. I remember everything about her. Her smell. The way she did her hair. How she'd pull it up in a ponytail when she cleaned the house, but she usually wore it down all other times because Dad liked it like that. Probably kids do that when they lose a parent. Or at least they do if they have enough time with them. I'm glad I was old enough to have that. Daly was eight. He doesn't remember as much as I do. And I hate that for him. I hate that for Mom. I wish he had more. But I remember. I remember how much she loved being with her family. Being with her boys. What I didn't know until a lot later, when I was old enough to know it, when Dad felt he could share it, was how much she wanted a girl."

No, this was not starting as he'd expected at all.

Coert forced himself to continue staring into the man's eyes.

"Dad wanted one too," Moreland said quietly. "But he was her husband and he had to look after her. She wanted kids, a lot of them. They both did. And with three boys they were really wanting a girl. Mom liked the idea of a girl being the last. Of her having three big brothers to look out for her. And Dad having a daughter to walk down the aisle. I could see that. Mom wanting it. Dad wanting the same. He still had to stop her having more, because as much as she loved kids her body wasn't good at making it easy for her to have them."

Shit, shit, shit.

"She had three boys and two miscarriages in between," Moreland told him. "She nearly…things went bad with my baby brother, Daly. So after Daly, Dad put an end to it."

Coert remained silent.

But he knew where this was leading.

He knew.

Shit, shit, *fuck*.

The man's voice was thicker when he said, "It took her years. But he loved her. He was like that. Dad was. He was like that with everyone he loved. He gave in. Gave them what they wanted. It might take time, but if they didn't give up, they'd always get there eventually. So she talked him into it in the end."

He needed to give the guy something but with the way this was going he knew he had to hold what little he had in reserve so Coert just jerked up his chin.

"She was six months in when it happened. Died giving birth to my baby sister."

Shit, shit, fuck.

"The baby lived but just for three hours."

Coert felt his jaw flex.

"Her name was Katy."

And there it was.

Coert looked to his boots.

"Yeah," Moreland whispered.

Coert forced his eyes back to Cady's "brother."

"Dad told me about her," Moreland shared. "Cady. Months before it all happened. We were at the office. We were having trouble with one of our employees. We had a lot of those and Dad had all the patience in the world but he must have been having a bad day. He said he wished all of our employees were like the girl who worked at the convenience store where he got his coffee in the morning. Where he always stopped to get gas. Not a great job. Not a job where every day you acted chipper and like you didn't want to be anywhere but there. He said every time he saw her she smiled and was friendly, and she learned his name and called him Mr. Moreland when he came in and asked about his day and she just gave a shit." Moreland swallowed before he repeated, "She gave a shit."

She did.

Cady gave a shit about everything.

Even that job and that job sucked. Her schedule all over the place. The other employees not caring, so she was doing overtime all the time, doing their jobs along with hers half the time.

But she'd had plan.

She'd had a path.

She'd had a direction.

And she was going to get where she was going no matter what it took.

And then she met Coert.

"So, obviously, when he went to the store one day and found her hysterically crying on the sidewalk, he was a little shocked, not to mention alarmed and upset."

Coert felt his jaw flex and dropped his eyes to his boots again.

"He went in. That was Dad," Moreland told him. "It wouldn't matter, pretty girl, young kid, old lady, if someone was hurting, he'd wade in." He paused. "He waded in."

He did that for certain.

"We were not good to her."

Coert lifted his eyes back to Moreland.

"We hated her," Moreland admitted. "We saw her play. We were sure of it. Dad told us her story and he saw it a different way from us. But, I mean, her best friend had just got arrested by her supposed undercover cop boyfriend and was going on trial for murder and drug dealing? And she didn't know her boyfriend was a cop, thought he was a drug dealer and that was okay with her? What else would we think?"

Nothing.

Nothing else.

Just like Coert thought what he thought to protect himself and nothing else was going to get through.

His mouth filled with saliva.

"We were…it was…" Moreland cleared his throat. "It was bad. We should have known. Dad told us. But we loved him so we were protective of him and she took it. Boy did she take it. *Christ*," he suddenly spat. "We hid it from Dad but we laid it on her, all us boys. Kath and I were married already, Shannon and Daly engaged, so the women did it too. We piled it on her. And she took it. She didn't breathe a word to Dad. She just took it."

Coert focused on breathing.

"Her parents were, God, her parents were…" Another pause then, "Did you meet them?"

Coert jerked up his chin.

"So you know," Moreland whispered.

Coert jerked up his chin.

He knew.

Fuck him.

He fucking knew.

"Dad wanted to adopt her." Moreland gave a sharp chuckle at that that was genuinely amused. "That was Dad. She was twenty-three and he wanted to adopt her. Suggested that to her first. Knew her first name and her story and was in her life in a real way for about *a day* and he's all up for adopting her. It was about Katy. It was losin' Mom and Katy. But it wasn't just Mom and Katy. He knew *Cady* and what she was about and he wanted a daughter. He wanted his sons to have a sister. But mostly, he listened to all that was happening to Cady and wanted Cady to have a family that'd look out for her."

Coert felt something foreign hit the back of his throat and he swallowed it down, a strange feeling at the backs of his eyes, but he beat it back.

"She wouldn't have it. Even if you can actually adopt an adult, and I don't know if you can, she wouldn't give up on them. Flatly refused. And she never did give up on them. After I met them I didn't get that. But then I realized that was just Cady."

That was.

It was just Cady.

Obviously they'd turned their backs on her when she'd needed them the most and just months ago she was up in Waldo County trying to build a bridge to her brother.

Yeah.

That was Cady.

"So he talked her into becoming a part of the family by marrying him."

When Moreland waited for a response, Coert just nodded.

"It wasn't that," Moreland said quietly.

Coert said nothing.

"They didn't even sleep in the same room together. It was never that."

He was getting that from all the rest.

But still.

Shit.

Shit.

Fuck.

"We boys thought that was even more indication she was playing him." He shook his head and ended that looking to the wall. "We learned."

It took some time for Moreland to pull himself together. He did that and looked back at Coert.

"It was crazy and maybe it was wrong but it was Dad. Half the people who worked for us were ex-cons or ex-junkies or stuff like that. He just…he, and Mom too when she was alive, they just took care of people."

Private investigators.

Cady dropping a load on renovating a lighthouse, a load she'd inherited from Patrick Moreland.

This was not lost on Coert.

It was just not Patrick Moreland's job to take care of Cady.

It was his.

"He tried to divorce her."

Coert's legs locked.

"By then, well, we boys got it and she'd become part of the family, but she still wasn't and she felt that. And by this time he'd also told us. He couldn't hide it anymore like he'd been doing. It got bad, and Cady lost her mind on him and made him come out with it because she saw it, she didn't know what was happening either and she was worried sick. So when Cady finally forced it, he told us about the cancer."

Christ, it just got worse.

"And then she wouldn't. She wouldn't divorce him. She wasn't a member of the family and if she wasn't, she couldn't have access to him at times or couldn't help us make decisions at times. I got it sorted for her to do that legally, even if they were divorced, but she wouldn't have it. She got it in her head and I know what it was with Cady. She was all about payback. You didn't get something and give nothing. So she gave everything to him, the prime of her life, when she should have been meeting a man and having babies. It tore Dad up. It tore all of us up. But she wouldn't disconnect from him. She absolutely refused. No matter how often we all talked to her about it, Dad tried to push her on it, how often we told her she was one of us, that wouldn't change no matter what, she held on. She wouldn't let go."

Coert understood that.

She'd let go once.

And lost everything.

"He had a nurse for the medical stuff but the rest, Cady wouldn't allow anyone but her to do it. He'd get better and we'd have hope. Then he'd get worse. And each time that worse was *worse.* I don't know how she did it. Sometimes, and it doesn't say a lot about me, but it's the truth, sometimes it'd take me days to get myself together to go see him. But Cady acted like nothing was different. Like he didn't look like he looked, didn't get weak like he got weak. No biggie for her she had to help him walk or get to the bathroom or up his morphine because he was in so much pain. Just another day for Cady. Just another day, one after another, up and down, good and so bad it broke our hearts, for twelve freaking years."

Coert looked to his boots again.

"But he beat it back, my old man. Lived past eighty, Dad did. But Cady helped with that. Cady gave him a reason to wake up every day. Cady was always there to babysit our kids in order to keep his family around him and because she loved those kids like they were her own. For every one of us, she did the birthday parties and did them up huge. Threw slumber parties Kath, Pam and Shannon were invited to, all the girls. Slumber parties. Adult women invited. God, she made every opportunity to keep that house full and alive so Dad was surrounded by that. By us. By his family. Her family."

Coert looked at him again.

The second he did, Moreland stated fiercely, "Best little sister a man could have. Best daughter a father could have."

Coert felt his Adam's apple jump.

"But she calls us the family. *The* family. Sometimes Patrick's family," he stated.

Maybe it was all Coert was giving to dealing with all this.

So he didn't have it in him to get that.

And his "What?" came out choked.

"*The* family. Not *my* family," Moreland explained.

Shit, shit, *fuck*.

"All her life, she never belonged anywhere. Not anywhere. Not with her family, who didn't allow her to belong. Not her *real* family, *my* family, who wants her to belong. The only time she ever belonged to anything, to anyone, was when she belonged to you."

Coert forced himself to stand strong after that blow landed because if he didn't, it would have rocked him back and taken him to his goddamned knees.

"She's always been sad," Moreland whispered. "It's always under the surface. But now, something's wrong. She's trying to hide it but she's failing. She talked to Kath and we know something happened with you. So I'm here, not to be a jerk, not to get in your face, not to drag you into it. But because I'm worried as all hell and I gotta know what happened with you and her so I can fix my little sister."

"You need to get your family out of that lighthouse."

Coert's words made Moreland blink.

"Sorry?" Moreland asked.

"Take them to dinner. If they've had dinner, take them out for dessert. A drive down the coast. I don't give a crap. But I need a few hours. And during that time I need you to get them out of that lighthouse."

"I…sorry…*what*?" he asked again.

"You lead the way, I'll follow. You get them out. I'll take it from there."

The two men stood staring at each other in the glow of a gorgeous, mismatched Christmas tree a little girl started to put together when she was two years old.

Then Moreland asked, "Are you gonna fix her?"

"I'm gonna try."

Moreland's face went hard. "You need to fix her."

"I broke her," Coert said low. "I did this. All of it. From the beginning. And I've known it. From the beginning. When she stops doing what her mother taught her to do, blaming herself for everything that happens, and she realizes that this isn't on her, I don't know how that's gonna go. It's something I've been avoiding since she showed here in Maine and it doesn't have to be said it's something I avoided for eighteen years. But it's gotta stop. And I'm gonna stop it. What goes from there…" It took him a beat to be able to finish. "Goes from there."

"You can't make more of a mess," Moreland warned.

"I'm in love with her."

Moreland blinked again, this time with his chin jerking back in his throat.

Coert kept talking.

"I've been in love with her since she poured beer all over the yard the first time she looked in my eyes. She's my world. She's been my world for eighteen years even when she wasn't close to being part of that world. And it was me. It was all on me. I kept her in something that was wrong and dangerous and made her think she was falling in love with a criminal. She was on the right path and it was me who jerked her off. I loved her but I lied to her with practically every word out of my mouth, and I played her to get what I needed. Then I got my pride stung and I was too fuckin' young and too fuckin' destroyed by all I'd done to do anything but lay that square on her shoulders. So this is my mess, Moreland, and I've lived with that for eighteen years, and I've lived with knowin' I made a mess of Cady for all that time too. Now I gotta go in there facing the very real possibility that just seein' me is gonna make more of a mess. But you and your family have spent all that time pickin' up the pieces so no matter what happens from here, the only way I'll go is knowin' *you* got this if it turns even more to shit."

"She's never stopped loving you," Moreland told him quietly.

"You say that thinkin' it makes it better, but *I fucked up her entire life*," Coert clipped, leaning forward but then pulling back, pulling himself together, taking everything he had to do it, because he was close to flying apart and right now he could not fall apart. "She told me she still loved me days ago and it only made it worse."

"You can salvage this."

"Maybe, but should I?" Coert fired back.

"Yes."

He said it instantly and he said it straight, and when he did, that was when Coert took a step back like he'd suffered a blow.

"She's my little sister and I want her to have what she wants and what she wants is *you*," Moreland declared.

"Then get your family outta that lighthouse," Coert growled.

Moreland stared at him.

Then he smiled.

Then he said, "I'm in a black rental Denali SUV. Think you know the way, but you're right. It's best I lead."

Coert walked right to the door and opened it.

Moreland followed him but stopped and looked him again in the eyes.

"My wife Kath said if you two quit squabbling, you'd jump each other's bones. Dad said the second you got your head out of your ass and came back, Cady would be gone in a flash so we'd have to gird our loins to hold on so we didn't lose her. But just to say, the whole family's here for Christmas so do us a favor. Cady cooks a mean bird and the kids are looking forward to it. She won't be able to lift it if she's exhausted by a reunion sex-a-thon."

So that explained the "sister" Kath, and the other wives were the other two "sisters" and the entire Moreland clan "the family" coming out for Christmas.

He loved Cady had that.

Still.

"How about I salvage this and we joke about it in, I don't know, say fifteen years?" Coert suggested.

"Maybe a good call," Pat muttered, lips curling up, and then he walked out the opened door.

Coert closed it, locked it, went into the living room, turned out the Christmas tree lights and hustled to the garage, not even grabbing his jacket.

He got in his truck, hit the garage door opener, pulled out and got behind the black Denali that was idling in his road.

In all his years to come, looking back at that ride from his house to the lighthouse, he'd never remember a second of it. He gave Cady shit for driving emotional but he was lucky he had those Denali taillights to focus on, because Lord knew with all the shit infesting his head if he'd have made it.

But he made it and Moreland must have had a remote to the gate because he coasted right through.

Coert followed him.

He'd been right, the Christmas lights were amazing.

And it was clear the "whole family" was a big one because there were two more Denali SUVs crowding the space around her two-car garage, both doors open but only Cady's Jag was parked inside one bay.

Coert parked and Moreland swung out as Coert did the same.

He followed him to the covered walk that led to the door to the lighthouse on that side.

Moreland stopped and Coert stopped with him.

"Ready?" Moreland asked.

"No," Coert answered.

"Dad liked you for her."

Coert suffered that blow too with a miracle of no movement.

"He lived long, the last years of his life not the greatest. I hope we made them not as bad as they could have been. I know Cady did. But I'd put money on the fact that he left this world with only two regrets. Giving in to his wife, planting Katy in my mother and then losing them both, and that he didn't live to see this."

And with nothing further, Moreland opened the door and moved through.

Coert heard Midnight bark, not a warning, a welcome.

He also heard someone shout, "Hey, Dad! Where you been?"

But as he moved in, all he saw was Cady in the kitchen with two other women and a kid. She was doing something at the island, and the minute she turned her head and saw him, she froze.

So he froze two steps in from the door.

"Who's that?" A child.

"Everyone, jackets on, we're going into town for dinner." Moreland.

"But Auntie Cady's making spaghetti pie!" Another child.

"What's goin' on, Pat?" A man.

"Right! Dinner in town! Everybody get suited up!" A woman.

"What've you done, Pat?" Another man.

"Let's go. Now." Moreland.

"I think—" Another woman.

"*Now.*" Moreland.

"Holy cow." And another woman.

"Who's that guy?" A young woman in a loud whisper.

"Jackets. Now!" Moreland's voice was rising. "Let's go."

"Yeesh, Uncle Pat's freaking *out*." A young man.

Midnight woofed.

"Come on. Come on. Let's go. Mike, Daly, got your keys?" The first woman.

"This goes bad, bud, we're having a family meeting." A man, growling.

Coert heard it, felt the movement, commotion, footfalls running upstairs and voices encouraging others to get jackets and move out, footfalls down the stairs.

It seemed it took years for it all to quiet down, for the brushes of people to stop moving past him to get out the door, for the door to close.

And all that time he and Cady just stared at each other.

When the door closed he said gently, "Is the stove on, baby?"

Woodenly, she nodded.

"Turn it off, Cady," he ordered.

Her body jolted but she forced it to move stiffly to the stove.

She turned knobs.

Then she turned to him.

"Come here," he urged quietly.

Slowly, one foot in front of the other, her eyes to his, she moved his way.

Midnight moved to her and crowded her but Cady didn't stop until she was two feet away.

Coert looked into emerald eyes.

Christ, how did he start?

Christ, how did he fix something that he broke before he'd even started it?

"I should have let you explain. I should have explained myself what—"

He didn't say any more.

She threw herself at him.

Grabbing his head on either side, burrowing into him, fucking *climbing him*, she did everything she could to wrap her arms around his head and pull it down to hers.

Their mouths collided and hers was already open, her tongue darting out.

And he tasted her.

Cinnamon and toffee and moonlight and warmth and *Cady*.

And for the first time in eighteen years, he hit home.

She shuffled him back, her movements jerky, desperate.

He didn't make her work for it and shifted when she turned him.

He also fell when she pushed into him. The backs of his legs hitting the arm of the couch, they went down, Coert on his back, Cady on top of him.

She was hungry for him, fucking *starving*, kissing him, her hands moving on him, shoving up his sweater to dive under and get to the skin of his stomach, his chest.

Midnight woofed and snuffled them with her nose.

They both ignored her, because Coert was right there with Cady, hands to her ass, up her sweater, along the skin at her sides, her ribs.

She sat up abruptly, straddling him, tore her sweater over her head. Her hair flying, she threw it aside, her hands going immediately to his sweater and yanking it up.

He did a half-curl to lift his back off the couch, his arms over his head. She tugged his sweater to his forearms and he pulled it off from there, tossing it away.

Hands back to her, she was hands and mouth back to him, fingers trailing, nails scratching, biting, licking, *feeding* from him.

God, it was beautiful.

It was Cady.

Coert drove a hand in her hair, pulled back, arm around her waist hauling her up his body. He kept his fingers in her hair as he took his arm from around her, ripped down a cup of her bra, lifted his head and sucked her nipple hard in his mouth.

God, her taste, her moan, the way she was grinding herself into his stomach.

All Cady.

His cock was hard and chafing against his fly, and that and Cady and getting more of her were all that filled his thoughts when she suddenly tore away, took her feet at the side of the couch but only to put her hands to her belt to undo it.

He watched her, her face flushed, her eyes dilated, locked to him, so fucking beautiful in her want, and he slid a hand under him, in his back pocket, pulling out his wallet.

A growl surged from his throat when she bent to yank her jeans and panties down her legs, exposing herself to him. She kicked them off and leaned over him, frenzied as she worked his belt.

He slid the condom out of his wallet then tossed the wallet aside.

She unbuttoned his jeans then slid down the zipper.

He dug his heels in to lift his hips off the couch as she wrenched his jeans and shorts down his hips, thrilled beyond reason when she'd freed his hard, aching cock from its confines.

She swung over him, her eyes again glued to Coert's.

His eyes to hers, he'd barely rolled the condom on before she was grabbing hold of his dick. She positioned it with one hand, leaned over him, the fingers of her other hand curling around his neck.

He put both hands to her hips when she found his head.

And then he had her.

She pulsed down, her head flying back, filling herself with him.

Giving him her, buried inside her, Cady all he could see, all he could feel, his entire focus, finally again his world.

"Cady," he grunted.

She looked to him and moved, hard, slamming down on him, her hand at his neck spasming, her pussy spasming, harsh breaths escaping parted lips.

He raced both his hands up her back to her head, holding it at the sides, holding her steady, holding her eyes, not about to lose those eyes, not about to lose her.

She rode him fast, frantic, reckless.

He yanked her face closer to his and saw it race up in her.

"Cady," he whispered.

Her head shot back as she let out a soft cry.

He pulled it forward, resting her forehead on his and holding her close as she panted and whimpered her orgasm against his lips, her hips still slamming into his.

When she started to lose it, the beauty drifting away, he rolled her to her back and took over.

Too far gone for her—the feel of her, having her under him again—to go gentle, he rode her rough and she held on. Both her arms circling his head again, she shoved his face in her neck. Her legs rounding his back, cinching tight, lifting her hips to give him more, he thrust into her, feeling each one push her breath out into his neck until he groaned into hers as he bucked into her body and came really fucking hard for his Cady.

He let it happen, it was fantastic, but it was so enormous he feared he'd hurt her. So he pushed back at it so he could gentle his movements and glide inside her as his orgasm slipped through him until he could settle in deep.

Finally again buried inside the only place he was ever supposed to be.

After he was done coming, the room didn't come back, the lighthouse, her dog, Magdalene, anything.

It was just Cady and him and that couch. That was all Coert could take. That was all he wanted. That was all he'd wanted for years.

And there they were.

They had it.

He brushed her neck with his nose, smelling hints of her perfume that were clean and earthy but also mellow and floral and it was so totally her, different than the scent she wore back in the day, it felt like a gift. Having it be so her, *this* her, after having *her* and feeling her soft body under him, his fingers in her hair, her pussy sleek and tight around his cock.

That was it felt like a gift until suddenly she made a strange noise, forced her hands between them and shoved up hard.

Not prepared for that, Coert lifted up farther, thinking his weight was too much, and still unprepared, she slithered out from under him, his cock lost her, and he was losing the rest of her.

He made a grab to hook her at the waist but was too late and she was too fraught. Practically falling over the side of the couch, she escaped him and he'd just gotten up on a forearm to turn to her, follow her out of the couch, find out what the fuck was going on, but he froze when he saw her awkwardly snatching up the clothes on the floor, holding them to her body.

And his heart felt like it exploded when her tortured eyes hit his.

"I'm sorry." The words were dripping shame and embarrassment. "I'm so sorry."

She then took off running to the stairs and up them.

Midnight followed to the foot of the steps, ran back to Coert, then changed directions and raced cumbersomely up the stairs after her momma.

"Fuck," Coert bit out, pushed up from the couch, saw a door under the stairs and hoped it led to a toilet.

He went there and entered the smallest half bath he'd ever been in, but it was still freaking nice.

He didn't take the time to admire it.

He pulled off the condom, flushed it, rinsed his hands and didn't bother drying them, closing the door to the bathroom or even doing up his jeans as he ran out and took the steps two at a time, holding his pants together at the fly.

He hit a room that had a big circular couch in it, some side tables with a curved TV that was still on, affixed to the wall.

But no Cady.

So he sprinted up the next winding set of stairs and came right into the smallest bedroom he'd ever seen that was dominated by a bed, but it was amazing the economy of space and the magic brought to it with fairy lights under sheers draped over the bed on the ceiling, and compact furniture that was all gorgeous but all useful.

He did not admire that either because Cady was at the foot of the bed and had her panties up, the other clothes in a pile in the minimal floor space at her feet, but she was holding his sweater.

Slowly her eyes came to him.

"I took your sweater," she whispered like she'd just admitted committing murder.

"Cady," he said carefully.

"I shouldn't have done that," she kept whispering.

"What?" he asked softly.

"Done that. That. To you. Touched you. Made you…made you…I shouldn't have touched you like that."

Was she insane?

"Cady, honey, think. I was right there with you all the way."

Her eyes were on him but he could tell she wasn't looking at him but was somewhere else, somewhere very not good, when she murmured, "I shouldn't have done that to you."

"Look at me, honey," he urged.

She didn't look at him.

"Cady," he said, taking a step toward her.

Her eyes focused on him.

And her words broke when she said, "I'm so sorry."

Okay.

Done.

He had to go all of two feet but he went there, scooped her up, turned and planted his ass on the end of her bed with her held in a tight ball in his lap against his chest.

"Stop that," he growled into her hair. "I was right there with you every step of the way."

"You…you're…the investigator. His reports. Patrick's reports. I read them. I know how you got your daughter."

A surprise but not a surprise.

"This was not that," he said firmly. "That wasn't even what you're thinking."

"You…you…women haven't done right by you."

He put hands to either side of her head and forced her to look at him.

"Stop it," he bit out.

"Coert—"

"It was me."

She stared into his eyes.

"Me, Cady. I did it. I broke us. It was *me*."

"You didn't—"

Shit.

Fuck.

Shit!

Fuck!

He felt it and he could no longer stop it.

His body bucked and his voice cracked when it forced itself out.

"It was all on *me*."

Gone was his Cady who was twisting shit in her head.

Suddenly in his lap was Cady who was all about him.

He could see it in her face.

And he couldn't handle it.

"Coert—" she said urgently.

"I fucked us up. I fucked *you* up. From the beginning. Used you. Knew it was wrong. Knew it would break us. Knew it. Did it anyway."

"Coert, honey, look at me ."

He was looking at her but she wasn't there.

She was in his lap, as close as she could be, but he was in hell.

"After, after you knew, after you knew every time you said the name Tony it was a lie, I was a lie, *we* were a lie, I was a piece of shit, I wanted to go to you. I knew you. I knew what you'd do. Malc and Tom, they said dig right back in. Don't give you time. Get right back in there. But Cap, my captain, said to give you time. He said if I gave you time, you'd see it was my job. You'd understand. It'd be all right. You'd be open to me fixing us, starting again. If I went too early, I'd go in when you were pissed and hurt and fuck shit up even more. Malc and Tom were right. I should have listened to them. Cap was wrong. You needed me and I knew it, and I listened to him and it was fuckin' *stupid*."

She adjusted in his lap, straddling him. His hands still on the sides of her head, she reciprocated that and put her face right in his.

"Coert, honey, *see me*," she begged.

He didn't see her.

"Christ, every time, every time I moved inside you and you called me Tony, I died a little."

"God, *Coert*," her voice broke, her thumbs moved over the wet on his cheeks, "please, look at me."

He was looking right at her but he wasn't seeing anything but a black pall of blame and shame.

"I blamed you because I couldn't take it. I laid that shit on you because I couldn't live with the fact I'd done that to you. She fuckin' *murdered her boyfriend.* You wanted out, I made you stay in. I made you a part of that. I made you live that right there. *In it.* Covering you in filth. In shit."

"Stop it, please stop it," she pleaded, her fingers frantic on his face, her body burrowing close to his.

"I'd come home and you'd smile at me and throw yourself in my arms and call me Tony. You'd look at me with Lars, and when I caught you, you'd look away. God, so fuckin' sad. Every day hoping that I'd give you reason to believe and every day I gave you reason to walk away, and you stuck by me and I was *using you.*"

She shook his head. "*Stop it!*"

He finally looked into her eyes. "I loved you and I made you live a hell."

"I loved you and I was happy to be in that hell if you were there with me."

Coert shut up.

"I shouldn't have married Patrick," she declared.

He slid his hands to her jaw and shared, "Your brother explained it to me."

Her head jerked in his hands when he said the word "brother" but he kept talking.

"And back then, I didn't let you explain because I wanted an excuse to let you go, let you live your life, not have the shit I did to you that infested every second we'd had together go on to infest every second we would have. I wanted to set you free."

"I didn't want to be free," she whispered.

"I thought you'd be better off without me."

"And I thought the same, so after I hurt you with Patrick I didn't go back to you and make you listen to me because I was young and stupid. We were both young and stupid and scared and that was insanely crazy and messed up, and we fucked up and now we're here."

He stared in her eyes.

"We're here, Coert. So what are we going to do about it?"

It wasn't that easy.

With them it had never been easy.

"I hurt you again just days ago, Cady. It wasn't about talking to you. It was about facing you after what I'd done to you. After what I'd put you through. Facing myself and admitting I'd acted like a piece of shit. Seeing Lars, having it all brought back, he said it straight to me. He gave it to me straight. I did what I did to him and that didn't matter. He's trash. He did what he did and deserved what he got. But not you. And I had to face that again. And face what I thought I drove you to with Moreland."

"He wasn't my husband, Coert, not really."

"His son shared that but you didn't because I didn't let you, and you tried back then and when you came back to me, and I didn't let you give it to me then either."

"Can you see how all this is intense?" she demanded. "It isn't like we were too young and hadn't learned how to communicate yet, how to compromise, how to be in a relationship. There was murder and felonies and my family didn't help, and Patrick was suddenly there and dealing with his own grief so he was being overprotective, and all this was just *crazy insane.* So maybe we need to both understand that and realize it happened. It went wrong. Okay so it went horribly wrong, devastatingly wrong. But now we have a choice. Keep letting it go wrong or make it right."

"What's right, Cady?"

"I think what's right happened on my couch."

Coert went still.

"And Lars can go fuck himself," she carried on. "I don't know what he said to you but I mean, *God.* He was firing a swath of vengeance across the country because *he* was a *nimrod.* I mean, really?" She settled back on her ass on his thighs and slid her hands down to either side of his neck. "Don't think another second about whatever Lars said. He's always been a jerk."

Firing a swath of vengeance.

Nimrod.

She was being funny and sweet.

But Coert was not near to a place he could laugh.

"Cady, honey, can you honestly say you can move on from here and every time you look at me not see how I threw your life right in the garbage and did it willfully?"

"Coert, can you honest to God move forward from here and every time you look at me not see *I* didn't believe in you when I knew. *I knew.* You were right. I knew who you were."

She moved in, burrowing closer, and kept talking.

"You knew me too, and I did the exact thing I always did. Rash. Reckless. Whatever I could do to make the hurt go away. Better yet, find someone else to make the hurt go away and I did that the *very day* it all went down. That morning you left, Maria called me, screaming at me,

'*What did you do! What did you and that pig do?*' I had no idea what she was talking about and I was so freaked I went to her before I went to work, and I saw you there with your badge on your jeans, talking to cops, Lars and Maria and Sharon on their knees with their arms cuffed behind their backs in that dirty yard and I got *more* freaked. Then I barely got through the doors, trembling, not even knowing why I went in to work, and Jaime came into the Sip and Save right behind me, getting in my face, saying he'd cut me. I'd go down. My cop boyfriend would go down. And he took off and I lost it and went out to the side of the shop. I couldn't even stand. I was sitting on the cement sobbing so hard and Patrick found me there. And what did I do?"

"Cady," he whispered.

"I betrayed you. Right then and there. I didn't go home to Casey's that night and wait for you. Patrick took me to my parents' and they kicked me out, '*For good this time, Cady, and never come back*,'" she mimicked her mother and kept doing it. "'*Not ever. If you love us at all, don't bring this kind of thing in our lives. Not ever.*' So I went home with Patrick and that was it. I didn't even go back to the Sip and Save. He took care of everything. He was there when I finally went back to Casey's to get my stuff and you showed, and you saw him and the ring and rightfully lost it on me and that was it." She shook her head. "That was it."

"Honey," Coert murmured, gathering her closer.

But she wasn't done.

"So you know, it's a lot easier for me to see you were doing your job, as filled with landmines as that was to negotiate, I understood. It took some time but I completely understood. It was your job and it wasn't an easy job and you told me as best as you could tell me I needed not to let go, not to give up on us, to stick by you, and I didn't. You were doing your job. I was just being..." she huffed out a breath and finished, "*me*. So where does that leave us when you look at me?"

"Do you wanna find out?"

"With everything I have even though it's completely terrifying."

Coert relaxed but did it still holding her close.

"Then let's find out."

She shook her head. "I say that but I can't…I can't…if it doesn't…"

"Cady, I love you. I never stopped loving you. You said you read the reports now read between the lines. I was never able to commit to another woman because I was still in love with you."

She jerked then went solid in his arms.

"And that happened even when I convinced myself you married a man three times your age for his money," he told her.

She stared in his eyes.

And Coert looked into them and made a decision.

"Now, this is what's going to happen," he declared. "I'm gonna go down and get my wallet because I have one condom left and this time when I make love to you, it's not gonna go that fast. That was fuckin' fantastic, but it went way too fast."

She stayed solid in his arms but her hands at his neck convulsed.

He kept going.

"Then you're gonna text your family to tell them to come back and I'm gonna go home and leave you with them. You're also gonna tell them that even though they're here for a visit, you're gonna have dinner with them tomorrow but then you're gonna come to my place and spend the night with me. And we're gonna spend Christmas Eve together until I gotta go to Kim's to be with my kid in the evening. When I go to Janie, you can come home and be with your family. And I want time with you on Christmas so you need to figure that out, because I'm doing presents with Janie at Kim's and then I got a couple of hours where she has her before she brings her to me in the afternoon. And those hours I'm gonna spend with you. And I want you to meet my daughter and do that soon. But we'll plan that after Christmas. So your family can have you and Janie needs me but any time we have in between, it's ours, and when they're gone, it's you and me and when I have her, we'll have Janie."

He stopped talking, and when she said nothing, just stared at him, her pretty face stunned, he felt his own face get soft.

"And soon as I can," he said quietly, "I want you to make me spaghetti pie, whatever that is."

He barely got the word "pie" out before he was on his back in her bed because she'd attacked him straight from his lap and she was kissing him.

She was all over him.

And Coert might have wanted to slow it down that time but he didn't get that chance (and again had to sprint on her stairs, taking them two at a time, this time to grab his wallet) because it had been a long time, too long, way too long and they might have had a taste, but Cady was still very hungry.

And Coert...

Coert was still *starving.*

AGAIN ONLY IN his jeans, done up this time, Coert moved up the stairs to Cady's bedroom and this time found her where he left her in bed.

He got in it with her, stretching out beside her, but she was under the covers he'd pulled over her.

He laid on top, handing her phone to her.

"Thanks, Coert," she said.

It came out shy, she didn't meet his eyes and he sighed.

They'd had fantastic sex twice and they'd have more fantastic sex, a lot of it, but that didn't erase the fact that they'd both jumped from their opposite sides of the shore into the raging waters of everything that came in between and neither of them had life vests.

They just had to have the determination, since they'd made it through the rapids to each other, to hold the fuck on.

"Kath," she said softly, and Coert focused on her. She moved her eyes from her phone that had been beeping, he'd heard it go when he'd run to get his wallet, to him. "I think considering she's sent eleven texts, she's worried."

"I bet," he muttered, pulling her and the covers over her closer to his body.

"And I think Pat's in some big trouble with Mike and Daly, and maybe Pam."

"You need to text her."

She nodded.

Turning her attention back to her phone, he watched her text with her thumbs.

"You can text with your thumbs?" he asked, and her eyes tilted back to his.

"I have seven nieces and nephews. They all have phones, except Melanie and Ellie, but they're getting one when they turn ten, like their brother Riley did. And I'm cool Auntie Cady. I spoil them, to their parents' chagrin. Thus they text me a lot. And even Melanie and Ellie do it, when they steal Riley's, Pam's or Mike's phone to do it."

"So you have lots of practice."

She nodded, went back to her phone. He heard the whoosh, and then without her phone to take her attention, she looked like she didn't know where to put her gaze.

"Cady," he whispered.

It slid to his.

"If we do this, we have to learn something from what came before."

"What's that?" she asked quietly.

"We have to learn, even when it gets hard, we can't give up and we can't let go."

She got it and he knew it when her eyes widened and her body relaxed against his.

"I spent so long not even thinking that this was a possibility, it's hard to wrap my head around it being a reality," she admitted.

He touched his mouth to hers before he said, "I understand that feeling."

He watched her swallow and it looked painful.

"You get freaked, worried, anything starts twisting the wrong way in your head, use your thumbs and text me," he urged.

"I think that might mean you'll get a text every ten minutes."

"After not having you for eighteen years, do you honestly think I'll mind hearing from you every ten minutes? Christ, Cady, you lived in the lighthouse in my town, and I'd convinced myself I was pissed at you and I made every excuse I could find to come here just to see you."

He didn't mean to do it, but he got it when his words made her eyes fill with tears. It looked like she'd try to beat them back but she gave in and shoved her face in his throat, her body wracking in his arms.

He rolled to his back, pulled her over him and held her.

After he gave her some time to get it out, he pushed up so his shoulders were to her headboard and he took her with him, pulling her even deeper into him, holding tight.

"I never once considered the thought you'd forgive me," he told her.

She pulled her head back and looked at him through watery, brilliant green eyes. "I thought the same. I thought you hated me."

"Two sides of the same coin, they say, love and hate. Let's move to the other side, yeah?"

She nodded.

He needed to get her where she felt safe and solid enough for him to leave her to her family but also so she could look past the part that was scary as shit and precarious as hell and keep on going.

"I'm committed to this, Cady," he said gentle but firm. "I'm committed to working on this. Getting us through the whitewater and finding us somewhere safe. I would not have come here with your brother if I wasn't all in. I'm looking you right in the eye and I'm saying that to you. It's been a long time but I know what I feel. How I've felt since you came back. How I couldn't get you out of my head, stop thinking about you. I know where I'm at even if I understand we have to get to know each other again, we have history to share and some of it might not be easy. Though," he grinned at her and teased, "since you had an investigator, that might not be as tough on you."

She ducked her head and tucked her face in the side of his neck.

"Teasing," he whispered, lifting a hand to stroke the side of her neck.

"I know," she whispered back.

"Too soon?" he asked.

"No, just that I missed you teasing me."

He stopped stroking and wrapped his arm around her.

That was something he'd missed too.

He cleared his throat.

"To finish what I was saying, I wouldn't be here, I wouldn't have put you through all this, if I wasn't all in, if I didn't still love you. You said you still loved me too. So we have that. We hold on to it. And we ride these rapids until I can get us to safety. You with me?"

"I'm with you."

"Good," he muttered.

"I'm with you," she repeated.

"Heard you, Cady."

She lifted up and looked him in the eye, raising a hand to catch him hard on the head behind his ear.

And he thought he was alert.

But at her hold he became more alert.

"I mean that," she said again.

Shit.

She was back there. Back where she'd promised she'd stick with him.

And then didn't.

"I know," he said gently.

"Seriously."

"Stop it," he urged softly. "You hear me? That's twisting shit. That's staying where we were. Apart. Separate. With too much in between. We're coming together. We're moving on. You with me?"

It took a second but she nodded.

"Did you tell Kath that they could come back?"

"I said I was good, they shouldn't worry and I'd text soon when they could come back."

"Text them," he ordered. "They wanna see you're okay. You text. Get dressed. Walk me to my truck. And I'll get outta here so they can have you to themselves to see you're okay."

She nodded again.

He gave her a squeeze.

Then he gave her a kiss.

That kiss led to another one and a few more, all soft, quick, sweet.

But it eventually led to them making out before he unfortunately needed to pull away and say, "Your family needs to see you're good, Cady."

She thought it was unfortunate too, gave him that, it made him smile so he touched his mouth to hers one more time before he found her phone she'd dropped in the bed and gave it to her.

He got out of bed, put on his sweater, socks, boots and gave her privacy after she texted, doing this stroking Midnight while she dressed.

She put on the thick socks she'd been wearing that he hadn't noticed until the second time when he'd taken them off and when they got downstairs draped a shawl around her shoulders before she started to walk outside in her socks with him to his truck.

He stopped her before he even opened the door.

"Cady, shoes," he said.

She looked to her feet then to him. "I'm okay."

"It's not even twenty degrees out there."

"Am I hanging out there for an hour?"

"No."

"I'm good."

"Cady, there's snow out there. Put on some boots."

"Coert, they're at the Lobster Market loitering over whoopee pies. They probably stopped loitering two seconds after I gave them the go ahead to come home. They'll be back any minute."

"Boots," he ordered.

"These socks are thicker than my boots.

"What'd I say?"

"Coert!" she snapped.

"Cady."

Her frame went still.

Then she bowed her head.

He grew instantly alarmed.

Shit, he shouldn't have pushed the boots.

When she lifted her head, she was on him again. Hands in his hair, yanking his mouth to hers and kissing him wet and heavy and deep.

He turned her, pushed her against the door and participated avidly.

He eventually tore his mouth from hers saying what he had to say, not for him or them.

For her.

"I gotta go."

"Love you," she whispered.

That was when Coert stilled.

"Love you, Coert," she whispered again.

"Love you too, Cady," he whispered back, went in for another touch of the lips and said, "Just stay in. Stay warm. And I'll call tomorrow."

"Okay."

Another lip touch like he couldn't exist unless he had that connection and finally he pulled her from the door, set her aside and gave himself one last moment to give Midnight a quick rubdown. He moved his eyes to her, shot her a smile, waited and watched her face get soft.

And then he turned to the door, opened it and walked right out.

He was halfway to his truck when he heard the door open behind him.

He turned and started walking backward seeing Cady in the door.

“Get inside!” he called.

“Text me when you get home,” she called back.

“Right.”

“Talk to you tomorrow!” She was yelling now.

“Right!” he yelled back.

“‘Bye!”

“Later, baby!”

He nearly ran into his truck so he turned to watch where he was going, got in, started her right up to get her warmed up, because it was freaking cold, and he looked to Cady’s door.

She stood illuminated by the light behind her, the Christmas swags, the spiral pines, Midnight sitting at her side.

She waved.

Coert waved back.

It looked like Midnight woofed.

And he was smiling when he reversed out and drove away.

HE WAS STILL smiling when he got into his house, turned on Janie’s tree and pulled out his phone.

Home safe. Sleep tight. Love you, he texted.

He was in his kitchen pouring a needed two fingers of bourbon when he got back, *Family’s back. Impromptu meeting. Although they see me breathing, Pat’s in trouble.*

He strikes me as a guy who can take it, Coert returned.

He is, thank God, she replied.

After taking a sip of bourbon he told her, *We’ll scratch a meeting with your family on the agenda before they leave.*

I'm feeling a good deal of happy right now and Mike can be more overprotective than his dad. So maybe you can meet them over Skype when they're a gazillion states away.

Coert grinned. *Fortitude, honey. We can do this.*

Yes we can.

Coert kept grinning and sipping as he turned on his TV but sat not watching it, rather smelling Cady on him, his phone in his hand, Cady on the other end.

And just to say, he texted, *I'm liking that good deal of happy.*

She didn't text for a while and Coert didn't like it until she did, and it stated, *Daly put me on the hot seat. I was just grilled to within an inch of my life and then had to endure Kath shouting, "For God's sake, Daly, can't you see you're ruining her afterglow!" Thank God the kids are at Elijah's or that would have been bad.*

Coert burst out laughing.

And when he was done, he tried to think of the last time he'd laughed that hard with that sense of freedom.

It wasn't even when he was with Cady, no matter how funny she could be, and she'd always been funny, because all he was doing to her was standing in the way.

Was Elijah there tonight? he asked.

Out on a date but he's back and I'll tell you about it, but this date was not good seeing as I think Verity got a huge crush on him the second she laid eyes on him.

Which ones are Verity's parents?

Kath and Pat.

Was in his presence five minutes and still can say, she catches his eye, they should count themselves lucky.

Yes. I SO agree. He's SUCH a good guy.

Coert was again smiling. *Yeah.*

I should let you go. Kath's opening another bottle of wine and she's demanded the men go to the studio so I think I'm about to be on a different kind of hot seat.

More smiling *Right, Cady. Don't worry about your afterglow, honey. I'll give you another one tomorrow.*

Her reply didn't come as quickly, and he got why when he read it and felt it deeply when he saw, *Love you, Coert. A lot.*

I know, Cady. Love you too. Talk to you tomorrow and see you tomorrow night.

Can't wait. See you.

Don't get drunk. Afterglows aren't as good through a hangover.

It was then she sent him a cartoon picture that looked a lot like her, smiling big, but wearing a dragon outfit with a sword in her chest with the words YOU SLAY ME! hanging over it.

A shock of laughter exploded from his throat and he asked, *What the fuck is that?*

He got rapid texts.

Bitmoji.

Nieces and nephews.

Learn to cope. I can have entire conversations through Bitmoji.

Coert chuckled and returned, *Go get drunk with your girls. But not too drunk.*

Okay. Sleep tight.

Oh, he would.

Will do. Night, honey.

Goodnight, Coert.

He didn't text her back to hold their connection even when he wanted to, letting her go to be with her family.

But he did stare at the cartoon of Cady in a dragon suit and he did it a long time.

Then he couldn't stop himself from leaning over, elbows to his knees, pressing his bourbon to one temple, his phone to his other, his mouth engaged with sucking huge amounts of oxygen into his lungs.

It happened.

They did it.

They were committed to negotiating the in between and finding each other again.

Which meant rediscovering each other.

Which meant Cady sharing Bitmojis.

He stopped deep breathing and started laughing then he grunted twice to hold a different emotion at bay and folded deeper into himself holding the phone and glass to the back of his neck.

"She forgives me," he muttered to his knees.

Love you, Coert. A lot.

It was ragged when he repeated, "She forgives me."

He drew in breath, sat up, sat back, set his phone aside and trained his eyes to his Christmas tree.

Then he flipped off his boots, lifted his stocking feet to the coffee table and turned his attention to his TV.

Seventeen

TOTALLY SHOW ME

CADY

Present day…

Midnight roaming my back seat, a pie in the seat beside me, the next night, I drove to Coert's.

No matter all the good that had happened the night before, part of that being after it happened I had the girls right there to process it with over wine, I still hardly slept at all.

I couldn't believe in it.

I couldn't believe it was real.

I eventually fell into a fitful sleep sometime in the early morning hours.

And I did this only to have Coert not waste any time proving to me it was real.

This came through a text at six thirty that made my phone on my nightstand buzz.

I woke immediately, saw his name and snatched it up to read, *Morning, honey. Hope you slept good. I'll give you time to have breakfast with your family and call around 10:30 or 11:00. If you need me sooner, you have my number.*

That was so sweet, so wonderful, so *everything*, I didn't hesitate to text back, *Good morning back to you. Hope you slept well too. That time will be great. Look forward to it. Love you.*

And I immediately got back, *Love you too. Talk soon.*

I was up on an arm in my bed, the sun not yet even a promise in the sky, my dog awake and knowing I was as well thus sharing with some nudges it was time to be let out and then provide doggie breakfast, and in my hand as I scrolled down with my thumb, I saw the proof.

Ample proof.

In writing.

This was real.

Coert and I were *real*.

On that thought, regardless of the little sleep I'd had, I'd bounded out of bed.

The morning had been interesting, assessing the two camps that had formed around this situation.

Kath, Shannon and Verity (the last now of an age that her mother and I had allowed her to be a part of the women's discussion, but it was just her mother who let her drink wine) were all in, Verity going so far as to declare it, "Like a Christmas romance movie, Auntie Cady. With a lighthouse and everything!"

The night before, Pam had fallen when I shared Coert broke down under the crush of emotion he was feeling and all he'd given me when he did.

That morning Pat, I could tell, was happy it happened, but still watchful.

Daly and Mike did not hide they had yet to be won over.

The rest of the kids didn't really know what was happening, but they'd seen Coert and sensed it was something. Though they had pancakes, were staying at a lighthouse and Christmas was around the corner so the conversation about Coert had been limited, starting when Ellie asked, "Who was that tall man at your house last night, Auntie Cady?"

To which, under smiles from the women, a thoughtful look from Pat and glowers from his brothers, I replied, "Since I've been here, I've reconnected with somebody I knew a long time ago. We had something important to talk about so we had to do it alone. But you'll meet him soon, sweetie."

"Gross, a boyfriend," Riley declared.

"Not gross, he's an old guy but still it was right there to see Auntie Cady scored herself some hot," Bea, my fourteen-year-old (in truth), twenty-five-year-old (in her head) niece announced.

"Sick." Riley.

"Lush." Verity.

"He was really tall! Taller even than Daddy!" Melanie.

"He jacks you around, I'll break his neck." Dexter (or my now eighteen-year-old nephew who'd lived with a sister who was a serial girlfriend who (until her crush on Elijah) had chosen poorly so he'd also lived through the dramas and tantrums of many a breakup).

"He's the sheriff, Riley," Verity declared a little smugly, rubbing the youngsters noses just a tad bit in the fact that she was now an "adult" so was in the know.

"The sheriff! I change my mind! That's *awesome*!" Riley cried.

"Let's stop talking about the sheriff and start talking about bacon," Daly cut in to put an end to a discussion he didn't like (as any mention of bacon would do). "Who wants some and how many pieces?"

This prompted a cacophony of shouts and a feeling of relief that when we'd gone to the grocery store, we'd bought eight packets of bacon.

And I lounged on the sofa in the studio sipping coffee and eyeing Daly and a grumpy-faced Mike while Shannon made silver dollar pancakes for everybody, Daly fried up enough bacon to feed an army, and I decided to let Coert be Coert, which would bring Mike and Daly around.

And if the unlikely event occurred that he didn't manage that, I could not let that faze me.

Fortitude, honey. We can do this.

We could.

We would.

We had to.

And I had to stop thinking about what everyone thought about me. I had to make my own decisions, live my own life, and if doing that meant I'd need to, bear my own consequences.

Last, I had to stop believing what my mother (and brother) thought of me and I had to start believing in *me*.

I was a good person. I'd done things that might be unwise, but the person I was, I'd earned happiness along the way.

Now it was *my* time.

And it was the time to stop thinking so much about what others thought of me, trying so hard to earn the love of certain people—two of which were now dead, one I'd never win over—and concentrate on what I'd already earned, how precious it was.

And what it said about me.

As promised, Coert had called at ten forty-four and it wasn't a quick chat, a duty call because he'd promised to do it.

We talked for over twenty minutes.

I told him about the family. How they were taking it. Then got into who was who with husbands and wives and kids.

He told me how he'd had a chat with Kim about getting along better for Janie, how well things went at Thanksgiving and how Janie wasn't acting any differently but it still felt like things were healthier for all of them.

This was the only time when we were talking that things turned sticky, because I needed to know and Coert was giving every indication he wanted us communicating frequently, but more importantly openly, so I had to ask.

What I asked was if Kim knew about me.

I'd be sharing his life. I'd be sharing his daughter's life. And thus I'd have to be in her life.

So I needed to know what I was facing.

"That's a talk for when you're with me, honey," he'd replied.

That didn't seem like open communication, and I didn't know what to make of it so I fell silent.

"I told Darcy," he shared into my silence.

Darcy. His fiancée that he'd never married.

Because of me.

"There's a lot to this," he continued when I said nothing. "And I'd like you close when I explain it. But so you understand now and don't get anything twisted in your head, it was her and it was me doing it to her. She knew she didn't have all of me and that's on me. How she handled it is on her. And when things got tough, her throwing you in my face all the time instead of trying to talk to me about it, using you as a weapon which kept you sharp in my mind, including the guilt I felt, rather than understanding you'd been a part of my life and finding our way with that made matters worse. So I learned from what happened with Darcy and I never told Kim."

"I…that…I," I stammered, because I was thinking too much and feeling too much to put any of it into words. The only thing I could push out was, "I'm sorry about that."

"I'm not because if I was married to Darcy, I wouldn't have you."

That made me grow silent for a different reason.

"But that would never have happened," he went on, "because all I ever wanted was you."

That made me grow warm.

"Coert," I whispered.

"I know that it happened as it should now. I hurt a good woman along the way and that really sucks. I have to live with that. The worst part about that is that I let it go on too long. With her and with Kim. I should have let them both go long before I did so they could find someone to make them happy. But to deal with that, I have to look at the bottom line. And that's the fact that, since I was in love with you, it took too long but it turned out better for Darcy in the end too. She's married to another guy. They have a kid and one on the way. I hear this from others. She doesn't stay in touch with me. But I also hear she's happy."

With this news I knew Coert was actually very right.

So all I could say was, "Yes."

"I'll have to tell Kim and I'll have to go into detail, and just like we'll deal with Mike and Daly, we'll deal with that too," he finished.

"Yes," I whispered, loving his strength, feeding from it, letting it fill me, making me think this was easy.

We'd had so very much that was almost too difficult to bear.

So now was not my time.

Now was *our* time.

Coert's and mine.

He had to go back to work so I let him go, and then I came up with my plan to bring him a pie, something I'd made him a lot when we were together, a touch of yesterday that I hoped was sweet to bring into today.

But this meant I needed a pie carrier and a pie carrier was not something Paige and I had stocked in the kitchen.

There was a kitchen shop on the jetty that was one of the shops that hadn't burned down, but it had sustained some damage they'd had fixed since and reopened, and I told the girls we needed to load up and go there.

It was shopping, so in the end we had to take two cars to fit me, Kath, Pam, Shannon, Verity, Bea, Ellie and Melanie.

I was on a mission for a pie carrier and I also had to go to the grocery store to get ingredients, but the others were on a mission just to spend money.

I'd gotten what I needed in five minutes.

This meant I was standing by the door, getting antsy to get home and get cracking on my pie when two blondes approached me.

"You're the lighthouse lady," the bolder of the two stated (and brasher, if I was being honest, but even so you could tell it was an endearing trait of hers right off the bat).

"Uh, yes," I agreed.

"And you're giving our handsome sheriff a run for his money," she declared.

I stared.

I'd lived in Denver all my life. It felt small town-ish but it was a big city.

I hadn't lived in Magdalene very long and events were such that I hadn't been especially social and thus had not met very many people.

In other words, this was my first indication of how small of a town Magdalene really was.

"Alyssa," the other blonde murmured. She was just as pretty, but in a more refined way (in fact, her outfit didn't seem Maine at all, but instead Paris in wintertime), her eyes blue to the other blonde's brown.

"You are, yeah?" the other one, Alyssa, pressed me.

"I…um…" I mumbled.

"Finally!" she cried. "It's high time that hot hunk of lusciousness got his hands on a fiery one. *Need* to know that story, babelicious. I'm the woman behind Maude's House of Beauty. Half-price mani-pedi you come in and spill all. And to sweeten that pot, I'm talkin' *gel* mani. Not stuff that'll chip off in two days. Make it late afternoon, then we'll all go out and get drinks."

"Erm, *we?*" I asked.

She jerked a thumb to the blonde with her. "Me, Josie here and our other girl, Amelia. She's got some man problems right about now too. Me and Josie'll be cool that we're livin' the dream with our fellas, though, while we help you sort yourselves out."

I found myself sharing, "I think my situation has sorted itself out."

Her face fell.

Her friend Josie's brightened.

"So you aren't givin' Coert a run for his money," Alyssa muttered.

And for some reason, I kept sharing. "It took us nearly two decades to get sorted out."

That was when Alyssa's face brightened but Josie's grew distressed.

"Brilliant!" Alyssa cried. "It'll be a three martini night for sure." She pointed at me. "Maude's. After Christmas. Now I gotta get my ass home 'cause I got seven thousand presents to wrap. Laterzzzzz."

And on that she sashayed out the door.

Josie got close. "Alyssa is…" she smiled a small smile, "Alyssa. Big heart. Big mouth. Big everything. She's a love and what she's trying to say is, we'd like to welcome you to Magdalene. So I hope you call and make an appointment."

Brash but sweet.

Soft-spoken and also sweet.

I made a decision. "I guess…I will."

She smiled and offered a hand. "I'm Josie Spear."

I took her hand. "Cady Moreland."

"Lovely to meet you," she murmured as she squeezed my hand and let go. "We'll speak soon. Have a Merry Christmas."

"You too."

She touched my arm briefly then followed her friend.

In Magdalene I had Jackie and Amanda, but Amanda didn't live close so we saw each other, but not that much.

Now I had Coert.

And with Coert (eventually) would come Janie.

But a girl needed her girls and as wild as what just happened was, it felt nice to have some strangers walk up to me and essentially offer to be my girls.

"Do I *need* this?" Kath shouted from across the store.

I looked her way to see her holding up a deep-purple ladle that she absolutely did not need.

"It's Christmas and you're buying stuff for yourself?" Pam shouted from her place across the store in the other direction.

"Pat won't think to buy me a purple ladle," Kath shouted back.

"I hope not," Shannon put in.

Verity walked up to her mother, took the ladle from her hand and moved to the cash register, saying, "Merry Christmas, Mom."

Kath beamed.

As hilarious and sweet as my family was being, I tried not to scream at them to hurry up.

In the end, we got out, to the grocery store, home and I had to make three pies, two to leave for the family.

One for Coert and Janie (and maybe Kim).

So now I was on my way to Coert's and I had a variety of things cluttering my head.

One, I was on my way to Coert's and I was fiercely curious about where he lived. I had the address he'd texted me programmed in my sat nav (at the same time he thoughtfully invited Midnight to come along and I was glad, I'd been worried, since I'd had her we barely spent any time apart).

But I'd had the address before. It was in the investigator's reports.

I'd just never tortured myself and gone.

I also had Mike's parting shot to me in my head, this being him pulling me aside after I'd said my farewells but before I got out the door.

"Tell that guy he's coming for Christmas dinner."

I really needed to get Mike past referring to Coert as "that guy."

However, right then was not the time to do it.

"Mike, he has his daughter."

"She'll be in your family, our family, a family you want us to let him be a part of, so she should meet our family too."

"It's too soon," I told him, because it was and I had to admit to being a little miffed because he had to know that too.

"She won't know what's going on. She's five. She'll just know there's family and love around."

"And she'll also know you're giving her father the stink eye," I retorted.

Mike had no reply.

Which meant there'd be stink eye and I was going to have none of that.

"You agree to be fair and give him a shot, I'll broach this with Coert," I offered. "If you don't, Mike, then you'll meet Coert before you go home but when he's ready to do that, and you'll meet Janie when he makes the decision that time is right because I haven't even met her yet, officially, so he may not think that time is right."

"Showing her how much people love you and how much you love your family is the perfect time, Cady," he'd returned. "But I'll make you that deal."

On that, me, Midnight and the pie moved out, got in my car and I texted Coert I was on my way.

But now I was not only thinking I shouldn't have made that deal, I was thinking I shouldn't have told a perfect stranger in a kitchen shop that it had taken Coert and I nearly two decades to sort ourselves out. They both obviously knew him. He was the sheriff. I didn't need to be offering up gossip for the gristmill.

In other words, no matter what, I was going to make this trek to his house nervous as hell.

But by the time I reached his block I was making it *nervous as hell.*

Those nerves flew away when I counted house numbers and finally caught sight of Coert's house.

I'd never allowed myself to imagine us together again and I'd also never allowed my mind to go other places, especially not after I'd learned he'd had a daughter.

And one of those places was never allowing myself to think about where he might live, the home he'd give his daughter.

But seeing a house that looked like a farmhouse, painted yellow with white trim, huge trees in the front, lots of paned windows, a red-framed door fit mostly with paned glass, steep gables in the second story, all this tufted with the snow we'd been getting, took my breath away.

However, it was more.

There were candles in all the windows. White Christmas lights on two small pine trees beside his front steps, their illumination muted by snow. A thick pine wreath with a red bow on the door. Two red rocking chairs on a front porch that was recessed from the façade of the house.

Like most of his block, he decorated for Christmas and he did it gracefully, cheerful but not garish; handsome and subtle.

The odd thing out, prominent in one of the windows, even proud, was a big Christmas tree lit with multi-colored lights, shining behind the white lit candles in the window, incongruous with the rest that seemed planned and executed so perfectly.

He probably did all of this for his daughter, but the fact he did it at all stunned me in a way that thrilled me.

But that wasn't it.

The two lights on the outside of his house were lit bright, beating back the dark night, the lighting in the recessed porch lit too.

A beacon for me.

He didn't want me to miss his house.

He wanted me to come home.

And I knew this was true when I made the turn into his drive at the side and did it while one of his garage doors was going up.

I'd texted I was on my way and he'd been watching for me.

I wanted to laugh. I wanted to cry. I wanted to shout with glee.

But I didn't do this.

I guided my car into the garage by a miracle, doing it staring at the tall frame silhouetted with light coming from behind as it stood framed by the inside door.

I parked, turned the car off and heard the garage door going right back down as I watched Coert step into the garage and come toward me.

He passed my door and I knew why, so I made sure the locks were unlocked as he opened the back passenger door to let Midnight out.

I took that opportunity to turn and grab the pie. I would have to go around to get my bag that Kath had advised I pack, doing this stating, "It's been a long time for me but not a century and I'm thinking you need to be with the program from the start. So here it is from memory of a boyfriend sleepover. Nightie. Clean panties. In this weather, slippers or thick socks and maybe a cardigan or robe. Cleanser and moisturizer and a toothbrush. At least."

So I didn't just have my purse.

I had an overnight bag I hoped communicated the right things.

When Coert opened my door, I twisted with the pie but had to stop because he was in my door, blocking me.

I looked to his face to see his eyes aimed at the pie carrier.

"Coert—" I started to greet (as well as ask him to get out of my way because it was cold and I wanted my dog and I to get indoors, but after seeing the outside, I also was dying to see the inside).

I spoke no more and not only because he interrupted me by whispering, "Pie."

Suddenly I was a nervous wreck again, wondering if I should have reminded Coert of something we'd had, something that was sweet, but it was also a reminder of what had come in between.

I didn't get to wonder long because half a second later, the pie was not in my hands, though one of my hands had been captured by Coert's and I was being pulled out of my Jag.

I just had enough time to slam the door before Coert was dragging me toward the door of his house, Midnight moving excitedly alongside us.

We were through the garage and in a laundry room that was relatively spacious but a complete disaster with shopping bags and rolls of Christmas wrap and not one, not two, but three hampers of laundry, men's clothes intermingled with little girl's.

I had no time to experience what a treasure it was to have that first look into Coert's everyday life, a life he shared with his daughter, that first look being an actual *first look* since I'd never even had that before, considering when we were together he'd all but moved in to his friend Casey's with me, because I was in a kitchen.

I saw it was dark and masculine, various gleaming woods, open shelves, iron mesh fronted cupboards, pounded iron over a big stove, when I was stopped in front of a stainless steel fridge.

"This need refrigerating?"

I was thinking about wood, laundry, little-girl tights, the bag I'd left in my car, the fact Coert had a glass trifle bowl filled with oranges on his kitchen island.

In other words I wasn't following.

"Sorry?" I whispered.

"The pie, Cady. Does it need refrigerating?"

"It's…um, for you. And Janie. And Kim. For tomorrow night, if you want to take it with you. It's a butterbeer pie. I don't know if Janie's old enough for Harry Potter but I thought—"

I emitted a small cry when my arm was yanked and I went flying, slamming into Coert's front.

I looked up at him to see his chin in his neck looking down at me, holding the pie to the side.

"Does this pie…need…refrigerating?" he growled.

"Yes," I breathed staring up into his eyes.

Heated eyes.

Oh my.

He let me go long enough to open the fridge, shove the pie in among a lot of other stuff, and close the fridge.

Then my purse was taken from me, tossed to the island, he had my hand in his and he was tugging me.

I was looking around, not taking much in, but I glimpsed the Christmas tree in the living room across the hall, which from that close looked even less like the subtle holiday décor on the outside of the house.

It was bright and jolly and lively and playful.

That was all I took in before I was dragged up some stairs.

Midnight followed us.

Coert turned right at the top, and as I was attached to him, I went with him.

We entered a room that was also masculine. Painted a dark, coastal blue, it was dominated by a huge bed.

And that was all I could take in before I was twirled around with my back to that bed and my knit cap was torn from my head.

I felt my hair flying (and frizzing) but all I did was stare up at Coert.

My gloves were pulled off and thrown to the side. Then my jacket tugged down my arms.

Once that fell to my feet, Coert took a step away and ripped his sweater off his body.

I stopped breathing.

My sweater went next with Coert taking it.

I started panting.

Coert put his hands under my arms, lifted me straight up and then he was on me in his bed.

On me.

And *all over me.*

So I took that as my invitation to attempt to be all over him.

He'd wanted us to slow down the second time last night, a goal he did not achieve.

He didn't achieve it this time either.

The only difference between the three was that the last two times I got my opportunities to have the top, to take what I wanted.

But this time, even when I tried to roll him over, Coert kept me pinned to my back and he took from me.

And took.

And *took.*

His hands. His mouth. His lips. His tongue. His teeth.

It was *glorious.*

He'd divested me of my bra, and I was arching a nipple into his mouth and moaning when I lost that mouth because I lost Coert completely.

When I'd opened my eyes and searched dazedly for where he'd gone, my search wasn't long.

He was beside the bed, tearing down his jeans.

Shakily, my hands went to the belt on mine.

I got it undone and was working on the fly when he lifted a leg and yanked off one of my boots.

The other one.

My socks.

Then latching onto the hems, he hauled off my jeans.

And when he did, the denim scored a path of fire down my legs that chased right back up between them.

Oh *my.*

I whimpered.

He bent over me to tug my panties down my legs.

He was naked above me, tall, lean, beautiful.

I was naked on his bed and I knew by the darkness in his face he liked what he was seeing.

He tore his eyes away from me, opened the drawer to his nightstand and then treated me to something I never would imagine would be so sexy to watch that it was *excruciating*.

That being watching him roll a condom on his cock.

My mouth watered as between my legs grew even wetter and I nearly came out of the bed to get to him.

I didn't get a chance because Coert surged over me, kicking my legs open with his knee.

He settled between them and stared at my face as I felt his hand go between us.

And then I was squirming, looking into his eyes, feeling him rub the head of his cock hard against my clit.

Simply amazing.

"Coert," I breathed.

He rubbed harder.

"*Coert*," I begged, lifting up my knees, rounding him with my arms, pressing down on his cock.

He slipped it down, and then as fast as it had all gone, he slid inside and he did it just that slowly.

I felt my lips part, my scalp tingle, my stomach drop, my arms tighten and my pussy convulse as he filled me.

He hooked a hand behind one of my raised, bent knees and gripped tight as his gaze imprisoned mine and he started thrusting inside me.

I locked my thighs against his sides and held on, mewing then gasping.

His other hand slid over my belly, down, his finger hit my clit and started fluttering.

And right then I felt it rise inside me.

I pushed it away.

It pushed back.

Staring into Coert's eyes as he kept driving inside, his finger making miracles, my hands slid up his spine to hold on to his hair, and I again pushed it back.

It threatened to consume me.

I started panting.

Coert broke eye contact to slide his temple down mine and say in my ear, "Please, baby, give that to me."

And I let go.

Turning my head to shove my face in his neck, my fists tightened in his hair, my legs convulsed against his sides, and just like the two times the night before, my orgasm engulfed me, blistering through my body, sweeping me away into nothing.

Nothing, that was, except a world where there was a Coert and me.

Vaguely, I felt his finger at my clit go away as I heard his grunts turn into altogether different noises, the driving force behind his thrusts growing more powerful but uncontrolled and I shivered anew knowing he was coming with me.

Together we flew and together we drifted down to earth, to his bed, his room, this world, this life.

Ending still with a Coert and me.

Yes, it was glorious.

It was as I felt his breath turn steady on my neck that it occurred to me that, outside of kissing him back, doing a lot of squirming, moaning, holding on and some touching, he'd given me that and I'd given him nothing in return.

"I just held on," I whispered.

"What?" he murmured against my neck.

I realized my fingers were still tight in his hair and that probably didn't feel great so I let him go instantly, suddenly mortified.

"Cady?"

I slid my eyes to him to see he'd lifted his head and was looking down at me.

And I sounded just as mortified as I was when I announced, "I just held on. You did all the work. You gave me all that and I didn't give you anything."

He stared down at me.

Then he burst out laughing.

I stared up at him.

Then I glared up at him.

And finally I pushed at his shoulders to slither out from under him because really…

How embarrassing!

He let the back of my knee go to plant his forearm in the bed so he didn't give me all his weight when he clamped an arm around my waist and held me right where I was.

"Oh no, you're not takin' off on me this time," he muttered.

I looked to his nose, his shoulder, the ceiling.

"Cady," he called.

"I'm out of practice," I stated.

His body started shaking again.

It felt very nice.

I was still mortified.

"Cady," he repeated.

"I'll get in the swing of things again," I promised his ear.

"Cady, honey, are you being serious here?" he asked, still sounding amused but also sounding incredulous.

"No man wants a woman who just lays there and…" I didn't know how to finish that so I mumbled, "Lays there."

"Don't know about other guys, but this guy, the one who's still inside you and likes it there, gets off on his woman bein' so into what he's doin' to her she latches onto his hair and clamps on with her legs and, I'll note, when you do that other parts of you clamp too. So you might not think you did anything, Cady, but you did a lot of things and they were all really fuckin' good."

I finally looked at him.

"Really?" I asked skeptically.

"I think if pressed a guy can fake it but just sayin', I'm not that good of an actor."

And as suddenly as I grew mortified, his words made me dissolve into hilarity and I giggled underneath him, liking very much how his face got soft while he watched me.

My giggles were fading away when he kissed me deep and sweet then lifted his head.

When he did, I saw he was no longer amused.

"You made me pie."

I moved a hand to cup his cheek. "Yes. Is that okay?"

"I wanted to give you a tour of the house. Make sure Midnight was good. Show you the tree my kid made since she picked all the ornaments."

So that explained the tree.

And that made me *adore* his tree and I hadn't even taken it all in.

Coert kept speaking.

"Pour you wine. Relax. Make you comfortable in my space. But I saw that pie and dragged you to my bed. So yeah, honey. I think it's safe to say that's okay."

Even if it was okay, I still felt the need to explain.

But I did it quietly.

"It went bad for us, but before it did, it was pure beauty and I want to stop that from causing pain and start remembering the way it really was."

"Yeah," he agreed.

I slid my hand back and stroked his hair. "I'm glad you liked it."

"I liked it."

I grinned at him. "Especially that much."

Coert grinned back. "Definitely liked it that much and I haven't even tasted the pie."

He'd like it even more when he tasted the pie.

We looked into each other eyes, sharing a moment of nostalgia and togetherness and intimacy that made me want to laugh. To cry. To shout with glee.

I kept silent and let it just…be.

After long, beautiful moments, Coert whispered, "You want wine?"

I nodded.

"I'm losin' you so I'm gonna slip out and deal with this condom."

"Okay," I said softly.

He kissed me. He slipped out. He pulled a throw spread over the bottom of his bed over me and I watched him walk to and through a door before I saw the light go on, sharing what I knew. It was his bathroom.

Midnight, quiet and absent during the excitement in bed, as she'd been the night before (couch and bed), shambled after him.

I held the throw to me and sat up, realizing that the lights were on at both nightstands and they had been when we entered the room.

I also felt something lovely and warm niggle inside me because Coert's favorite color was blue. I knew that back in the day and I saw it now all around me. The walls were deep, dark blue. The covers and sheets the same.

The throw a shade darker, but the same. Even the button-backed accent chair and matching ottoman in a corner were the same. All the way to the tile I could see in his bathroom.

The only change in color was the dark wood baseboards, headboard and footboard and the taupe shades on the lamps.

My eyes drifted to the light on his nightstand (the base was glass, but it was blue) and it occurred to me the lights were on outside, in the kitchen, in the hall, the living room where the tree was, everywhere.

Coert came back and I wasn't thinking about lights.

I was seeing him naked in a time where my world hadn't been altered in an impossibly magnificent way so it was a time I could enjoy the view.

And I was watching him walk to me thinking he'd seemed leaner years ago, but now he seemed bigger, not large or stocky, just like there was more to him. His stomach was flat, and if not boxed to cut perfection, there was definition down the center, and up in his pectorals. His hipbones came out in slight relief. His chest and stomach were lightly furred (as they had been years ago).

And his shaft was perfectly formed, nestled in dark curls that made it stand out even when it wasn't hard or it was semi-erect, like it was now.

His body was beautiful, head to foot.

I liked it all. I loved some parts more than others (forearms, behind, pectorals, to name a few).

But I'd always adored his cock.

I blinked when I lost sight of it because I was abruptly tangled up in Coert's blue throw, as well as Coert's limbs.

I looked to his face.

He was smiling.

Widely.

He had amazing teeth.

Another part of him I loved and not just because they were attractive to look at.

"Afraid you're gonna have to give it a rest, honey. As much as it wants to show you its appreciation for the look you just gave it, it needs more than ten minutes to recuperate. And that's not because I'm not twenty-seven anymore. If you'll think back, it needed more time than that then too."

"Sorry?"

"My dick."

I felt my eyes get wide. "Sorry?"

"Baby, you were staring at my dick like you wanted to pounce on it."

I undoubtedly was.

I looked to his ear again, and again I was mortified.

He started laughing, pulling me close and tangling us tighter.

"You have a lot of lights on," I declared in some desperation to get us off the subject of me staring at his cock.

"Yeah," he agreed, still chuckling. "Got a kid who can't reach switches, not to mention a lot of the lamps. Learned she wants to go somewhere without breaking her neck, or even taking a header, both I'd really prefer she not do, and feel free to go anywhere she wants, that I need to keep the path lit whatever she decides that path will be. She's not here I do it anyway to keep in the habit."

I felt myself melt into him, sliding a hand to rest it at the base of his throat and saying, "I'm beginning to think you're not a good dad, you're an amazing one."

"That's the goal," he muttered, gazing into my eyes.

I gazed into his and allowed myself to enjoy the show.

Coert broke it asking quietly, "Midnight taken care of with goin' outside?"

"It probably wouldn't hurt to give her another go as well as a tour of your house so she knows the lay of the land."

I said this last because my dog should know the lay of the land.

And I wanted that too.

"Then let's get dressed. I'll take her out. Then get you wine. And I'll give you and your dog a tour."

"That sounds like a plan, Coert."

"Yeah," he agreed.

But he didn't set about doing it.

He kissed me.

He did it for some time.

And only after he'd done that did he set about instigating our plan.

"IT'S A GOOD idea."

"It is?" I asked.

It was after Coert took Midnight out in his backyard.

After, while he was doing this and I was out getting my bag, I noticed two stainless steel dog bowls on a mat on the floor by the door to the laundry room that he'd clearly gotten just for Midnight since he clearly didn't have a dog himself.

One bowl had water. The other had food.

It was after I dealt with that lovely show of thoughtfulness.

After he poured me wine, got himself a beer and walked Midnight and me through his house that was very attractive, very masculine, very *him*, every corner, every nook and cranny.

Except a little girl's room, which had white wallpaper on the walls that had big bright blue and pink flowers on it, a little bed with a pink satin comforter that had ruffles on the edges, a princess canopy hanging from the ceiling, and a white nightstand with a pink drawer that had a big swirly pink and white knob (among other equally very little girl things).

A room so perfect for a little girl, it was ridiculously perfect and there was no way it would have come about unless it came about like Coert had explained the Christmas tree had come about and she'd picked everything in it.

Yes, definitely yes.

He was an amazing dad.

"You do know, Sheriff," I said softly, standing in the doorway of Janie's room, "that evidence is clearly pointing to the fact you've got a great daughter because she's got an amazing father, and since she gets that, she gives it back."

These words came out of my mouth.

A growl surged up his throat.

And we then made out in the doorway to Janie's room.

But before I poured my wine down his back or did something highly inappropriate in the doorway to his daughter's room, Coert ended it and led me back downstairs to his couch.

It was after all that, the Christmas lights and the blazing fireplace with lamps turned low making it cozy, Coert pulling a blanket over us cuddled in the corner making it cozier, I'd told him about the deal I'd made with Mike.

I was certain he'd refuse.

But he'd immediately said it was a good idea.

"She has a lot of people in her life, Cady. So she's learned to be social," Coert explained. "Kim has a big family and they don't all live close but they get together a lot, especially during holidays. We both work so Janie goes to preschool and has a lot of friends, which means birthday parties and play dates and stuff like that. She comes into the station with me, and I have to keep a close eye no one takes off with her because the guys love her, everyone loves her and wants her sitting in their lap at their desk or hanging at the bench with them."

He pulled me closer and kept talking.

"She'll love having a big Christmas dinner even with people she doesn't know. She's used to things like that. But more, even at her age, I think it'll get in there that she's glad her dad has that. I live alone. I have friends. They love her. But it's not the same as what her mom's got. And the last time she saw you, you burst into tears. I don't know if she remembers it, but she probably does. She asked when I got back from you if I made you okay. It'll be good she sees you're okay."

I didn't want to think about that or how I'd go about explaining that if she remembered me.

We had to think about other things.

"You haven't had the chance to talk to Kim about me," I pointed out. "I'm not sure if I was Kim that I'd be good with this going this fast."

"First, I have news on that for you," he started interestingly, but when he went on it was not about that. "And second, this feeling is sure to fade but I have it and I'm aware I need to ride it out for now. This urgency to make up time, to build on what we got and make it stronger so it'll withstand if anything comes and shakes it. It feels like running to catch up because that's what we're doing. I don't know if we'll ever feel we're caught up. I just know we have enough on our plates to fight that back now so I'm gonna let that be what it has to be. But part of running to catch up is the fact that you're in my life. It's real. It's happening. It's not going to end. And Janie's a part of my life the same way. In other words, I'm not feeling like waiting, being cautious, hanging back. This does not mean I want to blindside my daughter with what's happening. But I don't have to think too hard on the fact this is gonna shake up her life and it's honestly a good idea to introduce you into it without putting too much pressure on her or you."

He stroked my back and kept speaking.

"We could do one on one. And knowing my kid, she'd be good with one on one. But we got this shot to make it fun and happy and about family and holiday and not just about you and her. I'm thinkin' it's a good idea we take it."

That made sense and it was his daughter, his choice, and last, I liked that he felt that way but only because I felt the same and it was a good strategy to deal with it, just allowing ourselves to feel it, "ride it out" and run to catch up because that was how it needed to be.

However, there was something else he said that took my attention.

"If that's what you want, I want what you want and you know Janie so you know best. But, Coert, what's the news on talking to Kim about me?" I asked.

He nodded in a way I suspected he nodded to his deputies quite often, matter of fact, and there was something confident about it that made my belly settle.

"Called Kim after we got off the phone this morning, asked if her sister or one of her friends could look after Janie after work so we could talk. She arranged that, and while you were having your dinner with your family, I took some chicken from Wayfarer's over to Kim's. We ate and I told her about you."

Okay, well, it was becoming very apparent that when Coert said he was riding out the urgency of running to catch up, he was not lying.

"You did?"

That came out squeaky and because of that, it made Coert grin.

"How did she take it?" I asked.

His grin died, my stomach went from settled to clenched and he took in a deep breath before he said, "She did not get up and do cartwheels before declaring she was going to plan our wedding shower."

Now my stomach dipped at the words "wedding shower."

Coert couldn't feel that so he kept on.

"But she understood. She told me she had a feeling what was holding me back was something like that. She already knew there was no chance for us. So now she's aware there's a you. She's aware that this is serious and it's gonna last. She's aware that you're gonna be a part of Janie's life and be that imminently. And honest to God, it threw me, but she also put together me working shit out with you was what pushed me to work shit out with her. So in the end she said she was grateful you came back so she and I could build something more for our daughter and just…" he shrugged, "find something that made me happy."

I had not allowed myself to think anything about Janie's mother because I had not allowed myself to think I had the right to think anything about Janie's mom.

If I had, from what I'd known, it would not be much.

But at that time I was glad I hadn't formed an opinion, because what she did was wrong but I knew how you could do things that were wrong, and if you allowed it time, they could turn out right.

"That's fantastic, Coert," I said quietly. "And I'm glad that's done for you and her. But I'm still not sure she wants this to happen for her daughter on Christmas."

"You got dinner sorted?"

I was confused at his question. "Sorry?"

"Christmas dinner. You already bought everything?" he asked.

I nodded.

"You skimp?"

I was again confused. "Skimp?"

"You skimpy in hopes there's no leftovers?" he explained.

"There are six males in that equation, and of those six, three are still growing boys, even if Dexter might never speak to me again if he knew I called him a 'growing boy.' They eat. A lot. So no. I don't skimp."

"Then you'll have enough if another male and a five-year-old show for dinner."

I understood him then and smiled.

I also nodded again.

"I'll call Kim tomorrow," he stated. "Share that with her and see where she's at. If you feel you have to make another pie or whatever, we'll go to the store before you go back home to get the stuff. But regardless, if you're good either way, then it's just good either way."

"Yes," I agreed.

His voice dipped low when he said, "If we make it hard, Cady, if we make a big deal of it, if we communicate there's something to worry about or we feel we might be doing something wrong, Janie'll read that. If we just are what we are right here and right now, and your family is good to her and me, which I know they'll be because they love you, then we've got nothing to worry about."

How marvelous that would be.

To have nothing to worry about.

"That said," he carried on. "I'd get the duty call with your folks done before Janie gets there because Pat made mention of them in a way I know they haven't changed. I also know Caylen was pulling his usual shit just months ago. So if they upset you, that'll upset me which in turn will upset Janie. And if you feel you gotta do it, I won't advise you this soon back into us not to do it. But I don't think it's good at this juncture that I see it, definitely not Janie seeing it, and I'll warn you now that when we got more time under our belts, we'll be talking about them."

As he spoke, my body grew more and more still but he didn't notice it until he was done talking.

And I had an idea what my face looked like when his eyes narrowed on it before they became angry.

Which prompted him to whisper ominously, "What?"

"They're dead, Coert."

The anger vanished while he did a very slow blink.

"What?" he asked.

"Both of them."

"I..." he trailed off then noted, "Christ, they can't have been that old."

"Dad suffered a stroke and Mom, well Mom..." I swallowed then told him the story of Mom.

When I was done, his repeat of, "Christ," was deeper.

"Yes," I whispered.

"So it's just Caylen," he remarked.

"Thus my attempt to confront him and force a reconciliation, which failed. This part of why I'm out here, why, when he knew he was close to the end, Patrick urged me to come, saying it was no coincidence two important men in my life lived just hours from each other but entire states away from me."

"So he brought you back to me," Coert murmured.

It was awkward but I had to get past that.

So I turned in his arms, pressing closer and saying, "He was a good man, Coert."

"You have a family who loves you, that Jag, that lighthouse, all the beautiful parts that were always you intact, not bitter, not broken, not sad, I got that a long time ago, honey."

It was then I did not want to laugh or shout with glee.

I just wanted to weep.

Coert saw it and I knew it when he reached a long arm to his coffee table to put down his beer so he could put both hands to my face, thumbs to the apples of my cheeks like he was preparing in case he had to sweep away tears.

It was shaky when I said, "He'd be happy this was happening."

"Yeah," he said gently.

"Ecstatic."

"Yeah," Coert repeated.

"I'm not going to cry," I lied.

A small smile and another, "Yeah."

A tear fell.

Looking in my eyes, Coert swept it away.

Another fell.

And Coert swept it away.

Another and a repeat from Coert.

Then I got myself together.

Coert saw that too, which was why he told me, "My parents are still alive and I got myself a younger brother who has a wife and four kids. Mom and Dad spent Thanksgiving to after New Year's last year with Janie and me, so they're spending the holidays with Braylon and his brood this year. They're retired and they like spoiling Janie so they come not frequent, but they aren't strangers. You'll meet them."

I'd never met his parents. For reasons that were obvious after, not during, he didn't talk about them.

I never even knew he had a brother.

And it was learning that and knowing I'd meet his parents that I realized that not only had I got Coert back, in getting him back, I was getting *Coert.*

Not just him or him and his daughter.

All of him in a way I'd never had him.

Knowing this, another tear fell.

"Honey," he murmured, sweeping it away at the same time pulling my face closer.

He gave me a soft kiss before he pushed me an inch away.

"They'll love you," he whispered.

God, I hoped so.

The two syllables were trembling when I replied, "Okay."

"You need to feel this. I get that," he said. "We'll have tough times navigating our way back to us together. I get that too. They might bite us in the ass down the line just because they were that tough. But once we get through that, we'll be fighters so we'll know how to keep fighting to keep it good."

With my face still held in his hands, I nodded before I decided a change of subject was in order and forced out, "Braylon?"

He understood me and I knew it when he answered, "Dad."

"Yes?" I prompted.

"His name is Richard. When he was growing up, people called him Dick. Obviously, time wore on, that wasn't something he was feelin' like sticking with and he was determined his boys would not get the shit he got, so John was out. Willy. You get the picture. It goes without saying he went way overboard. But at least none of our teachers growin' up got us confused with anyone else."

"I love the name Coert."

His handsome face got soft before he pulled me to him again and gave me another light kiss.

When it was done, I stared at that handsome face so close, right there, all mine again, made more handsome with the tenderness he was showing, the moment we were sharing, and I decided I had to do it because he had to know it.

And maybe it was wavering courage or maybe I just felt I needed to be as close to him as I could get when I did it.

But I pushed through his hold so I could put my lips to his ear when I said, "Obviously I love Coert. But I loved you as Tony too. I love you no matter what because the simple matter of fact is, I just love *you*."

His fingers gripped me around the back of my neck. They pulled me back and I held my breath when I saw his face.

"You done with your wine?" he asked abruptly and rather harshly.

I took in the expression on his face and someplace very private quivered.

"Are you, um…going to ravage me again?" I asked.

"You want me to sit here and try to find words to tell you how much I love you or you want me to show you?"

Totally show me.

"Can I take my wine?" I asked, and at our movement, with a surprised woof from Midnight who'd been woken from her nap lying by the fire, we were up.

Then he had my hand in his and was dragging me to the stairs.

"I'll come get it after," he said.

I grinned at his back not only because Coert was dragging me to the stairs in order to ravage me again.

But also because he was holding my hand.

Eighteen

TERMINALLY IN LOVE

CADY

Present day…

I opened my eyes and saw dark-blue sheets.

I rolled to my back and looked to the other side of the bed to see it mussed, the pillow depressed, but the space was empty.

I sat up holding the covers to my chest and looked around, realizing there was sunlight coming around the closed drapes in Coert's bedroom.

I'd slept late.

Not a surprise since I'd had little sleep the night before, and when Coert took me back up to his room to ravage me, he'd finally gotten to a point where he could take his time.

This he did.

We did.

So when I'd conked out naked in his arms after, I'd conked *out.*

On that thought, I heard a faraway whistle.

I threw the covers aside and saw Coert's sweater on the floor.

Way back when, I wouldn't hesitate to pull on one of Coert's tees or shirts and Coert didn't hesitate to share he didn't care. He liked it. To the point sometimes he'd pick up his own shirt and hand it to me when we were done doing the things we'd been doing and I needed something to put on.

So right then, I grabbed that sweater, tugged it over my head, pushed my hands through the arms and moved to the back of the room.

I pulled the curtains aside and saw Coert outside with another sweater on, jeans, a scarf wrapped around his throat, snow boots on his feet, throwing a stick to Midnight, who was bounding through the high snow to grab it.

She got it and brought it back to him.

I'd never played fetch with her.

I didn't even know she knew how to play fetch.

But I was arrested by the beauty of her jumping through the snow, this enthusiastic and graceful, the thick bed of soft flakes taking away the lasting results of a terrible injury and giving her freedom to move again.

Not to mention I was arrested by the vision of Coert out in the snow in the morning playing with my dog.

I made the decision to play fetch with Midnight every morning, hopefully doing this with Coert, before I moved to my bag that Coert had brought up and thrown on his chair. I got out the fresh pair of panties and my bathroom stuff and headed to his bathroom to take care of business.

When I was done, I went back to the bag, pulled on some socks, and still in his sweater, I moved out of his room, through his house, taking it in in the light.

He'd been there awhile, I saw. He'd taken that time to make every inch of it his, I saw that too. It was all very masculine but it was homey and comfortable.

I could live there, happily. With her room like it was and the rest with her dad all around, Janie undoubtedly already lived there happily when she was with her father.

Making my way to the kitchen (and coffee and hopefully Coert since the back door led from the laundry room), it made me feel good he had this. That he'd created this. That he'd lived his life without me but made it a good one in a variety of ways. He had a job of influence and authority. A great house. A beautiful daughter. He said he had friends. He said his men loved his daughter but I suspected they also felt some of that for him, and surely respect.

With warmth filling the pit of my belly at these thoughts, waking up in Coert's house, knowing I was moving to the only man I'd ever loved who was in my life again, I made it to the bottom of the stairs and started toward the kitchen to see Coert and Midnight had come back in since she was rushing toward me exuberantly, tail wagging.

I gave her cold coat a rubdown then straightened, and she fell to my side as I walked into the kitchen.

Scarf gone, Coert was sitting at the opposite end of the island, and the minute I hit the door, his eyes went from the newspaper spread out in front of him to me.

They then instantly dropped down to his sweater on my body.

I was not surprised at that.

But I was still surprised.

"You read the newspaper?"

His eyes came back to my face. "You don't?"

Absolutely not.

I had enough bad news in my life. I didn't need to seek it out daily.

"No. But what I mean is, you read an actual newspaper? You don't just go online?"

"Got my face in technology a lot of the day every day. On my phone. On my computer. On my tablet." He put fingers to the edge of the paper spread out across the island and gave it a shake. "Gotta give myself a dose of old school or I'll turn into a microchip or something."

I smiled at his quip and walked to the other side of the island, spying the trifle bowl of oranges when I did.

"The trifle bowl is a nice touch, Coert," I told him.

He was studying me in a strange way and I didn't think that strange came from his confused, "Pardon?"

"The trifle bowl with the oranges."

He glanced to it and then back to me. "That's called a trifle bowl?"

I grinned at him. "Yes."

He did not grin back when he explained, "Mom. She says my place looks like a man puked all over it. That's why I got that bowl. Rocking chairs out front." He lifted a hand and flicked it to the sink where my wineglass from last night was sitting on the edge. "And really cool wineglasses."

I kept grinning at him.

He still did not grin at me.

He raised his brows. "You gonna come here?"

I definitely was.

After I got coffee.

I looked to his mug and was about to scan for the coffeemaker when he said, "C'm 'ere, Cady."

His voice was deeper, richer, and I forgot all about coffee.

I went there.

Coert swiveled to the side on his stool when I did. His heels were up on a rung with his legs splayed wide.

When I got close, he curled an arm around me and pulled me between those legs so I was a whole lot closer.

"You sleep good?" he murmured, looking at my mouth.

"Yes," I whispered, seeing him looking at my mouth so I looked at his.

Another part of him I loved. He had beautiful lips.

Those lips moved.

"Midnight's been out," he told me.

"'Kay," I breathed, my gaze dreamily rising to his.

His eyes lifted to mine just as his hand dipped, then went up and under his sweater.

My breath hitched.

"Like you showin' in my kitchen wearing my sweater," he shared.

I hadn't been cold and I still wasn't.

But my legs were trembling.

"I…good," I pushed out.

His hand went from the skin of my hip to the small of my back and he pushed me so I was pressed against him from crotch to chest.

"You hungry?" he asked.

I might have felt morning peckish on my way down the stairs.

I felt something else entirely in that moment.

I still forced out a wispy, "Yes."

His mouth moved forward and touched mine, his eyes so close we almost gave each other butterfly kisses with our lashes, and with his lips moving against mine, he muttered, "Me too."

He brushed my lips with his before I let out an involuntary squeal because I was suddenly going up.

And then I was behind to his newspaper, Coert bending over me, successfully pressing my back to the island.

He didn't kiss me. His breaths skimming across my lips, his eyes staring into mine, both his hands went up the sweater, the skin of my sides, his thumbs splayed to skate over my ribs to come to rest right under my breasts.

My breath hitched again then came uneasy as I stared up at him, lost in the sight of him, his cold-of-outdoors-still-clinging, warmth-of-Coert smell, the feel of his hands, this together moment of morning decadence.

His fingers moved back down, caught at the sides of my panties, and I skimmed my teeth over my bottom lip, watched his eyes darken as he took that in, and whispered, "Coert."

"Yeah," he growled, the dark in his eyes deepening, his fingers curling into the material of my panties, stretching them against me, causing a shiver to slither between my legs. "Coert. Say it again, Cady."

Feeling my panties bite in, looking into his eyes, it came almost as a whimper. "Coert."

He started to tug my panties down.

"Again," he ordered.

"Coert," I panted.

He touched his lips to mine, a dark fire burning in his eyes.

Then he disappeared and my panties were pulled down my legs, my calves. I felt them catch at one shin before they fell to the floor and I lifted my head to follow Coert and saw him toss one of my thighs over a shoulder, press the other one gently aside…

And his mouth was on me.

My head hit the island with a *thunk* but I didn't feel it.

I felt other, vastly better things.

I slid a hand into his thick hair and moaned, "*Coert.*"

"Yeah," he grunted his approval into my sex and then kept at me.

I dug a heel into his back, pressed myself into his face and felt it.

God.

I felt it.

He'd been good at this before.

But now…

Amazing.

As he built it in me, my noises filled his kitchen, my heel plowed into his back, my fingers clenched and unclenched in his hair and he wrapped his arms around the backs of my thighs.

Running his hands over my belly, up under his sweater, his mouth working beauty between my legs, his hands found my breasts, curled around. Thumbs moving hard over my stiffened nipples, electricity shot between my legs to add to the sparks he was making and I cried out.

"Say it," he growled between my legs, putting fingers to thumbs and pinching my nipples.

God, that felt good.

I squirmed under him and gave him what he wanted immediately.

"Coert."

He went at me with his mouth, sucking, licking, darting his tongue inside and then again, against my clit, he demanded roughly, "Say it."

My hand pressing his head to me, I gasped, "Coert."

He gave me back his mouth, his fingers squeezing and lightly twisting. I ground into his face and wrapped my other leg around his shoulder.

"Coert," I breathed, putting my other hand to his head.

He ate.

He squeezed.

"Coert," I panted.

His hands left my breasts to go to my ribs and pulse me down into his mouth.

Yes.

My back arched, the top of my head dug into the island, my hips bore down on him and I cried, "*Coert!*" as it rolled over me, through me, sweeping me away in wave after wave of ecstasy.

When it started to leave me, my back relaxed, my eyes opened, but they'd only go hooded. I felt Coert trailing his lips along my inner thigh, his hand across the top of the other one, his other arm coming from around me.

I then felt his finger between my legs, running from clit down through the wet folds, dipping slightly in when he found me. My hips jerked then sought his light touch as the finger traced back up and became a warm hand cupping me intimately.

Coert removed my leg from his shoulder, slid out from under the other one and came up, kissing me on the skin over the curls between my legs.

And then he had hands to my waist and he was lifting me, turning me. Gravity pulled at the sweater and Coert adjusted his hands to let it, allowing it to cover me again. I ended up seated on his thigh as he resumed his position on his stool, my legs dangling between his spread ones, my head tucked under his chin, his arm wrapped around me holding me close.

I worked at steadying my breathing, which had gone slightly erratic again at being held so casually yet so tenderly, and I watched with dazed eyes as he reached to his coffee mug.

It disappeared as he put it to his lips.

It reappeared as he set it back on the island.

And after a bit, he turned the page on his newspaper.

I cuddled closer, and the instant I started to do that, his arm around me got tighter, he adjusted his jaw to fit my head closer to his neck, and I was breathing deeply for a different reason, fighting back emotion at all he was giving me.

I honestly didn't know whether to laugh or sob that Coert would make me come with his mouth while I was on top of his newspaper, then set me in his lap and resumed drinking coffee and catching up on the news.

We'd had an active and highly enjoyable sex life when we'd been together before.

But we had not had the kind of life where you could eat out your woman and then read your newspaper while you carried on caffeinating yourself in the morning.

"You good?" His voice still mildly rough from what he'd done to me cut through my thoughts.

"If you have to ask, you weren't paying attention," I replied.

The roughness was still there, but he'd added amusement when he muttered, "Oh, I was payin' attention, honey."

"Mmm," I mumbled, cuddling closer.

"You want coffee?' he asked.

I did.

But much more, I never wanted to move from where I right then was.

"In a minute."

He reached out to his mug but didn't take a sip.

I saw it come straight to me and I looked into its creamy depths, seeing not even half of it was gone and it was still steaming.

Back in the day, we took our coffee the same way.

I wrapped my hands around the warm mug, Coert's fell away, and I lifted it to my lips to take a sip.

And discovered we still did.

I fought back an audible sigh at that knowledge and the sweet intimacy of sharing Coert's coffee.

But I still sighed.

Silently.

But happily.

Coert turned the page on the newspaper again.

"What about you?" I whispered after taking another sip.

"Never read another newspaper again without thinking of going down on you on it, so trust me on this, I'm all good, Cady."

I grinned smugly into the coffee mug.

And right then, sadly, living our impossibly real dream of being together again was broken when Midnight barked.

I heard her start to move and bark again before a loud, clearly angry knock came at the door.

Coert's body went solid and mine followed suit.

Midnight again barked and I heard her nails against Coert's wood floors as she headed toward the front door.

The knocking stopped, started again, Midnight went into a continual bark, and I pulled my head from his neck to look up at him and see his jaw was set, his eyes aimed in the direction of the front door.

He didn't like our impossibly real dream broken either.

He got up, his arm tightening around me to hold me to him as he slid me off his lap and put me on my stocking feet.

"Stay here," he ordered over Midnight's barking, not looking at me, eyes still aimed in the direction of the front door.

He moved that way too, and when he did, I put the mug down, glanced at the floor, found my panties, bent to grab them and stepped into them, quickly pulling them up my legs.

Midnight stopped barking only to give out a happy, welcoming *woof.*

I would know why when I heard Coert's murmur (if not the words) and then a loud, demanding, "She in there?"

Elijah.

It was then *I* was on the move.

"I just heard about this shit," Elijah bit out before I made it to the door from kitchen to hall.

I moved into the hall and Midnight dashed to me to share the good news Elijah was there.

I gave her head a rub even as I carried on walking toward Coert, who stood in the open door, Midnight trotting beside me.

But my eyes were aimed at what was on his porch.

Elijah filling the doorway.

And Verity standing beside him, uncomfortable to the point she looked like she was fretting.

"We were having coffee in town," she said fast, the instant she laid eyes on me. "I told him. I didn't think he'd get mad because it's, well…*awesome.* But he got mad. I tried, Auntie Cady. I promise I tried to talk him out of coming. But he called Uncle Mike, and Uncle Mike gave him the sheriff's address and now…" she looked like she gulped, "we're here."

How Mike had Coert's address I didn't have to guess.

It was how Pat had it and used it to go talk to Coert.

The investigator's reports.

It was Christmas Eve.

And that evening Mike's early present that he wouldn't want was going to be getting a piece of my mind.

"It's okay, honey," I murmured, coming to stand by Coert who immediately put an arm around my waist and pulled me to his side.

Elijah was staring down at Coert's sweater on my body with a comical look of disbelief.

"Go back to the kitchen, Cady. You stand here, you'll catch a chill," Coert said quietly.

I didn't get the chance to refuse this request because Elijah announced, "A week ago, you were movin' back to Denver because of this guy."

"Elijah—" I began.

"And now you're bringin' Midnight over to his house," Elijah spoke over me, saying this like I was taking my dog with me on a trip to have tea with Satan.

"This is complicated," I told him.

"I explained that," Verity put in quickly. "I…it probably wasn't mine to tell, but when I shared I thought it was good news," she went on to explain just as quickly.

"Really, it's okay, honey," I said to her.

"Verity, I'm Coert," Coert put in, and I watched Verity look to Coert and her eyes danced a little before she smiled a shy smile.

"I'm Verity, Aunt Cady's niece."

"Got that," Coert muttered, amusement back in his voice.

"Jesus, are we serious here?" Elijah clipped, jerking a thumb at Coert. "Because of this guy, a week ago you were *flippin' out.*"

"I'd invite you two in to give you time and explain but I hope you get that this is our first morning together in a very long time, and I kinda want it to be just me and Cady," Coert said.

"And I kinda want your assurances you're not gonna dick her over," Elijah reported.

I felt my body stiffen but Coert's didn't, not even a little bit.

Relaxed and very easily, he simply, but very firmly, said, "You don't have my assurances that I'm not gonna dick her over. You have my promise I'm not gonna dick her over. We're together. That means something to me because I'm in love with her and I have been for years. But this time, I'm going to do everything in my power to protect it."

Elijah's head jerked at that.

Verity smiled at that.

And I pressed myself in Coert's side at that.

"I…well…uh, shit," Elijah mumbled.

"I cannot tell you the relief I feel that I won't be alone in looking after Cady," Coert continued. "Her family's here now but they live far away, so until she can build her crew here, you and I are all she's got and it's good to know I'm not alone in giving her that."

It was then I melted into his side (even though he wasn't correct, I had Walt and Amanda, Rob and Trish, Jackie and maybe the two blondes from town, and I made a note to share that with him, just later).

Verity looked like she was fighting clapping her hands together and jumping up and down.

Elijah was staring at Coert with his mouth hanging open.

"Sometime later you and me'll go get a beer and get to know each other. But now it's cold, the door is open, I haven't given Cady breakfast yet so I hope you don't take offense when I ask us to end this here. For now," Coert finished.

"Right, uh…" Elijah took in Coert's sweater on my body again before he shifted awkwardly and lifted a hand to scratch the back of his head, "I'll just take Verity back."

This brought to my attention that Verity and Elijah were getting coffee at all.

I looked to her and widened my eyes.

She looked to me, now beaming, and widened her eyes back.

I fought giving her a thumb's up.

Midnight danced around all of us excitedly, probably wondering why Verity and Elijah weren't coming in.

"Have a good Christmas Eve," Coert drew a line under it, also drawing me away from the door.

"Right, yeah, uh…you too," Elijah said and looked at me. "Later, Cady?"

"Later, Elijah," I said softly and turned my eyes to Verity. "Later, honey. I'll be home around five. Okay?"

She nodded. "Have a *great* Christmas Eve, Auntie Cady."

I gave her a different kind of smile and said, "I will, sweetie."

"Midnight," Coert called while closing the door.

My dog dashed in.

I spied Elijah turning stiltedly to Verity but then reaching a hand casually to take hers before he guided her to Coert's steps as Coert closed the door.

When he turned to me, I tipped my head back and my body forward, pressing into my hands in his chest and lifting up on my toes whereupon I whispered conspiratorially, "They're *out* for *coffee*."

Coert slid his arms around me, doing it grinning.

"Yeah."

I looked to the door then to him.

"He was holding her hand," I shared.

"Yeah," Coert agreed.

"I…do you…you're a guy. Would a guy take a girl out for coffee if he wasn't, you know, interested in her?"

"She's young but she's cute and my guess is he hasn't missed that so that answer would be no. But he's all about you, though not in that way, in the way he thinks the world of you and she's your young, pretty niece. So that answer is different since no way in hell he's gonna go there. Sorry to burst your bubble, but gotta share that coffee was a friendly with his landlord slash woman he feels he needs to look after slash friend's pretty niece."

I felt my face fall as I fell back to my heels.

"She the one in Connecticut?" Coert asked.

"She's at Yale."

Coert's expression went guarded.

So I asked, "What?"

"That guy is a solid guy but he's rough and I bet he knows it. She's at Yale and she dresses like you and I bet he hasn't missed it. So baby, think you best let it be what it is now and don't get your hopes up. Definitely don't raise hers."

"Verity's not like that," I shared.

"She's at Yale. She's a Moreland. He didn't have the money to get his own place after his girl got shot of him. Again, Cady, don't get your hopes up or hers."

"She won't care," I told him.

"He will," he told me knowingly.

"Oh," I muttered, seeing the wisdom in this statement, my gaze again drifting to the door.

His arms gave me a gentle shake so I looked back at Coert.

"She's young. She'll find the right guy."

I nodded.

"And he's a good man. He'll find the right girl."

I nodded again.

"Now can we have breakfast?" he asked.

I made a mental note to have a chat with Verity so she'd manage her expectations when it came to Elijah.

And I made another mental note to hide my disappointment when I did that.

Then I nodded one more time.

Coert's arms went from around me but his hand took mine and he led me back to the kitchen.

He sat me on his stool.

He made me my own cup of coffee.

And I read his paper as Coert made breakfast for me.

COERT

"IT'S OKAY BY me."

Coert looked from his place in his living room to the kitchen where Cady was, paper, ribbon, bags and the presents he'd bought Janie and hadn't yet wrapped strewn all over his island, Cady hard at work wrapping.

Her choice.

And she'd made it with apparent glee.

Something that made Coert gleeful because he freaking hated wrapping presents.

"You know you can say no," he said to Kim.

She was silent.

He turned his back to Cady and his eyes to Janie's tree before he said, "I bought this, where we are now, I get it and it sucks that I did that to you, making you think you have to agree to important shit so I won't get ticked."

"This isn't that, Coert."

"Okay, you say that but I gotta believe that's true before I tick you off by doin' something you say is okay to do but you don't think it is, and then that bites me in the ass later and I got no ground to stand on because I bought that too."

"Coert," she said slowly. "Okay, I'll admit, this is going very fast. You told me about her yesterday. You want our daughter to meet her family tomorrow. Which is Christmas. But…I think…well, I guess that, uh… you know…I have to put the shoe on the other foot. I mean, I know it's not the same as you falling terminally in love with a girl while you were undercover, and then all the drama that happened after your cop status was outed, but I was really, *really* into my high school boyfriend. And he broke up with me because his family moved to Spokane. And say he came back to live in town and told me he'd been in love with me all this time and couldn't live without me. And his family was here for Christmas but they were going back to Spokane, and who knew when they'd all get to meet me or Janie. If I had that shot to let Janie meet him and his family when everybody's buzzing on the Christmas vibe and it's sure to be all good, I'd wanna take it and I'd hope you'd get it."

Coert felt his lips twitching. "Terminally in love?"

He heard the smile in her voice when she replied, "Well, you kinda died for all other women when you met her."

"Yeah," he muttered, liking the smile in her voice, the amusement she gave him and he really liked that was where they were when they were talking about something like this.

But mostly, he was liking that description because it was true. That happened.

And now Cady was back, wrapping Christmas gifts at his island.

"You sound different."

She sounded different when she said that and all amusement fled at how that was.

"Kim—"

She spoke over him.

"Like a new Coert. I can tell you're being sensitive to me but I can still hear it."

"Kim—"

"You're happy."

Coert fell silent.

"She gives that to you. You give that to Janie. If she and her family give that to Janie, Coert, how can I say no?"

It was then, for the first time in a long time, Coert remembered why he'd spent four years with Janie's mom.

"I appreciate this, Kim, but still, think on it. We'll talk more after Janie goes to sleep. Okay?"

"You mean, at one o'clock in the morning when her Santa excitement has worn her out?"

Coert smiled. "Maybe earlier. We'll talk quiet."

He heard her laugh.

Yeah, he remembered why he gave her four years and more, why he took them, and it might be selfish but listening to her laugh he was glad he'd had them.

Because now he could focus on that while he was building something more solid under the family Janie had rather than focusing on something that wasn't like that at all.

"Right, we'll talk quiet," she agreed. "And I'll let you go. Bring your appetite. Christmas Eve dinner is beef tenderloin."

"I'll come hungry," he assured. "And Cady made us a pie."

He heard her chuckle before, "Perfect. Janie's like her dad. Loves cupcakes but it's always been about pie. Good start to this Cady earning devotion from our girl."

He liked the chuckle.

And he liked the idea of Janie giving something like that to Cady.

"Right," he muttered, but even muttered it too came out amused.

"Okay, Coert. Do you wanna talk to Janie?"

"Yeah."

She gave him to his daughter.

His daughter talked his ear off for ten minutes.

Coert barely said a word until he said goodbye.

When he'd disconnected, he stared at Janie's tree.

Then he walked into his kitchen to give Cady the news.

"I KNOW IT'S you."

Coert looked from shoving clothes into the washer to Cady, who was standing at the counter beside the dryer, folding a pink pair of Janie's tights.

"Pardon?" he asked.

Her eyes to Janie's folded tights that she was putting in a hamper, she reached to the pile of clean clothes and grabbed a pair of his jeans.

"Inside me," she said softly to the jeans. "Touching me. I know it's you, Coert."

He had no clue what she was talking about, but the words she was saying didn't sit great with him.

So it came out edgy when he asked, "Who else would it be?"

She turned those green eyes to him.

"Tony."

Coert stilled.

She held his gaze.

"I'll say your name over and over as much as you want, again and again for years and years if that's what works for you. I didn't have your name before so I can imagine why you wouldn't want that kind of thing before. But if you're demanding it now because you want to make sure I'm with us, *us*, here, now, Coert and Cady, I want you to know I know it's you."

He'd given her everything he could give when they were together.

And he'd kept everything from her just the same.

But it felt good knowing that regardless of that, she knew him down to the bone.

Still.

"I might need that for a while, honey," he said quietly.

She nodded and looked back to his jeans. "Then that's what I'll give you."

He stared at her profile, the gentle curve of her jaw ending in the thick waves of her hair.

That was right there.

In his laundry room.

Folding his goddamned jeans.

"You get I love you?" he asked.

"I love you more," she said to the jeans she was now stacking on a pile of others she'd folded.

"That might not be right," he gave her the truth.

She looked at him again. "I'll take that too."

He reached out an arm, hooked a hand behind her neck and drew her to him.

Then he took her mouth.

He ended the deep kiss with a succession of quick, soft ones before he let her go.

He turned to the laundry detergent.

Cady turned back to a pile of unfolded, fresh, clean clothes.

"RIGHT, I'LL FEEL her out, make sure what she said on the phone is what she means, and I'll call you later to let you know for sure if me and Janie are comin' to dinner tomorrow."

It was quarter to five. It was time for Cady to leave and Coert to get over to Kim's for Christmas Eve with his daughter.

They were standing in each other's arms beside her Jag in his garage. Midnight was already loaded up.

He didn't want her to go.

But he would soon be gone, he couldn't take her with him, so there was no reason for her to stay.

"Okay, Coert," she replied.

"If she gives a vibe she's not down with it, you good to come here around one to have some time with me on Christmas?" he asked to be sure.

She pressed closer and smiled up at him. "Definitely."

"I'm taking your time away from you with your family."

"They may be going home after New Year's, but they're really not going anywhere."

She was right about that and he was not only glad she looked at it like that, he was glad she had it.

He bent to her and touched his mouth to hers.

He lifted a hint away and looked into her eyes. "Thank you for giving me today."

"Thank *you* for the same thing."

That was when Coert smiled at her.

"I should go, honey," she said softly.

Yeah.

Shit.

She had to go.

"All right, Cady," he murmured.

But then he really kissed her.

He took his time and he did not get his fill.

He'd never get his fill.

But he ended it because they had to end it, and he shifted her from her door so he could open it for her to get in.

She climbed in.

He shut it behind her, moved to the pad on the wall and hit the button for the door to open.

She started the car and waved at him.

He lifted his hand back.

Cady reversed out and Coert watched, walking a few feet from her front bumper as she did it, stopping in the open door to the garage.

Snow was falling lightly and he watched through it as she reversed into the street and then drove off, doing it after looking to her side and giving him another wave.

Midnight sniffed the crack in the window at the back.

Coert lifted his hand again.

He watched her go, and when she turned at the end of the street, Coert retraced his steps back to the house, closing the door and moving into his mud room.

The Christmas wrap was bunched in a bag in a corner, the only bag left, all of Janie's presents were wrapped and loaded in his truck.

Cady had wrapped every one. She'd acted nearly ecstatic to do it (and she was good at it, something he was not).

Coert's participation in this was that he'd cut strips of tape and line them on the edge of his island so she could grab them. And often, she'd say, "Need your finger." He'd give it to her and she'd tighten ribbon around it.

That was it.

There was also only one hamper of clothes left, the rest had been laundered, folded and put away.

She'd helped him do that, the only time anyone had helped him do that outside his mom when she was around, a chore he wasn't big on that had been on his agenda on this day off that he had no intention of doing when Cady became the whole of that agenda.

But she'd wanted to, it was weird but it was clear that was true, so they'd done it.

They'd wrapped presents and done laundry and took a walk with her dog and ate breakfast and lunch and had a shower and sex after in his bed and made out repeatedly and talked.

She'd made him laugh.

He'd returned the favor.

Now she was going home and he was going to his daughter.

He hadn't even gotten to Janie yet.

But still.

It had already been the best Christmas Eve of his life.

And hitting Kim's where Janie was with Cady's pie in tow, it was just going to get better.

Nineteen

"FAST CAR"

COERT

Eighteen years earlier…

Cady's head came out of the fridge before the rest of her body did, and she did this holding up a half filled jar of Smucker's caramel sundae sauce.

"We have this," she stated.

Coert grinned at her. "French toast infused, your word, baby, with cinnamon and topped with caramel sauce. I think that fits, but just to say, next year we gotta be more on top of this Christmas thing. Pretty sure it's a major Christmas foul not to have maple syrup."

She grinned back but she didn't seem to have a problem with that.

On Coert's part, he was trying not to think of next year.

His vision of next year, Cady would be in it when they again celebrated Christmas and she'd be in it every day in between.

But that vision was hard to force into focus. There was too much in the way. Too much that could go wrong. Too much that could take them away from each other.

Too much that could drive them apart.

He forked the soggy bread out of the cinnamon and vanilla egg batter that Cady made and dropped it on the sizzling skillet. He then tossed another slice of bread in the batter.

As he did that, Cady came up behind him and wrapped her arms around him.

"Love the perfume you got me, Tony."

She was so short, she couldn't see him if he turned his head, so Coert did that before he closed his eyes to fight back the pain.

They'd been together just a short time.

And it seemed like just that sometimes with all the things he was learning about her.

Like how damned funny she could be.

Like how he never stopped marveling at how hard she worked and how much loyalty she had for a job that plain sucked.

How, as much as she had to understand in a rational way it was a lost cause, she refused to give up on a family who treated her like garbage (this too close to the bone, Coert tried not to think about much…and failed).

And how generous she was in bed. How sweet it was she didn't have a lot of experience, but she had a lot of exuberance and she had that because she was into him. So focused on him and what they were doing, giving and getting, the way they were connecting, it was unreal.

And unbelievably beautiful.

But other times it seemed like they'd been together for years.

He was practically living at Casey's with her. He didn't have all of his stuff there since he had his own place, but he had a good supply of clothes, all the bathroom stuff. He ate breakfast or dinner with her there (or took her out to eat) when she wasn't working. He spent nearly every night there. Which meant he woke up there nearly every morning.

With Cady at his side.

They'd fallen into that and it was insane how easy it was. She wasn't moody, demanding, immature. When he forgot, she rinsed his whiskers out of the sink and didn't bitch, like his last girlfriend did. She didn't call him all the time to find out where he was or make certain that he was going to be where she wanted him to be, like the girlfriend before that did. She gave him zero shit about anything.

If she was home and he came to her, she acted like he'd been away at war for years.

And in the mornings when they woke up together, she did it like she'd just come out of a really good dream only to find she'd opened her eyes to a dream come true.

In their short time together, they'd had one tough time.

This was when he'd come to her for dinner, she'd been in the kitchen and it was the only time she hadn't rushed out and right into his arms.

The radio had been playing, and when Coert hit the doorway to the kitchen, he stopped there, leaned a shoulder against the jamb and stared, partially frozen, partially suspended in fear as she kept her back to him, her hands involved in making dinner, but she wasn't giving herself to him.

Tracy Chapman's "Fast Car" was playing on Casey's radio.

Coert hadn't moved.

He'd leaned right there, his gut burning, his throat closing, waiting…

Waiting for her to turn and say she was done. Done with pretending something she didn't know was all pretend. Done keeping her mouth shut even when her eyes searched his for a reason to keep believing.

Done with him.

He wanted to tell her. Who he was. What he was doing. Move away from her but in a way he knew she'd understand. Do that so he could get her far away from him, Maria, Lars and his crew, get her safe and come back to her after it was all over.

Cap wouldn't let him. Cap told him she couldn't be trusted. Cap said Coert met her through that crew and he had to assume her loyalty was at least with Maria, maybe Lonnie too. Cap said telling her could put Coert in more danger, he wouldn't be doing his job if he let Coert put himself in more danger. Cap told Coert he was young, inexperienced, in deep in his first undercover job, he wasn't thinking clearly, she could be pulling one over on him.

And nothing Coert said would change his mind.

He'd even fucking begged.

No go.

Tom and Malc agreed with him. Agreed that Coert should let her in on who he was, cut her loose, go back to her when it was safe.

But they couldn't sway Cap either.

So now he was stuck.

Stuck falling deeper in love with a cute redhead with amazing green eyes, who had no idea who he really was but in the first vulnerable, sleepy, open moments of her every day, she looked at him like he was a dream come true.

But now, the situation was worse. What he was learning Lars was capable of. What he was learning were Lars's goals. The vibe he was getting from Maria that grew creepier and more threatening every time he was around the woman.

Now Coert wasn't getting off on the adrenaline of being on the hunt, building a case, walking the minefield of undercover work with the end goal of taking down the bad guy.

Now Coert was living in fear. Fear he'd be found out that wasn't fear for himself, but fear for what they'd do to Cady if he was.

And fear that every day he spent with her he was falling deeper and doing it faster.

She'd already burrowed into his heart. She'd done that before he gave her their first kiss. She'd started doing that in a hallway in a filthy house, telling him she had goals and didn't wear red.

Now she was clawing into his soul.

And when it all blew up, what then?

Where would Cady be when she learned every second was a lie? Every word. Even the name she said when he had his hands on her, his mouth, when he was inside her.

When, like right then, she had her arms wrapped around him.

Christ, he hated the name Tony. Now not only when she said it, but when anyone did, he had to fight back a flinch, a snarl, a bite.

And that night, the night of "Fast Car," watching her make their dinner but for the first time leave him out, keep him away, distance herself from him even if he was essentially in the same room with her, Coert struggled with letting it all hang out or letting it just play out. Reaching for the relief he would feel when she got shot of him. Knowing he could come back to her later, fresh, clean…no one but Coert. Knowing after it was all done she'd hold the understanding he'd let her go. He'd kept her safe. He hadn't pushed the lie to the point of no return.

But this was Cady.

She couldn't even move the first time she'd looked into his eyes.

So when the song was over she'd just turned to him and said softly, "You're home."

She'd let the words to the song say everything. She'd let them deliver the message.

But her message, Cady's message, the one that came from her own lips was *home*.

Coert had tasted bile in his throat, his feet itching to walk away, his fingers curling into his palms to make fists.

They'd started from less than zero.

But they had everything to lose.

He should walk away.

He should act like a dick to drive her away and explain later.

He didn't do either.

Because he was trapped by his job.

And he was weak.

And most importantly, he was in love with a cute redhead with emerald green eyes.

"Believe," he'd whispered.

Without hesitation, she'd whispered back, "I believe."

She came to him. Cady always came to Coert.

Right then, that night after "Fast Car," he'd not gone to her.

He'd rushed her.

Caged her.

Forced her against the counter to take his mouth, endure the desperation of his hands.

Then he'd taken her to the floor and she gave him it all.

And when Coert had made her come, she'd called out the name Tony.

Oh yeah.

He hated the name Tony.

"Tony?" she called, giving him a squeeze when he didn't reply to her telling him she liked his not-so-sterling Christmas gift of a bottle of perfume.

"Glad," he forced out, made a noise in his throat and finished. "Next year I'll do better than perfume."

And he would.

Next year, he'd give her diamonds.

He felt her press her face in his back. "But I just said I like my perfume."

Coert fished the soggy bread out of the batter and tossed it into the skillet with the other. He nudged them so they wouldn't stick.

Then he turned in her hold and wrapped his arms around her.

"Happy about that, honey," he murmured, bent his neck and touched his mouth to hers.

This was what they had. This was who they were. It was the real them, she just didn't know how real it was in the way that it right then wasn't.

But that was what Malc had told Coert he had to keep hold of to stop from losing his mind.

So he did.

Right then, literally.

And he also did it by saying, "I think you should call your folks and tell them we can't make Christmas dinner."

Something flashed in her eyes that told him she wanted to do that but she wasn't going to do that.

He'd met them once. At a family dinner that Cady had set up prior to Thanksgiving with the hopes they'd ask Coert to share Thanksgiving with the family.

They had not and he'd spent Thanksgiving pretending to get drunk with Lars and two members of his crew.

During the dinner they'd had, her dad had been okay. He was a smart man but he was weak and pretty much checked out to anything that was important, like his daughter.

Her mother was a haughty, controlling bitch.

And her brother was the worst of them all.

He wasn't an asshole. He wasn't a dick. The word hadn't been invented for the smug, arrogant, condescending, critical, sniping pissant that he was.

Coert detested him. How Cady tolerated him, he didn't know.

But he knew it was part of why he was falling deeper and doing it faster.

She didn't give up on people.

Case in point…him.

"We have to go," she told him.

"We don't have to do shit," he replied.

"They invited you," she fibbed.

"You made them invite me by saying you weren't coming without me."

She shut up because she couldn't argue that seeing as it was fact.

Coert wanted to laugh, howl, put her in his Chevy, take her to Montana and lose themselves under big sky.

"Cady—" he started.

"Tony, it's Christmas."

That was when he shut up and it was part about Christmas, part that he had to recover from the blow of another Tony.

He wished she'd come up with a pet name for him. He didn't care if she called him pookie. Even pookie was better than Tony.

She knew she had him when she got up on her toes, brushed her lips on his jaw and rolled back, saying, "You need to flip the toast."

She was right.

This was the them they had right now, the real them, and one day, and he hoped to God it was soon, he could let her in on how *real* they were.

But now he had to flip the toast.

He did that as she moved in and tossed another piece of bread in the batter.

This was part of them too, part of what felt settled, right, like he'd had her for years. They moved around a kitchen together, cooking or cleaning up, like they'd had decades of practice.

"The knife you bought me was sweet too, baby," he murmured, pulling down plates.

And it was. She couldn't afford the Swiss Army knife she'd gotten him for Christmas but she'd silenced his objections by jumping him to shut him up, a tactic that worked.

She couldn't afford more and he knew it (outside filling a stocking for him), so he'd only given her perfume.

He'd made a note of the stocking thing since he didn't do shit for her stocking, and he felt like an ass because he didn't. When he'd shared that, she'd silenced that with a kiss. Fortunately, she'd only put little or zany stuff in that. Candy. Silly string. Deodorant. Shave cream.

But the bottom line was that he could afford more than perfume, but he didn't go there. Not this year. She didn't know where his money came from and she didn't ask. But he didn't want her thinking some grand gesture gift was bought for her with dirty cash, especially when it wasn't.

And he didn't want to leave her with something that might be an ugly memory someday if things plummeted south.

Next year.

It'd all be next year.

"Every man needs a good pocketknife," she replied.

"Cady."

She turned to him.

"I know that dug deep, it's a good knife. And it means a lot," he told her quietly.

The smile that bought him was bright.

He fought back the urge to make out with her because that usually led to a lot more and they'd slept in, they'd already done it under the Christmas tree and they needed to eat and get ready for their command performance at her parents, starting at noon. "No later, please, Cady. I know you have a habit of running late," he'd heard her mother say over the phone.

He also needed to scoop out the toast.

He did that.

She tossed two more slices in.

They sat with their filled plates at Casey's kitchen table, where, under it, their knees brushed.

"This is *amazing*," Cady breathed after her first bite.

Coert had no idea if it was the cinnamon "infused" egg batter. It was probably the sprinkle of cinnamon she put on top.

It was definitely the caramel syrup.

But she was right.

He bumped her knee with his and kept his lips over his teeth to hide the chewed French toast behind his grin.

She bumped his knee back and dug in.

They ate.

They cleaned up.

He made her come again with his fingers while they were in the shower.

Then they got ready and went over to her folks' house.

THEY WERE SILENT on the way home.

She waited for them to get through the door, for him to close it, lock it, and start unwrapping his scarf from around his neck before she started, "To—"

He cut her off not only because he didn't want to hear that name on her lips but because he…was…*pissed.*

"Next year, no."

Needless to say, Christmas dinner did not go well.

Not with the Webster clan.

It had been four hours and seventeen minutes (he'd timed it) of sheer torture.

Christ, her mother was a piece of work and that brother of hers?

Christ.

"Tony," she whispered, still in her jacket, her eyes locked to him.

"And when we have kids, Cady, that asshole gets nowhere near them. And by that asshole, I mean Caylen."

She shut her mouth and started at him, her eyes growing wide.

Coert was too ticked to notice that response or wonder at it.

He just tossed his scarf on the back of one of Casey's chairs and put his fingers to the buttons of his coat. "Your mom and dad, I'll have to stomach that because maybe they'll be better grandparents than they are parents. Your mother starts her bullshit, Cady, it ends for them too. A kid has got to find out who they are. Along the way, they don't need some battle-ax badgering them to be…I don't know. What the fuck is it she's all fired up about you being?"

"Having a college education, for one," she shared.

"Mark Twain didn't graduate college."

She blinked at him.

"Neither did Ansel Adams," he went on.

She stared.

"Frank Lloyd Wright, Henry Ford, even frigging Benjamin Franklin."

Her eyes got round.

"For fuck's sake, Abraham Lincoln didn't have a college degree," he bit out.

"Wow, you know a lot of people who didn't graduate college," she whispered.

He did because he'd fought with his own dad about not going to college during the phase he'd had where he wanted nothing to do with it, he wanted to dig right in and be a cop. So he remembered an argument that came in handy now.

Coert had eventually gone but his argument at the time was still sound. Even his father had given in.

Though his mother had said the route to detective might be faster if he had a political science or criminal justice degree.

He'd majored in both.

Obviously, he didn't impart this knowledge on Cady.

"Have I made my point?" he asked, shrugging off his coat and throwing it over the back of the chair with his scarf.

"Next time I'll mention that Abraham Lincoln thing," she said. "And Ben Franklin," she added.

Had she not just spent the last four hours where he did?

"Next time?" Coert asked.

She bit her lip and shrugged out of her jacket too.

"They hate me," he declared.

"Tony, honey," she said softly, tossing her coat on the back of the couch and moving to him.

"They hate me and they don't hide it. They don't see what I am to you. They don't see what we've got. And Christ, Cady, you can't miss it."

She got up close and laid a hand on his chest, telling him, "Only I need to know that. Who cares what they think?"

"They think it's gonna be 'Fast Car.'"

She stilled.

Yeah, she'd delivered her message with that song.

And they'd spent Christmas together.

Now he was all in.

So Coert needed to deliver his message too.

He lifted his hand and wrapped his fingers around her wrist.

"It's not gonna be 'Fast Car,' Cady," he told her, his voice vibrating.

"I know," she replied, shifting closer.

"The thing is, the only person who needs to believe is you, and you believe. So if they love you, *they* should believe."

"They're being protective."

"They're not being protective. They're being judgmental."

"They'll get it," she assured.

"They won't get dick."

"Maybe not," she allowed.

"Not ever, Cady, they won't get dick. And what makes it worse is that they don't even have it in them to be polite. Jesus, how did they even make you?"

Her other hand went to his waist and started curving around. "I don't know but that might be the nicest thing anyone's ever said to me."

"Don't be funny when I'm this pissed," he returned.

"I wasn't being funny."

Jesus.

Her hair. That face. Those freckles. Her ass. Her generosity. Her loyalty. Her sense of humor.

Those fucking eyes.

And her not being like her parents was the nicest thing anyone had ever said to her?

He took his fingers from her wrist to frame her face with both his hands and he bent his face to hers.

"We're gonna have to make a decision about them, Cady. This is us. You and me. And I can take it. But I'm not gonna sit at a table or be in a room or even be breathing and know you're taking it. Not that. Not from them. Especially not that brother of yours. Are you getting me?"

Her nod moved his hands but she didn't lose his eyes.

She got him.

So he let her go, grabbed one of hers and pulled her to the couch.

"Now we're gonna find a movie," he announced. "*A Christmas Story* or *Scrooged* or *It's a Wonderful Life* has gotta be playin' on some channel. And we're gonna erase that Christmas shit with pink rabbit pajamas."

Cady burst out laughing.

Coert did not.

He collapsed on the couch, pulling her down with him.

He stretched them out, getting her right where he wanted her, tucked close to his front.

And only when he had her there did he reach for the remote.

He did this thinking that the perfume was lame. It wasn't a cheap brand, like the one she owned, and it was pretty and all her, but it was still lame.

But not more lame than the hundred dollar check her parents gave her.

Her mother handing it over (not even in a goddamned envelope) saying, "We know you need this, Cady."

They hadn't even gone out to get her cash. They gave her a check.

And a hundred bucks?

Cady had given her mother a bracelet she couldn't afford and her dad a Bronco's baseball cap she also couldn't afford.

And Coert reckoned what she'd spent they didn't even reimburse with that lame-ass check.

It blew his mind and not in a good way.

Her brother didn't even get her anything and she had way less than he did and she'd bought him a bag of his favorite coffee beans and a grinder.

To which he'd said, "I have a Cuisinart at home but I guess it's the thought that counts."

Fuck, Coert had wanted to plant his fist in the guy's face and right then he thought it was a Christmas miracle that he'd managed to stop himself from doing that.

"You want a beer?" Cady asked, fortunately taking his mind from his thoughts.

"We'll find a movie," Coert answered, flicking through the channels that going over recent memories he hadn't been seeing. "Then I'll get us a beer."

"It doesn't matter," she said.

"It does," he told her. "I think a funny one. After that shit with your family, we need funny."

"No, honey, I mean *it doesn't matter.*"

At her tone, he looked down at her to see her neck twisted to look up at him.

"What?" he asked.

"This matters. Cinnamon, caramel French toast matters. They don't matter. We have cinnamon, caramel French toast. And since we do, we can take whatever else comes."

God, he hoped she was right.

God, *fuck*, he hoped she was right.

He felt the tension ebb out of him, he relaxed into her and he bent his face closer to hers.

"You're right."

"You find a movie, babe. I'll go get us beers."

Before he could stop her, she gave him a quick touch of the lips and scooted out of his hold.

She brought them beers and tossed a throw rug over him (because Cady kept the heat down low to save money, even if he was giving Casey money to pay the utilities, something she didn't know about, so she felt it wasn't fair to saddle Casey with high utility bills when she felt he was doing her a bigger favor than she was doing for him).

She climbed under it, burrowing into him.

Coert toed off his boots.

Cady followed suit.

And Coert found *A Christmas Story.*

They'd missed the leg lamp bit but not the rabbit pajamas bit.

And next year, Coert vowed, they'd start their Christmas with cinnamon, caramel French toast, but he'd make sure they had all they'd need to veg out in front of the TV and then make a big feast before they'd again veg out in front of the TV.

This meant no Christmas dinner with her folks (though, maybe one with his).

But next year, they'd start their Christmas like they'd started that Christmas.

And they'd end their Christmas just like this.

Twenty

YOU DID THE RIGHT THING

COERT

Present day…

The text came in at nine thirty on the dot, like she was waiting, not wanting to intrude but wanting to say what needed to be said.

Merry Christmas, honey. Love you. See you guys later.

Coert felt his face get soft as he read Cady's text and he knew that wasn't only a feeling, but a look when he felt Kim's hand curl around the back of his neck.

He bent back his head, her hand falling away as he did, to see her standing beside him where he was sitting on her couch, and she was staring down at him.

"Terminally in love," she murmured.

His eyes flicked to the tree where Janie was amidst a sea of spent wrapping paper, her bottom ensconced in a flannel mermaid's tail that was mostly aqua with a pink flipper at the end, her attention centered on taking stick-on outfits off a mermaid drawing (her Santa list that year definitely had a theme).

He turned them back to Kim in time to catch her asking in a whisper, "Is Coert in love gonna make me wanna hurl?"

"Shut up," he whispered back, feeling his lips twitch.

Her eyes danced. "It is. It's totally gonna make me hurl."

"You mind if I text Cady back?" he asked dryly.

"I'd have a heart attack at the thought you're actually asking if you can do something, but since you aren't and you're being sarcastic, then I'll give you the unnecessary. An answer. That being no."

He grinned up at her.

Then he bent to his phone and texted back, *Merry Christmas, baby. Hope you're having a good day so far. Love you back and see you soon.*

"Daddy!" Janie called, and he turned his eyes to her to see she was holding up her board, the mermaid wearing a purple mermaid outfit, but Janie's other hand was also up and she was holding a green and blue mermaid outfit. "Purple or green?"

If someone told him that in his life, one day he'd be asked to give an opinion on a mermaid outfit, he might have laughed and silently hoped to God that never happened.

And he would have been totally wrong thinking that.

"Absolutely purple," he said firmly.

Janie looked unsure, lifted her gaze to her mother, and asked, "Mommy?"

"Purple, Janie. Always purple, sweetie. For sure," Kim replied, and for Kim it was always purple since that was her favorite color.

Janie put the things down and declared, "I'm gonna try the green, just in case."

Neither Coert nor Kim were surprised their daughter ignored their advice.

"More coffee?" Kim asked Coert.

"Yeah," he mumbled, pushing out of her couch. "And I should get on breakfast."

"Can we have butterly pie for breakfast, Daddy?" Janie asked.

To say his daughter liked Cady's pie was an understatement.

To say when he and Kim told Janie she and Coert were going to a big family party for Christmas dinner that she was ecstatic even though she had no clue who that family was, was an understatement too.

This proved him correct again. She understood her mom having a big family with lots of people around on special occasions was good to have.

And she understood that as fun as it was to go to Jake and Josie's, with Jake's kids around (especially Ethan, Jake's youngest, who Janie had a crush on), or having Coert's parents there, it wasn't as good as what her mom had.

And she wanted her dad to have that.

So Christmas dinner with Cady and her family was all good.

If her brothers kept it good.

"Butter*beer* pie, Janie," Kim corrected. "Daddy's friend Cady made butter*beer* pie."

And Kim was all in with this, something Coert couldn't wrap his mind around, even if he could wrap it around his feelings of gratitude that she was.

But maybe she was just glad Coert was going to have this too.

She loved him and it was coming clear she'd never stopped, she was just working hard to adjust that into something that was right and good and healthy, not only for Janie, but for her and Coert.

Suffice it to say, Coert had had the best Christmas Eve of his life the day before.

And it wasn't even ten in the morning and his Christmas was shaping up the same way, because he had hope, real hope this time, that it was just going to get better.

Janie scrunched her nose at her mother. "I've smelled Daddy's beers and that pie doesn't smell anything like Daddy's beers."

Kim chuckled.

As did Coert.

"In a few years, we'll start reading *Harry Potter*, sweetie," Kim offered.

Janie loved her books so she brightened. "You can read it to me now!"

"It can get a little scary," Kim told her.

"That's okay. I never get scared," Janie returned.

That was when Coert let out a bark of laughter, because his baby girl defined scaredy-cat to the point she demanded they go trick or treating at Halloween before the sun went down because some of the other kids' costumes made her skittish.

And that was when Janie scrunched her nose at him.

"I don't," she stated.

"All right, cupcake," he muttered, grabbing his empty mug, the one from Kim's hand, and moving toward the kitchen with both.

"I don't!" she yelled at his back.

Coert stopped, turned and looked, stunned at his daughter's face set cute…and stubborn.

He'd never seen that expression in her life.

And unless she had a genuine need to be heard or was overly excited about something, she'd never yelled in her life.

He felt the surprise coming off Kim too.

The expression melted, Janie looked upset, then a little scared before she turned her head away and whispered, "I don't."

"Okay, baby, you don't. So how about when you turn six next summer, your mom can start reading that to you?" Coert suggested.

She brightened again and did a little bounce of her booty on her calves in her mermaid tail. "Okay!"

He lifted the mugs. "You want cocoa?"

Her "Okay!" that time was louder.

He glanced at Kim who was still staring at their daughter then he moved into her kitchen.

Kim followed him, having well cleared of the door before she said, "Six is too early for those books, Coert."

"Haven't read 'em but she'll probably forget by then anyway," Coert replied, replenishing both their mugs from her coffeepot.

He was shoving it back into the maker when he felt her punch his arm lightly.

He looked at her.

She was grinning hugely.

"We're making a monster," she said like she was delighted about this beyond reason.

He doubted that was right. Janie just didn't have monster in her.

But it had to be said, even if it sounded crazy, that her feeling free enough to openly share she was annoyed about something was a step in the right direction.

Coert felt his lips twitch again, handed the mug to her and lifted his to his lips before he said, "We might regret this," and took a sip.

Her eyes slid to the door of the kitchen before coming back to Coert, and she lifted her mug too, but before taking a sip she said, "Better get on that cocoa for our budding little mermaid princess."

Coert chuckled.

Kim threw him a smile before she took a sip of her coffee.

"Mommy!" Janie yelled from the other room in a manner they were far more used to. "Can I take my ballerina box upstairs and put my jewelry in it?"

"Yeah, sweetie," Kim yelled back.

Coert went to the fridge, doing it asking, "How much jewelry does she have?"

"One necklace and a bracelet. But she asked about getting her ears pierced. Get ready for that."

He looked to Kim. "That's a no."

Kim nodded but queried, "Six?"

"Eight," Coert returned.

She gave him a cocky smile. "Then seven it is."

Oh yeah.

This new gig with Kim was much better.

"Deal," Coert replied and pulled out the milk.

"Coert Yaeger's famous cinnamon, caramel French toast?" she asked.

Coert stilled in closing the fridge door, memories gliding through him in a new way that wasn't yet pleasant, but they didn't burn like they used to.

He forced his body to move and looked at her.

Kim took in his face.

Then on a wry grin, she said, "Let me guess. Cady's recipe."

It wasn't, exactly.

It was *their* recipe.

Something he made every Christmas since that first, he thought, because he was a moron and he was torturing himself. Now he knew it was to spend time with Cady even if he didn't have her. But regardless, since Janie had been born and could chew real food, it had taken on another meaning as it was her favorite breakfast.

"Kim," he said softly.

She shrugged. "I promise I'm not lying when I say that it's good to have the blanks filled in. And just to say, Coert, I thought that French toast came from Darcy. You're a man who can cook but you're no Emeril, and you never failed to make a face when I had Food Network on. So I always figured they came from somewhere and that somewhere had girl parts."

"Some were Darcy's too," he told her carefully.

She tipped her head to the side and righted it in a nonverbal, *So?*

He quirked his lips at her. "And now I got some of yours as well."

"You can make my inside-out burgers for her," Kim declared.

Coert didn't know how to take that until she finished, her eyes lighting.

"But don't tell her they aren't mine like I didn't want you to know they aren't mine. They're Guy Fieri's."

"Crushed to know that, Kim," he teased.

Her eyes stayed lit. "Always your favorites."

"Just to say, I didn't make a face when 'Diners, Drive-ins and Dives' was on. Now I know why."

She laughed.

"Cinnamon, caramel French toast?" he asked quietly.

"Absolutely," she said firmly.

He studied her, totally having a lock on how he felt about how hard she was trying to put things right between them.

And she should know it.

"You can't know how much it means to me, you being this cool," he told her, still going quiet.

"And you can't know how happy I am that you're happy, Coert. You're a tough guy but you also can't hide you're a sensitive guy, so I'm guessing you're sensing that this isn't quite easy. But that doesn't make what I said less true."

"You got my gratitude for it, Kim."

"Anyway," she turned to a cupboard to pull down a bowl, "I'll one day find another hot guy and make him cinnamon, caramel French toast and claim it all for my own."

Coert burst out laughing.

She shot a big smile at him over her shoulder.

"What's funny?" Janie shouted, coming to a skidding stop on Kim's floors, mermaid tail gone (unfortunately, his girl couldn't swim up the stairs), now only wearing her thick purple socks and pink jammies with dancing snowmen on them.

"Your momma, cupcake," Coert replied. "Now come over here and help me make French toast while your mom makes you cocoa."

"'Kay!" she cried and dashed to him.

They made a mess of Kim's kitchen.

Later, they helped her clean up.

KATH

"JESUS, IS SHE gonna come out of her skin?"

Kath turned from the sink where she was tidying up some Christmas dinner prep utensils to her husband who'd come up at her side.

They'd done presents and breakfast all gathered around the tree in Cady's living room at the lighthouse.

Now all the kids were scattered to the winds.

But the women and men were at the studio where they'd pulled back the furniture in the living room, put in some sawhorses and topped them with plywood Elijah had procured for them. They'd topped that with tablecloths and covered it with the stoneware and glassware from two different houses. This was so they could all have Christmas dinner together by the glow of the tree Cady and Elijah had put up before they'd arrived.

Cady's friends Walt and Amanda had brought over folding chairs on Christmas Eve's eve so they were all set, cooking Christmas dinner for fifteen in two different kitchens.

Since dinner wasn't until three and it was just past one, and the birds were in the oven, the prep work was just completed, Kath looked over her shoulder and saw Cady nervously readjusting the bright Christmas crackers that were on every plate.

This was, as far as Kath could count, the fourth time she'd done that in the last fifteen minutes.

And in the mere seconds that Kath watched her, Cady's eyes went to the window at the back of the studio twice.

The window that faced the front of the property where the gate was.

Needless to say, Coert and Janie were going to arrive imminently.

"Did I do the right thing?" Pat asked under his breath.

Kath looked from her sister to her husband.

"Yes," she answered.

"She's a nervous wreck," Pat muttered.

"She's excited," Kath returned.

He jerked his head behind him. "That's not excitement. She's freaking out."

"She's going to meet the love of her life's daughter in T minus about two minutes."

Or meet her again, this time (hopefully) without bursting into tears.

Pat glanced over his shoulder, whispering, "But she's great with kids."

"You know this is different," Kath told him.

He looked to her. "How?"

Men.

Clueless.

"Okay, so if things go right this time, she's gonna help raise that child, Kathy," Pat stated. "But she's done the same with seven of them. And she sees what they've become. She has to know she's played a part in that."

"Nothing can go wrong with this," Kath shared.

"It won't go wrong. She's Cady. That little girl is gonna fall in love with her in about T minus two minutes," Pat returned.

"Nothing can go wrong with this," Kath repeated. "Because everything that was important went wrong before in a huge way so now they need everything, absolutely everything, Pat, but especially the important things, and this is the most important of all...they need them to go right."

That got in there, Kath knew, because she saw the light dawn in her husband's eyes.

Because he was clueless, but cute, and cuter since he was worried about Cady, she leaned up on her toes and touched her mouth to his.

As Pat was wont to do, the second she did, his arm curled around her to pull her closer.

Before she could return the favor, they both heard a strange noise come from the living room.

They looked there to see Cady running toward the front door, Shannon and Daly, in that room with her staring after her.

Kath and Pat moved to the opening to the living room to see Cady at the door, yanking on her coat, her dog dancing around her legs.

They felt Pam, who'd been working at the opposite counter, come up beside them just as Cady looked their way.

"He's here," she whispered, her face lit with a happiness so extreme, Kath actually had to blink against its brightness.

Then Cady was out the door, having closed it behind her, keeping Midnight in.

"Let out the dog, Pat," Kath ordered.

"What?" Pat asked.

"We gotta let out Midnight," Pam murmured, moving herself to do it and moving quickly.

Midnight danced around her, sensing she was going to get what she wanted, and when she got what she wanted, she raced out behind her momma.

Mike came in right after her, returning from taking out the trash, his face a scowl.

He knew Cady's man was there.

Kath didn't give that a second thought as they all moved to the window to see a big, silver Chevy Silverado parked at the edge of the garage beside one of their snow dusted Denalis, the tall, handsome Coert Yeager walking around the side toward the studio.

He was holding the hand of an adorable little girl trussed up in pink and purple winter gear, his knowledge of where to find Cady explained because Riley was also with them, pointing toward the studio, Corbin, who was with his cousin, trailing up the rear, his eyes on Coert's back.

The little girl was walking forward with her daddy but looking behind her at Corbin.

Until Midnight bounced through the snow excitedly, pausing only momentarily to sniff an approaching Cady as she passed her, and the little girl looked around.

And it was love at first sight.

Love at first sight for a little girl and a German shepherd who would be her dog and only hers for the rest of that dog's life.

Kath knew this because Midnight knocked Coert's little girl into the snow, and although Coert moved to separate them at first, they could hear her peals of laughter as Midnight danced around her, snuffling and giving her doggie kisses everywhere and Janie tried all she could to get her arms around the excited pup. Snow churned all around them and Corbin, Riley, Cady and Coert stood around watching dog and child disappear in clouds of white.

"Good call on Midnight," Pat mumbled.

Kath chuckled.

"Christ, that dog's gonna bury the kid," Mike, joining them from behind, muttered.

Kath glanced up at her brother-in-law to see his eyes trained out the window.

His jaw was set hard and Kath glanced back to see Coert's face had disappeared in Cady's hair.

He was either talking in her ear or kissing her neck, Kath couldn't tell.

But she could see Cady leaned against him, her arm around his waist, his around her shoulders, her head turned toward him, chin dipped down, but that was all she could see.

It didn't matter. The way they were standing so naturally together in their casual embrace, that focus they had on each other, it spoke volumes.

"You're not gonna be a dick."

Kath turned from her awesome view when she heard her husband order this firmly in the big brother voice he had not broken himself from using even if he was fifty-three and his brothers were closing in on that number right behind him.

"Pat," Kath warned.

"I'm not gonna be a dick," Mike spat.

"Mike," Pam warned.

"Oh my God! Do you see the cuteness outside?" Shannon cried from her place probably at the window in the living room.

She dashed into the kitchen to join them.

Daly followed his wife more sedately.

All eyes went back to the window to see Coert was now hunkered low, righting a snow-covered, still clearly giggling Janie while Cady was squatted down too, trying to hold back a still licking and snuffling, snow covered Midnight.

"Okay, goin' on record that that dude has got it going on," Daly noted. "Dogs, baby daughters, and all that's happening, and in about thirty second he's got time to make Cady's face look like that? Shit. Boys, we may need lessons."

"You do all right," Shannon told him.

"Thanks, darlin'," Daly replied. "But 'all right' isn't exactly a crowning achievement."

Shannon giggled.

With Shannon and Daly joining them, they crowded closer together around the window and watched as Coert dusted the snow off his daughter and Midnight started licking Cady, with Janie smiling at Cady before Midnight's excitement got the better of Cady and she landed on her ass in the snow with Midnight snuffling her.

Riley and Corbin waded in, as did Coert, the boys holding Midnight back and Coert pulling Cady out of the snow.

At this point, both Cady and Janie were giggling at each other.

"Christ, it's like a Hallmark movie," Mike muttered.

"Shut up, Mike," Daly muttered back.

Kath felt Pam lean into her.

"I think it just got super dusty in here," Pam whispered.

Kath felt her pain. What she was witnessing outside was suddenly wobbling.

Coert said something that made Corbin and Riley laugh, and Coert grinned at them and clapped Riley on the back.

Riley, head tilted back staring up at the handsome sheriff, slid visibly right into hero worship.

Cady reached out her hand to Janie, and Janie hesitated not one second to take it.

Shannon sniffled.

Kath felt her husband's arm slide around her waist and then she felt her side pulled tight into his front.

"You women better get your shit together. That little girl walks in and you're all bawling, this good start is gonna go up in smoke," Mike warned.

"Shut up, Mike," Daly repeated.

Kath stopped watching Cady and Janie, hand in hand, Janie's head tipped way back, her mouth not stopping moving, Cady's chin dipped down, her eyes locked to the girl, a smile radiant on her face, walk toward the studio with the males following them, and she looked at her husband.

"You did the right thing," she whispered.

That time, it was Pat that bent to touch his mouth to his wife's.

When her husband pulled away, his eyes slid to his brother. "And you're not gonna be a dick," he repeated his warning.

"I'm about to be a dick by punching you in the sternum," Mike retorted.

"Oh, great, you two in a fistfight when Cady's hot guy and his daughter walk through the door," Pam said sarcastically. "Perfect."

Mike turned to his wife. "That guy's not hot. He looks like every cop out there."

"If that's true, then I should have married into law enforcement, not heating and air conditioning," Pam shot back.

Mike scowled.

"You're not helping," Shannon told Pam.

The door opened, they heard a dog woof and Melanie's excited voice, "Santa came here for you too!"

"Really?" a child's voice came at them, sounding excited and amazed.

"Yeah! The presents are under that tree," Melanie replied as the men and women moved as one from window to the large opening to the living room.

Cady's eyes were riveted to Janie.

Coert's eyes immediately turned to the adults.

Janie's eyes went to her dad.

"Can I open them, Daddy?"

Coert looked to his girl. "In a minute, cupcake. How 'bout we meet the rest of Cady's family first, yeah?" he asked.

Oh man.

He called his cupcake-loving daughter "cupcake."

How cute was that!

"Yeah!" Janie cried then rounded a mittened hand to the room at large. "Hi! I'm Janie!"

Kath moved forward. "Hey, Janie. I'm Kathy."

"*Aunt* Kathy, Janie," Coert murmured.

His daughter's eyes got huge. "*Aunt* Kathy?"

"This is Cady's sister," Coert explained.

"Oh," Janie breathed, almost preternaturally adorable with her eyes that wide.

"And I'm Uncle Pat, I guess," Pat said, coming to stand by Kath's side. "And that's Uncle Mike, Aunt Pam, Aunt Shannon and Uncle Daly," he introduced, indicating each in turn.

Janie looked through them all and then tipped her head way back to look up at Cady. "You have a super big family. Like my mommy."

"Yes I do, sweetheart," Cady murmured.

"Let's get your coat off, baby," Coert said, hunkering down next to his daughter to help her off with her coat.

After Coert extricated his girl from her gear, more introductions ensued for Janie with Cady introducing the kids, who'd all crowded in, and Coert coming forward to shake hands with the adults.

Mike wasn't a dick.

But he wasn't overtly welcoming.

Pat made up for it. "We're real pleased you guys could come."

"Thanks," Coert replied. "We're real pleased to be invited."

The men locked eyes.

Something passed between them that, having a vagina, Kath would never understand, and age and the wisdom you got from it taught her years ago not to even try.

But it was Christmas. There were still gifts to be unwrapped, then cleanup to happen, food to prepare, more cleanup to endure and breakdown of the table before they could all pass out from their food comas scattered between two homes and the RV parked behind the garage that Mike and Pam had rented so they'd have more room to hang or sleep and they could all be together doing it.

So Kath announced, "Right. Santa did show here last night for one Janie Yeager and he told us we were to be sure you didn't miss a present. So Melanie, how about you find the presents for Janie and Coert under the tree and we'll get that sorted before we dive into cooking."

"*Daddy* got presents from Santa too?" Janie breathed.

"Santa knows everybody's a kid at heart, Janie," Cady told her, and Janie's dazed eyes drifted to Cady. "He always leaves something special under our tree for everyone."

Janie looked back at her dad. "Can we have presents here *every* year?"

Cady's eyes flew to Coert.

With his attention on his daughter, Coert's handsome face went so soft, for the first time (except when she met George Clooney watching the premiere of *ER*), Kath questioned her commitment to Pat.

"Do not *even* go there," Pat's lips said at her ear.

She turned and grinned at him.

He rolled his eyes to the ceiling.

"How about we let Cady get her coat off and you settle in with everyone and Midnight for a few minutes? I gotta talk real quick to Cady's brothers," Coert told her.

"Oh shit," Daly muttered from behind Kath.

Coert looked their way. "Can I have a minute, men?"

"Sure," Pat said immediately, moving toward the hall tree where there were stacks of jackets, mittens, hats, gloves and a tangle of boots around the floor.

"Of course," Daly said.

Mike said nothing, just headed to his coat.

Cady looked searchingly at Coert.

"It's cool," he murmured, touching her hip with a gloved hand before turning toward the door.

The men went through it.

Kath saw Janie watching her father leaving.

She started to open her mouth, but Cady got there before her.

"Okay, you tussled in the snow with Midnight, let's get you warmed up. You want some hot cider? Or cocoa? Or are you hungry? A little snack before dinner?"

"Do you have butterly pie?" Janie asked.

Cady stared down at her.

Shannon bumped Kath with her shoulder.

The dust was again rising.

"I…no, honey. I don't have any of that," Cady answered.

"You made us butterly pie and it was *yummy*. Mommy and I *loved it*. Mommy said to be sure to say thanks, so *thanks*!"

Well thank God.

The ex said to say thanks.

It just kept getting better and better.

"You're welcome, Janie. I'm glad you enjoyed it," Cady replied softly. "Your mom too."

Janie gave a short nod and continued, "But we had cinnamon, caramel French toast for breakfast so I didn't get any today," Janie told her.

Cady went visibly still.

"Oh shit," Shannon whispered.

"You did? We had tha—!" Melanie started to shout.

"Right!" Pam said loudly, clapping. "Let's get on cocoa and you can give Midnight a dog biscuit, Janie. How's that sound?" Pam asked, reaching a hand out to Janie.

"We don't have a dog," Janie told her, walking toward her and taking her hand.

"Well, then, live it up," Shannon put in, moving with them toward the kitchen.

"Hey, Mom, can we have cocoa too?" Ellie asked.

"Sure 'nuff, cute stuff," Pam replied.

One faction broke off to move into the kitchen. Another broke off to throw themselves on the couches and chairs shoved to the walls. Melanie was still arranging the presents under the tree for Janie and Coert.

Kath went to Cady.

"You made him your French toast, I take it?" she said under her breath to Cady.

Cady turned her gaze to Kath. "We came up with the recipe together."

Hmm.

Good?

Not good?

"And we came up with it on Christmas," Cady finished.

Oh boy.

This was foreign territory.

So Kath treaded lightly.

"It's fantastic French toast, Cady." Kath brushed the back of her sister's hand with the back of her own. "It's good he gives it to his daughter."

"I've been with him," Cady stated.

Kath didn't get it.

"Sorry?"

"This whole time, I've been with him. He's kept me with him. And me him. Me giving that time he and I had to you guys making that for you this morning. Him giving that time we had to Janie and Kim. I mean, we both made that French toast for our families, Kath. Because that's the way it's supposed to be."

So it was good.

Or at least Cady was making it that way.

Kath got closer. "That's a good way to look at it."

Cady looked confused. "What other way would I look at it?"

Kath wasn't going to touch that one.

"Get your jacket off, babe," she ordered instead. "There's present unwrapping to be done."

Cady spoke while shrugging off her coat, saying words she'd already said when she'd found out they'd done it.

"It really was great of you guys to go out and get some things for Coert and Janie yesterday."

"Can't welcome them into the family without at least spoiling a little princess rotten. Patrick would turn in his grave."

Cady shot her a smile as she hung her coat over Bea's, and since Bea's was over Shannon's which was over Dexter's, it fell right off and landed on the floor.

Cady bent to pick it up and tossed it on the seat of the hall tree and a pile of more coats.

Then she looked to the door.

With this at least, since she'd been married to a member of the male species for twenty-two years, she could advise.

"He needs to get the lay of the land," Kath told her. "It'll be fine."

Cady's head turned her way. "Mike—"

Kath grabbed her hand. "It'll be fine."

Cady looked again to the door then she turned her attention to the kitchen and finally back to Kath. "She loves Midnight."

Kath gave her a big grin. "Yeah." She tugged her hand. "Let's go make cocoa. Verity's still pouting in the observation deck. I need to text her and get her over here so she can meet Janie and the family can be together for presents."

They moved to the kitchen, Cady took over with Janie and cocoa and Kath texted her daughter.

The whoosh on her phone barely sounded before the men could be heard coming in.

Cady's eyes went right to Kath.

So Kath walked right to Pat.

Pat and Coert were jacketless inside the door, and Coert was looking around when Kath made it to them.

Coert asked, "Where are my girls?"

His girls.

Plural.

God, she was thinking she totally loved this guy.

"Kitchen. Cocoa," she answered.

He smiled.

Yep.

She was totally loving this guy.

"Thanks," he murmured, dipped his chin to Pat, to her, and he moved toward the kitchen.

Kath bellied up to her husband.

Close up to her husband.

"Jesus, sweetheart," he muttered as she crowded him, but he did it not moving from his spot and smiling down at her.

"That go okay?" she asked, shifting her eyes to the door and back to him to explain what he didn't need explained. That she was talking about what happened outside.

"Uh, yeah," Pat answered.

But he said no more.

"Can you elaborate?" she pushed.

Pat pulled her slightly to the side, turned a shoulder to the room and bent into his wife.

"Well, clearly he's a take charge guy because he took charge. Said straight up he gets we won't trust him with Cady and he gets why. He told us he knew he'd have to work for it and he was all in to do that. He told us he loves her. She loves him. They were going to make it work and he's going to make her happy. And he thanked us for buying his daughter Christmas presents."

After that, Pat stopped talking.

"That's it?" Kath asked.

Pat shrugged. "Pretty much."

"You were out there longer than that," she pointed out then narrowed her eyes. "What did Mike do?"

"Mike glared at him silently. Yeager was game and ignored it so I think Cady warned him about Mike. And Daly cracked about fifty stupid jokes about how it was good we didn't have to use any of the research we'd done on how to make a body disappear that Yeager laughed at. Then, when it came clear he was restless to get back inside to his girl and Cady, we came back inside."

Kath held her husband's eyes.

Then she declared, "I love you."

He smiled and moved farther into her. "Love you more."

"Impossible," she whispered.

He took her into his arms just as Janie cried out while dancing out of the kitchen, "Daddy says we can open presents!"

It was Christmas, so presents it was.

Verity showed, they all settled in, and for the next half an hour they discovered Janie wasn't discerning when it came to presents. She loved *everything.*

But the purple Easy-Bake Ultimate Oven with its purple, cream and blue circles and swirls on the door still was hands down the winner.

And Mike didn't miss it.

"Cady told Santa specifically you'd like that," Mike announced.

From her place sitting on the floor, Janie turned huge eyes to Cady, who was also curled on the floor close to Janie.

And, of course, Coert, who wasn't quite touching her, but that didn't mean he hadn't wrapped his long body around her to watch his daughter open presents over his woman's shoulder.

"You did?" she asked.

Cady didn't.

She'd told Kath, Pam and Shannon that Janie liked making cupcakes. Cady was so involved with going to see Coert, she'd only thought about pie, not presents.

So her family did.

But when Cady opened her mouth to answer, Mike got there first.

"She did. Sent a letter straight to the North Pole direct," he shared.

"Wow," Janie breathed. "You have Santa's address too?"

Cady gave her a smile and a murmured, "I never forgot it from when I was a little girl like you."

"Awesome!" Janie replied.

Cady kept smiling at her before she turned it to Mike.

Coert was gracious about his two new sweaters and lined leather gloves, regardless of how uninspired they were. But they'd learned, in Maine, you couldn't have enough sweaters or gloves and they figured Coert very well knew that.

When Kath was about to announce it was time to peel potatoes, Janie proclaimed, "Now, Daddy. Santa's presents are done. So you gotta do it now."

"Maybe later, cupcake," Coert murmured.

"No!" she cried, turning from her rump to her knees and bouncing up and down. "It's present time! So it has to be *now*."

Coert studied his little girl with an intensity that was a little bizarre.

Then he said, "Okay, Janie, baby. Go get it out of Daddy's jacket."

Janie was a streak of cream top with pink and green polka-dotted Christmas tree and red pants with pink and green polka-dotted hem, as she raced to her father's jacket and came back with a small box wrapped in elegant green foil paper with a white velvet ribbon wrapped around it.

Store wrapped, but who cared?

The little present was gorgeous.

She dropped to her knees in front of Cady and held it out, stating, "That's from Daddy and me. I don't know what it is." She glanced around before she looked back to Cady and went on, "We didn't bring everyone prezzies but Daddy said it'd be okay, once everyone saw that."

Cady took the box and sat in the curve of Coert's body, Coert positioned in a way she could have leaned back against the leg he had bent up with wrist resting on it.

And this, Kath hoped, was what she would do during Christmas a year from now, then many more to come.

What she didn't do was unwrap her present.

"*Open it!*" Janie nearly shrieked. "I can't *believe* there's a present that little that will make *everyone* happy and I can't wait to see!"

"Oh, Christ, he's not gonna give her a ring in front of his daughter, do you think?" Pat murmured.

Men.

"That's not a ring box," Kath shared in a whisper. "Maybe necklace. Maybe bracelet."

"Right," Pat muttered.

Cady twisted her neck to look at Coert.

"When did you have ti—?" she started.

"Just open it, honey, or Janie'll burst," he interrupted on a grin.

It was no ring.

But it was going to be something.

She kept her eyes on him then she looked to Janie, gave her a sweet smile and bent her head to unwrap the gift.

Kath looked at Pam.

Pam looked at Kath then looked at Shannon.

Shannon looked at both of them.

"Oh my goodness," Cady breathed.

They looked at Cady.

"It's a *necklace*," Janie stated reverently, leaning forward on a hand to peer around Cady's hands to the box. "A sparkly one!"

"It is," Cady whispered, staring at it.

"I like sparkly things," Janie informed her.

"I do too, honey," Cady replied then looked back to the necklace. "Put it on," she said, her voice sounding funny.

"Cady, you can—" Coert began.

She twisted to him. "Please. Will you put it on?"

They'd had a Christmas together.

One of them.

Kath didn't know much about it just that one hadn't been enough.

But she could guess it was nothing like this.

Cady pulled what looked like a delicate gold chain out of the box and handed the dangling thing to Coert.

She then put the box on the floor, lifted her hair and Coert's hands came around in front of her, disappearing at the back of her neck.

And it was then Kath saw the simple solitaire diamond that hung from the chain. It fit snug in the indent of Cady's throat.

It was perfect.

"Someone needs to clean this place," Pam mumbled, and Kath tore her gaze from Cady to look at Pam to see her swiping under her eye. "Dust everywhere."

"I hear that," Shannon mumbled.

"It seems clean to me," Riley noted.

Shannon sent her nephew a watery smile and tugged him into a hug.

"Gross! Aunt cooties!" Riley shouted.

"You've got a big mouth, Riley," Melanie told him.

"*You've* got a big *face*," Riley shot back.

"That'll do it," Mike growled.

The kids shut up.

Kath looked back to Cady and Coert just in time to see Cady leaning toward Janie.

"What do you think? Does it look okay?" Cady asked.

Janie reached out a finger and said, "It's real pretty." She dropped her hand and her attention shifted to Cady's face. "But maybe if we come for Christmas with your family next year we can get you one that's bigger."

Pat and Daly roared with laughter.

The startling sound made Midnight woof and for some reason shuffle toward Janie, who she was lying beside. She then got up on all fours and rained dog kisses on the little girl's neck.

Janie giggled.

Cady turned to Coert and whispered something Kath couldn't hear.

They needed a moment.

It was time to peel the potatoes.

So Kath pushed out of her place in the couch and shared that.

"Right, potato duty. Who bought it?" she asked.

"Me!" Riley cried, got up from his place and raced into the kitchen, this happening because Riley had always been a big fan of getting stuff done he hated so he could concentrate more time on doing stuff he liked.

"And me," Corbin groused, pushing up from sitting on the arm of the chair his mother sat in and slunk into the kitchen, this happening because Corbin was a master procrastinator.

Verity just slunk into the kitchen.

Elijah heading to Bangor last night to be with his family and doing it after he had a conversation, just him and Verity, after they'd come back from getting coffees that had caused her to have a lot of alone time in the observation deck (and managing this by shouting at anyone who came up, "Can't I just get a moment's peace?") meant a mother-daughter chat was imminent.

But not on Christmas.

Christmas was for family however that came, however it morphed and changed.

And this year, apparently, diamonds.

Kath smiled.

"You're lucky. I got an Easy-Bake Oven when I was six, and the box says eight and up so Mom wouldn't let me bake my own cakes without her around. Santa must like Auntie Cady a whole lot that you got one when you're *five*," Melanie declared.

"Maybe Daddy told her I'm real good at making cupcakes so Santa knows I'll be good at baking *real* cakes in *my own oven*," Janie suggested enthusiastically.

"Well, it's something," Melanie told her authoritatively. "Mom says Santa's real stuck on giving toys at the right ages so she had to promise him she'd watch over me when I used mine."

Janie turned to Cady and Coert. "Daddy, are you gonna hafta watch over me?"

Coert's deep voice rumbled. "Absolutely."

Janie made a face.

Then she made a face to Melanie.

Melanie giggled.

Janie's face melted and she giggled too.

Pat's lips came again to Kath's ear.

"How 'bout you give Janie and Melanie something to do so Cady can suck face with her man after he gave her that bling?"

He pulled away and she turned her head to catch his gaze.

"Excellent thinking, Mr. Moreland."

"I'm not just a pretty face, Mrs. Moreland."

She grinned.

Then she pushed out of the couch. "Right, kids. How about we do real baking and get on Jesus's birthday cake? Who's with me?"

"Me!" Janie cried, jumping up, making Midnight dance and follow her as she raced toward Kath.

"Me too!" Melanie yelled.

"Me three!" Ellie shouted.

"Okay, you're my cake troop. Let's move out. Destination," she pointed in that direction, "kitchen."

The girls rushed to the kitchen.

Kath followed them but looked over her shoulder.

The table was in the way and Coert and Cady were still on the floor.

So the girls in the kitchen couldn't see.

But Kath could.

And Coert knew his daughter couldn't.

So they sucked face.

Of a sort.

It was short. It was soft. It was still wet.

And it was sweet.

Kath moved into the kitchen and she did it grinning.

"Time for assignments," she proclaimed. "We need someone in charge of batter patrol. Someone in charge of icing patrol. And someone in charge of decorating patrol. We all help but you always gotta have the one in charge. Now, who's batter?"

Three hands went up.

Kath's lips again tipped up.

And they made a hella mess of the kitchen.

But they also made a delicious cake for Jesus.

THE FOOD WAS on the table. They were getting ready to pray.

And that was when Pat stood up, grabbing his glass of wine as he went.

Kath looked up at her husband, who was at her left side, then her eyes darted to Cady, who was staring up at Pat with eyes slightly wide, apprehension on her face.

"Something needs to be said," Pat announced.

Kath could feel mixed emotions spring up around a table that had just been mayhem of laying food, filling glasses, finding seats, and the anticipation of feasting.

She looked to Coert, who sat to Cady's left, and then Janie, who sat on a bunch of toss pillows to Coert's left.

Janie was staring at the gravy.

Coert was looking benignly at Pat.

Pat cleared his throat and it wasn't just because he was about to make a speech.

When he first spoke, Kath knew that throat clearing was about something else.

"Dad's not here."

Kath immediately looked down to her plate as the dust again flew.

Pat continued, "And every year we're gonna feel it, Dad not being here, Gramps not being here."

Her husband's voice was getting thick so Kath reached out a hand and rested it on his waist.

She heard him draw in breath so she tipped her head back to gaze up at him again.

"The years will pass but it'll never be the same, not just Christmas, every day. But especially days like today," Pat carried on. "I know this as much as I know Dad would hate that. He'd want us to celebrate with no sadness. But I say he earned that sadness by being the best dad there is, the best grandfather, the best father-in-law, so he earned us missing him now that he's gone."

"Hear, hear," Shannon whispered and the way she did, Kath knew the dust was flying for her too.

She also knew it was flying for Bea when she heard her niece try to swallow a whimper.

"So every year," Pat went on, "before we tuck into Christmas dinner, I say we build a new tradition, raise a glass and take a moment to remember the finest man who ever walked this earth. Patrick Moreland."

He raised his glass.

Everyone reached out, grabbed their glass and followed suit.

All except Janie, who whispered loudly to her father, "Where is he?"

"I'll explain in a bit, honey," Coert murmured, his own glass up.

Coert Yeager sitting with Patrick Moreland's family, lifting his glass in memory of the man.

And, Kath thought, this proved, no matter how old you got, you could bear witness to Christmas miracles.

There was silence and everyone took their own time thinking about Patrick before they brought their glasses to their lips and took a sip.

Pat waited until they were all done but he didn't sit down.

He continued.

"In life, you sometimes lose. If you're lucky, more often you win. And even as you note the losses and try to move on, you should make sure to celebrate the wins. So this, our first Christmas without Dad, I'm pleased just because I'm pleased, but I'm more pleased because I know Dad would be pleased that we had to lay two more place settings. We're down one but up two. It isn't the same. It's different. But it works great. So I'll make my welcome formal, Coert...Janie. Thank you for joining our family."

"Hear, hear!" Kath exclaimed, breaking out into a teary-eyed smile and lifting her glass Coert and Janie's way.

"I second that emotion!" Verity chimed in.

"Yay for Janie and Mr. Coert!" Ellie yelled.

Looking confused, Janie turned to her father. "Are we being adopted?"

Coert chuckled and bent to her, saying, "In a way, cupcake. I'll explain that later too."

"Is Mommy gonna be adopted too?" Janie asked.

Coert's good humor took a hit but Cady leaned forward and said, "Maybe next year."

Janie sat back in her seat, crying, "Neat! Mommy loves family!"

God, Kath hoped so.

Pat smoothed over that by finishing.

"Now let's raise our glasses to Coert, Janie, family and another very merry Christmas!"

Glasses were raised. Sips were taken.

Pat sat down and ordered, "Now for the prayer."

Everyone bowed their heads.

And more dust flew, because in years past, all of them when this family was this family, except the last one when he'd been too ill, Patrick said the prayer.

So this year, Pat made quick work of it before there was a round of murmured amens, Pat lifted his head and encouraged, "Tuck in."

Food was passed, forks were raised and the Moreland family…

No, the Moreland/Yeager family…

Tucked in.

COERT

"SO I BOUGHT it because of this," Cady whispered.

Coert took his eyes from the view where he and Cady were finally alone, cuddled together in the observation room in her lighthouse, and looked down at her head resting on his shoulder.

He had one boot to the floor, one leg up on the built-in seat, Cady snuggled between them, half twisted, resting on his chest, her eyes aimed to the glass surrounding them.

She had one arm wrapped around him.

However, the other hand was up and fiddling with the diamond at her neck.

"I can see that," he replied.

And he could. The minute she'd taken him and Janie on a tour after the cake was in the oven but before the dinner preparations heated up, and they'd climbed up to this room, he'd thought, if he'd had that kind of money, that was what would have done it for him too.

And as unbelievably amazing as the lighthouse was, he was getting a sinking feeling about it.

Their future was together.

And their future included Janie.

Further, he hoped their future included their own child, something at their ages they were going to have to discuss a lot sooner than would be normal in their circumstances.

And if they both agreed, they'd have to see to that a lot sooner too.

But more, he had Janie, *they* had Janie, but they had her in a way where they'd also have time to just have each other.

Coert always wanted his daughter with him but that wasn't the reality. And as much as it wasn't the best situation, with Cady back in his life it worked in its way so they could have that time to relearn each other, share about what had happened in the time in between, build their life as a couple.

In a perfect world, he'd take time to have that alone with Cady.

In their world, which had never been perfect, they didn't have that much time.

That lighthouse, no matter how cool it was, it was not a place to raise a family. There not only wasn't enough room, there would be no privacy, not for Janie, not for Coert and Cady.

The studio might work, at a pinch, but it wouldn't be optimal either.

His house was not large but it did have three bedrooms. He'd renovated the whole thing himself over the ten years he'd had it. He was only five years from paying it off. He had a good deal of equity in it.

It'd cut Cady to move from this place.

But for the readymade family he had to offer her, they'd need Cady to move from this place.

He felt her head leave his shoulder as she pulled slightly away from him and also pulled him away from his thoughts.

"You don't look happy," she observed.

Her hand was still at her pendant so he didn't share his thoughts, not then, that was for later.

Instead, he asked, "You like your diamond?"

"Of course I like my diamond," she answered.

It was one carat.

Moreland could probably have afforded to give her one that was four.

But it was becoming apparent that that wasn't what Moreland had been about.

Coert was beginning to realize the man lived in a big house because he had a big family that just got bigger.

From their clothes and their manner, the Moreland family wasn't about four-carat diamonds.

They were about love and family and humor and togetherness and baking cakes.

"Why would you ask that?" she queried quietly, and she did that studying him closely.

"I wanted to give you something like that the Christmas we had together. I didn't want to give you perfume. I wanted to give you something like that," he shared.

He saw her face grow gentle and she melted back into him. "Well then, now it's even *more* special and it was already amazing."

"What I didn't want to do was give you something, if you hated me after, that you'd hate and get rid of because it brought back ugly memories."

The gentleness went out of her face and sadness washed in.

"Coert," she whispered.

"It totally sucks, how awesome this is, at the same time it's a reminder we gotta run so hard to catch up."

She lifted her hand to rest it at the base of his throat. "That's because it's fresh. We'll settle in and that will fade away."

He hoped so.

"I'm sorry I didn't get you a present," she said, and he knew she was changing the subject. "And it wasn't me who bought those things for Janie. The girls went shopping while I was at your place Christmas Eve. All I could think about was the pie," she admitted.

When she admitted that, suddenly Coert felt like laughing.

"You do know that for birthdays, Christmas, Valentine's Day, whatever, all you ever gotta do is make me a pie," he shared.

She grinned at him, noticeably pleased she'd taken him out of his mood. "I probably should have gotten that message when I gave you the last one and you dragged me up the stairs and ravaged me."

He grinned back, bent his neck and touched his mouth to hers before pulling away and agreeing, "Yeah. And Janie thinks Santa rained that goodness on her. So it's all cool."

"'Kay," she said softly.

He drew her deeper into him, murmuring, "Your family's been great, honey."

"As ever," she replied, her eyes bright. "You'll see."

He might see more but he'd already seen. Janie especially had been folded into the clan with no hesitation. And, except for Mike, who was being unapproachable, they'd done the same with Coert.

"We need to think about me…meeting Kim," Cady noted hesitantly.

"Yeah," he said. "That'll be good, but for Kim, she's hanging in there, she's adjusting, she's supportive, but we gotta give her time. This all went fast. Now we gotta slow it down, only for her, but that has to happen."

She nodded.

"And it's late," he told her. "So my girl needs to be closer to her bed. So I need to find a way to extricate her from your family, most notably your dog, and get her home."

She nodded again, but even with his tease about Midnight, she looked a lot less happy about that.

Coert understood that feeling.

He pulled her up and more fully around before he continued, "I gotta work tomorrow and tonight's mine with Janie, but she goes back to her mom and regularly scheduled programming tomorrow. You need to be with your family. But wanna meet me in town for a drink after dinner or something?"

Another nod, this one a lot more enthusiastic.

He smiled.

Then he dipped in and kissed her.

Cady kissed him back.

They necked for a while with the sea and the lights and forest of Magdalene all around.

When Coert ended it, he lifted his head and said quietly, "Best Christmas of my life."

Her eyes, those green eyes warm from his kiss, got wet as she breathed, "Coert."

"Best Christmas Eve too, and it only had a little bit to do with the fact I didn't have to wrap all Janie's presents," he teased.

She got hold of the wet in her eyes in order to smile at him.

He kissed her again.

Yeah.

Best Christmas in his life.

Then, unfortunately, Coert had to guide Cady down the stairs through her bedroom to the family room and hang with his daughter while she and her "new cousins" finished watching *The Muppet Christmas Carol.*

This had benefits, since Janie fell asleep before the end.

So it was gently that he carried his daughter downstairs and pulled her jacket, hat and mittens on with Cady helping. And it was quietly he carried her falling-back-to-sleep body to his truck with Cady and half her family following, saying goodnight and their last Merry Christmases. The women (with Cady being the last) laid kisses on Janie's cheek then stretched up to do the same with Coert (this allowing Cady to do it too, after a day where they'd been careful with displays of affection in front of his daughter), before he strapped her in his truck.

But the others drifted away and it was only Cady standing outside in her jacket, her gloves on, a long scarf wrapped round and round her neck, waving as he drove to the gate Daly had opened for them.

Leaving Cady behind.

On Christmas.

Next Christmas, he'd wake up beside her.

And as soon as Coert could manage it, that would happen every day.

Twenty-One

THE TIME IN BETWEEN

COERT

Present day…

Coert tore his mouth from Cady's, pulled her ass off the basin where he'd planted it and put her feet to the ground.

He barely got her there before he turned her to face the sink, put his hands to her belt and started to undo it.

His cock jerked when he heard her sharp gasp.

Being quick in getting them undone, he yanked her jeans down to her thighs before he reached for his wallet.

He'd tossed it in the basin and was pulling his own pants down when he heard Cady ask breathily, "Is it legal to have sex in the bathroom of a bar, Sheriff?"

His eyes went to hers in the mirror and his hand went to his dick.

She looked turned on, hot, bothered, and sexy as all hell with her face like that and her pants yanked down.

"Anything's legal if you don't get caught, honey," he answered. "So be quiet."

"I think it's doubtful you're going to say that at the next sheriff convention."

He fought a grin as he rolled the condom on and warned, "You're not being quiet."

"Are there sheriff conventions?" she asked in a way he knew she was screwing with him because it was even breathier and her face was getting hotter and a lot more bothered.

She wasn't going to shut up.

So he dipped his knees, slanted one arm across her chest, hand curling around her jaw, thumb gliding across her lower lip.

Her tongue came out to touch it.

He felt that touch drive through his balls, and he watched as he guided himself to her and drove inside at the same time he slid his thumb in her mouth.

Her head fell back.

And then Coert watched himself fuck her, gliding his other hand around her hip and honing in.

She whimpered against his thumb when he hit his target.

Jesus, she was spectacular.

He fucked her harder while his finger circled her clit.

Her eyes found his in the mirror and Cady sucked his thumb deeper.

"Christ," he bit out low, going faster.

She got way up on her toes, angling her ass to get more of him and Coert gave more to her, staring at her taking him, front and back, in the mirror.

He flattened his thumb against her tongue then slid it out, raking it across her bottom teeth, forcing her mouth open so he could hear her rasping breaths.

She brought her top teeth down and nipped the pad of his thumb.

"*Christ*," he grunted, and watched as Cady took one of the hands she had braced against the basin and wound it behind them, grabbing on to his bared ass and holding tight.

She turned her head and he lost the look on her face as she tucked it in his neck so he dropped his head and listened to her beg, "Fuck me, Coert."

"Again," he growled.

"Fuck me, honey."

He bowed his knees further and powered up, taking her off her toes and getting off on her abrupt gasp.

"Yes, Coert, I'm...*Coert*."

He used his jaw and chin to force her head back and took her mouth right when she came. The whimper sounded soft and muted in the room but it tasted fucking *phenomenal*.

She returned the favor, grasping his ass, taking his thrusts, wrapping her other arm around his head to hold his lips to hers. Pumping her tongue into his mouth in tandem with his drives, she muffled his grunts and swallowed his deep groan when everything disintegrated and his world became nothing but Cady's hand at his ass, her tongue in his mouth, his cock buried in her pussy.

Coming down he glided inside awhile before he pulled out and away, steadying her as he did. When she had hold of the basin and was firm on her feet, he yanked his jeans up, helped her right hers and she finished doing them while he dealt with the condom and grabbed his wallet out of the sink.

She leaned against the basin as Coert was washing his hands and she did it sharing, "That was the hottest thing we've ever done."

She was not wrong.

They'd always run hot.

But bathroom-in-a-bar sex?

Nothing was that hot.

Having squirted soap in his hands, he turned his head to her and grinned.

She must have liked the way he did because her gaze dropped to his mouth and her face gentled but her eyes flared with heat.

But her mouth kept moving.

"Except, maybe, me attacking you on my couch."

Coert shook his head, and still grinning, he turned his attention to his hands.

"Or when you dragged me up to your bed after I gave you a pie."

Coert continued grinning as he rinsed his soapy hands.

"Or when you dragged me back to your bed not letting me finish my wine."

He turned off the faucet, leaned into her, and she didn't move as he reached for some paper towel.

"Then there was that time on the kitchen floor at Casey's house," she carried on. "And the time we didn't make it up the stairs after we came home from that party at Lonnie and Maria's. And that time we found that waterbed at, what were their names?" She didn't wait for an answer. She said, "We need to find another water bed."

He twisted at the waist, brushing her with an arm, they were that close, and tossed the spent paper towels to the bin, refusing to burn brain cells thinking about how great it was they were at a place where these memories were hot and sweet and not hard and painful.

Cady kept talking.

"And under the Christmas tree. And in the bed of your truck. It was cold that night, but you kept me warm. And—"

He hooked her with an arm and yanked her to his body, dropping his head and saying, "Baby, you want a drink?"

"I think we should celebrate Sheriff Coert Yeager's first unlawful act, so yes."

That was when he started laughing.

But he'd barely started doing it before he dropped his head farther and kissed her right through it.

"UH, JUST TO say, although I'm beyond thrilled you were so impatient to get in my pants, Sheriff Yeager, I've been released from family duty for the evening primarily because Mike and Pam want to sleep in a real bed, not in the back of an RV. So they essentially kicked me out."

They were out of the bathroom sitting at a high table on tall barstools at the Adam and Eve, the oldest bar in Magdalene, claimed as such even though it was a couple miles outside the city limits, inland from the sea.

It was popular with the townies, who kept quiet about it so they'd have a place to go that the tourists wouldn't find. It was mostly a dive, but only in a been-around-awhile-and-the-owners-didn't-feel-like-redecorating kind of way.

And fortunately the bathrooms were clean, there were four of them, and all of them were single occupancy.

Coert had bought Cady a glass of wine and he had a bottle of beer in front of him.

"So I have my overnight bag in my car," she finished.

"Am I gonna get that until I get Janie back Monday night?" he asked, hoping he would because it was Friday and he'd be freaking thrilled to bed down with Cady and wake up with her the next two days.

"Do you want it?" she asked back.

He shot her a look and didn't bother to answer a question that stupid.

She smiled at him. "Then you're getting it." She reached out a hand to his and the second she touched him, he turned his wrist and curled his fingers around hers. "And can you spend some time with us this weekend?"

He shook his head but said, "I can but not much. To give my guys time with their families on a weekend after a holiday, I'm in the office both days and on call all weekend. You'd think things would slow down around the holidays because they're the holidays and because it's frickin' cold outside. But it's the opposite, mostly because people drink a lot, and drunk people do stupid shit. Stupid drunk people do really stupid shit. And both kinds get really drunk around Christmas."

"Ah," she murmured.

"So maybe if you want me for dinner, I can do that. But if I get a call, I gotta roll."

She nodded.

"I'll give you a key to my house so you can get in."

At that, she smiled again and her fingers curled tighter around his.

"And I'll give you one to the lighthouse too and order another remote for the gate," she told him.

And at that, Coert tightened his fingers around hers.

He then gave her hand a tug and leaned in. "By the way, when your family is gone, we have a command performance meal at The Eaves with Jake and Josie, Amelia and Mick and Alyssa and Junior."

For a second she looked confused then it dawned on her and she looked sheepish.

"I meant to tell you that I met Josie and Alyssa at a shop on the jetty."

"I know. Alyssa had a break at the salon today and took it to stroll to the station. Apparently we should have picked something other than the town's beauty salon to have a drama right outside their window."

Her eyes got big.

Coert leaned in and gave her a quick kiss before he pulled away.

"It's okay," he said softly.

"You're the sheriff."

"Baby, I fucked you in the bathroom of the Adam and Eve. You didn't have sex hair when you walked out but you sure had sex face. We're sitting here holding hands. We're not a secret. We're also human and shit happens. It's against the law to have sex in a public place. It isn't against the law to shout at someone on the street."

She looked alarmed.

"I had sex face?" she asked.

She still kinda did.

He didn't tell her that.

Through his chuckle, he answered, "Trust me, it's a good look."

"Oh my God," she breathed.

He kept chuckling, and to move her past that, told her, "They have a reservation. And Alyssa says she's waiting for your call to make an appointment at the salon so she's not only nosing into our business, she's recruiting a new client. She's crazy, but she's a really good person. Great wife. Great mother. Far's I can tell, great friend. She's on a bent of adopting all the new women around her age that come to town, and there's been a few of them recently, Josie and Amelia namely. My impression is she's done that because they needed a girl close to get them through some rough times. She's making it clear they want to take you on, and I'll say, you could do worse but not sure you could do better."

"So you know all of these people?" she asked.

"Jake's one of my closest buds. Mickey's the same. So yeah. Josie and Jake didn't get married too long ago and Josie adopted Jake's youngest, his two older kids have a different mom. Amelia's newer but she and Mick have been together for a while now. I say that because you won't feel new or like you're coming into a group that's established and you're the odd man out. Except for Alyssa, all the women are all new to Magdalene and they're all mostly just starting out together with their men. So in a way, we'll both fit right in."

"I know I shouldn't share, about us, I mean, with you being a public figure. An elected figure. But I have to tell you that I might have let slip—"

"Honey," he whispered, leaning closer to her. "I know what you said. Alyssa alluded to it. I don't care. It happened. What happened with us happened. You didn't do anything wrong, now or then. I didn't do anything wrong. We didn't go on a killing spree. We got caught up in something extreme that we were too young to cope with. I've got nothing to hide. Neither do you." He grinned. "And if it gets out, which with Alyssa is a crapshoot, it'll wrap up the female vote for me. Long lost loves reunited. They'll all swoon."

She leaned back, took hold of her wine in her free hand, but even pulling away, she kept hold of his hand.

And she did all of this stating, "Women do vote for people for more reasons than they're attractive or they're heading toward the happily ever after, living a real-life, mostly tragic, finally brightening romance novel, Coert." She took a sip with her eyes directed away and slanted them back before concluding, "And it's been some time since women regularly swooned and they did it before mostly because they had to wear corsets."

Coert busted out laughing.

Cady rolled her eyes.

He erased the distance she'd put between them by kissing her lightly again, tasting wine and Cady, before he shifted away and grabbed his bottle of beer.

After taking a swig, he said, "So we're on for the fourth of January at The Eaves. It's dressy. Is that cool?"

"The guys and the kids are leaving the second but the girls are staying until that weekend for some girl time. Do you think they could come?" she asked.

"I think Jake and Mick are my best buds but if we put Alyssa together with Kath, Pam and Shannon, and they have to sit through that, they might not think the same way about me."

She blinked at him.

"Kath, particularly, is nuts," he told her. "But in a good way," he added.

"They're lovely," she retorted.

"They are," Coert agreed. "But I haven't lived forty-six years of life not figuring out what kind of women should not be thrown together when there are people with penises in the mix."

Her upper body started shaking, and her voice was too when she replied, "Alyssa struck me as someone who would be Kath's best friend in the entire world in about two seconds, and that world should watch out when that happens."

As she spoke, something struck Coert and the smile he had on his face died.

"Was she the one who was with you when you went to see Caylen?"

Cady had watched his smile die and her face grew concerned. "Yes, but honestly, Coert, he was being—"

"I'm glad."

She shut up.

"Don't go see him again," he ordered.

She shook her head. "I already told you I won't."

"When I told you before you shouldn't, I didn't mean it the way I mean how I'm telling you now you just *won't*."

Cady stared at him.

"I get it," he said. "You're your own woman. Got your own money. Your own home. Your own car. Your own life. Your own mind. And it may seem the way I'm saying all that that I'm patronizing you. But I promise, I really do get it. But back then, Cady, I was not in a place to put a stop to that asshole being an asshole to you. Now I am. He called the fucking sheriff to warn his sister off just to make trouble for you. Your parents are dead. As far as he knows, he's all you've got and that's his response?" Coert shook his head. "No. You have a family now. One that's growing with me and Janie and then maybe Jake and Josie, Mick, Amelia, Alyssa, Junior, and all that may come from that. You don't need him. You have all you need."

She stroked the side of his hand with her thumb. "I already gave up on him, Coert."

"Good," he bit out.

"Kath called him a fool to his face."

"Good," he repeated.

"And, well, also a dick."

"Good," he clipped.

She stopped talking but continued studying him.

Coert took another swig of beer.

When he put the bottle back down, she noted softly, "You wanted to protect me back then."

"I thought I made that clear," he reminded her.

"You did, I just..." She looked away and grabbed her glass again. "You did."

He waited for her to take a sip and then squeezed her hand to get her attention.

She looked at him.

"What?" he pushed because he knew she'd left something unsaid.

She didn't make him push harder.

"I was so young, even with all these years, so much pain was covering it that I didn't see underneath it to see that you kept your promise."

Coert felt something twisting in his gut. "What promise?"

"That I'd never be safer with anyone than I was with you."

It was then Coert looked away as that twist in his gut made him feel suddenly sick.

She jerked his hand but Coert just took another swig of his beer to keep down the bile threatening and kept his eyes unseeing across the bar.

"Coert," she called gently.

"I didn't keep you safe, Cady."

"At dinner, both times with my parents and Caylen, you can't know. I'm glad you'll never know. But I used to lose it, lose my temper, or get beaten down. But when I was with you, I just endured it because I knew I'd be going home with you. I knew my life was just us and they didn't matter anymore. If my mom said something or Caylen said something, all I did was look at you and I could handle it."

That got her Coert's eyes.

"And when we were out with Lars's crew," she continued. "I didn't like it but I knew you knew it and I wasn't there for them. I was there with you. So I didn't care. I didn't feel unsafe. It was the same thing. I could handle it because you were there with me and in the end, always in the end, Coert, we'd be together and just be...us."

"And that ended not as an always," he returned.

"And now it's begun again and it'll forever be an always."

He didn't have anything to say to that because he hoped to God she was right.

She leaned closer to him. "You bought all the food and you took out the trash and you helped me do the dishes, and you got out of bed early to take me to work that time my car wouldn't start because it was so cold. I loved that. I loved everything about you. Which means I loved how you took care of me and you didn't make a big deal of it. You just did it like you just breathed."

"And the time in between I didn't."

"Stop it," she hissed.

Her sudden change of tone made Coert's head jerk.

"You told me not to go back there, but you keep going back there, Coert. So stop it. We're not there. We're here."

She shook his hand hard and kept speaking.

"And we're never going to get from here to wherever we're going if you stay back there. You gave me my diamond and all you could think about was that you wanted to give it to me before. But that doesn't matter." She lifted her free hand to her throat where his diamond lay. "*I have my diamond.* I have *you.* If you stay in a place where we didn't have each other, what we have now is going to get bitter and twisted and ugly when, if you were right here with me, in a bar in a beautiful town with a beautiful person you love, you'd see that all we have left of the time in between is just that. *Beautiful.*"

He took his fingers from around his beer and cupped the side of her face.

And again he had nothing to say because she again was absolutely right.

Though he had something to say about something else.

"That time in between made you wise," he murmured.

"That time in between made you more handsome, which I find annoying since it just made me older."

He felt his face get soft. "You're beautiful, Cady. You've always been beautiful. And you always will be."

She slid her eyes to his ear, muttering, "Right."

"I miss the freckles though."

She slid her eyes back.

And when she did, they were wet.

"I love you," she whispered.

He dropped his forehead to hers.

"Now you know that I wasn't happy because I didn't have you," she told him. "But I was taken care of and I was loved and there were a lot of really good times and you left me to that. You left me with Patrick. It wasn't your choice and it wasn't the way it should be, but it was the way it was and what came of that is beautiful. And you got your job and this Jake person and Mickey, and you got Janie. We both suffered but neither of us stopped living our lives and we got so much out of them, so, so much. And now we have each other. So we have it all. If we believe that we can have it all. And I believe. Now, are you with me on that?"

"I'm with you, Cady," he told her quietly.

"Good, because I'm going to have to get angry if you slip back there again."

He felt his eyes get lazy with his smile and he adjusted so he could touch his mouth to hers.

But he didn't separate the connection of their foreheads when he pulled his lips away.

"I'll try not to make you angry," he promised.

"See to that," she ordered, being irritable, he knew, to fight another emotion still in her eyes.

"Yes, ma'am," he mumbled.

He watched from close as her eyes narrowed. "Are you patronizing me now?"

Coert slid his hand to curl it around her neck. "Baby, chill. I'm good. We're good. We're having a drink, and then we're going to my place and sleeping together and waking up together, two days straight, so we got a lot to look forward to."

"Right," she said, disconnecting them to the point he removed his hand, and reaching for her wine. "So drink up. I want to get home because I get the top when we have sex in your bed again. You've only let me have the top when I attacked you on the couch. I like the top. You go too fast. If I'm in charge, we'll take it slow."

He couldn't believe it, but his dick was getting hard.

However.

"Cady, you're so not gonna take it slow."

She swallowed her wine and turned to him. "You do things that escalate things. I'll do things that elongate things."

If she didn't quit talking about sex, something was going to elongate to the point he couldn't walk out of the bar.

"Cady, stop talking about sex."

She ignored him. "And you don't get to touch me."

Christ.

"Cady, stop talking about sex."

"Maybe I'll make you hold on to the headboard."

Jesus.

"Cady, *stop talking about sex*."

She gulped back some wine and looked at him again.

"Do you have handkerchiefs?" she asked. "I'm thinking I'll tie you up."

Coert looked to the ceiling and puffed out a breath.

"Oh, right, so it's only the woman who's supposed to be tied up," she declared.

He took hold of her again, this time with his fingers curled around the back of her scalp, and when he pulled her to him it was more of a yank.

"No. It isn't. But I can talk to you about how I'm down with you tyin' me up and ridin' my face and then ridin' my cock and taking yourself there as often as you want usin' me to do it, and I can see that look in your eyes, baby. You like that. And you can walk outta here likin' that, gettin' wet for me, your panties drenched you want that so bad, and no one will know, but me. But I like that too and I can't just walk outta here with a drop of pre-cum on my dick and no one will know. You hear what I'm sayin'?"

She got closer, sliding a hand up the top of his thigh which was *not helping*.

She did this saying breathily, "Wow, dirty talk is fun."

"You are not getting me."

She gave him a hooded-eyes, sexy-as-fuck grin and leaned back, dislodging his hand and removing her own, going again to her wine, murmuring, "Oh, I'm getting you, Coert."

He hated his name. All his life he'd hated his name. No one knew how to pronounce it. No one knew how to spell it.

On Cady's lips, which were curved up in that hot way, he loved it.

She'd played him.

Got him hard on purpose.

A new discovery from Cady.

He liked it.

"Hurry up with that wine," he ordered.

She looked at him again. "You can't chug wine, Coert."

He lifted a brow.

She grinned and took another sip.

He lifted his beer and didn't take a swig, he took a glug.

He also managed to control his erection by the time they walked out of the bar.

But just barely.

CADY FLEW OVER the edge.

Coert kept bucking up into her as she did and he continued to do it, digging his heels in the bed, his head in the pillows, his fingers curled so tight around the slats in the headboard, it was a miracle they didn't snap, as he shot inside her.

His grunts mingled with her moans, the sounds of their flesh connecting and Cady whimpering, "Coert."

So he kept exploding.

Finally, his hips settled. His muscles relaxed. She collapsed on top of him, her hair all over his face and neck, and Coert didn't care.

The room smelled of sex and Cady, her perfume, the scent of her hair. Her warm, soft body was heavy on top of him, her breaths harsh against his neck. Her slick pussy was tight around his dick, the taste of her still in his mouth, the vision of her lost in it, lost in him, so focused on what they had it was unreal as she rode him. With all that, he could be suspended in that moment for an eternity and he wouldn't have cared.

He could rub it in she went fast. She rode his face for about five minutes before she got so excited, she had to move down, fumbling maddeningly (but that was in a good way) in her excitement with the condom, and then climbing on his cock in order to ride him rough and hard, like they both had only minutes to reach orgasm before the earth careened into the sun.

But he wasn't going to rub it in.

At least not now.

Because now he was riding the high of learning there was something hotter than bathroom-in-a-bar sex.

Explosive.

And through it he got to watch her ride him, her beautiful body naked.

All except his diamond.

He turned his head and kissed whatever his lips encountered, which was her hair over her temple.

Then he muttered, "You get your way. You can have the top more often."

She took her time lifting her head like she didn't have the energy to do it (and this wasn't surprising, she'd gone gung ho, especially when she was riding his cock) and looked down at him.

"Well, thank you."

He knew she meant it snotty but it came out wispy so he smiled.

She shook her head then pushed up slightly, coming away from him. He felt her undo her wool scarf that bound his hands to his headboard.

When it went slack, he slid them free and rounded her with his arms but didn't move them any other way.

Cady settled back down, flicking her hair away from his face, which was too bad, but burying her face in his neck, which he liked.

"We need to do that again," she murmured.

"You get tied up next time," he replied.

She said nothing but she didn't have to since she also shivered and he knew it wasn't because she was cold.

He kept one arm wrapped around her waist and used his other hand to smooth over her back, trail through her hair, just touching her, taking her in, before he curved it around her upper back and stroked his knuckles against the side of her breast.

"We should probably not have so much sex and talk more, baby," he murmured. "There's a lot to talk about."

"Mm, but I like having sex," she murmured back.

He smiled at the ceiling.

She kissed his neck but otherwise didn't move. "We'll talk. Maybe I can meet you for lunch tomorrow. We'll go somewhere like Weatherby's where it would be terribly inappropriate for Sheriff Yeager to have an erection so I'll be certain not to make that happen. Instead, I'll share such important tidbits as, the lighthouse is beginning its tours in February but I'm beginning to volunteer at the Historical Society mid-January. And I still want a French bulldog, or a mastiff, or a Newfoundland. And since Janie has clearly stolen Midnight from me, I now have an excuse."

Coert heard all she said but it was only one thing that made him stop stroking her to twist his fist gently in her hair and give it a soft tug as he turned his head to the side.

She lifted hers and caught his eyes.

"Tours?" he asked.

"Yes. Two days a month. A Saturday and a Sunday, not the same weekend. Ticketed only. Small groups. And they'll be guided."

This wasn't getting better.

"Guided how?"

"Guided…*guided.* An attendant will be in the lighthouse with the people on tour."

Nope.

It wasn't getting better.

"You mean you're not opening the gate, you're opening *your home*?" he asked.

"Well, yes," she answered.

"I don't like that, Cady."

She looked perplexed. "Why?"

"That's your home," he said again.

"Yes," she unnecessarily agreed.

"And people do stupid shit."

She didn't have a reply to that.

"You have things," he stated. "Nice things. Things sticky fingers can grab. Or they'll come there to case the joint. And you just invested a lot to make that joint a really nice joint. They see that they'll think you have more. Cash. Jewelry. Whatever. You live alone. And that lighthouse is not close to town or really anything."

"I have Midnight and I have Elijah, and when you don't have Janie, I'll have you, and I have an alarm and again, there will be a volunteer doing the tours," she reminded him.

"Cady, it's not smart to open your home to strangers."

"And I have a gate and a fence, Coert," she went on like he didn't say anything.

"You've unfortunately been touched by it but it was in your life and then it was out. It's been my life, my career, since I graduated college and the academy so I know people can suck, Cady. I know there are some of them that, if they can't find ways to suck, they'll invent them. And it isn't rare they can do all that."

"You graduated college?"

Christ, he forgot how cute she could be *all the time.*

"University of Colorado, criminal justice and poli sci," he said shortly so he could get back to the matter at hand. "You need to ditch these tours."

"Coert, Jackie at the Historical Society is over the moon to be able to give tours. Not only that, I'm donating the proceeds of the tickets to the Society. She's already had her yearly budget approved with her estimate of revenue from this and it's substantial. I can't back out now."

"It isn't wise."

"It isn't foolish either. People in England give tours of private homes and they wouldn't do that if everyone was robbing them blind."

"This isn't England."

"I know. It's Magdalene, which is *New* England."

"Cady," he growled.

"Coert," she snapped.

They fell silent, and as Coert kept his silence, he remembered something else. This being that way back when, he and Cady had disagreed very little.

But regardless of the fact she didn't hold a degree she was sharp as a whip. No one with that quick a sense of humor wasn't highly intelligent.

The bad part about that was, she didn't use that intelligence just to be funny.

She was killer with a comeback in an argument.

Coert broke the silence.

"Am I gonna be able to talk you out of this?"

Cady responded immediately. "No."

"Then there'll be a sheriff's presence at the lighthouse on tour days."

Her eyes got huge. "That's not necessary."

"I'm the sheriff, Cady. So it's me who gets to say what's necessary."

"That's a personal abuse of resources. Which is an abuse of power. And it's a conflict of interest."

"It isn't a conflict of interest."

He had her there and he knew she knew it when her reply was, "Well, it's the other two."

It absolutely was.

That said…

"It's Magdalene's lighthouse, Cady, now being open to the public. And as Magdalene doesn't have its own police force, in these new circumstances, it's up to me to make certain it remains secure. To add to that, the land outside the lighthouse is officially unincorporated Derby County land, not within the Magdalene city limits, so it's not only in my jurisdiction, I think it's well within the purview of the county's sheriff department to see, with increased traffic, that that area is safe."

"That's ridiculous and extreme and I'm uncertain your voters will feel the same way you do."

"You gonna produce a campaign video to share it with the world?"

"No," she bit off. "But we had a drama in front of the beauty salon. I came out of a bathroom in a bar, a bathroom that I was in with *you*, with sex face, and we held hands and kissed through a drink. We're having lunch together at Weatherby's tomorrow where I'm not going to make you get hard. People will learn I'm your woman and they'll hear you're assigning deputies to guard my home. They'll question it and I don't think they'll like the answers they come up with."

"Your home happens to be the lighthouse open to the public and I'm not assigning deputies to give the tours, Cady. I said there'll be a sheriff's *presence*.

My boys might do drive-bys. They might park and remain. It's two days a month, not three hundred, sixty-five days a year. If there's a murder, obviously, they won't hang at a lighthouse staring down tourists. They'll roll out."

"There's murders in this county?" she whispered.

"There's murders everywhere," he replied.

"Oh my God, how many murders have you investigated?"

He didn't know whether to growl with frustration or bark with laughter.

So he just squeezed her tight and reminded her, "We're talking about you opening your home to strangers."

"I brought the old girl back to life, Coert. That needs to be shared. That's Magdalene's history. It's beautiful. Honestly, how selfish would it be to keep those views from the observation room just for us and our friends and family?"

They were getting into sticky territory here not only because she was making sense but also because the lighthouse wasn't his. It wouldn't ever be his. Maybe in nineteen, twenty years when their kid graduated from high school and they were empty-nesters, they could move in there.

But in the meantime, it wouldn't even really be hers because she'd be in the bed she was in right now.

"I'll share with Jackie you have concerns and that she or the other volunteers might see deputies around until you feel better about the situation," she carried on. "But except the winter months where weather can be extreme, she's expecting full tours for each day and she's doing that because quite a bit of them are already booked. She's been advertising this is coming for months. I can't let her down now. I just can't, Coert. And if you feel your sheriff's deputies have to stare them down in case a master burglar or a meth head looking to score some glassware and knickknacks he can pawn to pay for his next stash comes calling, then all right."

"All right?" he asked to confirm.

"All right," she confirmed.

"Can I be amused instead of annoyed at you now?" he asked to tease.

She narrowed her eyes.

He'd lost her between their legs so he rolled her to her back, stretching down her side, and all through this he was grinning at her.

"I can't imagine how you'd find it annoying that I would say what I'm going to do with my own home," she remarked.

"I can't imagine how you'd find it surprising that anything I think might cause you harm, or upset or aggravation, I'd want to do something to stop."

When she shut her mouth, she did it so hard he could swear he heard her teeth clack together.

Finally, he got her.

That was when he started laughing.

He just didn't do it out loud.

"Do you not have any women deputies?" she rapped out suddenly.

"Why do you ask that?" he returned, still chuckling.

"You call them your 'men' and your 'boys' and they aren't that if there are females among them."

"I wouldn't call them that if there were women, which there aren't," he answered.

"Why not?" she demanded to know.

"Because Liz moved to Annapolis with her husband a coupla years ago. He got the offer of a job at a firm that he couldn't turn down. He's a defense attorney, by the way, so you can imagine what it was like at their house. But she loved him and she managed not to kill him the five years I knew them while they were married, or the two years they've been gone, so go figure. And Jillian took leave to have a baby and decided not to come back, *and*," he stressed when she opened her mouth, "that was her decision. She was a loss. The guys still invite her to anything we have going on and she's still on the softball team. So now that I laid that out, maybe you can give Gloria Steinem a rest and I can have Cady back."

"Oh my God," she hissed. "You didn't just say that."

Coert dipped his face to hers. "Baby, you are just too easy to tease. You don't want your buttons pushed, your best bet isn't to turn on those blinking arrows pointing to them."

"I'm not enjoying discovering annoying, button-pushing Coert Yeager," she declared.

He moved in, burying his face in her neck. "Too late, honey. You're never getting rid of me now."

She lay tense under him only a second before she turned into him and wrapped her arms around him.

He kissed her neck.

She kissed his throat.

Coert guessed that meant they were done bickering.

"Gotta hit the bathroom, baby," he muttered in her ear.

"'Kay. I'll be in in a bit. Need to wash my face and brush my teeth."

He gave her neck another kiss before he slid away from her, out of bed and walked to the bathroom.

After he turned the water on to wash his hands, she came in wearing a nightie, and Coert wished she'd nabbed his sweater.

He dried his hands as she moved to the sink beside his that he never used and set her stuff down, lifting her hands to bind her hair back.

He reached for his toothbrush. "Lunch is good tomorrow. I'll text when I know I've got an hour free. Is that cool?"

"Yeah, honey," she replied.

He loaded toothpaste on his toothbrush but before he started brushing, he looked at her in the mirror and said, "I think Janie would like to see everyone again before they go so can you talk to the family? Set something up?"

She turned off the faucet and reached for the towel to dry her face, answering, "Of course. I'll tell you at lunch tomorrow."

Toothbrush to his lips, he didn't brush, he said, "She needs alone time with just you and me too. And I'd rather not wait until after your family leaves," and then he stuck the brush in his mouth.

She tossed the towel aside and grabbed her brush. "Whenever you're ready for that but I think the family night first. And also, you should be around the day before the men and kids leave. We'll probably do something up big. I'm not sure of the schedule. Do you have Janie on New Year's Day?"

He spit, rinsed, and told her, "Half day. The evening. Kim has her New Year's Eve this year. So you'll have me."

She pulled the brush out of her mouth, turned to him, and garbled, "Eggzelent."

Coert moved to her, hooked her around the waist, bent and touched her nose with his lips.

When he lifted, she went back to brushing but didn't move out of his hold.

"But you need to know, I'll be on call and just to say, New Year's is crazy town so I might be in and out or I might be in for the beginning and then gone until whenever I come home to you."

She kept brushing and nodded.

Coert kissed her nose again.

When he lifted away the second time, he murmured, "Meet you in bed."

She nodded again, grinning at the same time she was brushing.

Yeah, forty-one years old and his Cady was still cute.

He gave her a quick squeeze, let her go and left the room.

He'd pulled on pajama bottoms, walked the house, checked the doors, turned out the lights, and by the time he hit his bedroom, Cady was done in the bathroom and was under the covers in his bed.

It was the most beautiful vision he'd seen since his daughter waved good-bye to him at preschool that morning.

So Coert took it in as he moved across the room.

And met her there.

Twenty-Two

PARADISE

CADY

Present day…

Midnight woofed at the same time her body jerked, this jerking me awake in Coert's bed.

I got up on an elbow just as she woofed again and exited the bed.

It was mostly dark, but I could see faint light coming in from the hallway because I'd left the kitchen light on for Coert.

We'd had lunch together at Weatherby's that day and managed to get through it without finding a bathroom to have sex.

It was awesome doing something as everyday as meeting your man for his lunch hour. I'd never had that.

I loved it.

I still missed the sex.

He also came over for dinner that night, and I belatedly made my family (and Coert) spaghetti pie.

He'd approved.

Then again, I already knew Coert Yeager liked pie in all forms. I'd made him a shepherd's one back in the day and he'd loved that too.

However, he'd had a callout, which meant he'd left not long after Dexter and Corbin had their fourth servings, which meant around eight o'clock.

I looked at the alarm clock on Coert's nightstand and it said it was nearly one in the morning.

What I didn't hear was any barking.

I figured this meant Coert was home.

I threw back the covers and got hit with a blast of cold that washed whatever sleep that was remaining clean away.

Nevertheless, Coert was home so I left the bed, the room, walked down the hall and stairs and was wincing as I adjusted to the light from the kitchen when I hit the doorway to it. Through my wince I saw Coert in his light-brown sheriff's shirt with the beige thermal under it walking my way with Midnight prancing beside him.

"Baby, you shouldn't have left bed," he said, making it to me and reaching out a hand to the switch to douse the light in the kitchen.

He threw an arm around my shoulders and turned me around to go back up the stairs, guiding me that way.

"Is everything okay?" I asked.

"Suicide."

I almost stopped on the steps but pressure on my shoulders from Coert made me keep going.

"Oh my God. I'm sorry. That's terrible," I whispered.

"It happens. And you can guarantee at least one this time of year." His deep voice sounded both weary and world-weary.

To say the rigors of his job were not lost on me was an understatement. I'd been caught up in those rigors in a way that they couldn't.

However, learning this knowledge, the *full* rigors of his job *had* been lost on me.

Until now.

"I don't know what to say," I told him, feeling powerless to help, even in finding the right words.

"It's the job, Cady," he said, now just sounding tired. "It's actually the definition of the job. Bad shit happens, and that bad shit comes in a lot of forms, and then we wade in."

We'd entered his room and he gave me a gentle shove toward the bed.

"Go back to bed. Gonna walk through the house, make sure all is good. I'll be back."

I felt my best course of action was to do as he asked (or, more accurately, *told*) so I went back to bed. I didn't whistle for Midnight. I let her keep Coert company as he did what he had to do before he bedded down.

He came back, went right to the bathroom, and I saw the light go on before the door closed behind him (and Midnight).

He came out in the pajama bottoms he'd worn the night before that I'd put on the hooks on the back of his door and the bathroom light went out.

He and Midnight joined me in bed.

I turned to him immediately.

He pulled me into his arms the moment I did.

"What can I do?" I whispered.

"You can go back to sleep. I'm dog-tired, Cady. Need some shut-eye and an end to this day."

Well, you couldn't be clearer than that.

"Okay," I replied, snuggling into him.

He pulled the covers farther up our shoulders, tucking them in, and then his arm came back around me and he fell slightly forward, pulling me under him, covering me and weaving his long legs in mine.

"Love you," I said softly.

"Yeah," he replied in the same vein, his arms giving me a squeeze. "Love you back."

"'Night, honey."

"'Night, Cady."

I closed my eyes but I didn't sleep. Not until I heard his breath even. Not until I spent some time marveling that he could fall asleep after what he had to have just gone through. Not until I spent more time processing the fact this wasn't his first suicide, that murders happened everywhere, that his job of position and authority was a good one, a brave one, a necessary one.

But it was far from an easy one.

He did it. He laughed. He joked. He teased. He bought diamond necklaces. He called his daughter "cupcake." He fell asleep with relative ease after a tough night.

He had this.

It wasn't his job.

It was his life.

And he had me.

So I had to have it too.

And I had him.

So I would.

On that thought (or close to it), I fell asleep.

I OPENED MY eyes when I felt Coert (and Midnight) move away from me in bed.

"Honey?" I called.

"Gotta hit the shower and get into the station. Sleep. I'll call you later," he murmured, halting his exit of the bed to lean in and give my temple a kiss.

When he was done kissing me, I turned my head and looked to his shadow in the dark.

"I'll get up with you," I told him.

"Unnecessary," he told me.

"I'll make you breakfast."

"You can sleep, Cady."

I looked beyond him to the alarm clock to see it was before six.

He'd had less than five hours of sleep.

I looked back to his shadow which had recommenced moving.

"I'll make you breakfast."

He stopped and I saw his head swing to me.

"You wanna do that, honey, okay," he said quietly.

I was glad he didn't fight me on it because he'd lose.

I threw the covers back, declaring, "I get the bathroom first."

I took it first and walked out to a room that had the nightstand lights on, stopping to get a touch of the lips from Coert who walked into the bathroom after me.

I went to my bag, dug out the long cardigan I brought, the thick socks. I put them on and Midnight and I went downstairs. I let her out. I found the dog food Coert bought and put some in her bowl. I threw out her water and put out fresh. I made coffee. I let her in.

Then I got down to making Coert breakfast.

This was the good part of where Coert and I were in that moment (not that there were any bad parts, so I should call it the familiar part, which was *one* of the *many* good parts).

There was very little about him that I forgot.

Including what he liked to eat.

So I set about offering that, relishing in the old and the new. Getting back what we had and getting more, learning about each other again as we moved more deeply into what we were going to be.

Coert came down in a fresh sheriff shirt (a dark-brown thermal under it today), his hair still wet from a shower, and he came to me first. After I got a hard, brief kiss, he went to the coffee. Then he walked to the front door (with Midnight). Man and dog came back with the newspaper (though man was holding it).

"Lunch today?" he asked, his eyes roaming me from feet in socks to messy bedhead tamed only slightly by a ponytail holder twisted in a shock of hair on top of my head.

"Can you do that?" I asked back.

"Yes," he answered.

"Then yes."

He gave me a small grin and went to the stool at the end of the island to spread out his newspaper.

"Takin' you and your family to Tink's tomorrow night when we got Janie back," he said.

"We" got Janie back.

Lovely.

And having Janie back.

Lovelier.

I turned from skillet to him. "Tink's?"

"Tinker's. Burger joint. Place is a pit. But it has the best burgers in three counties, and I've done my research on that."

I smiled at him and went back to cooking the sausage patties. "That's going to work because everyone likes burgers and the more atmosphere a place has, the better it is."

"The atmosphere might be toxic at Tink's but you'll be salivating while sucking it in. The Health Department probably passes them because the smell of their burgers and fries has permeated the wood and the inspector can't think, he's so rabid to bite into a burger."

I started laughing softly as I moved the patties around in the skillet then went to toast the bread.

"You don't have to cook for me, Cady."

I pushed the lever down on the toaster and looked to him. "If you expected it, I wouldn't. I'd tell you to kiss my behind. Since you don't, I'll do it whenever I want."

Like every day I had the opportunity.

Because I liked cooking.

But more, because I'd spent half a lifetime wanting to take care of Coert Yeager and now that I had my chance, I wasn't missing any of it.

I didn't share all of that with Coert but I knew he got it when he asked gently, "Running to catch up?"

"As fast as I can."

That got me a sweet smile that I liked a lot so I took it in before I went back to the sausage patties and turned them.

I finished the meal and prepared the plates, mine with one less fried egg on toast (but not one less sausage patty because...*sausage*, enough said). I set Coert's plate beside his paper, mine in front of the empty stool next to him, and he folded the newspaper to shift it out of the way as I retrieved my mug and the pot of coffee.

I gave him a refresh, did the same with my own, put the pot back and then took my place next to him.

I was swallowing my second bite when Coert muttered, "Weird."

I turned my head to him. "Weird what?"

"Don't get pissed, honey, but little girls dream of mermaids and princess castles and knights in shining armor and I know this 'cause I got a little girl and it is just what it is. And little boys, they dream of flying to the moon and being a cowboy or bein' a cop and catching bad guys and I know that because I was a little boy. But it's weird because they got it all wrong and the trouble with that is that sometimes, even after they grow up, they don't realize they're never getting it right."

"Getting what right?" I asked.

"*This morning, with her, having coffee,*" he said as answer.

I felt my breath suspend in my throat so it was difficult saying, "What?"

"That's a quote," he shared.

"A quote from what?"

"A quote of what Johnny Cash said when he was asked to describe paradise."

My chest caught fire with the effort to keep breathing.

"Coert," I whispered.

"For me, it includes breakfast but only 'cause she made it for me."

"Oh my God, you're going to make me cry."

He turned to me, curled a hand around the side of my neck and pulled me to him as he dipped down to me.

"I missed your smell. I missed those green eyes. I missed holding hands with you. And I missed just having coffee with you. When I met you, I was in a place I was too old to dream of flying to the moon. I thought I'd made my dream happen by becoming a cop. But I was too caught up in what I wanted out of my career to take time to think about what I really should be thinking about. What my version of paradise would be and how to work towards that. And a job is only a small part of it. We had a version of paradise, but this here? This is the real thing."

I was breathing heavily so I could only reply quietly, "Definitely going to make me cry."

I saw his eyes smile then I felt his lips press against mine and then he let me go.

He turned to his plate.

I drew deep breaths into my nose and turned back to mine.

"Dispatch knows when I got Janie I can't leave but they keep me informed. When I don't, I have a lot of late nights, Cady. And people are people. They do bad things. They do sad things. So that happens a lot too," he said carefully.

He was sharing. Warning me this was him. This was his life. Last night would not be rare. I had to know what I was in for.

And I had to deal with it.

I kept my eyes aimed to my plate. "I can handle it."

"Okay, honey."

Just that, *Okay, honey.*

He believed in me.

And we were done.

I didn't feel like crying anymore.

We ate. We talked about getting sandwiches from Wayfarer's deli and taking them to his office so he could show me around, introduce me to the crew that was at the station, start the process of sharing the woman in the sheriff's life with the men he worked with.

Running to catch up.

He also told me he'd be at the lighthouse around five thirty to have dinner and hang with the family.

I kissed him at the door to the garage and that one we made a long one. But once he'd walked through it, I didn't stand in it to watch him pull out because it was too cold.

I did the dishes. I took a shower in his shower and got ready to face the day there. I left what I could leave because I was spending the night again and packed what needed to go home.

I took my bag out to my car in his garage and Midnight and I got in. I hit the remote Coert had given me at lunch the day before and started the Jag before I pulled out my phone.

I engaged it. I went to the texts. I went to Coert's string.

And I typed in, *This morning, the bed moved, I opened my eyes, and I was with him.*

I sent the text, reversed out, closed the door and headed home.

At the second sign where I had to stop, my phone binged.

I grabbed it.

Paradise, he'd texted.

My version, I texted back.

I was at a stoplight when I glanced at the text that came in while I was driving.

I was talking about waking up with you.

My heart turned over.

We're being gushy, I replied.

I was in my garage when I read his next, *I don't give a fuck.*

I sent a Bitmoji of me with a big smile on my face and two thumbs up.

Then I sent a Bitmoji of me with big smile, eyes closed, suspended in the air with chest arched out and a stream of pink with sparkles coming out of my chest with LOVE YOU THE MOST in purple streaming through the pink.

Midnight and I got out of the car. I grabbed my bag and I was opening the door to let her in the lighthouse, hearing greetings and also the bing of another text.

Christ, you're a goof.

"But you still love me," I whispered to the phone.

But I sent him the BIG TIME Bitmoji.

And then I followed Midnight into the lighthouse, doing it smiling.

I WAS DRIVING into town to meet Coert at Wayfarer's to get sandwiches.

He was already at the deli. I'd texted him my order.

My mind was on him. On having lunch with him. Dinner with him. Hoping that nothing happened that night to call him away, and not just because I wanted more time with him, but because I didn't want him to have to deal with whatever bad or sad it would be.

My mind was also on Verity, who had finally shared with me (privately, something she'd been holding to herself even if Kath had approached several times to find out what was wrong) that she'd been crushed when Elijah had told her before he'd gone to Bangor that they weren't "going there."

The "there" he was referring to was after he set her away when she'd made a pass at him in his apartment when she'd gone to visit him with the intent of making said pass while he was packing before he left.

This was, I was sure, incredibly humiliating.

This was, as Verity described, done in a sweet and gentle way that only made her want Elijah more.

Which was why, now that Elijah was coming home that day from his holiday with his parents, she was in a dither.

Because she couldn't wait to see him.

And she never wanted to see him again.

I felt for her but he lived there and she was staying there, and although he had to go back to work the next day, Elijah had already been adopted as a member of the family.

It would be difficult to avoid him.

I was wracking my brain to find ways I could assist her to do this as I finished parking, turned off the car, got out, beeped the locks and started toward Wayfarer's when my phone rang.

I pulled it out, saw the number was local, but not one programmed in. I still took the call.

"Hello?" I answered.

"Yes, hello, Cady Moreland?"

"This is Cady Moreland. Who am I speaking to?"

"I'm Terry Baginski. I'm Boston Stone's attorney."

Attorney?

Why was an attorney calling me?

On a Sunday?

My step on the sidewalk faltered as I asked, "Sorry?"

"Terry Baginski," she said impatiently like I was wasting her time, not like she'd phoned me out of the blue *on a Sunday*. "Attorney for Boston Stone. You haven't been returning his calls."

"Um…no. I haven't. I don't know Mr. Stone, and every time one of his people call they don't explain what the call refers to," I shared as I pushed through the doors to Wayfarer's, smiling at someone coming out.

"Well, allow me to share what he's referring to," she replied curtly. "He'd like to make an offer on the lighthouse and the surrounding property."

I was rounding the cash registers, the deli in sight—or more importantly, Coert in his jeans, boots, sheriff shirt and shiny, handsome sheriff jacket with a wool muffler looped around his neck, something that highlighted his strong jaw in sight—when I stopped dead and looked at my feet.

"What did you say?"

"He'd like to make an offer on the lighthouse and its surrounding property."

"I don't understand."

"He'd like to *buy* them," she told me like I was a dim bulb.

"I understand that," I snapped. "I don't understand why he'd approach me about a property he knows I purchased in order to invest heavily in renovating so I can live there."

Coert's deep voice said low, "Cady."

I lifted my eyes to him as I listened to the woman speak in my ear.

"He wants to build a resort there."

"A resort?" I asked, staring in Coert's eyes.

He lifted a brow.

"A resort-type area," the woman said. "An exclusive inn and spa with surrounding cottages that includes a fine-dining restaurant within the lighthouse itself."

I nearly choked.

"So I'd like to make an appointment for you and me and Mr. Stone to discuss this offer," she declared.

"He can't build a resort-type area with an inn and surrounding cottages and a restaurant at the lighthouse," I shared sharply, and doing it watched Coert's face turn stunned then hard. "First," I went on, "because it's my *home* and second, because there are riders on the deed that disallow building on that property."

"This is why he has an attorney, namely me," she retorted.

Why was this woman being so rude?

She was calling *me* on a *Sunday* to say some unknown man wanted to buy *my home*.

"Well, if he wishes to waste his money paying your—" I began.

She didn't let me finish. "And those riders are enforced by Magdalene's City Council. However, rezoning of the lands outside the lighthouse a year ago placed it in a precarious position considering only a slim line of coastal path and the lighthouse are within Magdalene city limits, which makes no zoning sense. And Mr. Stone, as well as a number of members of the Magdalene Club, sit on the board that governs the unincorporated land surrounding the lighthouse, and there's strong support not only to press forward rezoning *all* of that land but also to then null the riders so the area immediately around the lighthouse can be developed."

"And can I ask who rezoned that land?" I requested tersely.

"It was a county referendum."

"Written by who?" I pressed.

"Does it matter?" she shot back.

"I gazumped him."

"I'm sorry?" she asked irately.

"It's a British term I heard while over there that I liked very much so I remembered it," I shared curtly. "In other words, he was planning to buy the property, planning this all along, and I got in and offered, was accepted and I got the property, thus *gazumping* him."

"Mr. Colley made it clear that the family was resistant to Mr. Stone's offers, which was not acting in the best interests of the family." This was said threateningly.

The family being "resistant" to his offers meant he'd lowballed them lower than I had.

And Robert knew about this, made some move to stop it, but he didn't tell me about it.

That didn't matter. It wasn't necessary I knew and I wished I *still* didn't know.

But now, the lighthouse was mine.

End of story.

I looked to the bakery case that was next to the deli and announced, "I have absolutely no interest in selling."

"Mr. Stone is annoyed that his offer will have to be considerably more than it would have been if Mr. Colley hadn't intervened but he's quite intent on—"

I interrupted her. "It doesn't matter what he's quite intent on. I own that property. There's no lien on it. No mortgage. The deed is in my name, free and clear. And I have no interest in selling nor will I. And I'll be discussing with the Historical Society and Magdalene's City Council how to rezone that land so it's where it should be."

"Ms. Moreland—"

"Good day, and please, tell Mr. Stone and all of his minions to cease calling me. If I hear from you again, I'll make a record of how often this has happened and then I'll share with the sheriff I'm being harassed."

"I'm sure Sheriff Yeager will take that *very* seriously," she stated snidely.

She knew about Coert and me.

Not a surprise. We'd been somewhat out there, what with me shouting at him on the sidewalk and all.

But the way she said that was galling.

I looked back at Coert and retorted, "I'm absolutely *certain* of it. Enjoy the rest of your Sunday, which, by the way, is *not* the day to make such calls. But fortunately, this particular one is over."

And with that, I took the phone from my ear and disconnected.

"What the hell?" Coert asked.

"Some man named Boston Stone wants to buy the lighthouse and make it a *restaurant*," I answered.

His mouth got tight in a way that was as scary as it was sexy before he bit out, "Stone."

"Do you know him?" I queried.

"Yeah. Pure dick."

"Sheriff! Your sandwiches are ready," the deli lady called.

Coert grabbed my hand and drew me to the counter.

"Thanks, Shirl," he murmured, reaching out to take the bag.

"Shirl" smiled at him, gave me an assessing look, and I barely was able to force a smile at her before Coert dragged me to the cash register.

"Tell me," he ordered when we were standing in line.

Even though he heard most of it from my side of the conversation, I told him in fits and spurts as we waited in line and as he paid, having to stop repeatedly for him to return a hello or dip his chin at somebody.

It was nice to see he was so popular.

But frustrating when you had an irritating (or perhaps any) story to tell.

We were on the street and walking (hand in hand, I'll add) toward the station when I was finished.

"Wondered why that bunch pushed for the rezoning," he murmured like he was talking to himself. "And it wasn't popular. It barely passed."

"Well, it doesn't matter now. Though I'm going to share with Jackie about it. But the fact remains that it's mine and he could offer me fifty million dollars and I'd not sell it."

That made Coert stop us both dead and he looked down at me.

"Seriously?" he asked, and the expression on his face concerned me.

"I…yes," I replied haltingly, trying to understand that expression.

"You love it that much?"

Slowly, I looked to the horizon where the lighthouse lay, white against a backdrop of snow and sea, its black trim, red roofs and Christmas decorations could be seen all the way from there, and back to him.

"Coert, look at it. Can you imagine if that view changed and *how* it could change if someone got hold of it who just wants to make money off that land?"

He didn't look at it.

He didn't look away from me.

"That would suck and he's not gonna offer that high, Cady, but the man's got money and if he's determined to do something, he isn't easily shaken. So say he goes high, you'd say no?"

I shook my head but replied, "Each one of the kids say they want to live there when they grow up. Kath joked she wanted to talk Pat into retiring there when she was here this summer, but she told me just the other day that now that Pat has seen it, he was thinking the same thing. They love the place. They love the studio. And it was also a joke, but they called dibs on it during dinner one night. When they did, Mike looked ticked. So now it's a family place. But it's always only been a lighthouse. For over two hundred years. So no. If my family isn't interested should I need to let it go, I'd find another family. Not a developer. Never a developer. And to make that a certainty, it needs new riders written into the deed and perhaps the land around it zoned back to where it's supposed to be."

"So you just want to keep it as it is," Coert said.

"Yes. I mean, someone may want to redecorate it one day. I'm not going to go that crazy. But…yes. Keep it as it is."

Coert seemed extremely relieved. So much so, it worried me.

"Coert?"

He started us moving again and replied, "During sandwiches. They're hot and they'll get cold if we stand outside much longer. Meet the guys quick, we'll eat them and talk in my office."

Now I had my mind on all of this as he took me to the station.

The hot sandwiches weren't only in answer to the cold outside.

It was an indication of how sweet Coert was.

He had hot sandwiches in a bag held in his hand. It was lunchtime. They were men. They got all that in a big way. And thus the round of introductions was short, not prolonged, and relatively easy for me (not that they'd be anything else, all his men seemed very polite, respectful but familiar and friendly with Coert, respectful and friendly to me, but it was kind of Coert to maneuver it so there was no opportunity to put me under a microscope).

When we hit his office, he drew me to a chair and let me go so I sat in it, taking off my jacket and scarf.

He grabbed two cans of Fresca from a mini-fridge in his office (he still drank Fresca, we were both Fresca lovers back in the day, and this knowledge calmed me) and handed one to me. He shrugged off his jacket, but not his scarf, and sat beside me rather than behind his big wooden desk as he pulled out the sandwiches and two bags of kettle-cooked chips.

I waited until he'd peeled back the foil and paper and taken his first bite before I asked, "What was that on the sidewalk?"

Then I took my first bite.

Sliced prime rib with melted Swiss cheese, horseradish sauce and crispy onions.

It was divine.

And it was from Wayfarer's.

So it was even more divine.

"I'm not sure we should get into this now," he replied after he swallowed.

"I think from the look on your face outside, honey, that we need to get into this now," I returned cautiously.

He held his sandwich (it looked like shaved ham and cheese) in front of him with elbows on his spread knees but his eyes were on mine.

"I got a kid," he said carefully.

I smiled at him. "I know."

"I now got a woman. The only one I ever wanted."

My heart warmed and my smile remained in place. "I know."

"And someday, that day being very soon, if I can manage it without messin' up my kid or the solid ground I'm forming in raising her with her mom, my two girls, every other week, are gonna live together. But for me, every day, I'm gonna wake up next to my woman."

I nodded.

This was what I too thought was the unspoken but mutually agreed plan.

"Baby, we can't do that at the lighthouse."

My brows drew together. "I know."

He stared at me.

"When that happens, I'll rent the lighthouse," I shared. "I want it to be lived in, not let like a B and B or something. Find someone decent who loves it and wants to stay for a while. Elijah might want it and then he can move over when I leave and we'll rent the space over the garage. The studio can be rented like a B and B if the tenants in the lighthouse and garage are all right with that. Or it can be left open for when my family, or your family, come to visit for somewhere nice for them to stay."

"You're okay movin' in with me?" he asked like that shocked him.

But I couldn't imagine how it would shock him.

"I like having sex with you, Coert, and that can't happen if we convert the family room into Janie's bedroom. The stairs are open and we'll be right on top of her. But the only full bath is off the master bedroom and that simply won't work. And the studio is far too small. Last, we can't build on lighthouse land because, well…I think we went over that already. So unless you want to move to a new house altogether, which seems unnecessary to me since your house is fabulous, then that's the only option."

He grinned his crooked grin and it was the first time I'd seen it since back in Denver, before it all blew up, before it all went bad, and for a second my mind blanked of everything but that boyish grin on his handsome, manly face.

Then he scooted his chair forward with his boots without leaning back, which was somehow cute *and* sexy, and he kept scooting until one of our knees touched, and I came back into the room.

"I know you love it, baby, so I was worried about takin' you from there."

I was finding my Coert was a worrier. Especially when it came to me.

That was cute and sweet.

I leaned into my elbows on my knees with my sandwich in front of me too, just to get closer.

"That's sweet, Coert, but it isn't going anywhere and it's still mine. Maybe one day when Janie's gone to college or something, we can move back. We can talk about it then. But that's a long way away."

He pressed his knee against mine and the relieved look on his face changed to something so intense, it frightened me.

"Not for now, I'm just gonna say it now because you have to think about it and start doing that right away. We both have to think about where we are. What we want. Where we're goin'. And if you aren't where I am on this, I'm good with that, Cady. If you take anything from this discussion, I need you to take that. I got what I want when I got you back and I'm happier than I've been my entire life. Even havin' Janie. Love her but there was shit makin' that not all it could have been. So now I'm right where I want to be. But I still need to put this out there because you need to think on it. And what I need to put out there is that I want you to consider having my baby."

I wasn't moving.

Still, I froze solid.

"Not for now," he said quickly. "You don't have to give me an answer right now. But think about that. And we'll talk—"

"I want your baby."

It was then Coert, also not moving, also still froze.

"I've always wanted that," I whispered.

His voice sounded funny, thicker, when he reminded me, "We're not young."

"I don't care," I stated firmly.

There was a fire in his eyes but his lips said, "That means fast, Cady. Move in fast. Get married fast. Get pregnant fast."

"I'll make an appointment with a gynecologist next week."

He closed his eyes. He did this slowly. And something moved over his face that was so terrible and so beautiful in equal measure, it was difficult to witness.

But I still knew every day for the rest of my life I'd remember the beautiful part of it.

He opened his eyes. "A little girl with your green eyes."

"A little boy with your hazel eyes."

"Gotta have more of your green."

More of your green.

My nose started stinging.

"Oh no, I'm going to cry into my prime rib."

He tossed his sandwich on the Wayfarer's bag, took mine and did the same.

Then he had my head in both hands and his mouth on mine while we sat in chairs in front of his desk, our knees pressing into each other's so hard, it hurt.

I didn't care.

I loved that kiss.

I'd had a lot of beautiful kisses (all from Coert).

But that was the best.

By far.

When his mouth left mine, he stayed in my space and his thumbs swept in to rub through the wet under my eyes that had spilled over, even with the kiss.

"Doctor would be good," he whispered. "Get a sense of how much time we have so we can plan how we make this easy on Janie."

I nodded with my head in his hands.

Coert pressed his forehead to mine. "Right now, with her, in my office."

Fresh tears fell over.

And my throat was clogged when I replied, "Right now, with him, in his office."

His thumbs moved through my tears and I let them flow freely.

Coert held my gaze as I did.

I got myself together and he pulled me forward for a touch of lips before his thumbs swept my skin one last time and he let me go.

He moved away, only slightly, and grabbed my sandwich.

He handed it to me.

I took it.

He grabbed his own.

"So, baby, you been to England?" he murmured.

I grinned at him

Then I answered.

And Coert and I ate lunch in his office.

I HAD BOTH legs wrapped around the backs of his thighs, one hand trailing along the skin of his back, one hand with fingers in his hair.

Coert had one leg hitched, one hand curled around the back of my neck, one arm wrapped around my waist.

We were going slow.

He kissed me as he moved inside me.

I kissed him back.

He lifted his head away and stared in my eyes as he moved inside me.

I stared back.

"Love you," he whispered.

"Love you too," I whispered back.

He went faster.

I held on tighter.

He kissed me harder.

I kissed him deeper.

He ended the kiss and dipped his head. I felt his tongue pressing the diamond at the dent in the base of my throat into my skin.

I shivered and fisted my hand in his hair, raking my nails up his back.

His mouth recaptured mine and he started pounding into me, his thrusts smooth yet rough, his tongue in my mouth giving and seizing.

His cock hit somewhere deep inside of me, *Coert* hit somewhere deep inside of me, and I broke our kiss, whimpering, "Coert."

"Cady."

I was there.

My neck arched and my mouth opened but no sound came out as the blinding orgasm throbbed higher every time the base of his cock hit my clit, his shaft slammed into me.

His hand at the back of my neck shifted up, cupping the back of my head, righting it so he could again take my mouth.

He sucked my orgasm deep inside as he sucked my tongue in his mouth, and my climax throbbed higher again just as he released my tongue and his grunt pulsed down my throat chased by his groan that soothed it.

My orgasm slid away from me and when it did I found myself still kissing Coert, my fingers drifting through his hair, my other arm and legs holding him close as he slowed it down, stroking in and out, in and out until he connected us and stayed there.

Only then did his lips trail to my ear, down to my neck where he kissed me there and remained.

"That's how I wanna make her," he said softly.

My eyes floated closed, the sides of my lips coasted up and my hold on him got tighter.

It took nearly two decades.

But it was good to know way back when that God listened to me.

"Then that's how we'll make him," I replied.

I felt his smile against my neck.

We laid that way for a long time, content, silent, before I started losing Coert.

He pulled fully out then he shifted us both out of his bed.

Coert dealt with the condom.

I put on panties and a nightie.

We did what we had to do and I went back to bed.

Coert walked the house and then he joined me.

After he did, sensing the intimacy was done, Midnight joined us.

And then I experienced another version of paradise.

In his arms, I fell asleep.

Twenty-Three

LIKE YOU AND DADDY

CADY

Present day…

"Uncle *Jake*!" Janie screeched, and then twisted on her booty in her seat at the grease-stained picnic table that was one of three we were taking up at Tinker's burger joint.

She jumped to her feet and rushed around the table.

I watched her go, turning to look behind me to where she was heading, feeling Coert sitting beside me, do the same.

And when I saw Janie make it to a tall, black-haired, very built man who was bending to her before she arrived at him, a large smile curved into his extremely handsome face, I stilled.

I'd met Coert Yeager at age twenty-three.

And he'd ruined me for all other men in all ways.

Including the looks department.

I'd had the most handsome man I'd ever met fall in love with me.

And he'd done it the way he'd done it.

And I'd returned that completely.

You just didn't recover from that.

So although I'd obviously seen attractive men since then (and dated a few of them), I'd never seen any that had made me go still.

Until right then.

The black-haired man grabbed Janie under her arms and lifted her, to which she let out a squeal of pure delight. He swung her out, then in, and she wrapped her legs around his flat stomach, her arms around his neck and gave him a big kiss on the mouth.

He wrapped one arm around her bottom, one around her back and kept smiling down at her.

I wasn't sure because I wasn't thinking clearly, but I had a feeling my mouth was hanging open.

And maybe a little drool was coming out.

Coert and I were totally having a little girl.

Totally.

Absolutely.

"Jesus, what's in the water around here?" Shannon muttered (loudly, since I heard it and she was at another table).

"Please don't think thoughts that will require me asking for a divorce," Daly teased.

"Wait until you see Mick."

This was said in my ear, and I jerked my eyes away from the man who was now walking toward us, his light-blue eyes aimed at me, and looked at Coert, who was pulling his face out of my hair.

I caught sight of a pair of familiar hazel eyes that would never fail to dazzle me.

No.

Much better.

Much.

Still.

Janie had said *Uncle Jake.*

Oh my God.

That was Coert's friend *Jake.*

"Is Mickey better?" I asked Coert.

"I don't know. I'm a guy. But Liz said Mickey was the only man she'd ever leave her husband for. Jake's a boxer and he owns the local strip club. But Mick, he's a boxer and he's a volunteer firefighter."

"My," I breathed.

"I see dinner is gonna be interesting," Coert replied.

I came out of my daze to see Coert grinning at me, not angry or even annoyed at my reaction.

I got closer to him.

"You're the most handsome man I've known *and* slept with," I shared in a whisper.

Coert's shoulders started shaking and his lips also moved. "Well, glad I got that last distinction."

A deep rumbling voice came at us. "Coert, man, good to see you."

I tipped my head back, back, and back some more and stared into those blue eyes.

"Daddy! Look! Uncle Jake is here!" Janie cried.

"I see, cupcake," Coert murmured, and I felt him shifting to get out of the picnic table.

"You're Cady," Jake told me.

At that moment, with those eyes on me, I couldn't confirm that information.

Fortunately, Jake's blue eyes didn't have the same effect on Coert as they did on me.

"Yeah, bud, this is Cady," he answered for me.

Jake shifted Janie to his hip like she was a toddler, not a five-year-old, and held a large hand out to me.

I lifted mine and put it in his, remembering my brief meeting with his wife and thinking this man was incredibly good looking.

But he was rough.

She looked like she'd walk out of the kitchen shop to fold into a limousine and might pass out at the thought of a burger from Tink's.

He looked like he'd have not one thing to do with a woman who'd turn her nose up at the deliciousness of Tink's (Coert had not been wrong, I wasn't even finished with my burger and I wanted another one).

At any other time, this would give me pause about the Elijah/Verity situation.

But at that time, I had to think about it later.

"Yes, Cady. Um, I'm Cady. Sorry," I mumbled, feeling his fingers close firm but not tight around mine before he let me go.

I scrambled out of the picnic table and Jake and Coert moved away to give me room.

When I got up, Coert's fingers wrapped around mine.

This was the decision made at breakfast that morning. We'd been careful about how we were around Janie at Christmas. We'd talked about it Christmas Eve.

Coert didn't want her confused later when we started to show more affection for each other but he didn't want it in her face at first.

It was a delicate balance.

Now, he felt the time was right to give her stronger hints.

Holding hands.

Pecks of the lips.

Sitting beside each other at picnic tables.

"Cady's giving Daddy and me a whole 'nother family!" Janie declared, and Jake's head turned to her, my eyes shot to her and I felt Coert come alert at my side. "There's a lot of them," she carried on. "There's Dexter and Corbin over there."

She was twisted in Jake's arm and pointing.

"They're sitting with Bea, Aunt Shannon and Uncle Daly. And Elijah." She looked back to Jake. "He's new," she declared authoritatively. She twisted to another table. "And that's Uncle Mike and Aunt Pam and Ellie and Verity and Riley there."

Her hand was bobbing as she pointed from person to person. Each person she pointed to lifted a hand or a chin or sent a smile Jake's way to indicate who she was referring to.

"And that's Uncle Pat and Melanie." She slapped a hand on Jake's cheek, something that made his (very wide) chest start shaking as he pulled his full lips in to stop himself from laughing, and she got close to whisper loudly, "*She's my new best friend.*" She let him go and kept on, "And Aunt Kath and you met Cady and then there's Daddy!"

When she finished, Jake allowed himself to grin at her but the grin changed speculative when his eyes slid to Coert.

"So things are goin' well," he muttered.

"Yup," Coert agreed.

Kath burst out laughing.

She did a little choking through it when Jake looked at her but recovered enough to say, "Would you like to join us?"

"Thanks but can't. My boy's up from college and he wants his fill of things from home without leavin' his real home, so I'm pickin' up some grub and takin' it back to my family," Jake answered.

"Too bad," Pam murmured.

Mike shook his head, his gaze searching for sympathy coming to rest on—I could jump for joy—*Coert.*

"But hear I'll see you women at dinner next Sunday?" Jake asked.

"Oh yes, definitely," Shannon said.

"Be there with bells on," Pam chimed in.

"Abso-freaking-lutely," Kath declared.

"You do know it isn't 'what happens in Magdalene stays in Magdalene,' don't you?" Pat asked Kath.

Kath shrugged.

I giggled.

Jake looked to me with a grin playing at his mouth.

I stopped giggling.

Coert burst out laughing and Jake's smile got huge again.

"What's funny?" Janie asked.

"I'll show you a picture of Uncle Jake as he is right now in thirty years and remind you of this moment, cupcake," Coert replied then reached out and took his daughter, plonking her on his hip in the same manner Jake had handled her.

Oh yes.

Definitely having another little girl.

"But for now, we need to let Uncle Jake get food back to Josie, Con, Amber and Ethan," Coert finished.

"Con's home?" she exclaimed.

"Sure is, honey," Jake told her. "Get your dad to bring you over before he goes back to school, yeah?"

"Yeah!" she agreed.

"Cady," Jake dipped his chin to me then looked through the tables, "folks, good to meet you."

There were a lot of "you too," and "enjoy your evening," and such, but I took a step toward him, getting his attention back.

"It's really great to meet you. *Really* great to meet one of Coert's good friends."

And it was considering this was the first *real* friend of Coert's I'd ever met.

In response he stuck his hand out again and I took it again. But this time, when his fingers closed firm around mine, he kept hold of them.

"Pleased you're in Magdalene, Cady. High time I see a good man happy."

His eyes held mine and I pressed my lips together and squeezed his hand hard (so he could feel it, in case he was made of steel or something) and nodded.

"See you soon," I told him.

"You bet," he replied.

We let go, he clapped Coert on the shoulder, tipped his chin down to the family and moved to the window where you ordered food.

"Go back to your seat, Janie," Coert ordered gently, and I looked to them to see he was setting her on her feet.

"Okay, Daddy," she agreed easily then skipped around the table.

Coert let me sit down and then he climbed in and we went back to our food.

"I'm feeling a shopping trip coming on," Kath declared. "Is there a Nordstrom around here? You said this place we're going to for dinner with the Magdalene Welcome Wagon is fancy. I've decided I need a new dress."

"You. I can handle that she's half gaga over you," Pat said bluntly to Coert, leaning into the table to look across me to do it. "You belong to you-know-who so I can handle that because I know she's half messing with me and the other half I can ignore. Dwayne Johnson's better-looking partner from his last action movie…" he jerked his head toward Jake, "not so much."

Coert chuckled.

I wrapped a hand around his thigh and laughed softly.

"Can I go shopping with you and Cady, Aunt Kathy?" Janie, sitting between Kath and Melanie across from us, asked.

Kath glanced at Coert but said to Janie, "I don't know, honey. We'll talk to your dad about it later. Okay?"

"Sure," she replied, settled in her seat with a wiggle and went back to her burger that was at about mouth level since they didn't have booster seats at Tinker's.

"Can I go, Auntie Kathy?" Melanie asked.

"We'll talk about that later too, sweetie," Kath answered.

"Just to say, there's no Nordstrom anywhere near here," Coert told them.

"Dire," Kath muttered. "Well then, time to fire up the Internet. Overnight shipping."

"Kill me," Pat begged.

More chuckles from Coert (and me) and everyone resumed eating but I said to Janie, "We'll look at pretty dresses on the computer when we get back to the lighthouse. Does that sound good?"

"Can we do it in the room up top with all the windows?" she asked excitedly with her mouth full.

"Chew, baby, and swallow then talk," Coert murmured low.

She chewed fast, swallowed too soon and her eyes got big because of it.

I ignored all that, including the off-the-scales cute factor, thankful the Wi-Fi reached the observation room, and said, "Definitely."

"Yay," she replied and took another bite of burger.

Coert bumped my leg with his own.

I resisted resting my head on his shoulder.

"I'm gettin' another burger, anyone want anything?" Elijah, who'd been corralled into coming with us by the kids since he'd driven up as we were getting ready to roll out, asked.

He'd said no at first but he was too soft-hearted. So when Ellie and Melanie started begging, he'd given in but followed us there because he'd had to take a quick shower after work.

Verity had not been excited about this but she'd kept silent.

Almost totally.

Elijah's offer prompted a cacophony of kids asking parents if they could have more food to which the parents responded and then, for some reason, Elijah looked to Verity.

"Wanna help me, Verry?" he asked softly.

"Oh my," I whispered.

"Oh boy," Kath whispered.

"Hmm," Coert hummed.

"Freakin' great," Pat muttered dryly.

"I…all right," Verity told the table then got up from that table and stood still, not moving until she realized Elijah wasn't moving either because he wanted her to precede him.

Then she started with a jolt and stared at the floor all the way to the window.

I leaned immediately into the table and, *sotto voce*, asked Kath, "When did she become *Verry*?"

Kath leaned into the table and told me, "I've no idea. That's the first I heard that."

"Do you think he thought on this over Christmas?" I queried.

Kath's voice was rising when she repeated, "I've no idea." She quietened herself and went on, "I hope so. He's so cute and he so, *so* sweet. I mean, did you *see* how he caved when Melanie and Ellie were begging him to come? I almost propositioned him *for* Verity."

"You do know you're talking about my daughter," Pat declared.

Kath's gaze cut to her husband. "I do since I was there when we made her."

Coert chuckled again.

"What are you guys talking about?" Janie asked in a loud hushed voice.

I put a finger to my lips and took it away, whispering, "Girls' secret. Right now, we have to keep it very, *very* quiet. I'll tell you when we look at dresses on the computer later. Deal?"

Her eyes grew huge and her head nodded fast and she replied reverently, "*Deal.*"

"Can I hear too, Auntie Cady?" Melanie asked.

"Of course, baby," I answered.

Melanie smiled at me.

I winked at her.

Coert's arm came around me from behind, his hand at my opposite hip, pads of his fingers digging in briefly, then it disappeared.

I guessed that meant he was pleased at how things were going with Janie.

He wasn't the only one.

The world revolved around those eyes.

His.

And Janie's.

Yes, I wanted a little girl.

One that looked just like her sister.

Jake said another farewell as he walked out carrying three stuffed-full bags of food.

Verity and Elijah came back with two trays piled high with food.

She was still silent.

Elijah was shooting glances at her.

This meant I was shooting glances, or targeted with the same from Kathy.

We ate.

We went home.

And the girls (*sans* Verity, who headed to the studio since the boys were camped out in front of the TV or the fire on the first floor, the latter including Elijah) headed up to the observation room.

"SO THAT'S WHERE it's at," I declared.

I was sitting on the bench in the observation room with Janie tucked in my side, my laptop on her legs (precisely, on one of her thighs and on one of Melanie's, Melanie sitting next to her).

They were clicking through Nordstrom online like only children born in the computer age could do, in other words, expertly.

I kept talking.

"And we have to be really nice to Verity because Elijah is very sweet so she's chosen well. But he doesn't want to hurt her and we should help him out with that. He also might like her but not think the time is right. So we just have to be super quiet about it and super supportive to them both and wait and see what happens."

"Verity likes everyone," Bea muttered from where she sat with Ellie on the floor at her feet, her fingers in Ellie's hair, French braiding it.

At fourteen, Bea, too, had lived through a variety of Verity's boyfriends.

"Bea," Shannon said warningly.

"Well she does," Bea replied. "I'm not being mean. I'm just saying she's always got some crush on some boy."

"That might be true but if you're paying attention, Elijah's a little different," Shannon returned. "And anyway, no matter what a girl's going through, her girls need to see her through it no matter how they feel about it."

"This is very true," Pam agreed.

"Elijah *is* different," Ellie piped up. "He's taller than all those other guys. And he's a *man* and they were stupid *boys*. And I like his belly!"

I grinned at Shannon.

"So Elijah and Verity are like you and Daddy."

I stopped grinning at Shannon, whose eyes I saw grow large before I gave my attention to Janie, who'd spoken.

I tried not to make it sound strangled, but it sounded mostly strangled when I asked, "Sorry, Janie?"

She was still focused on the computer. "Elijah and Verity are like you and Daddy before you started making pies and Daddy started buying presents and you and Daddy started holding hands and stuff."

I was holding my breath so it was Pam that came to the rescue, asking carefully, "What do you mean by that, Janie?"

Janie gave a little girl shrug and clicked on a sparkly dress that was way too fancy for The Eaves, and I'd never been to The Eaves, I just knew it was because it might be way too fancy for the Oscars.

"Back at the ice cream shop, Cady saw Daddy and she got all funny and ran away. And Daddy got all funny when she got all funny, like if he didn't have me he'da run after her. But after he took me to the station, he did, to make sure Cady was okay. Like what Elijah did when he asked Verity to help him get burgers. He likes her and knows she likes him and the time isn't right but he wants to make sure she's okay. But he just likes her because the whole time we were eating burgers, he kept looking at her and you don't look at someone all the time if you just want to be sure they're okay. You look at them all the time if you like them. Like Daddy looks at Cady all the time. Except now they both know they like each other."

My gaze drifted to Kath who immediately mouthed, "Holy crap."

No one, Coert, Janie or I, had brought up the ice cream parlor incident.

Coert had advised me on Christmas Eve we would handle it should she bring it up but let it lie if she didn't, because that would indicate she forgot about it or felt he'd dealt with it at the time in a way she had moved beyond.

Apparently, it was Janie who had dealt with it but in her own way.

It was just that her way was extraordinary.

I heard clicking on the laptop and Janie spoke again so I dropped my eyes back to her.

"I'm glad the time is right. Daddy should hold hands with somebody. My friend at school, Ilaria, her mommy and daddy aren't together and her daddy got a new lady, and when he comes to get Ilaria at school he smiles a lot and makes Ilaria giggle. He was like that sometimes before, but he's like that, like, *all the time* now. And anyway, Ilaria and her daddy's lady play dress up and they have girlie movie nights. She says her mommy isn't very happy about this new lady but her daddy is, so I have it better because my daddy is super happy and my mommy's happy too because she likes Cady's butterly pie, and she told me Cady had to be super sweet and want me to like her to make sure Santa brought me presents at her house."

Janie tipped her head back and gave me those incredible eyes.

"Can we play dress up?" she asked.

Outside of having Coert, I'd never wanted anything more in the world.

"Yes," I whispered.

"Can we have girlie movie nights?" she pushed.

"Absolutely," I told her.

She gave me a beaming smile. "I'm gonna dress up as a mermaid. What are you gonna dress up as?"

I shook my head. "I don't know. Maybe a fairy godmother?"

She nodded once. "We have to find you a dress up fairy godmother outfit. Do you think they have those at Nodmans?"

"Nordstrom, sweetie," I corrected her gently. "And no. But that just means we'll have to find somewhere else to get a fairy godmother outfit."

"Yay," she replied, grinning.

She then went back to scrolling and clicking.

I stared at her dark head and then I bent in and kissed it.

I did this in an effort not to burst out crying or, perhaps, get up and dance a jig of joy.

It was the right choice. Janie tipped that head back and gave me another beaming smile.

"Do you know how smart you are?" I asked.

She nodded gravely. "My teacher says I'm sharp as a tack. And Daddy says I'm quick as a whip."

"Well, they're right," I told her. "But do you know how lovely you are?"

She looked confused. "Do you mean pretty?"

"Yes, but in a way where I can see it." I lifted a hand and touched a finger to her heart. "And I can feel it because you're pretty inside too."

She seemed to marvel at that. "No one ever told me I was pretty *inside.*"

"Well, you are and don't ever stop being that way because it really doesn't matter what you look like on the outside. It only matters how you are on the inside."

Another grave nod that made me need to kiss her again so I did, dropping to give her a touch of my lips on her forehead.

When I pulled away she looked like she'd come to a conclusion and she didn't make me wonder at it.

"Now I think I understand why you're prettier when you look at Daddy. Because what's inside is coming out."

All right.

That was it.

I'd completely fallen in love with Coert's daughter.

Not her eyes.

Not her off-the-scales cute factor.

Not the fact that Coert helped make her.

Because she was Janie.

"Your father is very right, Janie," I said softly. "You're quick as a whip."

She gave me a big grin.

Kath cleared her throat and declared, "I think it's time for pie."

I looked to her.

She shot big eyes at me and then aimed them at the stairs.

Janie gave my laptop to Melanie and shouted, "I'll help!"

"Oh no." Kath got up from her seat in one of the wicker chairs. "I need you to help me find a dress for dinner. That's priority one. Cady'll get some of the boys to help."

Janie was okay with that but turned to me. "What kind of pie did you make us this time, Cady?"

"Pecan," I told her.

Another blinding smile. "I love pecan pie!"

I smiled back. "Do you like it with ice cream or whipped cream?"

"Both!" she cried.

Of course.

I'd think "girl after my own heart" but she'd already accomplished earning that.

I got orders from the others then got up, avoiding Midnight who was curled at the base of the bench in front of me (or more likely, Janie, and this was proved true when she just lifted her head to give me a look as I got up, but she didn't otherwise move). Kath took my place with Janie, Melanie and my laptop. And after getting meaningful but happy looks from Pam and Shannon, I headed downstairs.

The younger boys were all rammed together on my sectional watching some movie on TV and I got their orders for pie with or without whipped cream or ice cream (or both).

Making it to the bottom, I noted that Elijah was no longer with the older men downstairs. Daly and Pat were on the couch. Mike was in front of the fire lounged on some huge pillows on the floor that I'd bought for that exact purpose prior to their arrival.

Coert was with the men, sitting in my armchair by the fire, legs stretched out in front of him crossed at the ankles, fingers wrapped around a glass of whiskey, eyes on me before I'd made it to the bottom.

Seeing him like that in my house, I thought it was really unfortunate we'd have to wait years to move back to the lighthouse.

But then again, I probably wouldn't care where he was kicking back, enjoying a whiskey.

As long as it was close to me.

"Where's Elijah?" I queried.

Mike looked to Pat then to me before he advised, "Don't ask."

"Oh," I mumbled.

Elijah had not retired to his apartment.

He'd gone to Verity.

An interesting development.

I spoke up when I announced, "It's pie time. I need orders. And Coert, honey, will you help me?"

He was studying me, but when I made my request, he didn't answer verbally.

He got up and walked to the kitchen, meeting me there.

I'd made two pies that afternoon and they were right there on the counter.

I didn't go to them nor did I go to the fridge to get the whipped cream and ice cream.

I went to Coert, grabbed his hand and pulled him to the sink.

His content, he-has-his-woman, he-has-his-daughter, he's-at-a-fabulous-lighthouse-chatting-with-good-men-holding-a-whiskey-in-his-hand expression changed as he grew concerned while he continued to study me.

He set his whiskey on the counter by the sink and asked, "Everything okay?"

"Well..."

Quickly, I ran down what happened with Janie in the observation room.

As I spoke, his gaze drifted to the stairs.

When I started to wind down, it came back to me.

I finished with, "I think this confirms a variety of things. One, you were kind of right. But she doesn't absorb everything, as such. She *observes* everything. And for a five-year-old, she processes it as it fits in her world with amazing perception. It's uncanny but also fantastic and I don't know, but it might be indicative that she has an exceptional IQ."

When I said that, Coert's lips quirked.

I liked the quirk but I wasn't done talking.

"And two, because of this, what's happening between you and me and even Kim is not lost on her in the slightest. She's right there with us. She gets it completely." I leaned into him and tried not to let my smile break my face. "And she's happy with it."

"I'd say it confirms all that," he murmured, no longer looking concerned, no longer quirking his lips, a smile was in his eyes too.

"And last, Coert, Kim is being really amazing with all this, and I don't know, but I think with the way she's handling this, we might actually be able to build something for Janie that's extraordinary. Most exes don't get along and there's usually not a nice division of Dad and Mom that the kids have to negotiate. But if there isn't that for Janie…I mean, wouldn't that be great?"

He slid an arm around my waist, pulling me closer, before he informed me, "Part of that might still be guilt, Cady. She knows I love Janie. She knows I can't imagine my life without my daughter. But that doesn't erase what she did or how I spent five years making her pay for that. She could still be making amends."

I was confused. "Is that bad?"

"I'm just saying, Kim's acted rashly before when she panicked or didn't get her way. And that rash was using me to get her pregnant without my consent in order to force me in one way or another to stay in her life, and then using our daughter to try to get me to fall in line when she thought I wasn't by threatening to take Janie away from me. So I'm grateful she's being so cool about this and she's demonstrating she's on board to help us settle Janie into her new reality. But I think it's going to take more than a couple of months of Kim being cool in response to me being cool now that you're involved in all that before I'm going to relax."

"What were you not doing to fall in line?"

"She wanted us to get back together."

I felt my lips part as I stared up at him.

"Yeah," he said. "She knew I was not anywhere near there and she said that didn't matter. Janie needed a mom and dad together. She told me we'd had something before. If we worked at it, we could get it back and she was ticked I refused to work at it. For me, I was ticked she'd think for a second I could get past what she did. So we can just say it was an ugly situation that was already that before it got uglier by dragging a judge into it."

His other hand came up to cup my jaw and he bent his neck so his face was close to mine.

"She made some nasty plays," he shared, and he could say that again. "But I spent as much time with her as I did because she's sweet and she's funny and she's a lot of other things. I think you and I both have learned anyone is capable of doing really stupid shit when they feel lost or jammed up. I honestly think she's grown up and she's a great mom and it's been a very long time since she's pulled anything. I don't want you to go in thinking the worst of her. Just knowing the story. But I want us both to go cautious. Does that make sense?"

I nodded.

He nodded back then said, "Now, as awesome as this is, knowing where Janie's at is a lot further than where we thought she was, we gotta get to the pie because Janie needs to be home and in bed soon, and she shouldn't eat real close to going to sleep. So we should get on that."

I nodded again.

He gave me a touch of the lips and when he moved away, he murmured, "It's still awesome."

I smiled at him.

He gave me another touch of the lips.

The door to the walkway to the garage flew open.

Coert kept his arm around me but twisted that way and I leaned to the side to see Verity storm in, close the door, spy us in the kitchen—or Coert in the kitchen—and come our way.

"Coert, do you have a guest room?" she asked.

Oh no.

"No, honey, I—" Coert started, going careful, and I knew he'd read the look on her face.

She interrupted him. "Do you have a couch?"

"What's going on?" Pat asked.

Verity turned to her father. "I can't stay here."

"Why not?" Pat asked.

"I just *can't*. All right?"

Mike and Daly were up (as was Pat) and they looked at the door Verity had come through.

Pat kept his attention on his daughter.

"Do you need your mother?" he asked gently.

"I need to stay with Coert," Verity answered and turned back to Coert. "I know it's rude to invite myself over. And I'm sorry. I won't be any trouble. I promise. But it's either stay with you or catch a plane back to New Haven."

"What the hell happened in the studio?" Pat asked.

"I'll find out," Coert rumbled, letting me go and beginning to move to the door.

"I'll go with you," Mike stated.

Oh no!

"No!" Verity and I shouted.

But only I continued.

"I'll go." I pointed at Coert. "You dish out pie." I pointed at Mike. "You help." I pointed at Daly. "You go up and get the orders again." I pointed at Pat. "You go get Kath. I'm going to Elijah."

"Verity, pack your things. After pie, Janie and I gotta go. You're going with us," Coert ordered.

I didn't know whether to kiss him or yell at him for getting involved in something none us knew what was going on.

"Thank you," Verity breathed.

The heartfelt words made me want to kiss him.

I didn't kiss him.

I headed to the hooks by the front door, grabbed my jacket, then moved across the room to the other door to find Elijah.

I didn't go to the studio.

I went to the garage where my Jag was parked, Elijah's beat-up truck was parked, and I walked through it to the door at the back that led to the stairs up to the apartment.

I hammered on the door.

"Elijah!" I shouted. "It's Cady!"

I heard footfalls. They didn't come fast, but they weren't taking their time.

The door opened and I took the hit of staring into Elijah's ravaged face.

My God.

What had happened in the studio?

They'd known each other barely a week!

"Honey," I whispered.

"No good for her."

Oh my God.

"Elijah—"

"She's so pretty and she's so sweet and she loves you so much, Cady. I don't think even you know how much she loves you. But I know the way she loves you, the way she talks about you, the way she talks about her family, she's got a big heart. She's got a big future. And because of that, I'm no good for her."

"How can you know that?" I asked.

He threw out an arm and I didn't know what he was indicating. Himself. His apartment over a garage. His truck. His life. Or all of that.

"You haven't even tried," I stated.

"What's the point?" he asked. "She's got the whole world laid out in front of her. What kinda guy would I be, she's twenty, and I narrow that down to nothing in nowhere in Maine?"

"That's taking it pretty far, honey. You've only known her a few days."

"A guy knows."

"He knows what?"

"He knows it when he meets the one."

I felt my middle shift back with the soft beauty of that blow.

"She's my one but I can't be hers," he declared.

"Why can't you be her one?" I pushed.

He threw his arm out again.

I still really didn't know what he was referring to but that didn't stop me from stating, "Elijah, I'll hear none of that and Verity won't either."

"Yeah, I know. She pretty much shouted the same thing with a lot more words in the studio."

Oh my God.

Elijah was Verity's one too.

I moved closer to him. "Elijah—"

"Cady, you're the shit, pardon my language, but you just are. What you aren't is a guy. And if a guy is any kind of good guy, he does right by the people he cares about. I'm doin' right and if Verity can't change my mind about that, you sure can't."

"Do you know Jake?" I asked abruptly.

"Say what?" he asked back.

"Jake…um, the boxer who owns the strip club. The one we saw at Tinker's tonight."

"The Truck?"

His words confused me. "Sorry?"

"Jake Spear. That guy tonight. He's known as The Truck."

"I…yes," I said but it was more of a guess.

I mean, he was big. But The Truck?

"Everyone knows him," Elijah told me.

"Do you know his wife?"

He gave a short shake of his head. "No."

"Maybe you should meet her. Because she lives in Magdalene and she gives me the impression that she doesn't think Magdalene is nothing in nowhere in Maine."

"What are you talking about?" he asked impatiently.

"I only met her once but she's beyond Verity and Jake's beyond you, and they're still together and from what I've heard, they're very happy with their together."

"Yeah, but The Truck is a boxer who had pay-per-view fights on TV and makes a boatload at that club and I'm just…" He let that lie but threw out his arm again.

"Elijah—"

He shook his head. "No."

"Elijah," I said urgently because he was closing the door.

He looked into my eyes. "One day, you and her, she will too…one day you both'll thank me."

At that, he closed the door.

"Elijah!" I cried, slapping a hand on it.

I heard footfalls ascending the stairs.

"Gah!" I shouted, turned and stomped back to the lighthouse.

I opened the door and stormed in.

Riley and Corbin were climbing the stairs, plates of pie in their hands.

Coert and Mike were at the counter with Dexter waiting to be loaded with plates, dishing out. Pat and Daly were doing whipped cream and ice cream duty, respectively.

All eyes came to me.

"Where's Verity?" I demanded to know.

"Your room with Kath. Packing up her stuff," Pat answered.

The kids were sleeping pretty much anywhere they felt like crashing between lighthouse, studio and RV.

But every night after Coert and I got back together, except the first one and when I was with Coert, Verity had slept with me.

I tossed the jacket I'd shrugged off onto the back of the couch and announced, "He thinks she's too good for him."

Coert's face turned knowing.

Mike, Daly and Pat looked to the door I'd just entered.

Dexter looked confused. "What are you talking about?"

He got three, "Nothings" from Mike, Daly and Pat.

Pat went on and he did it quietly, "Do I need to talk to him?"

"Not now," I told him and moved to stand by Dexter outside the island.

"Is there some way to suspend Ellie and Melanie at this age forever?" Mike muttered.

"My thoughts exactly," Coert muttered in return.

I'd find them funny if I wasn't so mad in order not to be so upset about my conversation with Elijah.

"Coert, can I talk to you?" I asked.

He handed a plate to Daly and then nodded to me.

He had pecan pie all over his fingers so he rinsed them before he joined me by the fire.

I situated us so his back was to the room, hiding me, and he got close, but I got closer.

"He says she's the one," I proclaimed.

"Oh shit," he murmured.

Apparently, a guy *did* know when he found the one.

I shouldn't have been surprised. Coert certainly knew.

And girls could know as well, because I knew too.

"Uh…yeah," I snapped. "You need to do something about that."

He did a blink that went very slow.

"Um…say that again," he ordered.

"You said you were going to have a beer with him. You need to have a beer with him and set him straight."

"Baby, I don't *know* him. I also don't know Verity very well. I'm not the person to wade into this."

"That's precisely why you *should* wade into this. You're an objective observer."

"An objective observer who kinda agrees with Elijah."

I snapped my mouth shut and felt my eyes bug out.

He got even closer and put both hands to my jaw.

"Cady, honey, they're both too young and if this got this intense between them without them even sharing a kiss, they both need to back off and let time guide them to each other or not, as the case may be."

"They *have* kissed," I informed him. "Verity made a pass at him. Elijah just deflected it."

He looked to the fire and mumbled, "Jesus."

"And I was twenty-three when I kissed you *once* and knew you were the one."

His attention returned to me.

"I think I kissed you," he corrected.

"Whatever," I snapped. "I still knew you were the one."

"And tell me, those three years you got on your niece were really like ten, weren't they?" He asked the question but he didn't want an answer because he continued, "And don't deny it because you know it. You were still growing up but you were paying rent and feeding yourself. She's two years out of high school. How old is Elijah?"

"Twenty-six."

He nodded. "And he's paying rent and feeding himself and getting his ass out of bed to go to work every day and finding ways to sort his life when it throws him a curveball. Pat was teasing Verity about paying her credit card bill after Christmas dinner. There's a gulf here, Cady, that he might be able to swim, but it's the man he is, and I'm saying it's a good one, he's not going to allow her to make that effort and maybe get drowned on the way. And don't," he said quickly, taking one hand from my jaw to put a finger to my lips, "get up in my shit about how I laid that out. It isn't a man thing like that. It's a *good* man thing looking out for a woman he feels something for, and you have to let him have that. *She* has to let him have that."

I opened my mouth to say something regardless of Coert's finger still on my lips but he kept talking before I could.

"If she doesn't, this plays out in one of two scenarios. She pushes, and right now it's heartbreak, but if he digs in, that could turn a lot uglier and be a hard lesson she never wants to learn. Or she pushes and he cows and wonders for the rest of his life with what he can give her if she could have done better even if that idea never enters her mind, it'll torture him and may turn things bad."

He took his finger from my lips and moved that hand back to my jaw when I returned, "And the other scenario is that they're both young but they're both smart and sensitive and aware of the emotions they're feeling, the draw they have to each other, and even if they're young, they could be happy."

"Maybe but she's on holiday from freaking *Yale* and he came home covered with drywall dust and had to take a shower before he could go out to dinner and they've known each other *days*."

"Jake and Josie."

"Sorry?"

"I've met Jake and I've met Josie, but I met Josie first. My vision of Jake would not have been the man I met tonight after I met Josie. But she didn't only marry him, she adopted his son so I don't know her at all but my take from that is her commitment to her husband and his family is pretty flipping strong. Are you seeing the correlation here?"

"Jake and Josie are in their forties. They understand their hearts and what they want out of life a whole lot better than Verity Moreland does, Cady. She's a great kid and I would say with Elijah she has great taste. She may be becoming a woman, but she's still a kid."

He had me there.

He also knew it so he gave my jaw a squeeze and said, "Now I need pie and I gotta make sure my daughter doesn't get pecan goo and cream all over herself, and then I got two girls to take care of tonight so I need to get that show on the road."

"All right," I mumbled.

"And you need to resolve to be Switzerland."

My brows drew together. "What?"

"He needs you and she needs you so you need to be Switzerland. Neutral. A safe place for them both. So you said whatever you said to him out there. And you had your chat with her. Now, retreat to that safe place for them and let them play it out."

He was right again.

I just didn't like how he was right.

I frowned.

Coert grinned.

Then he used my jaw to pull me up to him, gave me a kiss then said, "Need pie."

I nodded.

He let me go to slide an arm around my shoulders and guide me back to the island.

He took his pie up to the observation deck.

I gobbled mine down glaring at the door that led to the walkway to the garage.

Mike had already gobbled his down so he came to me when I was halfway through and wrapped an arm around my waist.

I turned my glare up to him.

His lips twitched.

"I like him," he stated.

I stopped glaring.

"Fits right in," he carried on. "He's got a nutty woman on his hands, meets her at the fire, talks soft, touches softer, gives her a kiss and brings her to heel. Totally fits right in."

I swallowed a bite of pie and asked, "Would you like a punch in the gut?"

"No," he said, now fully smiling.

"Coert talked sense," I explained.

"I'm sure he did. That happens when the talker has a penis."

He was totally teasing. That was Mike (and sometimes Daly). The two younger brothers, they were always pushing buttons to get a rise.

Then he became the part that mostly made up Mike.

He yanked me to him, kissed the side of my head and said softly into my hair. "She's gonna be okay. Elijah's gonna be okay. It'll all be okay and end up the way it's supposed to be." He pulled away and looked into my eyes. "Your job is not to worry yourself sick about it along the way."

I nodded.

"Am I talking sense?" he teased.

I started glaring again.

He burst out laughing.

Verity walked down the steps with a suitcase.

She scanned the space. "Where's Coert?"

"He's upstairs finishing his pie with Janie. Come here," I called. "Let me get you some pie."

She dropped her suitcase at the foot of the stairs and started toward me, but did it saying, "I can't eat any pie right now, Aunt Cady."

I set my plate aside and held out an arm. "Then just come here."

She came there and I folded her in my arm, and since Mike still had me in his, he shifted so he folded her in his arm too.

"You'll be all right, kid," Mike murmured, now talking against the side of Verity's hair.

"Yeah," she replied, not giving a lot of effort to sound like she wasn't lying.

Coert came down, and Janie came with him as well as a variety of other people.

But it was only Janie who was excited. "We're having a kind of *slumber party*!"

Verity went with that flow.

They prepared to leave and Coert commandeered Verity's suitcase.

Verity and I commandeered Janie.

We got her bound up in her winter gear and we both held a hand as we walked her out to Coert's truck.

It was me who helped strap her into the seat in the back and gave her a kiss before I said, "See you later, sweetie."

"Can't wait, Cady!" she cried.

I smiled at her, closed her in, gave Verity a hug and she climbed into the front.

I rounded the hood and gave Coert a hug and a kiss on the cheek.

He kissed me on mine and whispered in my ear, "I'll call after I got them settled."

"Thanks," I whispered back. "Love you. Drive safe."

"Will do."

He climbed in.

He started up his truck.

He pulled out and it wasn't only me this time that waved them away.

But it was only me who turned and looked up at the windows over the garage just in time to see a curtain fall back into place.

"Switzerland," I muttered.

"What?" Shannon, standing beside me, asked.

I looked to her. "Nothing. I need wine."

"No truer words have been spoken," Kath decreed, not quite hiding the worry on her face as she watched Coert's truck drive through the gate.

Mike raised a remote pointed at the gate and it started closing.

I went inside, straight to the wine.

Twenty-Four

MM-HMM

COERT

Present day…

When they walked into The Eaves that Sunday night, Coert should have been paying attention.

But he wasn't because Cady was wearing that green dress.

When they were together in Denver, they'd never had an occasion where Cady could get dressed up.

And since then, although she always looked nice, stylish, he could tell her clothes were good quality therefore expensive, and she'd sometimes wear heeled boots to dress something up, mostly she was casual.

He'd noticed she'd had lip gloss on a couple of times, saw her clean off her mascara at night. But she didn't even wear full makeup.

That night however, when he'd picked up the women from the lighthouse to drive them to The Eaves, he'd seen Cady standing in the kitchen holding a wineglass and he'd not wanted to go to dinner with seven women and three men.

He'd wanted to grab her hand, haul her out to his truck, take her to his house, remove that dress and tie her to his bed…again.

Simple, one shoulder bared, blousy at the top, overlaps in the front of the skirt, it wasn't tight, skin baring or in-your-face sexy. It showed a nice amount of leg (and Coert would admit to a good deal of infatuation with her gold sandals as well), arm and shoulder, but it wasn't about sex kitten appeal.

It was classy. Elegant.

Gorgeous.

And her hair all done up in soft curls and pulled back in a loose ponytail that fell over her shoulder, her face entirely made up…

Christ.

Coert hadn't thought about it because it was Cady. All he wanted was Cady. She could have third degree burn scars over most of her body and he'd want her back, and then be over the moon when he got her.

But she wasn't about primping and preening way back when and he knew now it wasn't just because she didn't have the money or the reason to do it seeing as she wasn't about that now.

It just wasn't her.

And seeing her made up like that for their meeting-of-the-friends dinner, he realized he liked that it wasn't.

She was just what she was, natural and beautiful.

But now he knew it was more because he knew he'd get the gift of seeing her like this when they were going to share something special.

Kath's announcement of, "Oh no, we're not meeting you there so you guys can go upstairs and have a quickie. I'm hungry and I have a daughter in love who's pining in New Haven and a husband who single-handedly needs to pry my teenage son out of bed and get him to school for a week without losing the will to fight back the urge to commit murder, so I need wine and we're running low. But restaurants have a ready supply so we need to go there, STAT," had killed any dream that Coert could last minute bow out of that evening and do that with Cady.

Kim had taken Janie a day early so Coert could go out which meant Cady was back in his bed that night. Her overnight bag by the door confirmed that plan hadn't changed.

So he'd have to wait.

And he could wait.

That didn't mean he was over that dress.

And snatching her into his arms and kissing the lip gloss off her lips after the other women had filed out of the lighthouse earlier hadn't helped even a little bit.

So Coert's mind was on Cady's dress, and taking it off later, not on the meeting of the friends, or the fact that Kath was Kath, Alyssa was Alyssa, and he should have paid attention.

But he didn't.

And Kath started it off being Kath.

Hilarious, but still, in the end he'd lose Cady being close (in that dress) for most of the night.

"Okay, well, not…gonna…work," Kath announced the minute they hit the long table where Jake and Josie, Mickey and Amelia and Alyssa and Junior were already seated. "First, let's not pretend that this isn't gonna be ninety-nine point nine percent gossip about Coert and Cady so this boy-girl thing," she had a hand lifted, finger pointed out, and she slid it side to side to indicate how the couples were arranged at the table, "is just gonna get in the way. Second, my eyeballs are attached to muscles and arranging all the hot guys together means I won't have to strain them by looking around too much. So up! Rearrange. This is the girls' end of the table, and that's the boys'."

She indicated where everyone was sitting, then tugged out a chair in the women's section and sat her ass down.

"Uh, this is my sister, Kath, and she's had a traumatic Christmas with her twenty-year-old daughter falling in love with the man who rents the apartment over my garage," Cady introduced.

Josie and Amelia turned concerned eyes to Kath.

"So she sometimes has *some* manners, but now, not so much," Cady finished.

Coert slid a hand along the silky material at Cady's waist and curled his fingers at her hip and he did this watching the men at the table smile at his woman.

"I think I love you," Alyssa stated, staying in her seat in the women's section at the same time shoving at Junior to move him out of his, her eyes not leaving Kath.

"I *know* I love you," Kath returned. "Any sister who's got it and isn't afraid to flaunt it receives premier status. But you have to tell me, how do you keep those girls in? Double sided tape?"

"That's for amateurs. Hairspray," Alyssa replied.

"Really?" Pam asked, taking her seat in the women's section.

"Really," Alyssa confirmed.

"What the hell are they talking about?" Coert whispered in Cady ear.

"Cleavage," Cady whispered in his.

He still didn't get it and her answer didn't make Coert look at Alyssa's display. He was a guy, he liked tits, that was prerequisite. But he was an ass man and Cady's ass in her dress was all his mind needed.

"Hi, I'm Amelia. You're Cady?" Amelia said to Cady as she shifted out of her seat and Mickey shifted one over.

Josie also came around from the men's section and gave Coert a touch of her cheek to his before she pulled away and also gave him a smile.

"We'll take care of her," she said softly, turning to Cady.

And also leading her away.

Cursory introductions were performed between the people who hadn't met yet and Coert sat next to Junior, who was now at the head of the table, Mick on Coert's other side, and Jake across from him in the men's section.

He looked down the table to Cady, who'd been seated opposite him and all the way down the table next to Shannon on one side, who'd taken the foot, and Alyssa on her other.

He would have preferred her next to him but the placement didn't suck since he could look at her all night.

She gave him an amused smile.

He returned it.

"She's pretty," Junior murmured.

"She's everything," Coert murmured back.

The men exchanged glances.

Coert ignored them, grabbed his menu from in front of him, opened it and studied it, even though he knew he would get the ribeye because he always got the ribeye at The Eaves.

"By the way, I'm paying and I don't want any backtalk," Kath called from her seat on Shannon's left.

"That's gonna go bad for her since we already gave the waiter our credit cards," Mick muttered.

Coert chuckled and looked to his friend. "How's things?"

"Bought her a ring and we're goin' to the Keys so I can give it to her," Mickey answered.

Coert smiled. "So they're good."

Mick didn't answer. He just returned Coert's smile.

Yeah. Things were good.

And a glance at Amelia, who was sitting next to Mickey but was turned to face the women, Coert was glad for him. She was a short, pretty brunette who had two kids and currently lived at Cliff Blue, one of the three great houses in Magdalene (now that Cady had done up the lighthouse and it could again be considered a house). Cliff Blue was situated across the street from Mickey's place and it was so spectacular, Coert reckoned even if Mick had grown up in the house he and his kids now shared, once the ring he intended to put on her finger was joined by another one, Mick and his kids would be moving across the street.

"Brother," Jake called and Coert looked to him. "How's Janie taking things? She seemed good at Tink's. That still goin' on?"

"Yeah. She gets it," Coert answered. "We had our first alone night this week with Cady coming over after me and Janie had dinner. She watched TV with us and left before I put Janie to bed even though she said she didn't want Cady to go. We're trying to take it slow but she likes her. And Janie loves Cady's family. Thought I'd have to pry them apart with a crowbar when Janie had to say goodbye to Cady's niece after the last dinner with the whole family New Year's night at Breeze Point. Cady's going to show her how to Skype." He paused before he finished, "And Kim's helping. Being cool."

"Kim's helping?" Jake asked on raised brows, the three men sitting at that table with him being the only men, outside Coert's brother and father, who knew all that Kim had pulled.

"So far she's been great," Coert told him.

"Hope that doesn't end," Mickey said.

"You and me both," Coert replied.

"That boy needs to get his head out of his ass," Alyssa proclaimed loudly.

Elijah.

Coert was suddenly glad the poor guy hadn't been roped in to be there with them and he hoped Kath and all of them made it through the rest of their visit without visiting him to extract, what they thought was his head out of his ass.

"Probably good whatever's goin' on with Cady's renter is goin' on or they'd be pecking over your carcass," Jake noted.

Coert watched the waiter move around the women taking drink orders and returned, "No doubt they'll get to that."

"And this eighteen years Alyssa's been on about?" Junior prompted.

Coert glanced at his menu, made his decision, closed it and looked at Junior.

The last week had been busy with Janie, New Year's, the madness that caused at work and Cady's family. But he'd found time to take Janie over to see Con before he went back to school. And when he did, Jake and Josie had gotten the full story while Con, his girlfriend (incidentally, also Alyssa and Junior's daughter) Sofie, Amber and Ethan had looked after Janie.

Now it was clear from Junior's question and the feel of Mick's eyes on him that Jake hadn't shared.

He had to wait to answer while the men gave their drink orders.

When the waiter left, he launched in.

"Eighteen, now nearly nineteen years ago, the high school friends Cady was beginning to realize were people she didn't want in her life were people she seriously didn't want in her life, because they were getting involved with a crew that sold dope. She didn't know that part. She was just coming to the understanding they were bad news. I was undercover to bring this crew down. This was a bad situation significantly exacerbated by me gathering evidence that proved her best friend murdered her boyfriend, another friend Cady'd had for years, as a show of loyalty to the ringleader. She didn't know any of that either and I was under orders not to tell her. And as you could probably guess, things did not go well when the truth was outed."

"Holy fuck," Mick muttered.

"Yeah," Coert agreed. "Neither me or Cady handled any of that well. She was young, I wasn't much older, the situation was a mess and ugly got uglier. We were together for a while as my undercover work was happening. It was intense, we both knew it was forever, but in the end it was too much and we couldn't deal. We both perpetrated fuckups of massive proportions. Cue those eighteen years."

Coert stopped speaking and when he said no more, Junior stated, "And now she's back."

Coert looked to him. "As soon as we think Janie can handle it, she's moving in, we're getting married and we're getting pregnant. Though considering our ages, I'm not sure those last two will be in that order."

Junior, a huge man with a bald head who looked more like a mafia enforcer than the devoted family man he actually was, smiled huge. "So she's *back*."

"She was the one then and nothing changed in the time in between," Coert told him.

"Happy for you, man," Mickey said.

"Thanks," Coert murmured.

"Oh my God, Coert, it's like a romance novel!" Alyssa cried.

Coert looked to her, to Cady at her side, who was grinning even if she was rolling her eyes, and felt his lips twitch.

"Now they're peckin' over you," Junior said under his breath.

"There are worse things," Coert replied, and Lord knew there absolutely were. He glanced at Junior then at Mickey before he looked to Jake. "We need to talk about something else."

"What's that?" Jake asked.

"Did you know Boston Stone was behind the rezoning of the land around the lighthouse?" Coert queried.

He felt the tension of the men and it wasn't just because they all knew Stone was pure dick. It was because Stone had made a play for Josie that turned very ugly and he'd also made a play for Amelia that hadn't turned as ugly, but Stone had tried.

So they really weren't big fans.

"No. Is there an issue?" Jake asked.

"Terry Baginski got in touch with Cady last Sunday. Told her Stone wants to buy the lighthouse because he wants to build a resort there," Coert explained.

"He can want whatever he wants," Mick said, and Coert looked at him to see him finish a shrug. "If she owns it, and she owns it, he can't do dick."

"That's what I thought at first," Coert told him. "But I looked into it and there's an application submitted by Baginski on behalf of some corporations

I've never heard of, but I probably wouldn't have to look too hard to find that they're cover for Stone in partnership with others, to have the parkland around the lighthouse stripped of its protections in order for it to be allocated as commercial."

"Are you shitting me?" Jake demanded.

Coert shook his head. "When I uncovered that, I made a few more calls and found that Stone and these others have already contracted with an architecture firm to have plans drawn up for a hotel, some shops and restaurants."

"That would change the entire face of Magdalene," Junior pointed out.

"Considering Stone and two of his four partners are on the board that governs that unincorporated land, unless there's a move to stop it, it *will* change the face of Magdalene," Coert shared.

"It's a conflict of interest for them to approve something like that," Jake put in.

"Not sure they mind stepping down but I am sure some of their buddies with membership at the Magdalene Club will step right in to push approval of all of this through without anyone in Magdalene having a say about it," Coert told them.

Jake's eyes were on him. "And you *really* can't have a say about it."

Coert shook his head but said, "I'm a human so I can have an opinion and I'm a citizen so I can vote, but in my capacity as sheriff I can't make any moves, especially in regards to this, considering the owner of the property that's going to be most affected if they build is my future wife."

Jake nodded. "I'll talk to Weaver."

"Arnold Weaver? The attorney?" Junior asked.

Jake lifted his chin to Junior in verification.

This was a good call. Coert knew Arnie Weaver. Born and bred and built his family in Magdalene, he'd also lost his wife there not long ago and he used to be a city council member who was dogged in preserving the town as it was. It probably wouldn't take much to talk him into spearheading an attack on whatever legal obstacles they faced in stalling anything happening to that parkland before they could get a new referendum on the ballot to recall the old one.

"You might ask him to get in touch with Jackie at the Historical Society," Coert suggested. "Cady explained the call she got from Terry and Jackie lost her mind. There are some heavy hitters in Magdalene who sit on the Historical Society's board, and if you corral them and Weaver gets Magdalene's City Council interested, you might be able to stonewall them long enough to get another referendum on the ballot for the election in November."

"I'll call him tomorrow," Jake returned.

"*Mickey*," Alyssa cooed. "I thought Coert was going to be my most favorite man of the night, notwithstanding you, my beautiful bruiser," she said to her husband before blowing him an exaggerated kiss and looking back at Mick. "But you're giving him a run for his money!"

"Now they're pecking over you," Coert informed Mickey unnecessarily.

Mick just lifted an arm and draped it across the back of Amelia's chair.

Amelia turned her eyes to her man and gave him much the same look Cady had given Coert minutes before.

Yeah, she was pretty.

And from the way Mick's face got soft when he caught her look, Coert had confirmation that things weren't good for his friend, they were awesome.

Coert liked that.

Mickey's ex-wife was a decent woman but she was also an alcoholic who was relatively functioning out in the world, if you didn't count the times Coert's deputies had pulled her over for driving intoxicated. And she was able to function because Mick smoothed so much over for her, especially with their kids.

But when the kids got older and Mick was finding it harder and harder to smooth things over, he'd given her an ultimatum. When he did, she'd chosen the bottle over her husband and family and Mickey had to call it done.

It was a bad situation and it had been shit, watching Mick deal with the decision of having to tear his family apart in an effort to make them stronger by giving his kids healthy for the part time he had them and dealing with the fallout after they came back from her.

He didn't know what was happening with Mick's ex now.

He just knew Mick wasn't a man to put his children through that with their mother only to find another woman that might bring anything into their lives other than the soft that came about Mickey when he took in her smile.

The waiter approached with a colleague, both bearing trays covered in glasses.

Coert looked to Cady, who was being served and receiving her wineglass with a smile, and he didn't look forward to telling her what he hadn't yet told her. This being what he'd just shared with the men about Boston Stone.

She was going to lose her mind.

She reached to her glass and lifted it, considering Pam was making a toast that the men weren't involved in, and Coert allowed the happy contentment in her face to settle in his gut.

That woman wearing that dress was in his life. Her dog was in his life. Her family was in his life. And all of that was a part of his daughter's life.

He did not want to be dealing with Boston Stone.

More, he did not want her to have to deal with Boston Stone.

But if they could get through what they'd gone through and she'd end that sitting at a table (far from him, but she was still there), with her family and his friends, wearing that dress with that look on her face, they'd get through whatever a dick like Boston Stone had planned.

No sweat.

So when Coert's beer was served, he grabbed it and took a drink.

And when the waiter came around to him, he ordered his meal and slipped him his credit card in order to share his quarter of the bill.

The waiter was walking away as Kath exclaimed, "No! The cloak room? My God!"

Mickey got tense at his side and did not relax after Alyssa declared, "Junior, after appetizers, we're checking this out. Mickey and Amy can't hog all the best make-out spots."

Mick muttered, "We got one. One fuckin' make-out spot."

It was then Coert took in the huge smile Cady shot his way and Coert settled in to enjoy an excellent dinner at The Eaves with his friends.

Even though Cady, in that dress, was too fucking far away.

"*WHAT?*" CADY FAIRLY shrieked.

Midnight woofed.

Coert sighed as he took this as indication he was going to have to wait even longer to get Cady out of her dress.

He'd shared Stone's plans on the way to his place after dropping the women off at the lighthouse and picking up Midnight.

Now they were in his kitchen and Cady hadn't even taken her coat off before she lost her mind.

"Cady, I told you he was pure dick."

She tossed her purse on his island and started to unbutton her coat as she returned, "Yes, you told me that he was pure dick. What you *didn't* share was that he's Magdalene's version of the antichrist. I mean, *do you know what he did to Josie?*"

"Jake filled me in," Coert murmured. "And I was kinda involved seeing as I arrested that asshole of an uncle of hers that Stone dug up to harass her."

She shrugged off her coat. "Her grandmother had just died."

"Cady—"

"And he tried to get funding cut at the firehouse just because Amy didn't return his phone calls," she snapped.

Midnight woofed again, like the good dog she was, sharing in Cady's irritation even if she had no dog clue what it was about.

Coert put his own coat on the hook by the door in the laundry room, where he still was, and moved to her.

"Jake's going to talk to an attorney in town. We'll get Jackie in touch with him. And you and Jackie can talk to the council to get rolling whatever ball they've got to get rolling."

He took her coat from her and moved back to the hooks to hang it up so it was to his back when she replied, "This rezoning might have passed for a reason, Coert. Building like that creates jobs. A hotel can accommodate more tourists and this town exists mostly on tourist trade. More tourists, more people, more money. It might not be that people will want to recall that referendum. And if there's no support to fight it, all will be lost."

Coert walked back to her and put his hands on her neck.

"First, they'd have a helluva job to get support because the referendum barely passed the first time it was up for a vote, and people didn't know then precisely why it was up for that vote. Now, they will. And this town has tourist trade because it's like stepping back in time two hundred years. It's also because, from anywhere you look, you have unadulterated views of that lighthouse. There might be some who don't see that this is the attraction and if it isn't maintained, like every other town that overdeveloped in order to milk that kind of cash cow to the point it died, that cash cow will just plain die when Magdalene gets full of fast food joints and crap fish and chips stands and loses the charm that's the draw in the first place. But I think most realize the people who will profit in the short run, before they cut and run, are the ones who will push this through and then be retired to their beach houses in Florida while everyone else deals with the fallout of their greed. So I think if it's brought to people's attention what the plans are, they'll recall the rezoning of that land."

"Greed breeds greed," she returned.

"No one had any idea why the referendum for that land to be rezoned was put on the ballot and it doesn't really have anything to do with them until something like this comes up. Now that it's come up, something that didn't matter will matter."

"People think in immediates, Coert. They think about what's going to put food on their tables. Not how their world is going to change when men from North Carolina stop coming up here to see the lighthouse in springtime because the view isn't what it used to be," she returned.

"People hate change, Cady. It's one thing to vote or abstain on that vote because you don't care because you don't think anything's going to change, and it's something else to have the understanding of why that was brought to a vote in the first place and be able to make an informed decision. We just need to put a stop to anything happening in the now so that people can be informed and then make a decision."

He knew she had no argument to that when she snapped, "Why hasn't this man been run out of town on a rail?"

He grinned. "Because it's not against the law to be a dick but it is against the law to run someone out of town on a rail."

"I don't find this funny, Coert. Not only is this very concerning, I've never even met this man and he's ruining a good night. Dinner was utterly delicious. The company was even better. And the unknown Boston Stone has cast a pall over all of that."

Coert ran a finger across the top of her bare shoulder, his gaze not leaving hers, and he murmured, "Then how about we stop talking about him and get back to having a good night."

He wasn't being vague but he knew she got him when he watched her eyes heat.

He got closer and his voice went low. "Did I tell you I like this dress?"

"In words, no," she replied. "The look you gave me when you walked into the lighthouse and the kiss you gave me before we walked out said it all, though."

He dipped his face to hers. "Pleased that message was conveyed, baby."

"I'm not sure I told you how much I like you in this suit," she shared.

"I'm pretty sure I like you in that dress more than you like me in my suit," he parried, his voice coming rough.

With the slight widening of her eyes and the sway of her body he knew he'd made his point.

"Are we going to go slow? I'm in the mood to go slow," she told him, trying to sound bossy like Kath, and failing because it came out breathy. "It's been a whole week and I'm thinking you can't go slow after it's been a whole week."

Now she was challenging him.

"We're totally going to go slow," he promised, running his finger back up and continuing on that journey along the side of her neck.

"You keep saying that and we go fast," she returned.

Coert dropped his mouth to hers but he didn't kiss her or release her gaze.

"It's you being tied to the bed this time, honey. So we're absolutely going to go slow."

He felt her breath come faster against his lips.

"All we have is wool scarves. You can tie a man up with wool scarves. When it's the woman, it has to be something else," she informed him in barely a whisper.

"You think after what we did and I knew I'd get my turn I didn't hit that place on the jetty that sells women's clothes, you'd think wrong."

"You bought scarves?" she breathed, leaning into him, but Coert inched back just to tease.

"Mm-hmm," he murmured.

"I accidentally went fast when I tied you up," she reminded him.

Accidentally?

Coert fought back laughter and ran his finger along her jaw.

"I'm not accidentally gonna do anything when you're tied up," he replied.

"Are you gonna kiss me?" she whispered, her eyes drifting to his mouth.

"Oh yeah," he whispered back.

He ran his finger down her throat to his diamond that was resting in the dent at the base.

Always resting there.

She never took it off.

She got up on her toes and he edged back.

Her gaze lifted to his.

"Like…*now*?" she pushed softly.

"Mm-hmm," he murmured, trailing his finger along the slanted neckline of her dress.

"Coert," she begged.

"Do you know how much I love you?" he asked.

Finally, she touched him, her hands coming to the sides of his waist, her fingers digging in.

"I love you the most," she said as answer.

He flattened his hand against her chest, stroked it up and caught her behind the neck.

Cady gasped.

"Not even close," he growled.

And then he kissed her.

Cady's green dress was still on the kitchen floor the next morning.

The black silk scarves were also still tied to the headboard.

And it's important to note, regardless of the overwhelming incentive to do otherwise…

Coert went slow.

Twenty-Five

BE HAPPY

CADY

Present day…

"What the fuck?"

I couldn't help but giggle.

Coert looked at me but jerked a head to the carnage that had just happened on my TV screen. "That's funny?"

No one on earth would describe the Red Wedding from *Game of Thrones* as funny.

But Coert's response to it was.

He looked back at the TV. "Why are we watching this again?"

"Because it's brilliant," I told him.

He looked at me. "Everybody dies."

"Weeeeellll," I drew it out. "You won't get this yet but it's worth sticking with it. One word. Ramsay."

"Do I wanna know?" he asked.

"It's a long row to hoe but the harvest is pretty sweet," I shared.

My phone binged with a text and I looked down at it as Coert scowled his way through the credits after the bloodbath of the Red Wedding.

Thanks, Auntie Cady, but I have something going on that weekend. Tell Coert and Janie I said hi!

I frowned at my phone.

"Let it go," Coert ordered.

I frowned at him.

His eyes dropped to my frown and then came back up. "What happened to Switzerland?"

"I'm completely Switzerland," I declared.

"This is the third weekend in a row you've pushed her to come up here, Cady. She just left a month ago."

"A month is a long time. Long enough of it to pass for her to come up for another visit."

"No. It's long enough of it for you to remind Elijah who his one is since he's still going out with that woman you disapprove of, not to mention, this is the third invite in three weeks, pushing for a visit from Verity," Coert retorted, then concluded, "That's not Switzerland."

"That girl's not right for him," I declared, looking back at the TV.

"What's wrong with her?" he asked.

She was not Verity.

Obviously, that wasn't the answer I gave Coert.

"She's grasping," I stated.

"How's that?"

I looked to Coert. "He told me she asked him to see if I'd let him move into the studio. She had one date with him before Christmas and Verity happened in between. But they haven't even been dating a month and she's asking him to move to a nicer place?"

"The apartment over the garage is essentially one room. It's a huge room and when he and I tossed some back while watching the game a couple weeks ago I saw it was a nice room. A really nice room. With a freaking killer view. But it's not as nice or big as the studio."

"Elijah needs a new truck and he's saving. Walt told me what rent I could get on that garage apartment and it's more than Elijah pays because he removes snow and helped us take down the Christmas decorations that he also helped put up, and he's going to mow the grass in the summer. But I also know the rent I could get on that studio, and I can't cut him a deal that would let him save up for a truck that would be a deal that wouldn't be a hit to his manhood. He's trying to get his life in order, including his financial situation, which is somewhat dire because he spoiled his last girlfriend rotten since she was also grasping and only kicked him out when he had to put his foot down that he couldn't carry on giving them a lifestyle he couldn't afford and she didn't contribute to. He doesn't need another woman giving it another hit."

I knew Coert saw my point when he looked back at the TV.

I looked back to my phone right when Coert's binged, stating, "We share the same birthday. I'm asking her up for then so we can have a big celebration."

"Uh, no you aren't."

Coert had his phone in hand but his attention was on me.

"I'm not?"

He fell slightly to the side toward me on my big, round sectional.

I liked watching TV at Coert's. I especially liked doing it when Janie was around watching with us, or not and just coloring.

But I liked it more that Coert was giving me my lighthouse for the time I could have it by spending the night with me most nights when he didn't have Janie after the men and kids left (including spending the night when the girls were there—after the rest left, everyone had a bed because Shannon and Kath didn't mind sharing since Shannon and Kath didn't mind staying up until the wee hours talking about everything under the sun).

And I especially, *especially* liked cuddling with him on my big round sectional in front of the TV.

I missed Elijah, who came over for dinner and to lounge when Coert and I were giving Janie a break from me (though, lately, most of the time Elijah was spending with this new girl, something I *did not* like).

But living life with Coert doing things like making him catch up on *Game of Thrones* and snuggling on my couch (or his when Janie was asleep and before I left to come home) I adored.

We just...were.

Life just...was.

After the drama of us coming back together again, it was like the nearly two decades in between melted away.

It was beautiful.

"Baby, my first birthday with you since we're back…I like Verity. I want the opportunity to get to know her better. More, I wanna see her with my own eyes and make sure she's okay because she didn't leave here in a good state. But I want all of that birthday action for myself."

And hearing that, he was going to get all that action to himself.

It had all fallen apart after I'd shared my birthday with Coert years ago, and I would look back at that day and see it for how it was, something I didn't see when it was happening.

This being Coert's bad mood that he tried to hide, which I knew after the fact was because he couldn't allow himself to buy me a present (though he went out of his way with a big store-bought cake with lots of icing flowers and he made me a big dinner after he made sure I took the whole day off, the rest of it when he wasn't cooking we spent in bed).

It was still the best birthday of my life.

And it was the best present I could ever have just to get it back again.

I slid closer to him and put my hand on his chest. "I want this birthday to be just like the last one we had together."

He grinned. "I'll schedule a day off when I get to the station tomorrow."

"Just like the last one, Coert. Bed, dinner, cake and no presents."

A shadow clouded his features before he forced it clear.

Oh yes, he'd wanted to buy me a present.

I pressed into his chest. "Running to catch up doesn't mean that. It isn't about presents. Running to catch up is about this." I threw an arm out to indicate *Game of Thrones*.

He raised a brow. "Marathon watching a fantasy show where everyone you like bites it?"

I grinned at him. "Yes. Precisely. Everyday stuff that just is. Being just us. Having just what we should have had."

"I should have been able to buy you a present that birthday, Cady."

I shook my head. "But don't you see? Having you do something special meant more to me. And it's my birthday so I should get what I want."

He stared in my eyes, looked at my mouth, covered my hand on his chest with his and curled his fingers around before he looked back into my eyes.

"It's your birthday, you'll get what you want, honey," he said softly.

I grinned again.

Then something occurred to me.

"But I get to buy you a present."

He burst out laughing, which nearly drowned out the second bing of his phone reminding him he had a text.

He also wrapped his arms around me and settled back, taking me with him.

I curled my arms around him as he muttered, "Why am I not surprised she's trying to pull a fast one?"

"I learned your birthdate from a private investigator's report," I told his chest.

His arms convulsed and the humor in the room slid away.

"I missed it again last year," I went on. "October."

"Cady."

"You got one. I was with you during the one I had with you and you didn't tell me I had that because you couldn't. You got to make the tradition for me. So I'm calling it. I get to make mine for you."

He didn't fight it.

But I was learning that about Coert (or remembering).

If I wanted it badly and he sensed that, Coert rarely fought anything.

"You gonna make me pie?" he asked instead.

"Yes."

"Stick candles in that thing?"

He was ruining my plans by guessing them!

"Maybe."

"You best quit making Janie and me pies all the time then, Cady. It won't be special."

I tipped my head back and saw his chin dipped to catch my eyes.

"It'll be special."

His eyes warmed with sadness and nostalgia and gratitude before he gave me a light kiss and pulled away.

He looked back to the TV. "We got a deal. Now you wanna queue up another hour of torture or are you gonna give me a break with this?"

"You really don't like it?"

He returned his attention to me. "It's brilliant."

"You're teasing," I surmised.

"Was a fan of Robb's, a big fan of Cat's," he shared, referring to characters on *Game of Thrones*, "so that wasn't all that fun. Your buttons, though, since Mike's gone, need pushing or they'll get stuck in the off position."

I lifted my chin and ignored Coert's lips twitching when he caught it.

"I love Mike but I do not miss his button pushing," I informed him.

"I'm just glad my girl got herself some *real* older brothers who give her shit in their different ways because they love her, not the asshole she had who treated her like shit because he was an asshole."

I relaxed into him. "I'm pretty glad about that too."

And I wasn't more glad he was glad but I was pretty ecstatic about that as well.

Unfortunately, Coert kept speaking.

"And it's good to understand it was them who drove her to be the screaming feminist she's become."

I tensed against him. "I'm not a screaming feminist. It's that you're a bossy, domineering chauvinist and it's my duty to point that out."

"Jesus," he said through a grin, "you don't even see it coming."

It was maddening, but I actually made a *harrumph* sound when I turned my attention to finding the remote in order to queue up the next episode of *GoT*.

Coert lifted his phone while I located it and aimed it at the TV, but I didn't go to the next episode when I heard Coert mutter a rather annoyed, "Fuck."

I looked to him. "What?"

"Kim," he stated.

Kim?

"What?" I repeated.

He took his arm from around me in order to stab irately at his phone and I heard a text whoosh before he focused on me.

"I told her that next week when I have Janie back we'd be doing our first sleepover with you. It's important to note I told her this. I didn't ask her if it's okay. But she took it like that," he stated then turned his phone to me.

I read Kim's text of, *Sorry, Coert. This is too soon. And it's too much too fast. I hate to say this but I really can't allow it.*

I also saw Coert's very recent response of, *I wasn't asking.*

"Maybe you should have taken a breath before you responded," I suggested carefully.

I didn't like the look in his eyes when he replied, "And so it begins."

"Coert—"

"I know her, Cady, and this is a sign that she's starting her shit back up again. Janie loves you. I had that callout last week and left you two together and all she could talk about the next day was how you ditched dinner and ate snack food and watched *Beauty and the Beast*, and you didn't care that she made you watch it twice, back to back. She's down with this. She's ready. The doctor says you're good. We have time to make a baby. But we don't have a decade. Things need to move. And I told Kim about it as a courtesy. I don't tell her what can and can't happen at her house. She can't tell me what can and can't happen at mine."

"And if she had a man in her life and had him stay over?" I asked cautiously.

"If she knew him a day, a week, a month…no, I would not be down with that. That said, I know she loves our daughter so I might not be down with it but I'd have no choice but to trust her to make the right decision. And bottom line, our lives are separate so I don't get a say in how she lives hers unless she's making stupid decisions that I know are gonna affect my kid. This is more, though. She knows our story. You aren't some woman I'm getting to know. You're Cady. The future is not in question. The future is set. She knows that too. But she's big on control. I haven't seen it in a while but this is not unfamiliar territory. I learned the hard way you don't give an inch because Kim won't take a mile. She'll go for a hundred of them."

"You have experience with this but even so, what would it hurt to, say, maybe give her a couple more weeks? Offer a compromise?"

He turned into me and replied instantly, "It hurts every day I wake up without you beside me. Yeah, I know now I'll get you back but I lost that for too long and I don't like it for even a day, much less every other week. If it was just me, I'd have asked you to move in the night we got back together. It isn't just me. I've been seeing to my daughter. And the time is right. You're not moving in. One sleepover next week. Maybe two the next time she's with me. And then we'll see about more and taking that to permanently. But Kim doesn't make that call. We do."

"I think perhaps we need to set a precedent with her that we're all in this together…for Janie."

"I see where you want this to go for Janie, Cady, but that isn't Kim. If she's backsliding and not genuinely…" he trailed off because his phone binged.

He looked at it and turned it to me.

It said, *Uncool.*

And as I read that, another bubble popped up with, *We come to mutual decisions about these things. Your actions affect more than just Janie, Coert.*

He looked at his phone and muttered, "I don't have to finish what I was saying. She's backsliding."

He then started stabbing his phone with his finger again.

"Coert, I really think you should take a second to consider your response before you reply to her," I cautioned as I watched Coert type out, *Give me one good reason.*

He hesitated.

I looked at him.

"You think I deserve one good reason?" he asked.

To be honest, I actually did.

So I bit my lip and nodded.

He turned his attention back to the phone and I heard the whoosh.

I stared at his phone, worried.

I didn't know what Coert was doing but I could feel he wasn't worried. I could feel he was still annoyed.

Kim didn't immediately reply.

I turned my eyes to Coert. "Do you want me to get you another beer?"

Before he could answer, his phone binged.

We both looked at it.

I haven't even met her yet.

"I hesitate to say…" I said hesitantly. "But that's a good reason."

"You up to meet Kim?" Coert asked.

Actually, no.

I wanted to like her because, until now (and she did have a good reason for now), she'd been great.

From afar.

It was exceptionally difficult to factor out the beauty of Janie, but regardless, what she'd done not only trying to trap Coert (and succeeding in doing that in a way she was still in his life, in that room, controlling his emotions at that moment) but also learning she'd attempted to use Janie as a weapon against him to get what she wanted was not conducive to me being objective about Janie's mother.

But this was it. This was life. This was us in the form of "us" being more than just Coert and me.

So I had to.

"Yes," I answered.

Coert turned back to his phone.

I did too and watched him type in, *Lunch, any day this week. Weatherby's. Your call. We'll see you there.*

He hit send and then he said, "Now I can use a beer but I'll get it."

A soft *whoop* signaled she'd immediately texted back and both of us looked at it.

Just her and me.

I wasn't a big fan of the "her" when "Cady" would have been nicer, and the use of "her" slightly worried me, but I wasn't going to point that out.

Absolutely not, Coert typed.

I darted a hand out to close my fingers around his wrist before he hit send.

I looked at him. Coert looked at me.

"It's fine," I told him.

"It is fuckin' not," he told me.

"Honey," I slid up to get closer to face to face with him, "you said she's a good mom. But you didn't have to tell me that. I see it in Janie. I'm watching *Beauty and the Beast* with her daughter while you're on a callout. I'm going to be spending every other week with her girl. She's entitled to meet me and do it without you glowering at her and waiting for her to mess up."

"I'm not going to glower," he bit out.

"You're glowering right now," I shared.

"I'm pissed at her right now," he returned.

"Let us do this," I urged gently. "I have this. Her reason for having a concern about this sleepover is valid. Just," I slid farther up to get eye to eye with him, "let us do this."

"You forgive. You let people shit all over you without calling them on it. I'm not saying Kim's gonna do that. What I'm saying is, you won't put a stop to it if she does. But if I'm around and it starts, I will."

"I don't do that."

"Baby, you forgave *me* and I destroyed your entire life."

I blinked.

"And you came back here and I was a total dick to you repeatedly in order to drive you away again, and you not once called me on that, not even once did we discuss it after we got back together. You just let it go, forgave me without saying the words. So I hear you but I gotta say no. This meet happens with me," he finished.

I felt him move his hand and my hold on his wrist tightened.

"I thought we got past that," I shared when he again focused on me.

"We did."

"We didn't since you just brought it up."

"Being past it doesn't negate it happened," he stated.

"Coert—"

He tossed his phone aside and twisted his wrist from my hold but only to cup my face with his hand when he was free.

"Look at me," he ordered.

"I am," I pointed out the obvious since I was staring right into his eyes.

"This is it. This is me. I'm your man. The man who loves you. The man you love. This is who I am. This is how it is. This is how it's gonna be. And if you don't understand what I'm saying to you, I'll spell it out. My job is to look after you. My job is to protect you. From bad shit. Or just from the crap of life happening. It's *always* been that since the first time we kissed. And when I don't, and there will be times when that's out of my control, like arguably that whole fiasco we endured, I'm gonna feel that. It's gonna live in me. I'll be able to hack it but that doesn't mean it'll go away. And you have to let me feel that because it's just plain…*me*."

My heart was beating fast, my stomach was warming, but my lips asked, "Do I get to protect you in return?"

"Baby, you forgave me. Yeah. That's your job too. And trust me, you're on it."

"Then let me take Kim," I requested.

He closed his eyes, shook his head once, opened them and said, "Do you not get why that has to be a no?"

"This is about you. This is about you and Janie. And this is about the future of you and me and Janie. Not Kim. *You* and *me* and *Janie.* We're setting a different precedent now. And I feel the right way forward is if I meet Kim alone. Please, Coert, I understand you. I promise. I love what you said more than I can ever express. But even so, I beg you to let me do this. Because I believe it's the right thing and I can do this and I want very badly for you to let me. But it's more. I want you to trust me to do this and in doing that, show you trust my instincts when it comes to protecting not only you, but you and Janie."

"Then you can meet Kim on your own."

He didn't even wait a second to answer me.

Not a second.

I didn't know whether to burst into tears or attack him and rip his clothes off.

I didn't do either.

I said, "God, I love you so fucking much."

His lips twitched. "Earned the F-word from my proper Cady."

I felt my brows draw together. "I'm not proper."

"Honey, you used to curse all the time. I'm not sure I've heard worse than a 'damn' from you since Christmas."

"Are you honestly teasing me about cursing right now?" I asked.

"Yeah," he whispered before he dipped in and brushed his mouth against mine. "I am."

"Text Kim back with my number so we can set up a time," I ordered.

"Thinkin' my Cady's feelin' bossy. Wonder who's getting tied up tonight."

"My headboard doesn't have slats."

"Worth braving the cold to ride back to my house then."

He was not wrong, and Maine cold was *cold* but it would be very much worth it.

I could argue both ways on the tying up score and we'd now had more experience with it. We were currently even. Me twice. Coert twice.

Maybe we should try wrestling to see who got to tie the other up.

He was stronger but I'd learned the last weeks I could do things that Coert found very distracting.

I'd suggest that later.

"Text her, Coert."

"Get me a beer while I do, baby."

I gave him a glare but started to move away to get him a beer.

He caught me, rolled me to my back and laid a hot and heavy one on me.

Then he let me go and said, "Beer."

I didn't have it in me anymore to glare so I didn't.

In other words, Coert did things I found very distracting too.

Coert turned his attention to his phone.

Midnight accompanied me as I got my man a beer.

TWO DAYS LATER, I made sure to be just a wee bit late so Kim could get there first and sit where she wanted to sit so she felt more comfortable.

This wasn't strategic.

This was sympathetic.

I had it all. The good man, and every other week, his beautiful daughter. I had a bright future—marriage and another child and living a life having everything I ever wanted.

I could afford to be sympathetic.

I saw her right away in a booth a few down. She was facing the door.

I also saw right away that she was prettier in real life than in the pictures Patrick's private investigator took of her.

She was studying me as I walked her way and she did it unsmiling.

I did not take this as a good sign.

That was until her eyes got wide and I realized she didn't know who I was until I stopped at her booth.

"Cady?" she asked.

"Kim," I replied. "Nice to meet you."

She slid out and offered her hand. "Yeah, you too."

We'd barely separated and sat in the booth and I was still setting my purse beside me when the waitress showed.

We ordered drinks and Kim said, "Sorry, this is rude and it's rushing you but I don't have a lot of time for lunch so have you been here before? Can you order? Or do you need to look at a menu?"

She was nice about it but I still got worried what it said that she was pushing me to order when I hadn't even taken off my coat.

Still, I looked to the waitress and said, "Patty melt."

"Oh thank God," Kim stated immediately. "You didn't order a salad making me feel like I need to order a salad."

Okay, that was promising.

She turned to the waitress. "Reuben."

"Gotcha," the waitress said and moved away.

I pulled off my gloves, scarf and coat and tucked them beside me on the bench seat.

"Let me guess, the lag time between texts, you had to talk Coert into letting you come alone."

I opened my mouth, closed it, opened it and closed it.

She smiled at me.

"I'll take that as a yes," she decreed. "And not surprised. When he and I were together, I got in a fight with my sister. Big drama. She was totally in the wrong, by the way," she shared chattily. "And Coert was pissed about it. To save face, when she reached out to apologize, she wasn't nice about it even though I knew she was reaching out to apologize and not doing it nice in order to save face. That just pissed Coert off more. He wouldn't listen to a word I said to explain where she was. To end, he didn't let me go meet her alone. Flatly refused. He came with me and stared her down the whole time. Weirdly, this didn't tick her off. She already loved him. It just made her love him more."

Something slid over her face, she looked away, gave a slight cough and then looked back.

"So I get it," she finished.

This was a strange opening and I didn't know where to go with it because there was no missing the something that slid over her face was her missing how protective Coert could be, and I had a bad feeling about that.

"I screwed up and I know it," she announced.

I continued to stare at her, still unable to speak, now because I wasn't sure precisely which screw up she was referring to and I was entirely taken aback she'd just announce she knew she did it (even though which "it" was in question).

"I got that text from Coert saying you were sleeping over and I sat on it because I knew it wasn't smart to reply right away because I was feeling sorry for myself that he found someone, or rather, you came back and I was still alone. But instead of sitting on it and getting my head together, I sat on it and stewed about it and let myself get angry and before I did something smart, like call my mom and talk it through, I did something stupid and sent him a text I knew would set him off."

I decided to try to say something.

"Kim—"

That was as far as I got.

She lifted a hand and waved it in my direction.

"I know this is okay. I know this is right. I know this is healthy. You and Coert, I mean. And not just for Coert, for Janie. And I know this because my mom and dad split up when I was thirteen and it wasn't good. Not for us kids. Not for them. It was ugly and got uglier. And then my mom got a boyfriend and the weird part about that was, it didn't get better at first. My dad got pissed and went off and got himself a girlfriend, I think mostly to make her angry like he was. And now, that woman is my stepmom and she's awesome. They're happy as clams and have been for years. And mom went through five boyfriends before she found the one who was a keeper and they're happy as clams too. Mom and Dad get along again. It's all good and has been for a long time."

"I appreciate you sharing all this with me but just so you're aware, I understood why you'd want to meet me before anything progressed with me spending more time with Janie. Being a bigger part of her life. Communicating on a deeper level who I am to her father."

"Glad about that, Cady," she replied. "But I think it's important that you understand that I get where this is at. Happy parents, happy kids. That was one of the reasons I was trying to stay cool about it all because I lived through it and I knew the best thing for the kid is to have parents who are where they want to be, including being with someone who makes them happy. Saying that, falling down on that with my text to Coert and what was behind it is actually a bigger issue."

Oh no.

I wasn't sure I wanted to know.

I asked anyway because I had to.

"What's that?"

"I was…" she trailed off, said no more, looked to the window at our sides, over my head, around the diner, giving the appearance she'd beg for the waitress to show with our drinks, before she finally came back to me. "Nervous as all hell about meeting you."

This surprised me.

"I think you can imagine that was my same feeling," I told her.

She couldn't imagine that and showed me this by openly displaying shock.

"You're Janie's mother, you're a part of Coert's life," I said softly. "I know he shared our story, but in the now, where things are going, it's important to us both, to all of us, that you and I get along."

"You know he shared your story and I don't know it, but I could guess, he shared our story with you."

Fortune wasn't shining on Kim but it was on me because our waitress took that moment to arrive at our table with our drinks, giving both of us a distraction that would allow me to hide my reaction.

However, when the waitress left, she pressed the issue.

"He did, didn't he?"

I wasn't going to tell her about Patrick's private detective and townsfolk talk. I also wasn't sure how Coert would feel about me disclosing our private conversations, even if they were about Kim.

But as she was being honest, I thought it safe to say, "I'm aware of the story."

"So you know what I did."

I knew what she did.

Times two.

I nodded.

"So, obviously, you being who you are to him, who you've always been, and you two finding your way back to each other, I'm cast in the role I created myself, being the evil ex," she declared.

Oh my God.

I leaned toward the table and whispered, "Kim—"

I again got no more words out because she again lifted her hand and waved it at me.

"It's the bed I made. I get it."

Coert was right.

She was still feeling guilt.

Quite a bit of it.

It could be said she should.

But then again, we all needed to move on from mistakes we'd made in our lives, and as I'd learned, sometimes even making them, something beautiful comes of it and there was nothing more beautiful in the world than a little girl like Janie.

Therefore I advised, "I think you need to move on."

She wasn't ready to do that and I knew it when she didn't do it.

She explained.

Thoroughly.

"I told you about my mom and dad. That's a bad time for a kid. A girl. Thirteen?" She shook her head. "I was dealing with being a girl at thirteen and all that came with that, and then my mom and dad break up and we have to sell our house because neither of them can afford it on their own and me and my sisters' and brother's life was totally changed. Mom told me I was a good kid. I didn't act out before that. She hates it that what happened with her and Dad was the catalyst for me starting to do stupid stuff. But she gets it. What I didn't get is that they were miserable before they broke up. They fought, tried to hide it but sometimes we heard. In the end, they weren't even comfortable being around each other. We felt that. I just chose to ignore it because I wanted what I wanted. I loved them both so I wanted Dad and Mom with me all the time. So in the end, Mom might be right but she's also wrong, because I was selfish and I had to be that way before it all happened, wanting just what I wanted. Not wanting them to go their separate ways so they could be happy."

"I think any child of that age would feel the same way and probably act on it, Kim. You may be being too hard on yourself."

"You can say that, but then I poked holes in Coert's condoms because I knew he was pulling away from me," she retorted.

I shut my mouth in an effort not to make a sound at hearing that brutal honesty straight from her lips.

She caught it and said, "Yeah. One thing to be a kid acting out because your parents have split and another thing to be an adult acting selfishly to hold on to a man who doesn't want to keep hold on you."

"I'm sorry," I said quietly. "But I can guess you would understand why I don't disagree."

"You, my mom, my sisters and you can imagine what my brother had to say about it."

This surprised me, so I asked, "Sorry?"

"They lost their minds," she shared. "At that and the time I threatened to move away and take Janie. They loved Coert and they didn't want me to lose him but they loved him and it was what it was. Then I did what I did and they flipping *freaked.* After the court thing, Mom eventually said if I didn't sort myself out, she'd disown me. Coert doesn't know this, but it was ugly. Things with my brother are still not the same. And that's what finally got me to take a good look at how I was acting and make a change. Mom told me I'd decided when she and Dad got divorced that even bad attention was attention and I wanted as much of that as I could get to try to make myself feel better about something I couldn't control. I looked it up. Read some books. And she was right. It was all about attempting to control something I couldn't control even if I did it in an unhealthy way. Coert pulling away from me, pull him back even if I have to do it in a way he'd despise me. Have a baby that reminds me daily of the stunt I pulled, try to force a reconciliation I know he's not ever going to go for just to try to force the situation to change, create a family I've no hope to create in an attempt to erase what I did."

I couldn't believe she was sharing all this with me.

I took a sip of my Diet Coke before I asked, "Have you told Coert any of this?"

She shook her head.

"Maybe you should," I advised carefully.

"What will it matter?" she queried. "What's done is done."

"He says you're a good mom."

She stared at me.

I kept at her.

"He says you're a good mom and there was a reason he spent so much time with you. Until the texting, he was relieved you were being so wonderful about all of this with Janie. He didn't say he was glad to have the woman back that he enjoyed having a part of his life, but if I'd given it thought, I could read that into what he's said. He's grateful you've been lovely through our reunion, letting us have that, facilitating things with Janie along the way." I dropped my voice. "He cares about you, Kim. It might not be what you'd hoped but it's a beautiful thing regardless, for you and for Janie and for what the three of us can give her if we allow that to be the foundation for us all. He'd want to know how much work went into you finding your way back to you."

"I get that he had every reason to be but he was really angry with me after all I did and he didn't let that go, Cady, not for a long time. So it isn't super easy to share things with him."

Boy, did I know how that felt.

But that I didn't share.

I said, "And he's putting effort into moving beyond that. Join him on that journey, Kim. Don't stay in the past when he's not there anymore. As the texting situation proved, it'll only serve to drag him back there and remind him of the reasons he had to remain angry, you'll react to that, and then where will we all be?"

"When you walked in, and I hoped to God you weren't Coert's Cady, then I found out you were, I thought it was because you're so incredibly pretty that he was hung up on you for so long. But it's not. It's because you're perfect for him. Honest and smart and sweet. And you don't play games. You lay it out there. That's pure Coert. Perfect for him."

I sat back and it was my turn to stare.

The waitress came and served our lunches.

I turned flustered eyes to my plate.

"Janie's falling in love with you," she said softly.

I lifted my gaze to her.

"I'm so glad because I'm gone for your beautiful girl," I said softly back.

"I know it's not my right to say this, but I'm gonna say it anyway. I'm really glad he got you back so he can be happy. Giving you more honesty, it hurt a lot, being with him and feeling the sadness in him and knowing it wasn't going to be me that would take that away. But I care about him enough that I'm glad he found what he needed to get rid of that. So thank you."

"That's very nice, Kim, and I hope you continue to feel that way," I replied.

"Why would I not?" she asked, picking up her Reuben.

"To be totally honest, we're aware this is going fast but we're even more aware of the time we lost so even if Coert's doing all he can to take care of Janie along the way, I think it's only fair to warn you that it feels like we're running to catch up and I'm not sure when that's going to end."

She chewed and swallowed the bite she took while I was speaking and then immediately grinned at me.

"Girl, if I was Coert Yeager's one and only and he looked like he looks when he gets a text from you, I'd break world records running to catch up."

I smiled back, feeling relief sweep through me, and feeling a lot more wondering what Coert looked like when he got a text from me.

"I'll add my gratitude for you being so lovely through this," I told her, going for one half of my patty melt.

"Beware our descent into the mutual admiration society because I can't tell you how relieved I am that you didn't come here thinking I was a total bitch after what I did to Coert, intent on hating me, and instead you're being so cool."

I chewed, swallowed and replied, "I don't mind being a member of that society."

"Good," she said with mouth full. But she swallowed before she inquired, "Can I ask you for something?"

I tried not to get visibly tense while I nodded.

"I absolutely have to see this lighthouse. Just because I always wanted to see the lighthouse. But Janie talks about it all the time. She says the 'window room,' her words, is the 'awesomest,' her word as well. So now I *need* to see this lighthouse. And meet your dog. Janie is drawing black dogs over all her coloring books and she says it's so she can have Midnight with her until she gets her back."

Oh my *God.*

I *loved that child.*

"Any time you like. I always have wine," I invited.

"That'd be *amazing*."

"You can't even *imagine*," I replied. "We'll set that up. I volunteer a couple of days a week at the Historical Society but other than that, I'm usually free."

"Awesome."

"Perfect."

We both took bites.

And then two new friends had lunch.

I HUSTLED ON my boots down the sidewalk toward the station but had to slow when my phone in my hand binged again with a text.

I looked at it.

Cady, text me.

I could actually *feel* the bold and underline under "text me."

This was because, close to the end of our lunch the text came in from Coert that ordered, *Text me the minute you're done.*

Which was after the text that came in *before* we had lunch that said, *Thinking of you. Hope it goes okay. Text me when it's over.*

I hit the microphone so it would type out my verbal reply without me having to stop and do it, saying, "Keep your pants on. I'm ten feet from the steps of the station. I'll be in your office soon."

I hit send.

Then I hit the steps to the station, trotted up them, pushed through the door, waved at one of Coert's deputies and called, "Hi, Matt."

"Hey there, Cady," he called back.

I ran up the steps and smiled at Monica who was in her small office next to Coert's.

"Hey, Cady," she said.

"Hiya, Monica," I replied.

I hurried down the hall, hit Coert's door that was open and saw him at his desk.

His head came up.

I smiled, walked in and closed the door behind me.

"Future," he growled. "I'm worried about you, don't tell me to keep my pants on."

I ignored his grouchiness and cried, "Kim knows a reporter at the *Bangor Daily News*!"

"Uh…what?" Coert asked.

I rushed to stand opposite him at his desk. "I told her about Boston Stone and the whole rezoning conspiracy and she got angry and told me she knows someone at the *Bangor Daily News* and she was calling her when she got back to work, and she hopes this reporter person will blow the story wide open!"

"You wanna share with me how your lunch went with my ex?" he demanded through a request, completely ignoring my fabulous news.

"Totally fine," I verbally waved it away. "She's lovely. It's all good. She's coming to the lighthouse for wine this weekend. Bringing Janie."

Coert blinked.

I kept talking.

"I know Bangor isn't close but Kim thinks like us, that this is corruption and Boston Stone has dealings all through Maine so she thinks it'll be so meaty, her friend will be dying to sink her teeth into it."

"Kim's coming to the lighthouse for wine?" Coert asked.

"Yes," I answered impatiently. "But Coert, did you hear me about Kim's friend?"

"I did. And it's a good idea that Amy already ran with. She did some huge house sale a while back and contacted all the local papers, so Mick phoned me this morning to say that she contacted them as a concerned citizen and shared this with them, and this morning a reporter at the *Derby Forecaster* called her back to tell her the paper is running a story next week. Now, let's talk about you having wine with my ex at your house."

"Do you think that's a bad idea?" I asked.

"Do you think it's a good one?" he returned.

"I can't imagine why not," I replied.

"Cady, she's my ex," he told me something I knew.

"Yes," I confirmed I knew it.

"And that road has been rocky."

"So has ours," I shared.

"Uh, yeah, I know. But just to let you in on something, a guy isn't real comfortable with two women he's taken to bed having wine at one of their houses."

I fell silent because I found this very interesting.

"The goal of this lunch was for you to get Kim's head out of her ass, not become best friends with her," he informed me.

"I doubt we'll ever be best friends, Coert, but I'm uncertain it's a bad thing that we become *friend* friends."

"I've slept with both of you," he retorted.

"Although I'll admit that when wine flows, tongues can loosen, but I do think it's doubtful we'll compare our Top Ten Favorite Intimate Times with Sheriff Coert Yeager."

His mouth got hard.

I tried not to laugh.

Instead, I went softly.

"You can trust me."

"I know that," he bit out.

My next was going to be harder.

"You can trust Kim."

"You've had one lunch with her and you feel you can say that?" he asked.

Yes, it was harder.

"She cares about you," I shared.

"Think I got that with how hard she found it, letting me go."

"Do you know her mother nearly disowned her after she tried to take Janie away from you?" I asked.

Coert sat back and he didn't hide this news stunned him.

"She says her relationship with her brother took such a hit, it hasn't yet recovered."

"Jesus," he whispered.

"She was terrified of meeting me, the reason she acted out in the texts, because she thought I'd hate her."

"Shit," he murmured.

I lifted my chin. "I like her. I'm going to be her friend. She's coming over for wine. And I promise I won't share my favorite time is a tie between bar bathroom sex, kitchen floor sex way back when, and the first time you tied me up."

"Don't try to distract me by making me hard reminding me of that first time I tied you up," he warned.

So his favorite time was that time.

Noted.

"It's over, honey," I reminded him.

"It's—"

"Over," I whispered. "Boston Stone could build a mall right next to the lighthouse. And Janie's no doubt someday going to have a bad flu. And I'm going to probably completely fail at being Switzerland with Elijah and Verity and not just in hopes of getting him to try things with my niece. But because I *really* do not like his new girlfriend because I heard her shouting at him when I pulled in last night before you came over that he never *listens to her*, and Elijah is an excellent listener. But that's it. That's all. Just life. We're through the tough stuff. Let's let go and be happy."

His expression was another mix of beautiful and awful when he whispered in return, "I'm not used to that."

"Then we'll get there together."

He stared in my eyes before he turned his head away and I saw a muscle jump up his cheek.

"Is it terribly inappropriate if I sit in the sheriff's lap at his desk?" I asked quietly.

He turned his head right back. "No."

I rounded his desk and Coert swiveled in his chair for me to have a clear shot at sitting in his lap.

So I did.

I also put my arms around his shoulders while he curled his around me.

"We're going to beat Boston Stone. And Janie will get over that future flu. And Elijah is going to break up with that awful girl. And we're going to move in together and get married and get pregnant and have a beautiful baby boy with your eyes," I told him.

"Yeah, except it'll be a girl with yours," he replied.

I smiled and snuggled closer, advising, "So, to end, we have to learn to get used to happy, Coert."

His arms separated, one coming up so he could pull me to him in a tight hold.

I rested my cheek at the base of his throat and felt him rest his chin on top of my head.

"I'll do my best," he murmured.

"Good," I murmured back.

"Sucks but it's probably 'terribly inappropriate' I make out with my woman at my desk," he kept murmuring.

"Yes, that sucks. Because that means sex is entirely out."

His arms gave me a squeeze and I felt his body shake with his laughter.

I cuddled even closer.

"Probably won't be too hard," he noted.

"Getting used to happy?" I asked.

He kissed the top of my hair and said there, "Yeah."

"Yeah," I agreed.

We stayed where we were for a while before Coert said, "Sucks again but I gotta get to work, because I got shit to do and I want to do it so I can come home to you and then watch Jon Snow probably meet an ugly, bloody death at the hands of some White Walkers or something."

I smiled into his chest at his *GoT* quip but said nothing about Jon Snow's bloody end. He'd have to be surprised.

I just shifted to kiss the skin of his throat above his Henley and then moved away so he could look down at me.

"Love you," I whispered.

"Love you most," he returned.

"Not even close."

We didn't make out.

But he did kiss me.

He also put his coat on to walk me to my car.

Then I went home.

And a few hours later, Coert joined me there.

We had dinner.

We watched three episodes of *GoT.*

He made love to me before we went to sleep.

And we were happy.

Twenty-Six

IN A NIGHTIE, CARDIGAN AND SOCKS

COERT

Present day…

"I'm not sure pissed is the right word. The way Arnie describes it, after Stone stormed into his office yesterday afternoon, apoplectic is the right word," Jake said in his ear.

Moving around Cady's kitchen as she made him breakfast, something she made clear she was going to make a habit and did, even on a day like that day—a Saturday he had off—while he refilled their coffee, Coert didn't bother to beat back his grin.

"So I take it Stone wasn't a big fan of the injunction Weaver filed on behalf of the citizens in unincorporated Derby County to freeze proceedings on reclassifying Magdalene parkland for commercial builds until an assessment of conflict of interest for the board of governors can be made?" Coert asked, finding Cady's eyes and watching hers taper in a smile.

"That and the *Forecaster* story followed up by the *Daily News* doing a three-part exposé on the shady machinations of Stone Incorporated to acquire land, some of it protected, and reclassify it for commercial or residential use across the state of Maine. Mick's dad is still a member of the Magdalene Club and Mick got him to make a few touch-base calls with some of his old buds, and there's some maneuvering going on with folks distancing themselves from Stone while this storm is hitting. So I'm thinkin' that's making Stone even testier."

"It's tough being a dick," Coert muttered just as the buzzer went, telling them someone was at Cady's gate.

He caught her eyes again and shook his head. So she stayed at the skillet frying bacon while Coert walked toward the console by her front door.

"Keep in touch, Jake," he said into the phone. "Especially if you got news as good as this. But now I gotta go. Someone's at Cady's gate."

"Right, let you go. But Amber and Ethan want you two over for dinner. Amber, because Josie digs your woman and has been talking about her so she wants to look Cady over. Ethan because he wants to impress you with some macaroni and cheese recipe he's made up that Josie assures him is gonna be the bomb, and he's decided you and Cady are gonna be his test subjects."

"We'll set that up when we got Janie back, sometime next week," Coert told him as the buzzer right in front of his face went again.

He frowned at it.

He might not have raced to answer the damned thing but it was eight feet from the kitchen, so it hadn't taken a year to get there.

"Next week," Jake agreed. "Later."

"Later," Coert replied, took the phone from his ear and hit the button to open the line to the gate. "Yeah?"

There was nothing.

"Hit the button to reply," Coert instructed.

"Who's this?" a man's voice asked.

Coert turned his head Cady's way.

She was staring at the console.

"Cady?" he called.

Her eyes moved to him and she opened her mouth to speak but the voice came through before she got anything out.

"I need to speak to Cady Webster. Doesn't she live here?"

Webster?

No one in Magdalene and no delivery person would call her Webster.

"You know who this is?" Coert asked his woman.

"I think…it sounds like…" She moved wide eyes from console to Coert. "Caylen."

Coert's neck instantly got tight.

Oh hell no.

He turned back to the console and hit the button. "Is this Caylen?"

"Again, who's this?" Caylen demanded, like he was ascertaining who was at his own freaking door.

"Remove yourself from this property," Coert ordered.

"Coert—" Cady started, and he knew she was coming his way so he twisted to her.

"Do not even say it," he growled.

"But—"

"I need to speak with Cady Webster," Caylen stated over the console.

Coert returned his attention to Caylen. "This is Sheriff Coert Yeager. And I'll repeat, remove yourself from the property."

He took his finger off the button and got nothing.

She didn't have a fucking window to the front of the property on any floor but the observation deck, which would leave Cady with the console if Coert went up to check that her brother was complying and that wasn't happening.

She'd talk to her brother if he left her with that console.

God damn it.

Fortunately and unfortunately, Caylen's voice came back, letting Coert know he hadn't left without Coert having to check, but also letting him know the asshole hadn't actually left.

"Yeager, that's the name of the undercover cop who—"

Coert cut him off by hitting the button. "You leave or I'll call deputies to remove you."

Cady's hand fell on his arm so he knew she was right beside him.

He didn't look at her because Caylen came back.

"I'm not on Cady's property. I'm *outside* Cady's property so unless you intend to abuse your authority, you can't have me removed and I'm not leaving until I speak to my sister."

"Right," Coert muttered irately to the room, not through the speaker, and he turned to Cady. "Do not speak to him. I'm going out there."

"Coert," she whispered, her beautiful green eyes big, concerned, and already ready to forgive.

He knew it.

God *damn* it.

"A week and a half ago. Red Wedding. You asked me to trust you. I reminded you of the man who's your man," he began. "Now I'm asking you to trust me. And I know it upsets you, honey, but I gotta dredge up the past and say, this being about your brother, I *need* to do this for you so you *need* to let me."

"Let me talk to my sister!" Caylen shouted over the speaker.

Cady looked at it.

"Baby," he whispered.

She looked to Coert. "I trust you."

Thank fuck.

He grabbed her head in both hands, pulled her to him, kissed her briefly, and gently pushed her away. "Do not talk to him over the speaker."

Her head nodded in his hands.

Coert let her go and sprinted up the stairs, Midnight coming with him.

He had on a Henley, socks and pajama pants.

He only took off the pajama pants before he put on some jeans and tugged on the turtleneck he left at Cady's house weeks ago that she'd washed and put in the drawer she'd cleared for him that was under the bed.

He pulled on his boots and then he sprinted back down the stairs, Midnight at his heels.

He gave her a look before he walked out the door.

"Jacket!" she called as he turned to hold Midnight back.

"Stay with your mom," he urged the dog.

She whined but edged back from the door.

Coert looked at Cady. "I won't be out there that long."

He knew she was going to say something but he closed the door before she could get it out.

He took his time walking to a gate that was not close to the lighthouse.

He was halfway there before he saw Cady's brother appear through the iron bars, walking in from the side as he came to stand in front of the Subaru that was parked outside the gate.

As he got closer, he saw the man had aged well.

However, Cady had already told him that.

Cady and Coert had had time. Time together. Time to binge watch TV. Mornings to share breakfasts. Afternoons to meet for lunch. Evenings to have dinner together. Nights to whisper to each other after they'd made love.

Running to catch up.

Sharing what was missed.

Relearning who they were.

Discovering who they'd become.

So Coert not only knew about the incident with Cady and Kath outside Caylen's home.

He knew Caylen had not only refused to allow Cady to meet his children (and how he'd communicated that), he'd disallowed her to come to her own mother's memorial reception.

And everything he learned, he thought that Caylen Webster had not changed. The man was not a dick and he was not an asshole.

There wasn't a word for a man like him.

"Let me in to talk to Cady," he snapped when Coert was within hearing distance.

Coert didn't reply until he was four feet from the gate.

There he stopped and explained, "You're in error. This is private property. That is public land. But as the sheriff of this county it's within my authority to have someone removed from public land if he's making a nuisance of himself by harassing one of my citizens, even if that citizen is the woman in my life. So my suggestion is, don't test me."

"I'm hardly harassing her," Caylen spat.

"You and I both know you're harassing her just showing here," Coert returned.

"And I wouldn't be here if I didn't need to be here," Caylen retorted.

"Yeah. And that's why I'm out here. Because Cady's gonna want to know why you're here because she's got a soft heart and you're her brother, even though you've got no clue that's a title you're born with, but to keep it, you gotta earn it."

Caylen's lips thinned.

Point scored.

Coert continued, "But I'm not gonna let you treat her like dirt, so to get to her you gotta go through me and if I don't like what you say, you'll need to leave, or as I shared earlier, you will be removed."

"You're not gonna like what I say," Caylen told him sharply.

"I already know that but for Cady I'm gonna listen anyway."

"I don't even like that I have to say it," he bit out.

"This tells me you want something from her so let's get this done because you interrupted Cady making breakfast and I'd like to put her mind at ease and let her get along with her day."

"You're the sharp one, Sheriff, deducing I want something from my sister."

Not asshole. Not dick.

Something a whole lot worse.

"I'm five seconds from walking away from you," Coert warned.

Caylen looked beyond the gates like he was wondering if he could jump them.

"Three seconds left," Coert told him.

Caylen looked into Coert's eyes and the new expression on his face made Coert immediately go wired.

"My son has leukemia. I don't want something from Cady. No one's a match. I *need* something from her. And what I need is for her to get tested for a bone marrow match."

Coert closed his eyes and dropped his head.

Caylen's voice sounded choked when he stated, "This is hard."

Coert looked at him.

Caylen kept going.

"And I'm fully aware I've made it harder. But…"

Caylen shook his head and didn't finish, and Coert had seen a lot of people in a lot of bad situations so he knew it wasn't discomfort that was in every word, every action, tightening the line of Cady's brother's frame.

It was pain.

"It's not good," he whispered.

"Get in your car," Coert ordered.

Caylen's face instantly turned to granite. "I—"

"Get in your car. Get warm. I'm gonna go up and break this to Cady. When I'm done with that, I'll open the gate and you can drive up. A warning, she's got a dog and the dog is protective and can get intense when she senses someone's around who Cady or I've got a problem with. She's got a bad history so I won't confine her. But I will contain her, though you gotta go in cautious."

Caylen nodded.

Coert didn't wait for him to get in his car.

He turned and jogged back to the house.

He got a woof from Midnight and Cady's immediate attention as he walked through the door.

He gave Midnight's ruff a rub down but she had to walk with him as he gave it because he didn't delay in making his way to Cady.

"Is he gone?" she asked before he got there.

"No," he answered, made it to her and lifted his hands to cup her jaw.

"Oh no," she whispered, staring into his eyes.

"Yeah. It's not good. I need to open the gate and let him drive up because, baby, I fuckin' hate to have to say these words to you, but he's here because he needs you because his son is sick and they can't find a match, so they need you to get tested to give bone marrow."

Her eyes filled with tears and her lips murmured, "Oh my God." She looked like she was about to face plant in his chest right before she jerked from his hold and started toward the door. "We have to let him in."

He hooked her at the waist but kept moving them toward the console and it was Coert who hit the button that would open the gate.

His other arm was engaged with curling Cady into his body.

When he got her there, her arms wrapped right around.

Midnight snuffled them.

"I don't believe this," she said into his chest.

"I know," he murmured.

Her voice was deteriorating when she repeated, "I just don't believe this."

That was Cady. She hadn't even met the kid and she was losing it.

Midnight stopped snuffling them and started barking at the door.

Caylen was there.

Coert bent his neck to get his lips to her hair. "He's not good, honey, so you need to pull it together and I need to get a lock on Midnight."

He heard and felt her draw in a big breath before she nodded and pulled out of his hold.

Coert caught hold of Midnight's collar.

Cady turned right to the door to open it.

Caylen was already out of his car, slamming the driver door.

Midnight barked louder and Coert held her back.

And Cady was in a nightie, a cardigan and socks, but she raced out the door.

"*Shit*," Coert hissed, but with Cady taking off like that he was having trouble containing Midnight, so all he could do was watch the shock freeze Caylen Webster's face and body when he caught sight of his sister speeding toward him so the man was forced back on a foot when Cady hit him head on.

Midnight kept barking.

"Shh, girl, it's okay," Coert soothed as Caylen stood there in Cady's arms for a full second before he lost it entirely, dissolved into tears and did it clutching his sister to him. "Shit," he whispered.

Caylen. Her parents. Maria. Lonnie.

Him.

She didn't give up on people unless her hand was forced.

To guard her heart, Coert might wish she was different.

But he knew there never was and there never would be another woman for him partly because of this.

So he wouldn't have her any other way.

He gave them ten seconds.

Ten seconds he counted in his head.

Then he called, "Cady's in her nightie, Caylen, get your sister inside."

Caylen's face was buried in Cady's neck but at Coert's call, he lifted it, took Coert in, Coert took in the red and wet of Cady's brother's face, and the man then disengaged just enough to turn Cady and walk her to the door.

Coert backed Midnight away, murmuring to her as they walked through.

He reached out and pushed the door closed himself as he demanded, "Crouch low and give her a minute."

Coert did this because Midnight was growling.

Caylen crouched low.

Cady came to Midnight and helped Coert talk to her.

"Lift your hand her way but do it slow," Coert eventually said.

Caylen complied.

Midnight kept growling but Coert let her inch forward, hand firm on her collar, so she could smell.

"He's my brother, baby, he's good. He's fine. He's welcome here. We like him," Cady cooed.

Coert stared into Caylen's eyes as these words came out of Cady's mouth and he watched the pain again become stark.

Caylen bought that pain and he knew it, which was why it burned deep when he spent a lifetime earning that pain and Cady still ran out of her house wearing a nightie in the freezing cold to throw her arms around her brother.

Knowing this didn't help Coert forgive. He wasn't like Cady. He was a practiced hand at holding a grudge.

But it ratcheted Caylen down from whatever he was to just an asshole.

At least right then.

Midnight sniffed him, did it some more then butted his hand before her tail started wagging.

Caylen patted her head and slowly came out of his squat. Coert kept hold on the dog to make sure it was all good.

When it was, he let her go and muttered, "I'll get coffee."

"Come sit down," Cady invited, taking her brother's hand and moving him to the couch.

Coert went to the kitchen.

Midnight went with Cady.

And in two hours' time, they'd had breakfast (with her fucking brother).

And Coert had called Kim and work because they also had two plane tickets to fly to Denver the next day so Cady could meet her niece and nephew and get tested to see if her marrow was a match.

"SHOULD I CHECK on him?"

"No."

"Coert, he's—"

"A grown man and you fed him three meals and stood over him like a mother hen making him eat them and you made his fucking bed for him and he's staying in a five star studio that's got the best view he'll ever see, and it's been a tough day, for both of you. So just let him have some time and give that to yourself while you're at it."

It was later, not late, but time to start winding down after a really shitty day.

Cady had talked Caylen into staying the night rather than driving home because the forecast was for snow.

And because she wanted her brother close.

This was probably not only because of the weight he was carrying, but also because he looked ready to drop. They'd settled him in the studio and then come back to the lighthouse where she finally got on the phone with Kath to let her know they were coming out.

While she was on the phone with Kath, Coert's phone rang and he walked up to the observation room as he took the call because his screen told him Pat was calling.

"I'm not liking this," Pat declared the minute Coert took the call.

"I'm not a fan of it either, man, but his son has leukemia."

"First, that's part of what sucks since she can't tell him to go fuck himself."

Coert felt his chin jerk into his neck because Pat was like Cady and not a devotee of the word "fuck."

"And second, Dad died of cancer so this is gonna mess with her even as it messes with her."

"I'm coming with her to Denver," Coert shared with him, coming to a stop in the observation room with unseeing eyes on a stormy sea. "And Cady's talking to Kath right now because she wants us to stay with you guys. So I've got her and then you'll have her so we'll see her through this."

"What if she's not a match?" Pat asked.

"We'll hit that if that hits her," Coert answered.

"What if it doesn't help?"

"And we'll hit that if it hits her."

Pat went silent.

Then he broke it.

"She asked them to dinner. Repeatedly over the years. Eventually that guy, the brother, called Dad and told him to tell her to stop it. They'd moved on from Cady and she was hurting her parents by trying to force herself back into their lives."

A pause while Coert tried to calm the heating of his blood because, since they'd been together, they'd shared a lot but not that.

Pat went on, "*Moved on*. From *their daughter*. Now they need something from her and that guy's sleeping in *my* bed at the studio?"

"If it wasn't bone marrow, he wouldn't be. But Pat, man, what are you wanting me to do here? Her nephew is dying."

"A nephew he withheld," Pat bit out.

"But the kid's still dying and she's Cady. I could chain her up in my basement, and if she thought she could help she'd find her way loose and get to that kid."

He heard nothing before he actually heard Pat blow out a breath.

And then he spoke.

"I'm just bitching because, Coert, buddy, how much more is she going to have to take?"

Coert knew what he wanted the answer to that to be, but he also knew with Caylen Webster in the studio and why he was there it just wasn't going to be that.

"I've got her," Coert assured.

"Only thing about this mess I feel good about," Pat muttered.

Hearing that, Coert had then closed his eyes to the view and their call didn't last a lot longer.

Cady had joined him with a glass of whiskey for Coert and one of wine for her, Midnight limping up at her side.

And there they remained, cuddled together in her observation room, Cady curled between his legs, her back to his chest, the beam of the lighthouse rotating round and round, illuminating the view.

Coert tried to put a better spin on things by noting, "While we're in Denver, I can finally introduce you to Malc and Tom. They always wanted to meet you. Now they can do it before they get invitations to the wedding."

"Okay," she said distractedly but finished it with, "That'd be nice."

Coert kept trying.

"And Tom's daughter married Malc's son, Malc's daughter married the nephew of a local crime boss, and fortunately Malc's oldest son married someone from Indiana, but I hear she's a spitfire. Maybe we can get a big dinner together so I can see how my old buddies are dealing with the insanity that they always thought would end when Indy and Ally grew up, but apparently they're intent to wreak havoc until the day they die."

"A cop's daughter married a crime boss's nephew?" she asked.

"Yeah. And she became a private investigator. Way Malc tells it, she's a badass. But I knew Ally back in the day, so at least that doesn't surprise me."

"Soothes the soul to know it wasn't only us who had it crazy, though it doesn't help because I wouldn't wish crazy on anybody."

"They're all happy, making babies." Coert gave her a squeeze, purposefully moving his hand to her belly while he did. "Life goes on."

"Life goes on," she repeated.

He didn't like the way she said that so he dipped his mouth to her ear and told her, "Pat called while you were on the phone with Kath."

"She told me she thought he was doing that when he stormed out after she shared what was happening with him while we were on the phone."

"He's worried that this is gonna trigger stuff with you after losing Patrick."

She nodded but kept her gaze to the sea.

"Is that yes it's triggering things for you or—?" he began.

"It's a yes it's not a surprise Pat would worry about that."

"Cady, this is a lot—"

He again didn't finish because he had to lift his head when she twisted to face him in his arms.

"I don't want Janie ever to get a bad flu but I still wish this was a bad flu and not the nephew I never met dying of leukemia. But it is. And this is life. And in all that's happened in mine, the one thing I've learned is, as ugly as it gets, as bad as you mess up, if you keep going, it'll get good again."

She slid a hand up his chest to his neck and kept talking.

"Caylen messed up. You're right. Everyone's right. He treated me terribly. But now I have a chance to show him the woman who's really his sister that he never allowed himself to see. And if he sees it for the length of time it takes for us to do this and then cuts me out or if this is the building block to me finally having my brother, I don't care. Patrick was dying for years, and through it he gave me a family. I lost you, you lost me, and through it you got Janie. When the bad comes, you focus on the good or you'll lose yourself forever. So today is today. And whatever will happen tomorrow will happen tomorrow. And like I've always done, I'm just going to keep on living. Then one way or another, good or bad, this will be over, I'll have you, I'll have my family, I'll have Janie, and so I'll be fine."

"Your family," Coert remarked.

"My family," she stated firmly.

"Caylen?" he asked.

She looked confused but said, "If that's what comes of this, then I want you to be open to that even though I know he's going to have to prove to you he deserves to be in our lives."

"That's not what I mean. When you said you'll have your family, I was asking if you meant Caylen."

"No, I meant my family."

"*Your* family," he stressed.

She was no less confused. "Coert—"

"Pat, Kath, Mike, Pam, Daly, Shannon and the kids?" he pushed.

"Of course," she stated like he'd temporarily lost rationality.

"Pat told me you called them *the* family or *Patrick's* family," he shared.

Her head jerked.

"But they're yours," he told her.

"Yes," she whispered, like that just dawned on her.

Christ.

"You held yourself apart, didn't you, because your parents and Caylen made you think you didn't deserve that," he guessed.

"I…I don't know," she replied quietly.

She might not know.

But Coert did.

"You did. And now you know. You know who they really are."

She nodded. "Pat went to you. He…he probably wasn't sure about you but he knew I was giving up and so he went to you. Like a brother would do for—"

Coert cut her off.

"I don't give a shit what made you believe. I'm just glad you get it now. And the only thing I disagree with you saying is you now have a chance to show Caylen the woman you really are. That's not what's happening. You've never been anything but you. The woman I fell in love with so deeply, I never let her go. The woman who earned her place in a family who's devoted to her. So this is happening but what's happening with it is not you doing dick to prove shit to your brother. You're just gonna be you. And if he wakes up to the woman you've always been and you want him in your life, I'll find a way to deal. But you're not jumping through hoops for the man who shares your blood. You got three brothers. It's up to him to prove he deserves to take his place and add to that number."

"His son is ill," she reminded him gently.

"And I'm a father, I feel that. But in this particular scenario, Cady, first and foremost I'm your man, so that factors, definitely. I'm still watching."

She slid her hand from his neck to his face and ran her thumb along his cheekbone and he saw in her eyes exactly how much she liked that, and it was a lot, but she didn't say anything.

"'Fast Car,'" he whispered.

Her eyes cut from her thumb to his but remained silent.

Coert did not.

"You never felt you belonged. They made you feel you were lacking. If anything good happened to you, you were always so surprised and acted like it was a miracle it dropped into your lap instead of being what it was, something you deserved because you're all that's you. So, baby, I hope you're learning that there was always so much to you, you never had to work so hard to be someone, prove you belonged, to have all the things you got along the way. There was always so much to you, it was up to everyone around you to prove we were worthy of belonging to you."

Her lips trembled, wet instantly filled her eyes, spilling over, but Coert wasn't done.

"You ran out to that man in your nightie, cardigan with socks on your feet. From near on the moment I met you, my life became a lifetime endeavor to prove I was worthy to be yours."

"Stop it," she whimpered.

Coert didn't stop it.

"Patrick Moreland knew that before I even did."

More wet came and Cady's entire body started trembling in his arms so much, Midnight sensed it, got up and started nosing her mom.

"Stop it, Coert," she whispered.

"I'm glad he caught it."

Her hand slid back down as the other one came up to grab tight hold on his neck.

"Stop," she begged.

"And I wish the man was alive so I could thank him for taking care of you after I fell down on that job."

He knew she wouldn't like it.

But Coert had to say it. He had to give it to her. He vowed it was the last time he'd bring it up, but he could do that because it was the last thing he had to do to put a line under the time in between.

And he had no regrets even as she melted into him, moving a hand so she could burrow her face in his neck and let loose her tears.

Midnight pushed into her as Coert turned his head so his lips were at her hair.

"Be forever grateful to him for taking care of my Cady," he murmured.

Her body bucked.

Coert absorbed it.

And he absorbed her tears, stroking her back, alternately giving Midnight some love so she'd calm down and settle back on the floor.

When it left her, Coert gave her more time before he turned her in his arms so they were both again facing the sea.

She allowed it but stopped when she was where she wanted to be by digging her forehead in his neck.

It took some time and her voice was so quiet, he almost didn't hear her.

But he heard her.

"I know how much you love me and I love you the same so I want you to have more green. But when we make him, would you please give me a boy with your hazel? Because I love looking in Janie's eyes but from the minute I looked into yours and fell in love with you, I wanted as much of that hazel as God would give me, so will you make that happen for me?"

Coert could talk to God about that but in the end it would all be up to the Big Man.

Still, he said, "I'll do what I can."

She took hold of his hand, pulling it from around her, bringing it to her mouth where she gave his knuckles a kiss.

She replaced it and only then did she say, "Thanks, honey."

To that, Coert stated the obvious.

"It's gonna be my pleasure, Cady."

She snuggled closer.

Coert held her.

And the beam of the lighthouse that was the last thing Patrick Moreland gave to the daughter he met at a convenience store went round and round, constant and tireless in offering safety.

SHE WAS ASLEEP in her bed with Midnight when Coert left her, got dressed and went over.

It still wasn't late, but it was too late to knock on a man's door.

He did it anyway, not hammering like only a cop knew how to get the door opened.

But he did it in a way it wouldn't be ignored.

Elijah didn't ignore it but he was barefoot, in sweats with a thermal he was still pulling on when he opened it.

"Shit, Cady okay?" he asked the minute he saw Coert at the door.

And so he'd be buying the man a peephole because for Christ's sake, no one should open a door not knowing who was on the other side. Even a man the size of Elijah with his door being inside a garage.

"Want you to know Cady got bad news today. Her nephew has leukemia."

When Elijah's eyes went from alert to alarmed, Coert quickly assured him, of a sort.

"Not any of the boys you know. Her biological brother's son. You might have noticed the lights on in the studio, her brother is staying there. We're all leaving tomorrow to go to Denver so she can get tested to see if her bone marrow is a match, and if it is, there isn't a delay in doing the transplant."

"Shit, shit, *shit*," Elijah cursed, leaning forward to look toward the lighthouse like he could do that and make sure Cady was okay.

"While we're gone, my ex and daughter are gonna look after Midnight, my buds Jake, Mickey and Junior are gonna keep an eye on the lighthouse, and you're goin' down to New Haven."

Elijah reared back and stared at him.

"Life is too short, brother," Coert whispered. "Don't waste a second."

Elijah started shaking his head. "Coert, man, I—"

"Don't waste a second."

Elijah shut his mouth.

Coert stared him in the eyes.

Elijah opened his mouth.

"What if I can't give her—?"

"All she wants is you."

Elijah shook his head. "She's too young to know what she wants."

"Then suffer the heartbreak of losing her if that happens. But trust me on this, the pain of wondering what could have been is a fuckuva lot worse than the pain of losing something that isn't working. And the thing about that is, at this juncture, you still got the chance to find out all it can be. If you don't go for it, you'll never know. You think you're not worthy so you're settling for something you've decided you're worthy of. So I gotta ask you to trust me on something else. You're worthy because I know the man you are and that's just the plain truth. But you won't believe that so you gotta learn to believe this. You're worthy simply because *she* thinks you are. So believe in what *she* sees and get your ass to New Haven."

"I'd never forgive myself if something happened with Verry and I lost her just because of that. But also because, at the same time, I'd be losin' Cady."

"You're never gonna lose Cady and if you don't know that by now, she'll just have to show you. But take it from me, I know. You're in her heart, Elijah, and once you find a place there, she never lets go."

"Verry reminds me of her," Elijah said quietly.

"Then get your ass to New Haven, man."

They stared at each other again.

Then Elijah looked beyond Coert to his truck.

And Coert knew his decision was made.

"The sheriff in me has got to ask you to get a decent night's sleep," Coert shared.

Elijah returned his attention to Coert. "You think I'll sleep?"

Coert grinned. "Right, then if you don't have a huge-ass travel mug, Cady does so we'll set you up with some coffee."

"I got a mug."

He said that but didn't move.

Coert lifted a brow. "You want me to help you pack?"

That was when Elijah grinned.

"Naw, bud, I'm good."

Coert nodded and started to move away.

"You'll keep in touch…about Cady and her nephew?" Elijah asked.

Coert looked back. "Definitely."

Coert was nearly to the door when he heard Elijah call his name.

He turned back again to see Elijah standing in the garage holding open the door to his place.

"Do *you* believe in what she sees?" Elijah asked.

From the minute I looked into yours and fell in love with you, I wanted as much of that hazel as God would give me.

"Absolutely," he answered.

Elijah dropped his chin and lifted his hand.

Then he disappeared behind his door.

And Coert returned to Cady.

Twenty-Seven

DRINK TO THAT

COERT

Present day…

He didn't want to do it. He really didn't.

But standing in the waiting room seeing Caylen at the window while Kath, Pam and Shannon performed an emergency adoption of Alice, Caylen's ex-wife, and Pat, Mike and Daly put herculean effort into not incinerating Caylen with their eyes (and not surprisingly it was Mike who was failing at this), Coert had to do it.

So he moved from the man huddle to Caylen at the window.

It was at the last second that Caylen started and turned to Coert, telling Coert his mind was planted firm elsewhere.

Also not a surprise.

Cady's part in the test for a match wouldn't take very long, and if Caylen wasn't involved, the entire adult Moreland clan probably would have just waited for Coert to bring her home.

It turned out good they'd come, however, because Alice was making clear she wanted to be involved in everything, including Caylen's estranged sister being tested. And since Caylen and Alice did not have a good relationship, the unique "You don't know us, but bad shit is going down, so we're not going to smother you and we're here if you need us" approach of the Moreland women was turning out to be a good thing.

So Alice had them keeping an eye on her and keeping her distracted, as well as her mother, who had come with her.

Cady also had them at her back when she'd met a gracious and exceptionally grateful Alice in that same waiting room twenty minutes before.

It was Caylen who was the odd man out in this and Coert didn't know him, didn't want to know him, and what the man could want was to be an island.

However Cady would want Coert to make sure that's where he wanted to be.

"You hanging in there?" he asked low.

Caylen slid a glance toward Cady's brothers before he looked at Coert. "I honestly don't mean to be difficult but is it really necessary for all of them to be here? The test is non-invasive and takes ten minutes to perform."

"Is them being here upsetting you or Alice?" Coert asked.

He didn't answer. He looked to the window.

Coert already knew it wasn't upsetting Alice, and if it had, they would have taken off.

But it was getting under Caylen's skin.

There were a lot of things Coert could say, not many of them nice, so he took a second to make sure he had it in check before he said, "Patrick Moreland didn't marry her to make her his wife. He married your sister to adopt her."

Caylen's eyes came right back to him.

Coert kept going.

"This is a bad time for you and I hope you understand that I get that. But years ago, Cady was in a really bad place and her family turned their backs on her. Patrick gave her a new family and those men and women consider her their sister. It's healthy. It's right. They're loyal to her. They love her. You're not unaware of how things have always been between you and Cady so I hope with that you get that they're understandably protective. So they're here. But if they're making you uncomfortable, I'll ask them to go order us some coffees and Cady and I'll meet them after she's done."

"Adopt her?" he asked.

"Patrick and Cady's relationship was entirely platonic. He offered to adopt her at first but she refused."

"She was an adult," Caylen scoffed.

"She was alone, terrified and heartbroken. She'd lost everything. Including her family," Coert returned.

Caylen looked back out the window and Coert watched his jaw get tight.

He sighed.

Caylen spoke.

"Now I get it. Thought it was weird, they showed here. If it was me, I'd hate her. Girl that age marrying my father."

Coert turned his own eyes out the window and crossed his arms on his chest.

He felt Caylen's regard but didn't look at him when Caylen asked, "Did you know that…the adoption thing?"

"No."

"Is that why you dumped her?"

"That was my excuse. But no." He looked at Cady's brother. "I let her go because I'd put her in harm's way, I'd lied to her and I thought she would be better off without me."

"But she stayed married to him."

"She stayed married to him because he got cancer and beat it back for twelve years with Cady's help, and she couldn't be involved in that as a family member unless she was legally tied to him."

Caylen's jaw got tight again as he looked back out the window.

"Maybe we shouldn't talk," Coert suggested, losing his hold on keeping it in check.

Caylen's attention came back to Coert and he looked genuinely confused.

"Why?" he asked.

"Not bein' harsh but you're still being judgmental about Cady when—"

"I'm not being judgmental about Cady. I'm being judgmental about them," he jerked his head to indicate Cady's family, "and you."

Coert's body locked.

Caylen went on.

"If they had some score to settle with my sister and were doing it by pretending to care about her, set her up for a fall, I don't want them here."

Astonished, Coert stared at Caylen Webster.

Caylen stared back but he did it talking.

"And I've got a lot on my mind and part of it is that I'm not sure how I feel about you. You think I'm an ass for turning my back on my sister but you did the same thing. Now you think you've got the high ground because you two somehow found your way back to each other but you're no different than me. You're being protective of her because you think I'm going to treat her like trash. But I'm in the position of having *no* ground to stand on because I'm concerned about the same coming from you and I can't do anything about it."

"That's the first time I've ever seen you behave like an actual brother," Coert remarked.

"That's because another part of what's weighing on my mind is driving the entire time from my place to her thinking that Cady would close the door in my face when I came to ask her for help about something that's life and death *for my son*."

He was losing it, his voice breaking on the last three words.

He took a second to gather himself, Coert gave him that, and then he continued.

"And instead she did the exact opposite, so I'm dealing with my son being ill and it hitting me in the face how I destroyed my family, all of it, including my relationship with Cady."

"There's only one thing I can put at ease in your mind and that's to tell you I love your sister. Truth, I'm not bein' a dick when I say it's not yours to have how we got back what we lost. But I'm making her happy and that's really all you need to know. The rest, straight up, is up to you."

"She dropped everything to be here. *You* dropped everything to be here."

"She lost hope in you just last year. Think on that. All that went down, just last year, Caylen. That's your sister. So think on that. But do it later. Because one thing I know, it'd cut Cady deep for her to think this is on your mind right now. She knows you have enough on your mind. So let it go for now. She doesn't live far from you. You want to build something with your sister, I think she's already proved that door is open."

"I'm moving back to Denver to be near my family."

"And that's the first time I've ever seen you behave like a decent man. I don't say that to be a dick either. I say it to encourage you to keep that shit going because right now there are a lot of people who are going to need to depend on it."

Caylen looked back out the window.

Coert kept going.

"And her family lives in Denver, so if you're here when we're visiting I'm sure she'd love to see you."

His face was hard when he turned it again to Coert. "I *am* her family."

"Prove it."

Caylen looked like Coert struck him.

"It won't be hard, Caylen," he told him. "All you gotta do is let her be there for you. I think you can probably manage that, don't you?"

Something changed in his face, started crumbling, and Coert's neck got tight.

"I have no excuses," he whispered.

"Cady isn't about excuses. She isn't even about explanations. She's about heart and soul and looking forward, not back."

"I'm not just talking about her. I'm talking about Alice. Orson. Camilla."

Orson, his son, twelve, very sick with leukemia. Camilla, his girl, she was ten. Neither of whom Cady had met yet.

"I'm not the man who can help you," Coert told him honestly.

Caylen turned back to the window.

And Coert watched him, thinking it sucked that he gave a shit that Caylen Webster no longer wanted to be the island.

It also sucked what he had to say next.

"But Cady can help you."

Coert saw the man swallow.

"And just to say, she might reject it but it wouldn't hurt you to give it a shot, go over there and try to sit with your ex-wife."

Caylen's eyes slid to him briefly before he nodded, turned and made his slow way to where Alice was sitting next to her mother, with Kath, Pam and Shannon hanging close.

The mother and Cady's sisters eyed him as he approached.

He didn't totally go for it. He just sat next to her and patted her hand awkwardly before he put both of his in his lap and stared at the floor in front of him.

The mother looked like she wanted to rip his throat out before she hid it.

But Alice reached out to grab his hand and pulled it to the arms of the chairs they were sitting in and held on.

Coert moved back to the man huddle.

"And he's a miracle worker," Pat muttered under his breath, swinging his gaze from Caylen and Alice to Coert.

"Man's coming to terms with four and a half decades of being a supreme asshole and doing it when his twelve-year-old son is in bad situation. So it tastes funny, but feel for the guy."

"That funny taste is bile considering you're trying hard not to puke," Mike murmured.

"Yeah," Coert agreed, wondering if it was in spite of himself or the fact they were seriously alike that he liked the guy so much. Then he suggested, "You men wanna go get us a table somewhere? Leave the women here. When Cady's done, we'll meet you for an early lunch."

"He doesn't want us here," Daly surmised.

"He's a man dealing with a lot of bad shit and the worst of it is out of his control but the rest of it is a pile of crap he built himself so he's in a bad way, and Cady wouldn't thank any of us for making that worse."

"Las Delicias," Pat stated. "I noticed you have no Mexican food in Magdalene and not only will that be our gift to you, Cady loves it there, and once we remind you of that, it'll guarantee at least once a year you'll bring her back to us."

Coert was not hungry.

He still said, "Sounds good."

The men moved to Caylen and Alice (mostly Alice, but as Caylen was in her vicinity they couldn't ignore that) and said a few words before they went to say goodbye to their women and took off.

Five minutes later, Cady came out.

He moved to her and grabbed her hand, walking next to her as she went to Caylen and Alice.

Alice hopped up. "How'd it go?"

Cady gave her a sweet smile and said, "We'll know soon." She looked to her brother. "And you have my number and we're sticking close so whatever happens…"

Caylen had risen to. "Right, Cady."

"Thank you," Alice said.

"Of course," Cady replied.

"No…I…no…" Tears filled Alice's eyes. Then she whispered, "Thank you."

Cady let him go to move in and give Alice a hug.

Kath moved into Coert to slide an arm around his waist.

He put one around her shoulders.

Cady let Alice go only to turn to her brother and give him a hug.

She pulled away but didn't break away.

She said, "I'm on the other end of the phone, yes?"

He stared her in the face like he'd never seen her before for long moments before he nodded.

She gave him a visible squeeze then came back to Coert.

He took her hand and made a flash decision.

"We're going to lunch," he shared. "Would you all like to come?"

Cady's fingers tightened around his.

Caylen cleared his throat and said firmly, "Alice and I need to get back to Orson. But thank you."

Alice's lips had parted as she looked to her ex-husband.

"Right. Then take care," Coert replied.

"We'll come for a visit later, if that's okay," Cady said.

"Yes, that'd be okay. Maybe when Camilla is out of school?" Alice suggested. "She comes every day to visit her brother. You can meet them both then."

"I'd love that," Cady said softly.

The women smiled at each other.

Coert (and it would also be Kath) gave them a moment before Coert opened his mouth but Kath beat him to the punch.

"Right, time to get these kids to food," she stated, tugging on Coert's waist. "You're in our thoughts."

Gratitude was expressed.

Coert moved Cady out.

Her sisters gathered close.

And Coert walked the women to his and Cady's rental in order to get his Cady some lunch.

COERT WAS TRYING to tamp down some pretty intense anger as he drove Cady back to Pat and Kath's that evening.

Caylen had done that to her, what she just went through. It had been Caylen who put her in the position of meeting that sick boy while he was in a hospital bed, his little sister who wore confusion and pain on her face like it had been etched there since birth. Caylen had made it so Cady had no idea what to do, what to bring, what they liked, and the circumstances were so dire it didn't matter what gesture she made, nothing could make it better.

But Cady had spent years around kids. None of them sick and frail and hospitalized after enduring months of intense radiation and chemotherapy, or mystified with no hope of grasping how life was so unfair it'd do that to your brother. But just like she took to Janie without hesitation, sure in herself and how to be around kids (apparently of all ages), she brought them bucket loads of candy of all kinds, Rubik's cubes, puzzle books and fun pencils and pens. Nothing that would take energy. Just a bunch of stuff that let them know she went out of her way and gave a shit.

Even so, it had been the most uncomfortable, saddest hour he'd spent in his life and he'd been a cop for twenty-three years. He'd seen people at their worst. He'd had to deliver news that would change lives forever in the cruelest ways imaginable.

But he'd never been with a family that broken, watching the woman he loved become a part of it knowing that there was a good possibility she'd never catch up on the twelve years she lost, no matter how much candy she bought or how fast she ran.

"I'm okay," she whispered.

He glanced at her to see her staring out the side window of the car and with just a glance he knew she was not okay.

Topper: the results were in and Cady wasn't a match.

"All right," he murmured, squeezing her hand that he held on his thigh.

"Alice is sweet," she said.

"Yeah," he agreed, and she was, and Coert wondered how Caylen had scored that woman even if he didn't have to wonder how he'd lost her.

"We'll go back to see them tomorrow," she told him. "Then dinner with your friends tomorrow night. But I think we should leave after that. They don't need to feel like they're entertaining and there's no purpose for us to be here now."

There actually was. Caylen had one person in his corner and that was Cady.

But Coert wasn't going to suggest that.

"When we get back to Kathy and Pat's, I'll get online and get our tickets," she said.

"I can do that," Coert replied.

"No, I—" she started but stopped when her phone rang. She didn't let go of his hand as she dug it out of her purse before she muttered, "Verity," took the call and put the phone to her ear. "Hey, honey."

She listened for a second and Coert listened to nothing while she did, and he listened hard.

He hadn't told her he'd visited Elijah. She'd had too much on her mind.

With life the way it was, Verity's call could be anything.

He just hoped like hell it was going to be what it should be.

"I'm all right. Just met the kids. Too much for now but I'll call in a couple of days. I'm not a match, honey, so I can't be of any help. We're going to stay another day and come home," Cady said into the phone.

She listened again.

He felt Cady's fingers clench his spasmodically before, "I'm sorry?"

She listened again.

Coert put on the turn signal and was preparing to execute a turn when he felt Cady's gaze come to him.

"I…he's *there*?" A pause, "Right *now*?" Another pause and then, breathy, "Oh my goodness, honey."

That sounded good.

Coert made the turn smiling at the windshield.

Another squeeze of his fingers before she asked. "He did?" She listened and then, "No, I didn't know." She squeezed hard. "He didn't tell me."

Coert kept smiling.

"Yes," Cady said into the phone. "Yes. It's fabulous. I'm so happy for you. You say Walt gave him the week off?" She waited for her question to be answered and then said, "Wonderful. Yes. Of course, yes, come up that weekend. Do you want me to send you a plane ticket?" She listened, then, "All right. Okay. Have you told your mom?" Silence then, "Okay, a week seems a long time but you'll find at the end that it isn't, so you go be with Elijah and I'll see him next week and you the weekend after that. We'll have a belated birthday cake." Pause. "Yes. Absolutely." Pause. "*Absolutely*, Verity. This is marvelous. Tell Elijah, Coert and I say hi and talk to you later." Pause. "Right. Love you too, like crazy. 'Bye."

Out of the side of his eyes he caught her dropping her phone and then he got another clench of her fingers.

"So, apparently you had a few words with Elijah," she remarked.

"Life's too short," he grunted, now fighting back his smile. "I take it Verity welcomed him with open arms?"

"They *did it* on the floor by her front door about two seconds after she opened it to him."

Jesus.

"Too much information," he muttered.

"She's straight with me," Cady told him.

"Still too much information," Coert repeated.

"They used protection."

"And now *more* too much information," Coert growled, though he was glad to know Elijah was the man he knew him to be and took care of that.

Cady giggled.

Thank Christ.

He glanced at her when he felt her leaning toward him and she stayed that way when she said, "She's very happy."

"Good," he said to the windshield.

"Do you know how wonderful you are?" she asked.

He bumped her hand against his thigh and answered, "You holding my hand, I got a clue."

He felt her warmth hit him at his words.

"He'd never have done that, made that journey, if you hadn't encouraged him to," she declared.

"He might have gotten there."

"No. He admires you. You two may have had a rocky start but he thinks the world of you. You talking to him about that was just the push he needed. He might have stayed stuck if it wasn't for you."

"I barely encouraged him to go before he was eyeing his truck, antsy to get in it and go to her, Cady," Coert informed her. "He was looking for an excuse. I just gave him one."

"Well, even if it was only that, which it wasn't, I'm glad you did it."

Since Cady was happy and Verity was happy, he was glad he did it too.

"Life," she said softly, righting herself in her seat. "We didn't get one match we needed today, but we got another one."

"Yeah," he replied.

Her fingers gave his another squeeze. "Love you, Coert."

"Love you most."

"Honestly, honey," that time she leaned deep into him and kissed his jaw, finishing what she was saying when she sat back, "I think that's impossible."

Coert drove her back to her brother's house thinking she was wrong.

"THEY OPENED FIRE?"

"They *opened fire*. I tackled Tod, who was, I'll repeat, in drag, and then Tex… you have to come to my store and meet Tex. He'll make a coffee for you. He's a genius barista and a total wild man. You'll love him. But anyway, and then Tex grabbed me and *threw me at Lee*. Like, *threw me*. Through the air. *At Lee*!"

The women around Malcolm Nightingale's table all started cackling at Indy's retelling of a pretty freaking scary story.

These women included Malcolm's wife, Kitty Sue, his daughter, Ally, his daughters-in-law, Indy and Roxie, and Tom's girlfriend, Lana.

The men, Coert noted, were not cackling. They weren't even smiling. What the women found a hilarious memory the men did not look at the same way.

Coert was right there with them and he hadn't even lived through the night of gunfire at a gay bar.

Coert caught Malc's eyes, and when he did Malc shook his head.

"I see Indy hasn't changed," Coert noted.

"A week ago officers were called to her location for disturbing the peace at a Starbucks," Malcolm returned.

"That wasn't me," Indy declared. "That was Tex too." Indy looked to Cady. "He doesn't like Starbucks."

"Why not?" Cady asked.

"Because he's Tex and you won't understand that's actually a thorough answer until you meet him," Indy replied.

"You didn't have to egg him on," Lee put in. Lee was Indy's husband and Malcolm's middle child, now very much a grown man and not just because he was old enough to have a wife.

"I didn't egg him on," Indy retorted. "Daisy did."

"You egged him on," Lee muttered.

"You weren't even there," she snapped.

Lee raised his brows. "Have I known you since birth?"

"Yes," Indy bit out.

"Have I been covering your ass since you were about six?"

"Yes," Indy hissed this admission.

Coert heard Cady stifle a giggle.

"You egged him on," Lee concluded.

Indy rolled her eyes at Ally.

She'd egged the unknown Tex on.

Ally sat in the curve of her husband Ren's arm and did it smiling.

Totally egged him on.

"I wish you wouldn't curse in front of Callum," Kitty Sue entered the conversation.

"Mom, my son is six months old. He doesn't know the word 'ass' from the word 'hello,'" Lee stated with a smile aimed at his mother. "Give it a rest. When it's time to teach him to curse properly, I'll be all over that."

At that, the men chuckled but the women did not.

"Lord, save me," Kitty Sue called to the ceiling.

This made Coert look to Cady to see her bouncing Lee and Indy's son, Callum, in her lap.

He was fascinated by the diamond at her throat.

With Cady's neck bowed and her lips to his dark-furred head, she was just fascinated by Callum.

"What Lee's trying to say is, you got two grown boys so maybe you should give it up with the cursing, Mom," Hank, Malc's oldest, waded in.

"You could stand to clean up your language too," Kitty Sue retorted.

Hank sighed.

Roxie, Hank's very pregnant wife, laughed.

Coert tore his eyes from Cady with a baby bouncing in her lap and caught Tom's gaze on them when he did.

Tom bobbed his head in a contented nod.

Coert dropped his arm from the back of Cady's chair to wrap it around her shoulders.

When he did, she fell to her side and her shoulder hit him.

And when she did that, Callum lost interest in Cady's diamond, looked to Coert, and launched himself that way.

When he thought he wouldn't get what he wanted, probably because Cady's hold tightened on him, he latched onto Coert's sweater and grunted to pull himself into Coert's arms.

Coert accepted him readily, even if the second he did Callum started punching him in the jaw.

"Totally having a little boy," Cady whispered in his ear.

He looked down at her before he bent to her and kissed her forehead.

Callum punched Cady in the jaw.

Her eyes got pretend big, she captured his hand and pulled it to her mouth, forcing his fingers open with her lips and blowing a raspberry in his palm.

Callum arched his back as he screeched out a giggle then patted Cady's lips for her to do it again.

Cady did it again.

And Coert decided that night was a good night to get her pregnant.

Or at least start trying.

"SO?"

Coert looked toward the man who asked the one-word question to see Malc and Tom had gravitated to his side.

It was just after dinner. The women had formed a huddle. The younger men had formed a huddle. And now Tom and Malc were forming their own huddle with Coert.

"She's not a match," Coert responded in a guess at the question.

"Shit," Malc whispered.

"But Cady's brother told us today that they found a compatible, unrelated donor in the National Marrow Donor Program so there's hope," Coert went on.

"This why you're leaving tomorrow?" Tom deduced.

Coert nodded.

"Right…and *so*?" Malc pressed.

"So…what?" Coert asked.

"Felt my son get tense when you and Cady had Callum, probably thought you two were conspiring to kidnap his boy. Is that where this is going?"

"Her birthday is the day after we get back," Coert shared. "She's demanded no presents, which sucks because I was going to give her the ring I bought her when I bought her that diamond she's wearing at her neck. So I'm giving her a ring the day after. But she's moving in in a couple of weeks and we're going to start trying as soon as possible. Cady isn't entirely in on those plans yet, but we'll talk tonight and she'll be in on them before she goes to sleep."

"Simpatico," Tom muttered.

"We always were," Coert returned.

"She's a great gal, Coert," Malc said. "Figured she was with all you said about her, but it's nice to finally be able to get to know her."

"Yeah," Coert replied, though the circumstances sucked for why they were in Denver, it had been a great night and that was one of the reasons it was.

"Is there a way to tell you how fuckin' happy I am this is where it's all ending?" Tom asked.

"No, since I'm living that and there's no way to describe how happy I am that we got what we lost back," Coert answered.

Tom nodded.

Malc clapped him on the shoulder.

"This division of genders thing is boring," Ally called out. "Next thing you know, you men are going to be thinking we're going to sashay into the kitchen and the miracle of clean dishes will be performed."

"That's my girl," Malc murmured, looking at his daughter with amused eyes.

"God doesn't send angels down to do the dishes?" Hank teased his sister.

"I'll remind you I took Luke down our last sparring match," Ally threatened her brother.

"You did that because Ava walked in, ready for their date night wearing a new dress," Lee returned.

"He shouldn't have let his guard down," Ally shot back.

"It was a nice dress," Lee muttered, his eyes crinkling.

"How nice *was* this dress, Lee?" Indy asked, her eyes narrowed.

"Very nice, baby," Lee replied, his eyes still crinkled, but he saved it when he finished, "But obviously, not as nice as any of yours."

"Luke's one of Lee's badasses," Ally explained to Cady, and incidentally, Coert, referring to the team of private investigators at Lee's firm. "And distracted or not, a takedown is a takedown."

"Agreed," Kitty Sue said firmly.

"You all kind of scare me," Cady admitted and smiled. "But in a good way."

"Trust me, you aren't the first person to feel that," Roxie told her.

"I love it. It keeps things exciting," Lana put in.

"And that's *my* girl," Tom muttered appreciatively.

Cady turned her smile to Roxie and Lana and then it went to Kitty Sue. "I don't mind helping with dishes."

"Malc and I'll do them after you all leave. I want to see pictures of this lighthouse. I can't imagine living in a lighthouse," Kitty Sue said.

"Do you have a laptop?" Cady asked. "There are tons of tourist shots online."

"Let's go to Malc's office."

The women trooped out after Indy deposited her son in his father's arms.

The young men joined the older and it was Malcolm who went in to take his grandson from his son's arms.

"We share a soft spot for redheads," Lee stated, gaze on Coert, this telling him something Coert had figured out since Indy was tall and curvy to Cady's short and curvy, but they shared the same hair color. "Just hope yours doesn't have her own code on police band."

Coert chuckled. "I'm the sheriff of my county and Cady's recently lost a loved one she inherited a load from. She dropped a load of that on renovating the town's lighthouse, which she made her home, and then opened it for tours two days a month, and I'm not talking just the grounds. She lets strangers inside. Dozens of them. Two days a month. Which means some of those pictures your mom's gonna be looking at are online photos of the interior of my woman's house, because she allows freaking pictures. So fortunately she doesn't have her own code but she's her own brand of nut."

"You allowed that?" Malc asked with not a small amount of surprise.

"You try *allowing* anything with Cady. If she wants to do it, she does it," Coert replied.

Or she talked him into being all right with it.

Or at least pretending he was all right with it but instead he found a way to put up with it.

"I feel that pain," Ren muttered, Ally's husband, who might be a crime boss's nephew but as Malcolm told it, was personally legit, and such a good-looking guy, Coert could even call that he was handsome.

"Me too," Hank said.

"It's in the blood. Kitty Sue and her best friend Katie made Indy and Ally look like amateurs," Malcolm told them.

Lee raised his bottle of beer between all of them, tipping the bottom out. "Here's to lives that'll never be boring."

The rest of the men lifted their bottles and clinked the butts.

They brought them to their lips.

"Malc!" They heard shouted from down the hall and all the men looked that way. "We are *soooooo* vacationing in Maine this summer!"

"When's your wedding?" Malcolm asked.

Coert turned back to him.

"Sometime this summer," Coert winged it.

The skin around Malcolm's eyes crinkled. "Then Maine in summertime it is."

"I'm feeling the need to give my sister a heart attack. I'm gonna go clear the table," Hank announced. "Do I got any help?"

"I'm in," Lee said.

"Yeah," Ren muttered.

They took off.

Coert, Malcolm and Tom watched them go.

"Finally, you're at the good part," Malcolm said quietly, and again Coert turned to him to see Callum had snuggled in to his granddad and was getting sleepy. "You get the fun of makin' 'em. Then you get the fun of watchin' 'em grow up and find the one they love. And then you get this." His hand on Callum's diapered bottom lifted the baby half an inch. "So it's been shit for you for a while. But that's over. And it's all good from here."

"That, I'll drink to too," Tom said, raising his beer, bottom out.

Coert would drink to that too.

So he and Tom and Malcolm butted beers again.

And then like old times but without the stress, tension and tragedy, instead with kids, grandkids and promise all around, they slugged some back.

COERT WAS NOT a big fan of watching Cady slide his cock totally out of her mouth.

Though he did like that she did it to use that mouth to work her way up his stomach and chest.

And he very much liked it when her lips hit his and he felt her adjust to straddle his hips.

But she didn't kiss him.

He put hands to her hips, sliding one in and up her spine and sliding one in the other way to hit a different target.

Both hands arrested when the fog of goodness that was Cady giving him head drifted away and he processed the look in her eyes.

"No condom," she whispered.

Coert felt his lips curl up.

Oh yeah.

Simpatico.

But his lips also asked, "You sure?"

"I'm sure," she said softly. "You sure?"

He felt a different kind of burn hit his gut as he took hold of her, lifted his head to give her a kiss, rolled her while he was doing it, got her to her back and slid inside.

Every time.

Christ.

Every single time.

Heaven.

Once he was planted, he murmured, "I'm sure."

That was when Cady's lips curled up.

He hitched a knee and thrust deep, driving a gasp between Cady's lips and feeling that gasp drive up his balls through his cock.

"She's a girl, she's Grace," he said against her mouth.

"Okay, honey."

"It's a boy, he's Dean," he told her.

Her fingers clutched his hair, her legs clutched his thighs, her hips lifted to take each of his strokes and her arm around his back held tight.

"Whatever you want. You get to name them."

He moved inside her faster, and since she was being so agreeable, he declared, "And the ring I'm giving you on your birthday isn't a birthday present. It's an engagement present."

That got another gasp and not only because on his last word he went in hard.

"Ho…kay," she forced out between two thrusts.

"Yeah?" he pushed in more ways than one.

"Whatever you want," she breathed, trying to take his mouth in a kiss.

He withheld, remarking, "Setting a precedent here to get what I want," he slid in and started grinding, "when I'm giving you what you want."

Her nails dug into his back and his hips flexed into hers in response.

"Stop being annoying," she warned.

"You love it when I'm annoying," he replied.

"Which is also annoying," she told him.

He smiled.

He felt the smile fade as he watched her heated eyes get hotter but nothing could burn away the love that shone from there.

"Grace," he whispered.

She pressed her lips to his and whispered back, "Dean."

He slanted his head and slid his tongue inside.

Minutes later, Cady tightened all around him and moaned down his throat.

Minutes after that, Coert buried himself deep and groaned down hers.

DEAN WASN'T MADE that night.

He was made two nights later in Cady's bed at the lighthouse.

On her birthday.

When it happened, Cady wore a diamond at her neck.

And one on her left finger.

Other than that, she and Coert wore nothing at all.

TWO WEEKS AFTER that, Coert and Janie moved Cady into their house.

Precisely, Coert, Jake, Mickey and Junior moved Cady into their house.

This was because Cady was dressed as a fairy godmother and Janie was dressed as a mermaid, while Josie was dressed as a film star, Amy was dressed as Snow White, Alyssa was dressed (it could only be described) as a slutty Greek goddess, and even Midnight had Supergirl's cape on.

So they were no help at all.

Twenty-Eight

NOT A FUCKING THING

CADY

Present day…

It was weird and it was concerning when I pulled into the garage, parked and entered the house, that when I turned to look into the kitchen, Coert wasn't there or sauntering in to greet me.

If he was home and I was not, this was what happened.

Usually I was in the kitchen when he came home, cooking him dinner. Over the last two weeks that we'd been living together, Coert said time and again that I didn't have to.

He'd stopped doing that when I finally convinced him that I knew I didn't *have* to, I wanted to.

And anyway, when Janie was home, I now picked her up from preschool and she helped me and that was my favorite part of those days.

Except when she was asleep in bed and Coert and I were alone in our own bed, of course.

But that night was late day mani-pedis at Maude's House of Beauty with Alyssa, Josie and Amy followed by drinks and dinner with the girls.

Maybe he didn't greet me because he wasn't expecting me to get home that early.

I was home early because the weather got weird.

It was March and we were having an unusual heatwave.

This "heatwave" consisted of it getting over fifty degrees the last two days but such was a heatwave for Maine, which meant the snow was melting fast. Making matters worse, on my way home, a thunderstorm had rolled in. There were weather advisories because apparently a cold front was getting ready to slam right into the heatwave and there were concerns that the rain would turn to sleet, hail or snow and the wet that was everywhere was going to ice over.

As another roll of thunder moved over the house, I looked to the ceiling thinking this was where Coert might be. If there was a possibility the roads would be bad, I'd learned that it was all hands on deck. People took stupid chances in weather and most of Coert's job was dealing with people doing stupid things.

That said, he'd normally tell me he had to go out.

I put my jacket on a hook by the door, walked into the kitchen and pulled out my phone before I tossed my purse on the island.

I checked it for missed calls or texts from Coert.

Nothing.

"Coert!" I called, tossing the phone on top of my purse.

"Bedroom!" I heard.

"Strange," I murmured and moved into the foyer, up the stairs and into the bedroom.

As usual, the house was illuminated everywhere even though we didn't have Janie.

Including the bedroom, although the bathroom door was open and the light was out.

And Coert wasn't anywhere to be seen.

"Coert!" I called again.

"Here," I heard his deep voice coming from the closet.

Very strange.

We had a small walk-in. It was nice and Coert had set it up so it was exceptionally functional, but it wasn't going to be photographed for any magazine because that just wasn't Coert.

Or me.

It was still better than what I had at the lighthouse (which had been close to nothing), and since neither Coert nor I were clothes hounds, it worked perfectly.

I moved to the closet but stopped dead in the doorway.

"What's happening?" I whispered.

And I whispered this, frozen in place staring at Coert on his side in the corner of the closet amongst a tangle of Coert's boots and running shoes, his long body wrapped around a visibly trembling to the point I wondered if she was in shock Midnight.

"The thunder rolled in and she lost it, raced up here," Coert replied, not moving, wrapped around our dog and stroking her full body from her head that was buried in Coert's shoulder to her rump. "She's actually better. She was keening, Cady, and fuck, it was the ugliest sound I ever heard. I can't leave her. If I even move, she starts making that noise again."

I went to them, dropped to my knees and instantly wrapped myself around Midnight, twining with Coert to do it when I felt the violence of her trembling physically against my own flesh.

While Coert stroked, I wrapped an arm around her and held her tight, pressing my body to hers.

"I take it from your response you haven't seen this before," Coert noted.

I shook my head.

I watched the expression on his face shift from troubled to something that, if I didn't know him, would have terrified me.

"Whatever those fuckers did to her, they did a number on her."

"Should we call the vet?" I asked.

I knew how bad it was when he replied immediately, "I've been waiting for you to get home to do that. Can't leave her, even if my phone is on the freaking nightstand, it's been that bad. But I also don't think we should make her wait until the storm passes. She needs to be sedated."

I nodded. "Do you want me to call or do you want me to stay with her and you call?"

"I've got her. You go."

I nodded again, bent my head, shoved my face in her fur and whispered, "It's okay, baby. We're gonna look out for you."

She didn't shift, just stayed shoved up against Coert, quaking full body.

I gave her a squeeze, carefully slid away, got to my feet and walked as calmly as I could out of the closet.

It wasn't until I got to the bedroom door that I ran.

I called the vet, explained the situation, told her there was no way we could take our dog out into the storm, begged for a house call, and I must have sounded as frightened as I was because I got one. I took my phone back up to stay with Coert and Midnight while we waited for the vet to arrive.

When the doorbell rang, that time Coert decided to leave me with her, and by then we knew it was the right call because the thunder had passed, the storm hadn't, and Midnight was no better.

The keening began again when Coert started to disengage from her and hearing it felt like my ears had started bleeding.

I flashed eyes I knew were wild with worry at Coert and tried to waylay him from moving.

"I'll go," I told him.

"Be back as quick as I can," he muttered and moved fast.

When he left, Midnight wailed like she'd been surprised by sudden and intense pain and she shuffled on her belly into the corner, burying her face under her paws.

I plastered myself to her back and wrapped my arms around her, murmuring, "Daddy's gone but I'm right here. I'm right here, baby. You're safe, Midnight. Daddy's going to be back. But I'm right here."

Coert was true to his word and he and the vet came into the closet within minutes. Since there wasn't enough space, I let Coert take over, watching Midnight scuttle into him whining and doing it feeling my heart swell as he accepted her fear into his big, strong body at the same time break at the sight of her having it. I moved to stand in the doorway as Coert held a shaking Midnight while the vet looked her over, asked a few questions and then administered an injection.

"Drag her dog bed in here, honey," Coert ordered as the vet straightened away.

I dashed out and down the stairs to the living room where we'd put Midnight's dog bed when she and I moved in.

The vet was standing just outside the closet when I got back. I pulled the dog bed in and Coert adjusted to his knees, lifting a calming Midnight in his arms.

I fell to my knees and shoved the shoes aside to position the bed in the corner. When I got it in place, Coert laid her down on it but then rearranged himself to wrap around Midnight and the dog bed while I moved out to talk to the vet.

"Do we have reason to worry?" I asked.

"Did the shelter give you any history on this animal?" she asked back.

"They mentioned this but we haven't had a storm since I've had her so this is our first time," I shared.

She nodded. "Animals display behavioral symptoms to psychological scars just like humans do. There are even studies that suggest animals suffer from PTSD after traumatic events. They also find coping mechanisms like humans do, which is why she's in the closet. I would hazard to guess it's not about the closet, but that your scent in there is stronger than anywhere else and she finds safety in that."

It was sweet to think of it like that but Midnight didn't seem to be indicating she felt all that safe even with the smell of Coert and me all around her, or even when Coert and I *were* all around her.

The vet carried on, "If this behavior is only exhibited during storms, I'll get you a prescription for an oral sedative that you can give her when a storm is coming. It should help. If it doesn't, call the office again and me or a vet tech will come out and administer another injection."

I nodded.

She nodded back, walked into the closet, checked on Midnight and then she came out and I walked her downstairs trying to hide how antsy I was to get back when we said goodbye at the door.

Once I closed it behind her, I went right back to the closet.

When I got there, Coert said, "She's better now, think she's almost asleep. Come in here and lay with her, will you?"

He moved out. I moved in. And my relief couldn't be described when I felt her resting peacefully on her dog bed.

This relief was short lived when I heard Coert clip, "This is Sheriff Coert Yeager. When you get this message, I want you to phone me with the details of who left the black German shepherd named Gorgeous Midnight Magic at the shelter, the dog that was rescued by Cady Moreland last year."

He left his number and then I saw his frame fill the door to the closet again.

"You called the shelter?" I asked.

"Yes," he bit out.

"Why?" I asked.

"Because I'm going to talk to the children of the man who got Midnight to see if I can find out where he got her, and then I'm going to investigate the assholes he got her from."

"And then what will you do?"

"Scare the fuck outta them by charging them with felony animal cruelty."

Oh my God.

"Honey," I whispered.

"It won't stick but I'm still gonna do it."

"Is that actually a thing?" I asked.

"It is. It's harder than hell to push through and the charge is usually brought in extreme cases where more than one animal is affected, dogs are used in fights or there's loss of life, which in the case of an animal means loss of property. But it's still a fuckin' thing."

It appeared my man was more than a little angry and even though his anger warmed my heart and I understood and agreed with what was causing it, I still had to do something about it.

"She's fine now," I said softly in an attempt to soothe him.

"She wasn't ten minutes ago and she's fine now because she's been fucking *medically sedated.*"

It was then, something happened.

His words and the force behind them made visions of Coert wrapped around our quaking dog in the corner of a closet pop into my head. These visions juxtaposed with memories of Coert sweetly admonishing Janie not to talk with her mouth open. And those juxtaposed with Coert not caring even a little bit when baby Callum used his jaw as a punching bag. All of this overlapped with demanding the shelter provide him information about an abused dog and Coert not allowing me to go downstairs and answer the door even though we knew it was the vet because he was just that protective of me.

More started crowding in but I stopped them when I whispered, "I love you."

"I know," he replied.

I kept whispering when I blurted out, "And I think I'm pregnant."

Coert went stock still.

"I'm a week late," I shared. "I was going to stop by the drugstore on the way home but the weather was nasty so I decided to do it tomorrow."

It seemed stiff somehow when Coert asked, "Are you ever late?"

"No."

He remained still and unmoving, and I did too, until he seemed to sag against the doorjamb but he did it without taking his eyes from me.

"I cannot believe you told me you might be carrying my baby while you're lying on the floor in our closet with our dog."

"I wasn't going to say anything until I knew for sure but you were being paternal so it just slipped out."

Coert raised a brow. "Threatening criminal charges against asshole animal abusers is being paternal?"

"Taking care of your baby, no matter what form she comes in, even if she's covered in fur…yes, it absolutely is."

His eyes traveled my body before they came back to mine.

And when those hazel eyes hit mine, they warmed every inch of my body.

"You might have told me you're having my baby while lying on the floor of our closet with our dog, but I'm not kissing you after you tell me that while you're lying on the floor with our dog so, Cady, baby, could you kindly get your sweet ass over here?"

I gave Midnight a stroke, got to my feet and walked to Coert.

He slid his arms around me so tight, it was a wonder they didn't wrap around twice. This meant I was held so close to him, I felt my flesh bunch at the back of my neck in order to look up at him.

"Do you want me to go out and get a test?" he asked softly.

In this weather?

No way.

"I don't want you to go anywhere," I answered in the same vein.

"Do you know how happy I am?" he went on.

"I know it's probably not a good idea to get too excited. It could be a false alarm. We haven't been trying that long. We should take a test and then get it confirmed with my doctor," I replied.

"I'm not talking about that, though it doesn't need to be said that a baby would just make that better."

Oh my God.

I closed my eyes.

I wouldn't have imagined I could get closer to him but his words made me melt right into him so much it was a wonder we didn't fuse.

Still, I opened my eyes and fretted, "Do you think Janie will be okay with it?"

"I think if she shocks the shit outta me not being okay with it, we'll find a way to make her okay with it."

I still fretted, even though I knew he was right.

"Okay, then do you think you can kiss me now?" I requested.

His lips tipped up, his eyes got warm (or warmer) and his lips came down to mine.

"Yeah," he whispered. "I can kiss you now."

He started to kiss me but it was interrupted by the doorbell going.

He didn't let me go but he did lift his head to look toward the wall beyond which was the hall, his brows knitting.

"A freeze is coming and there are weather advisories everywhere," I said. "Who, outside a vet on an emergency house call, could be out in that?"

"Is your brother still in Denver?" he asked.

"Yes," I answered.

"Anyone else would call," he muttered as the doorbell went again and then we heard the hammering. "Shit," he hissed, gave me a squeeze but didn't let me go.

He looked over my shoulder at Midnight.

"I'll stay with her," I told him.

He looked down at me, nodded, bent to me, touched his lips to my nose, then let me go.

I watched him disappear and then I moved back to Midnight. I squatted and ran my hand over her, feeling her chest rise and fall with her breathing, finding her heartbeat and knowing how sedated she was because no one would even get close to the door without a bark or at least a woof.

Her eyes were closed so I suspected she was sleeping.

I then wondered how Midnight would take to a new member of the household.

I wondered this for about two seconds. Considering how she was when she met Janie, I figured she'd like it a lot.

I was on my behind, in the midst of taking my boots off, doing this smiling, when I heard shouted, "I'll fucking have your *fucking badge*!"

Midnight didn't even lift her head.

Quickly, my heart racing as I heard Coert's low murmur of a reply, I checked for her breathing again just in case something went wrong with the injection, felt it coming steady, then I took off on stocking feet out the door.

"You'll leave on your own or you'll do it in handcuffs, your choice, Stone," Coert said as I kept my eyes glued to his broad back where he was standing in the foyer while hurrying down the stairs.

Stone?

Boston Stone?

Boston Stone was *here*?

"Using county resources to investigate commercial entities because your girlfriend doesn't want to live next to a hotel will be interesting to the County Commission."

"First, she's not my girlfriend, she's my fiancée," Coert corrected as I moved in behind him only for him to shift without even looking back at me, and he shifted in a way that told me he wanted me to stay behind him.

So even if I moved slightly to his side, I did it staying behind him.

And it was then I saw the man who was two steps into our foyer was tall, dark haired and quite handsome.

But the furious look on his face, the mean in his eyes, and the hardness of his mouth meant he wasn't *that* handsome.

Not to mention he was too slick. I'd never been attracted to slick men.

Then again, I'd only ever really been attracted to Coert, so…

His eyes flicked to me then went back to Coert.

"I'd congratulate you on the advancement of your relationship but I don't give a fuck," he snapped.

"Do not use that language in front of my fiancé," Coert bit out.

I did my best to have no reaction to Coert demanding this when he freely cursed in front of me and just stayed close to his back, eyes on Boston Stone.

"My apologies, Ms. Moreland," Boston Stone said to me snidely.

"Second," Coert rapped out and Stone's attention cut back to him. "I'm an elected official. I answer to the citizens of this county, not the County Commission. So although they might be interested in your bullshit for the sake of curiosity at how deep that bullshit can get, even if there was an issue, which there isn't, they can't do dick about it."

"You leaked private affairs of one of your citizens you illegally investigated using county resources to the press, which is impeachable," Stone declared.

"Are you making this up as you go along?" Coert asked derisively.

"I'm not certain the State Supreme Court will find this as disinteresting as you do when they hear it prosecuted," Stone retorted, these words making me put my hand to the small of Coert's back.

"Coert didn't leak anything," I piped up. "If you're angry about someone finding out your plans before you could push them through under the noses of the people of Magdalene, you should talk to the people who shared about them freely. You shouldn't show up at the doorstep of the sheriff to harass and threaten him."

"If it was *someone* finding out, I'd still be talking to them. But before I fired them, they shared it was the *sheriff* finding out."

"I didn't identify myself as the sheriff," Coert stated, and I pressed my hand into his back because I didn't think it was good he said that.

And Stone pounced right on it. "So you admit to calling?"

"It isn't illegal to call architecture firms to ask if any plans for the development of the Magdalene parkland were being drawn up," Coert retorted.

"They told me they wouldn't have shared if it wasn't a person of authority."

"That might be so but I didn't identify myself as the sheriff or mislead them by stating I was phoning as part of an investigation," Coert returned.

"Then it's a 'they said, you said' situation and you can use your version as your defense during your impeachment hearing," Stone fired back.

"I phoned them on my cell so my name will come up on caller ID and it isn't hard to find out I'm the sheriff of Derby County. But even if I did tell them I was the sheriff, me making inquiries about what might be happening on land that's under my jurisdiction would not be improper. Considering inquiries had already been made about reclassifying that land, I'd say it's not only not improper, it's also my job to know what's happening in my county. But I didn't call as the sheriff. If they're trying to cover their asses by talking shit about how they shared openly with a random caller about a client's business, that's their problem. But me making a phone call is not an impeachable offense. And me making this kind of phone call to be thorough in understanding what's happening in my jurisdiction is part of what I've been elected to do."

"Then you attempting to get re-elected next year after it's shared widely Magdalene's lighthouse was saved by the ill-gotten gains of a gold digger who married an old, sick man in order to inherit all his money, and then you married her will be an interesting proposition. But I'd suggest you start looking for alternate employment now. I hear there's always need for mall cops in Blakely."

I felt Coert's body tighten under my hand.

I did not get tight.

I moved instantly around Coert but he caught me with an arm around my stomach and pulled me back to his body.

So I used my mouth.

"You need to go," I advised.

"I'm not sure you're a threat," Boston Stone said, lip curled.

"I'm not the threat," I told him.

He lifted his brows. "Are you saying the sheriff is threatening me?"

"I'm saying if he was, he'd have every right to do that considering you're in his home and you've been asked to leave at least once and you've not left but instead stayed, continuing to harass him, threaten him and say foul things with the intent to bait him."

"You should have called me about the lighthouse, Ms. Moreland," he said ominously.

"Get over it," I shot back. "And also *leave.*"

He did not leave. He continued pushing.

And he did it leaned toward me, his face moving from snide to spiteful. "I'm going to ruin you and I'm going to ruin your *fiancé*."

Ruin me?

I'd already ruined myself, more than once.

And now…

Now the only people that it mattered what they thought knew me and loved me.

I was untouchable.

Coert, on the other hand, was sheriff. So he was not.

Still, this man was acting like a villain in a Victorian drama.

It would have been funny if it wasn't so irritating.

I mean, I'd just told Coert I might be pregnant, for goodness sake!

What Coert said next shared he agreed with me.

"Christ, you're a joke. Just go, would you? Jesus," Coert drawled impassively.

Stone leaned back with surprise drifting over his features and looked at Coert.

"You wanna report me to the County Commission? Do it," Coert invited. "You wanna try to impeach me? Try it. You wanna spread malicious gossip about Cady in an attempt to make me lose the next election? Go for it. The only person who thinks you have any leverage anymore is you, Stone. Everyone already thinks you're a snake. You want them to think you're a fool too, it isn't me that's gonna stop you. It's just me who's gonna say you got five seconds to walk out my front door before, honest to God, just because I'm sick of you boring me, I'm putting you in cuffs, arresting you for trespassing since I didn't invite your ass into my house, you shoved in, and I'm having a deputy come pick you up. Your choice. But trust me, I'm bein' very serious."

"I'm being very serious too," Stone spat.

"I don't really care," Coert replied.

Stone scowled at him.

Coert adjusted me so he was holding me casually at his side and when Stone continued to scowl at him, he sighed.

"Cady, my cuffs are in my gun belt in the closet. You wanna get them for me? And check Midnight while you're up there."

"The Magdalene Park project is moving forward," Stone declared.

"You beat down the injunction or we lose the election to recall the rezoning come November, you're right," Coert returned. "It probably is. Monsters who feed on greed like you win a lot, and it doesn't matter what devastation lies in their wake, as long as they can jot their win on whatever messed-up mental tally they got in their head, it's all the same to them. The joke's still on you because you think you're building a legacy when history will record it as Stone's folly or nothing at all. So whatever. Jot your win. But don't delude yourself you're writing the Declaration of Independence. Whatever you got planned is the same as a strip mall. It'll come and it'll go but that lighthouse will be that lighthouse until it crumbles to the earth. There won't be any plaques with your name on them put up in stone a hundred years after you die. Way you're goin', when you're gone, no one will give a shit at all."

Stone apparently had no response to that so he just stood there seething.

So Coert gave me a jostle before he let me go and prompted, "Cuffs, Cady."

"You're not arresting me," Stone snapped.

"I am if you don't get your ass out of my house," Coert replied.

Stone stared at Coert then glared at me before he turned and walked out the front door.

He slammed it, making the glass rattle.

"What an ass," Coert muttered.

I turned to him. "Coert—"

He looked at me and didn't allow me to say another word.

"Don't think about it for a second."

"But he—"

"Listen to me," Coert demanded.

And the way he did, I shut my mouth and listened.

"If you think that guy can do me dirty, you should know Jake was a professional boxer who built a junior boxing league and has been running it for years. Parents love him. And not just parents right now. Parents and the kids he taught how to box for the last however-many years he's been running the thing and kept them fit, helped them learn how to defend themselves and gave them a good male role model to use when it was their time to start to become good men. And Josie's family has been living in Lavender House for over a century and her grandmother wasn't beloved, she was practically worshipped in this town. And Josie adopting Ethan after his mother all but forgot him elevated her to that status in about a second."

Ethan's mother all but forgot him?

Josie hadn't shared that with me. Although considering she *had* adopted him, I assumed something like that had to happen, unless the woman had sadly passed. But I hadn't yet asked mostly because whatever had to happen would have to be sensitive and there hadn't been an appropriate time.

Still, how awful.

Coert kept talking through my musings.

"And Mick's a volunteer firefighter who's put his ass on the line repeatedly to keep people safe and save property, and his family owns Maine Fresh Maritime frozen seafood and not only is he loaded, his family helped settle Magdalene. Not to mention Amy is Amelia Hathaway, of *the* Hathaways, the oil gazillionaires. She's got more money than you and me will see in five lifetimes or Boston Stone could ever dream of conniving a way to get in his bank account."

I knew Amy was *a* Hathaway.

She'd seemed embarrassed when she'd shared for some odd reason, but she told me.

Coert kept at it.

"And you're loaded and not only used your money to restore what the townspeople consider their pride and joy, you opened it to the public which is something they've never had. So they're not gonna give a shit you married Moreland. You're you and one look at you tells anyone you're no gold digger. But you stayed married to the guy for seventeen years and anyone who meets you will know in about two seconds that was about love and loyalty."

Wow, that was sweet.

Coert continued, "But even if I didn't have all that firepower behind me, Alyssa's just gotta open her mouth at the salon and drop the right thing in a few ears and he's toast."

This was absolutely true. Everyone knew in a small town it wasn't the town paper, it was the town's beauty salon where everyone got their news.

Coert wasn't finished.

"That man doesn't scare me, Cady. And that man shouldn't scare you. He's a megalomaniac who thinks money means everything and the fact he has a lot of it gives him delusions of grandeur. I said he's a joke because he's a joke. If she had a mind to do it, Amelia alone could crush him. This project is not going forward. He's not going to get me impeached. And you're waking up in my bed every day, and hope to God for the next however many months, doing it pregnant with my child. I got that, nothing can touch me, Cady. Not a fucking thing."

He put his hands to my jaw and dipped his face close to mine.

"Now let's go check on our dog, and just in case all the energy we've been putting into it hasn't actually taken root, we should see about keepin' that effort going. And just to say, my call is to find out the sex. My boy is gonna be bedding down in a room that's blue. It's a girl, I've learned the drill, and when we do up the baby room, it's gonna be all about pink. None of that neutral yellow shit, lying in wait to see what we get. When they come home, we're gonna be ready for them."

When they come home, we're gonna be ready for them.

I stood in the foyer of an old, renovated farmhouse on the coast of Maine and felt the phantom wet of beer gliding over my fingers as I stared up into hazel eyes that I saw right there, I'd seen across a pillow from me, across a room from me, across a great emotional divide, and for almost two decades, in my dreams.

It had taken years and we'd lived through everything, even murder.

And we were right there.

Nothing can touch me, Cady. Not a fucking thing.

"Cady?" he called, the pads of his fingers digging into my flesh.

"I've made a lot of mistakes in my life—"

Coert dipped his face closer and it came in a whisper when repeated, "Cady."

"But I was spot on when I made the decision to believe in you."

His forehead came to rest on mine and he got so close, our noses rested alongside each other's.

And we stood in the foyer of an old, renovated farmhouse on the coast of Maine, so close, when Coert's eyes closed, his lashes swept through mine.

Then he kissed me.

He tasted of chill nights and wool sweaters and sea breezes and holding hands and playful teases and crooked grins and warm eyes and man and musk and sex and a million, billion other things that made Coert that I'd discovered, and a million, billion more I hadn't yet, and I couldn't have stopped my tongue from touching his in my need, my hunger, my *yearning* to have more.

He slanted his head and gave me more, wrapping his arms around me and pulling me deep into his body.

We consumed each other's mouths in the foyer until I broke the kiss, broke from his hold but grabbed urgently at his hand and tugged him toward the stairs. I was at the foot of them when he tugged me back around and his mouth slammed down on mine again.

His hands were everywhere, but his tongue was my entire universe, until I felt him yanking up my sweater.

I lifted my arms and took a step back to draw him closer to where I wanted us to go.

He pulled my sweater free just as the heel of my boot caught on the first riser.

I started going down but Coert caught me around the waist and he didn't stop my descent, he just controlled it, following me to the stairs.

We kissed and touched and tore at each other's clothes as we made our way up the stairs, and it wasn't until we were at the top that Coert came up to his feet with arms around me pulling me up with him.

I was in my bra and undies and his diamond, he was in his boxer briefs, our sweaters, jeans, socks and boots strewn along the stairs when we turned and kissed and turned and kissed as we made our short way down the hall, banging into walls, hitting the doorframe to his bedroom, each of us half groping, half struggling to get the upper hand.

Coert got impatient then and caught me just below my bottom and around my upper back.

He picked me up and strolled to the bed where he put me down.

"Don't move," he growled, towering over me.

I only let my eyes move to follow him to the closet.

He disappeared in it for moments but came out naked and hard, his thick cock rising proud from the spring of dark curls between his legs. That lumbering gait of his I loved so much and was such a part of him, his utter confidence in himself and his physique, his burning eyes intent on me, I felt a rush of wet hit between my legs and a whimper escape my lips.

He got to where I was lying horizontal across the bed, my calves over the side, and he bent to me.

He put a hand in the bed beside me and I watched the back of his strong neck, the muscles moving in his shoulders and back, as he put his lips to the skin just under my bra between my breasts and he trailed them down to my belly.

I held my breath as he stayed there, just his lips brushing my skin before he turned his head, and I felt the gentle abrasion of his evening whiskers grazing my skin. Claiming me. Staking his territory. Declaring me and what might lie beneath what he was doing and where he was doing it as all his.

My God, Coert Yeager was just…

Everything.

I slid my fingers in his hair and whispered, "Baby."

He lifted his head, his chin scraping my skin, his beautiful eyes hitting mine, as his fingers curled into the sides of my panties.

More wet saturated my sex as he slid them down my thighs and they fell down my calves and only then did Coert join me in bed.

Gathering me to him, his fingers flicked the hooks on the back of my bra. It came undone, he pulled it off my arms and tossed it aside as he hit a hip in the bed and rolled to his back, turning me, pulling me over, positioning me so I had his rock-hard cock in my face.

Before I could do a thing about it, his hands pressing in at my bottom, my knees slid down the comforter on either side of his head and his mouth was on me.

I pulsed into him, my neck arching back, then I rocked against him, reached to his iron shaft, curled my fingers around tight and sucked it deep.

He growled into my wet, instantly moving from lapping to hungry, insatiable *eating.*

Like we'd consumed each other's mouths, we consumed each other's bodies, Coert's fingers gripping the cheeks of my behind, biting into me, driving me against his tongue. I cupped his balls in one hand, stroked his cock with the other one as I bobbed and sucked.

And I sucked *hard.*

I didn't lick. This wasn't playing around. This wasn't going slow.

This was us, taking all we could get of everything we had *as fast as we could.*

I tasted salt on my tongue, knew he was ready and it was an enormous relief because I was so close to ready too, I was about to stop and beg him to take me.

I wanted to climax with him inside me, connected, looking into my hazel.

I was on my back before I could consciously slip him out of my mouth and Coert was dragging me up his thighs, looming over me, wrapping my legs around his hips. His eyes roaming, starving, all over me, one of his hands left my leg and went between us.

I felt him coating the head of his cock with my wet before his gaze locked on mine and he drove inside.

My back arched again, my hands went over my head, clutching the edge of the bed, using it as leverage to push down into his strokes.

He held my hips steady and slammed into me. I could hear his heavy breathing rasp in the room, grating against the sound of mine, when I felt him drift a hand over my hipbone, in, and his thumb hit my clit.

Oh *yes.*

"Coert."

"Yes."

"Coert."

"Yeah, Cady."

He pounded into me and I watched his face, flushed and hard, staring at mine like it was the only thing in the room, the only thing on earth, the only thing in the universe, and I understood that, because he was the only thing in mine.

His thumb pressed harder and circled.

"Coert," I whimpered, starting to lose our rhythm, needing to let go.

"Cady," he grunted, the muscles in his neck standing out.

He circled my clit hard, slammed into me, I let go and went flying.

I heard his growls turn to groans as he bucked between my legs and pushed my orgasm higher manipulating my clit, but it just added to the glory of floating on nothing but his cock buried deep inside, his cum flooding me, connected to Coert.

I was gasping and falling, again feeling the bed under me, when Coert's thumb left me and he fell forward into a hand on the bed, arm straight, his other hand still steady on my hip.

Dazedly, I focused on the top of his head, which was bent, staring down our bodies to where he was gently stroking me with his cock.

"Coert," I whispered.

Instantly, his head came up, his eyes sought mine, he buried himself inside and then he lowered himself to me, releasing my hip so he could brace some of his weight into a forearm.

"Yeah?" he asked softly.

"Yeah," I replied.

He brushed his mouth to mine and again and again, before he gave me a sweet, wet kiss. He broke the connection of our mouths to rest his forehead against mine.

"That hit the top five," I told him.

I watched the light of humor hit his eyes. "Agreed."

I grinned at him even if he was so close, he couldn't see my mouth.

Then I asked, "Did you have dinner?"

"Yeah."

"Was Midnight okay?"

"Yeah."

"Do you want to do that again?"

I felt his body shake with his amusement, a body still connected to mine.

But he answered, "Yeah."

Then he kissed me.

And we did it again.

But we went slower that time.

Twenty-Nine

IMPATIENT?

CADY

Present day…

The phone rang and I felt Midnight jerk, heard Coert growl, and I opened my eyes as he kept hold of me but twisted at the waist to reach toward his phone on the nightstand.

This was not unusual. At least once a week Coert got late night calls. Bad things happened all the time, but they had a favorite time of day and that time was nighttime.

It was the way of the world and it was the way of my life with Coert.

I had to admit in the beginning it took some getting used to.

But Coert was not one of those men who came home and complained about work. He did what he was meant to be doing. He was committed to it. And even if it didn't cause euphoria, I knew it meant something to him to be the man he was to the people of this county.

So I very quickly learned to get used to it.

That said, that night after Midnight had her turn, after we'd shared what we'd shared in bed, when the next day we'd learn if we were pregnant, and when the weather was nasty outside and the roads were grim (and I knew this because this was not the first call Coert had received, rain had turned to sleet then to snow, there was ice everywhere, the salt trucks had rolled out hours before, but people still needed to go places, and on ice, that wasn't easy), I didn't want him going anywhere.

"Yeager," he said into his phone.

I looked at the alarm clock.

It was just after midnight.

He listened then said, "Yeah. Right. How're the roads?" More listening and then, "Okay. That means I'll be there in half an hour, forty minutes."

Damn.

"Later," he finished, I heard a beep and Coert turned back to me. "Gotta go, Cady."

"What is it?" I asked.

"Car accident," he answered. "Alcohol is involved."

Alcohol?

"In this weather?"

"People drink all the time, even when it's snowy, baby. And if they do enough of it, they do stupid stuff."

This was sadly true.

"Go back to sleep," he ordered.

Normally, I did that.

The first few times he was called away, that hadn't come easy, but I got there. Then it just became par for the course.

But bad roads, I wasn't so sure.

However, he didn't need to know that.

"Okay," I replied.

He found my lips in the dark and kissed me.

Then he did what he always did when he left me in bed like this, sliding from under the covers so the cold didn't hit me then being careful to arrange them around me even though he didn't have to.

Midnight, apparently fully recovered after her ordeal (Coert had brought her to bed with us after we got finished with our activities earlier, she'd been groggy but awake), jumped off the bed and did what she always did when this happened. She followed him around as he went behind closed doors in the closet and bathroom to get ready without bothering me with any lights (something else he always did).

He came back to me when he was suited up, bent over me and gave my temple a kiss.

"Be home as soon as I can," he murmured.

"Okay, honey. Be careful."

"Yeah," he replied.

I felt him leave me but knew he was giving Midnight a rubdown when he said, "Stay with your mom."

It wasn't like she knew what he was saying. I heard him snap repeatedly and knew he was motioning to the bed when she jumped up.

I watched his shadow move to the door and called, "Love you," when he was almost out of it.

"Love you back," he replied.

Then he was gone.

MIDNIGHT AND I tried to sleep.

And when that didn't work, we tried some more.

And when that didn't work, I turned on the light on the nightstand, got out of bed, put on some socks and Midnight and I went to find my book.

I located it in the living room, assessed my alertness, then Midnight and I went to the kitchen and made some herbal tea.

As the kettle boiled, I looked over my dog to assess *her* alertness and was pleased to see she seemed no worse for the wear. The sedative had worn off and she was just Midnight.

My tea made, Midnight, my book, my mug and I went back to bed.

I tried to read.

I failed in trying to read.

I kept going, sipping tea, stroking Midnight where she lay stretched down my side, but I eventually gave up, stared at the curtains over the window and wondered what it was like out there.

Rain to snow, it was probably beautiful.

Beautiful and treacherous.

On this thought, Midnight's head jerked up, she woofed then she got to her feet and trotted off the bed and out of the room.

I looked to Coert's alarm clock.

It was now just before three.

No barking commenced, so I got out of bed, went to the chair in the corner, grabbed my cardigan and I was shrugging it on as I walked out of the room and down the hall to the mouth of the stairs.

It was there I saw Coert plodding up them with Midnight at his side. The house behind him was dark.

He sensed me, his head went back but his step didn't falter when he demanded, "Cady, get back in bed."

"Everything okay?"

"Back in bed and I'll tell you."

There was something about him that I couldn't quite read.

But since we were going to end up there anyway regardless of where we had our conversation, I retraced my steps, pulled off my cardigan and was throwing it on the chair when Coert came into the room.

He had his gun belt in his hands and was walking to the closet.

"Is everything okay?" I asked again when he didn't launch in, studying him as he moved into the closet.

"I don't know," he answered, hooking his gun belt where he always hooked it on the catch by the door and then pulling out the gun.

I moved closer to watch as he shoved it in the safe on a shelf in the closet (where he always shoved it).

I also watched him close the door to the safe and heard the electronic noises as he hit buttons.

What I didn't hear was Coert explain his, "I don't know."

"Coert—"

He turned his head to look at me and his hands went to his shirt. "Cady, you don't have to stay up when I have a callout."

"I normally don't. But the roads were bad and I couldn't sleep."

"Right," he muttered, unbuttoning his shirt.

"Coert." That came out sharper. "You're being strange."

He looked at me, rolling his shoulders to tug his shirt off.

Even doing that was attractive on Coert.

"How am I being strange?" he asked.

"I don't know," I replied, and I didn't, but he was.

"You're not normally up when I get back from a callout," he pointed out.

"That might be so but it isn't that."

And it wasn't!

He was now in jeans, boots and Henley.

He went for the Henley.

"It was just an accident on bad roads," he told me.

"That requires the presence of the sheriff?" I asked, because now I was curious about the answer seeing as that wouldn't seem to me to be a reason to drag the sheriff from his bed when he wasn't taking call.

As upsetting as it was, that would seem routine.

"Alcohol was involved," he shared.

"And *that* requires your presence?" I pressed.

He freed himself from his Henley and I was not accustomed to the brilliance of his bare chest right there for me to take in happily before I had more to take in happily when he shot me one of his crooked grins.

I grew still.

Coert stated, "The person drinking was Boston Stone."

I stayed still but felt my eyes get huge.

"*What?*" I breathed.

"Apparently, he went from here to Magdalene Club, probably to bitch about me to his cronies. He threw back a few and then threw back a few more. Fortunately for him, he also had dinner in between doing that. He was point one, not bad, but since the limit is point oh eight, he was definitely OUI and the other driver was not."

"OUI?"

"Operating Under the Influence."

Ah.

"Was anyone hurt?" I asked.

"None of them will feel good tomorrow," he told me. "The other car held a couple coming back from some anniversary party in Shepherd. The husband had been drinking, but he was well under the limit. They both reported they didn't want to go because of the weather, but it was her aunt and uncle's fiftieth so it was a big thing. They also both reported he was driving safely, maybe going twenty, twenty-five in a forty, due to the roads. The damage of the vehicles would say both cars were going the speed limit or slightly over, which meant Stone had to be going sixty or more."

"Oh my God, that's crazy," I replied.

Coert nodded. "Air bags inflated, seatbelts dug in, lots of damage to both cars and they were jerked around a lot. They'll all be sore and maybe bruised tomorrow but that's it. EMT says they were all good so they all went home, except Stone, who's in the tank."

Abruptly, a giggle escaped me.

Coert used his toes to flip off one of his boots and his eyes were twinkling. "I know."

"I…this is…I don't know what to say," I stammered.

"I do since he's been caught by a deputy driving just under OUI, breathalyzer put him at point oh seven, and he was warned. He's never been arrested before so he doesn't have a record of it, so also no conviction, but this isn't good for him and the last half hour I spent at the station I spent on the phone with reporters from the *Forecast* and the *Daily News*."

Now I knew why he was being strange.

He was setting me up for the good stuff.

"Poor Mr. Stone," I said smugly.

"Of course, Stone is saying this is police corruption, the breathalyzer reading in the field was full of shit since I have it out for him so I set my deputies on him, conspiring to pin an OUI on him when he wasn't over the limit."

I lost my smug feeling immediately.

"What?"

He shook his head. "Cady, don't worry. My deputies were nowhere near the scene when he hit that couple's car, so that's on him. But they did hit the Magdalene Club and got patrons and staff statements that Stone was there drinking regularly for several hours before he left, got into his car and drove away. And the idiot did this after the valet questioned his ability to drive, asked if he'd like him to call a taxi, and Stone demanded to talk to the Club manager and made a formal complaint against the valet for making such a suggestion that he was too inebriated to drive. He then demanded he be given his keys even if the valet and manager weren't comfortable with it. So not only was the man too drunk to drive, he did it even after the establishment he was drinking at advised him against it and made record of that advisement and the complaint, so they didn't get their shit in a sling should something like what happened happen. The manager had already typed out the incident report before we got there. A copy of it is in Stone's file at the station."

I couldn't believe all of this.

"How'd he get rich if he's this stupid?" I asked.

Coert shrugged, having undone his belt, he was yanking down his jeans. "He's not stupid. He's arrogant. And I'll admit, that's its own brand of stupidity and maybe a worse kind."

I cocked my head to the side. "So you don't think this will cause you trouble?"

Coert straightened from pulling his phone from the pocket of his jeans, came to me, hooked me at the belly, turned me and guided me to bed.

"I think he'll bluster and storm and do everything he can to make problems for me, and when none of it has any effect, he'll seethe and connive, and when none of *that* has any effect, he'll find someone else to bother with his crap."

I crawled into bed feeling Coert follow me, stating, "I'm not sure I want to get to the seething and conniving part of that."

Coert pulled the covers over us and replied, "I think it'll be funny."

I stared at him tossing his phone on the nightstand. "He has money and attorneys."

He turned to me. "He has money, yeah. And Terry Baginski is his attorney and her place on the tier of snakes and assholes of Derby County is second only to Boston Stone. That husband of my old deputy I was telling you about?"

I nodded when he didn't go on.

He then went on.

"He was a snake, best defense attorney in the county. Every law officer except his wife hated him and even she hated him after he won some of his cases. And he hated Baginski. Said she gave attorneys a bad name."

To that, he chuckled.

Although I could understand his amusement, I wasn't finding any of this funny.

"Coert," I said worriedly.

He leaned into me, kissed my nose and pulled back.

"Did I come home to you?" he asked.

"Yes," I answered.

"Are we in my bed together, about ready to go to sleep?"

I nodded.

"We gonna wake up together?"

"Yes, Coert."

"Are you having my baby?" he carried on.

"Well, yes, even if that might maybe need the addition of 'eventually,'" I replied.

"Then fuck 'em," he declared. "Some miracle happens and they cause problems for me, I'll become a mall cop. What do I care?"

I stared again.

Coert twisted and turned off the light, then he reached well beyond me and turned off mine.

He pulled me into his arms and deeper under the covers.

"You sure you're okay about all this?" I asked.

"Yup."

Midnight jumped up on the bed then lay down with a groan, head on our ankles.

"Go to sleep," Coert ordered.

I snuggled into him.

"Love you, Cady."

"Love you too, honey."

It only took a few minutes, but I heard and felt his breath even.

He was okay about all this.

Completely.

But that, I was learning, was Coert.

He had me. He had Janie.

So he was okay about everything.

I grinned against his shoulder where my head lay.

And then I fell asleep.

I WOKE UP alone in bed and I did this because I sensed movement in the room.

I opened my eyes and saw it was still dark outside, which meant early.

I pushed up to an elbow as I heard the pants of a dog.

"You awake?" Coert asked.

"Yes," I replied sleepily.

The bedside light went on.

I blinked against the bright and then saw Coert standing beside the bed, dressed in his work gear.

My eyes dropped to his alarm clock.

It was just after six.

He got up around this time every day, but by "up" that meant rolled out of bed.

I looked up at him again. "Wha—?"

I didn't even get the full word out when his hand came up in front of his chest and he waved a box in front of him.

"Out of bed, baby," he said.

I looked from the box to him and felt my lips curl.

Then I felt a brow go up.

"Impatient?" I asked.

He raised a brow back. "You want me to carry you to the toilet?"

"I think I can get there on my own," I mumbled, throwing back the covers, taking the hit of cold and tossing my legs over the side of the bed.

Coert met me at the foot, handing me the box but did it catching me at the back of the neck and pulling me up to him so he could touch his lips to mine.

When he lifted his head he said, "No worries about the results. If it's a negative, we got time for another go before I go to work."

I started giggling.

He let my neck go but only to pat my behind before he planted his hand there and pushed me to the bathroom when I didn't move fast enough.

I got behind closed doors, opened the box, read the directions, did my thing and then set the test on a few folded squares of toilet paper before I washed my hands and opened the bathroom door.

Coert sauntered in.

Midnight sat in the door.

"She go out?" I asked, grabbing my toothbrush.

"Yep," he answered.

"You feed her?" I asked, loading my toothbrush.

"Yep."

I brushed my teeth.

Coert leaned on the wall by his sink where I'd laid the pregnancy test, his arms crossed on his chest, his eyes on the test.

I took my brush out of my mouth and garbled through foam, "A watched pot never boils."

I got his hazel as he returned, "A smartass always can get spanked."

Something new to try.

I grinned at him through foam.

He shook his head and looked back down at the test.

I knew it the instant he did because the air in the room changed.

And this was because the world had just changed.

I was turning the faucet off after rinsing and it felt like it took a century to straighten from the sink and turn my gaze to him.

He was in the same position, casually leaning against the wall with his arms crossed on his chest, his attention on the test, but there was no longer anything casual about his posture.

"Honey?" I whispered.

His hazel hit me again, the fathomless depth to it now utterly fascinating, and I started tingling from head to toe.

"Yes?" I asked, but I knew.

"Yes," he answered even though he knew I knew.

"Yes?" I repeated stupidly, just because I wanted to hear him say it again.

"Yeah, Cady."

My eyes started filling and my feet moved.

Coert moved too.

He wasn't very far away but in that short distance both of us had gathered enough velocity, when we slammed into each other it felt like the whole of the earth shook.

He caught me around my thighs and back and lifted me straight up.

I grabbed either side of his face and brought my lips straight down.

Both of our mouths were open when they collided.

Midnight woofed.

She also scuttled out of the way as Coert carried me to bed kissing me.

He landed on top of me but shifted immediately to the side, though only to pull my nightie up.

When it was gone, he rolled back on top of me.

"Put that thing in my nightstand, we're never throwing away," he growled.

I didn't have to ask if he meant the test.

I knew.

"Okay," I breathed.

"Shimmy outta those panties, baby, this is gonna go fast," he ordered.

I moved instantly to do as told. "Okay."

"Love you, Cady."

"Love you most."

His hand settled at my belly. "I get that now, you not wasting any time giving me this."

"I think you had something to do with that, honey."

He grinned his crooked grin.

They were coming more often now.

Oh yes, he was getting used to happy.

"Yeah," he murmured.

Then he kissed me.

And we went fast.

Epilogue

MOST

CADY

Present day…

Coert slid out of the booth and stood the second I entered the door to join him for lunch at Weatherby's, and he did this because that was what he always did when he was there before I arrived.

I hurried to him, leaned into him with a hand at his stomach and one at his neck and accepted the light kiss he bent to give me.

He waited by the booth as I slid in my side before he slid in his.

"Well?" we said at the same time.

I started laughing.

Coert did not.

"You first," he ordered as I pulled off my coat.

I tucked it beside me and then looked right into hazel.

"My doctor confirmed it. We're having a baby."

He closed his eyes. Dropped his head. Lifted his head. Opened his eyes.

Love and gratitude.

His best look.

Bar none.

Though I'd take just the love part of that.

He reached across the table, grabbed my hand and held tight.

"Coke. Diet Coke. Cheeseburger. And patty melt," our waitress, who I'd come to know in all my meetings with Coert for lunch at Weatherby's was named Marjorie, said. "Or are we goin' out on a limb today?"

"Just water for me," I told her. "But yes on the patty melt."

"That works for me as is," Coert replied.

"Gotcha. Comin' up," she mumbled, turned and walked away.

I looked at Coert and resumed with my news. "So we're good, honey. I'm healthy. She foresees no problems. I'm on vitamins now and have all my appointments scheduled."

"You need to send those to Monica so she can get them in my calendar."

Coert wanting to be involved every step of the way didn't surprise me.

But it did make me very happy.

"I'll do that after I'm done at the Society this afternoon," I confirmed.

Coert nodded and asked, "No caffeine?"

"Just a cup in the morning."

His eyes lit up. "It's go time."

That was when I nodded.

It was go time.

Go time, destination—the arrival of Coert and my baby.

And there we were. Sitting at one of our lunches at a diner, holding hands.

Caught up.

"But otherwise good," he stated softly, but it was a question.

"No. You see, I'm pregnant so otherwise *great*."

At that, he smiled.

"Now your turn," I prompted.

He nodded yet again.

"Did what I said at breakfast I was gonna do. Went in, didn't have cause to request a warrant and didn't find cause to push anything when I arrived at the property. Still, to say the person who answered the door was freaked the sheriff was asking questions about a dog they gave up that showed signs of abuse, and then he pressed to know if they owned any pets, is putting it mildly."

Good.

I liked freaked.

Freaked in this case was *brilliant.*

"It was a woman," Coert shared. "She said Midnight was her husband's dog and they had to give her up because he lost his job and they didn't have the money to keep her anymore. He's employed now so he wasn't around. I pushed and she's sticking with the foot in a trap story but the longer I went at her, the more freaked she got. In the end I told her me or one of my deputies was coming around that evening to talk to the husband. She said they'd be out. I said we'd come back until someone could chat with her husband. So that happened. Now, did you tell Kath about the baby?"

I shook my head.

"The doctor says it's very early. I want to wait a few more weeks. She'd lose her mind if I pushed it through the first trimester before I told her but just a couple more weeks, make sure it's all going well, and then I'll give her the good news. Now, are you actually going back to talk to the husband?"

He nodded again.

"Good idea on Kath. And yeah, we are. Sending a deputy tonight. If the man's not there, we'll keep trying. We have nothing on them except the state of Midnight, so nothing is going to come of this. But that doesn't mean we can't put a little effort into scaring the shit out of them. The woman said they had no pets at this time, and I'm hoping scaring the shit out of them will make it so they don't feel the need for canine company again. There's nothing more to do but gotta say, I already feel better, seeing her face and leaving there making her think they're screwed."

I had to admit, I felt better too.

It wasn't going to change the state of Midnight, what she had to deal with in her doggie brain because of whatever they'd done to her. But it could mean those people never did that to another dog.

And that would be worth it.

Coert kept talking.

"Also had a chat with the folks at the shelter. They're gonna be reporting any concerns of abuse directly to me in the future."

God, how I *loved* this man.

"You're amazing, honey," I said softly.

"Not all the citizens in my county vote, but all of them breathe. So the way I see it, it's my job."

Coert thinking this way didn't surprise me.

But it did make me very happy.

"Now are we agreed that we've got a moratorium on sharing about the baby with everyone?" he asked. "Because I think we should keep it under wraps all around. Including with Janie."

"Yes," I agreed. "I'd like to have it just for ourselves for a little while but also give him time to get used to his new environs before we spread the news."

I took it Coert's crooked grin at the "have it just for ourselves" part of that, and did it happily, but also did it continuing to speak.

"That's done, and kudos for scaring the shit out of some animal abusers, honey," I said and that boyish grin stayed in place. "Now have you heard anything from Stone?"

"Nope," Coert answered with a shake of his head. "Told you he posted bail. His first offense with anything, it's probably not gonna go too bad for him. The worst he'll suffer is those follow-up articles coming out about him. But since it wasn't really big news he drove drunk, that wasn't a big splash, so it wasn't a big hit for him to take. Still, he's gone quiet. And I figure the reason behind that is that rumor has it the County Commission is getting close to finalizing the report on their investigation into the rezoning. And they shared a few things with Arnie who shared them with Jake who phoned me this morning."

He stopped talking when Marjorie arrived with our drinks.

"And?" I prompted after she walked away.

"Part of the application for a referendum for rezoning stated that, even within a new jurisdiction, those parklands would remain protected unless the governors of that unincorporated land could demonstrate a need for reclassification. And the Commissioners' investigation uncovered what I uncovered, that Terry Baginski was making inquiries into applying for reclassification on behalf of two corporations that have no assets or operations, and she did this very close to the vote, which makes it a logical conclusion that this was what they were considering *before* the vote."

"What does all that mean?" I asked.

"Arnie doesn't know for certain," he answered. "But he thinks that they've traced those shell corporations to one or more of the unincorporated land's board of governors, including Stone. The rumor is, due to this conflict of interest and the evidence suggesting corruption in the form of members of that board colluding to reclassify the land before submitting the referendum to rezone it, and not divulging that prior to the vote, all of this for their personal gain, the Commissioners will ask them to resign. If not, they'll be further investigated, this being something they'll put on my desk, which could bring criminal charges. And with this information coming to light, the Commissioners feel the only fair way forward is to resubmit the referendum for a vote come November. Arnie thinks that referendum should be pressed to write stauncher protections into the zoning. He also thinks applications should be submitted on a state or federal level to protect that land. He's going to call Jackie to get something going with that."

I stared at him, excited, but not quite believing this was actually going to work out the way that it should.

Therefore, I sought confirmation.

"So we're going to win?"

That got me another grin. "We're gonna win." He gave me that, let me enjoy it, but then his grin faded. "You hear from Caylen?"

My joy at stopping Boston Stone and his buddies from destroying the look and feel of Magdalene slipped away and I shook my head.

"Not since he told me Orson got through the transplant procedure okay," I shared. "Now I don't know what to do, Coert. We're the definition of *not close*. I don't actually even know him. But even if we were close, I wouldn't know what to do. Do I call him and ask? Or is that a bother? Everyone will be asking them. How many times do you want to tell someone how your sick son is doing? And I can't call Alice for the same reasons. She gave me her number but I barely know her at all."

"Just text him, honey. Tell him he's on your mind, so is his family, and if he ever needs to talk, remember you're there."

If our subject matter wasn't what it was, I would have laughed at the look on Coert's face because it was clear he didn't want to say those words.

He didn't want Caylen any part of my life.

But sometimes life didn't give you a choice.

And I'd learned to roll with it.

Because in the end, more often than not, it worked out.

And sitting across Coert, pregnant with his baby, I knew sometimes it worked out beautifully.

But I had to admit, it was just good to know Coert was on board with all of that.

"Good idea, I'll text them both," I agreed.

"August," Coert stated confusingly.

"Sorry?" I asked.

"Early August, weather's still good, kids are still out of school."

"Yes, that's what early August is," I confirmed when he didn't continue.

"For our wedding, Cady."

I stared at him again, something funny (in a good way) spiraling in my belly.

"Since we definitely have to have it at the lighthouse, would have preferred to do it when the tulips were out but I'm not waiting that long," he said.

Definitely have to have it at the lighthouse.

That spiral swirled out of control.

That said, there were some things Coert was willing to give into, and looking into his eyes I saw there were some things he was just not.

Even so.

"I'll be, I don't know, close to six months pregnant then," I shared.

"Perfect," he decreed.

I'd quit dreaming about what I wanted from life a long time ago.

But I'd never dreamed of being a pregnant bride.

"Coert—" I began.

"Wedding pictures with you, me, Janie and the baby. All of us there even if one of us isn't breathing on her own yet. It'll be perfect. No one left out."

No one left out.

And that was it. Suddenly it was what Coert said it would be.

Perfect.

"Do not make me cry in my patty melt," I whispered, seeing his handsome face start to wobble.

His fingers still around mine tightened. "Your patty melt hasn't been served yet, baby."

To fight back the tears, I declared, "I want Janie to be my flower girl."

His face went soft before he said quietly, "I think that can be arranged."

"I might need to have three matrons of honor," I warned.

"I don't care if you have ten of them," he returned.

"That means you'll need three best men," I told him.

"The guy's got one job, to look after the ring. That kinda thing means a lot more to women than it does to men so you can have as many matrons of honor as you want, but one best man is enough."

"They have to make a speech too," I reminded him.

"Then one of them is *definitely* enough. I'm not listening to three men try to crack jokes as they spill all my secrets when it'll be torture enough to listen to one of them do that shit."

"Do you have any secrets, Coert Yeager?" I asked through soft laughter.

"Yeah. Once I fucked this gorgeous redhead in the bathroom of the Adam and Eve but she'd later become my wife, so if anyone said dick about that I'd have to punch them in the throat. Though that's not a worry since no one knows about that except the redhead who's gonna be my wife."

At his words, I reached to my drink and took a sip.

"Cady?" he called.

"Mm?" I asked, putting my glass down and watching myself do this in an effort not to lift my gaze to his.

I heard him sigh before he asked, "Who'd you tell?"

I finally looked at him in order to admit, "I may have told Kath."

"May or did?" he asked, studying me closely.

I minimally lifted a shoulder.

"Right," he muttered, reading the shoulder lift. "And she definitely told Pat. Anyone else?"

I looked to the thermal at his throat this time.

"Shit," he mumbled and shook my hand so I lifted my eyes again. "Please don't say Alyssa."

"I'd had two martinis. You know I get chatty when I drink," I defended myself.

"So Josie and Amy were there," he noted.

He was right. They were.

I bit my lip.

"Which means Jake, Mick and Junior know," he declared.

Women talked to their men, so I guessed he was right about that too.

I pressed my lips together.

"Which means, since my brother is going to be my best man, I have to sequester him so none of those guys can get to him so he won't share that shit during our wedding reception, necessitating me punching my own flesh and blood in the throat. I don't give a shit people know I had sex in the bathroom at the Adam and Eve. But it's nobody's business I had sex with my *wife* in the bathroom at the Adam and Eve."

"Is there a statute of limitations on public indecency?" I queried.

"Don't be cute," he retorted, and that time I tried not to laugh.

Instead I told him, "Honestly, I had to. We were all tipsy. Alyssa was bragging about her and Junior's exploits. Amy piped in with something really good that happened in the back cab of the fire truck. And Josie's too classy to bare all, but Alyssa has no problem doing it for her. So she told us it's known widely that Josie and Jake *do it* in the locker room after practically every one of his fights. I had to protect your reputation by sharing you could be creative with location. It was a matter of pride."

"Your pride or my pride?" he asked.

Totally my pride. I knew Coert couldn't care less.

But in this case it was my *tipsy* pride.

"Honestly, the fire truck thing sounded fabulous. And Alyssa and Junior could write a very thick handbook on how to keep the sex in your marriage fresh over the years. Not to mention, Amy chimed in that fight night is fabulous, since Mickey's a fighter too and apparently things get pretty heated. But ours was the best."

That got me back his crooked grin.

"Yeah?" he asked.

I nodded, grinning back. "Absolutely."

"If I didn't know those women were some of the best women I'd ever met, I'd worry about you making them your Magdalene posse."

"You've got nothing to worry about," I assured.

"I know," he replied.

"I'm wearing white," I proclaimed.

His face changed instantly, his gaze grew intent, but his lips moved to say, "Wear what you want. You always look beautiful. The only important thing to me is that you show up."

I twisted our hands so that my thumb was hooked around his, my fingers tight around the side of his hand. "And my bouquet is going to be huge. Gigantic. I've always wanted an extravagant bouquet. Everything else can be low key. But I'm carrying an enormous bouquet."

"Whatever you want, baby," he said softly.

"Is there anything that you want?" I asked.

"You to show up," he answered.

"You said that, and that will definitely happen. But anything else?"

"I have everything I want already so not really. Though food like sliders and street tacos, a ton of it on a table people can go to and pig out, is a lot better than making people sit with people they don't know and share a meal. It should be a party. We have a lot to celebrate. And I'd want people comfortable doing it."

"That works for me," I told him.

"Sure?" he asked.

I nodded then stated, "We're planning our wedding."

His hand released mine, but only so he could slide it up and curl his fingers around my wrist.

So I did the same with his.

We did this as he whispered, "Yeah."

"I'm going to be Cady Yeager."

His fingers pulsed deep into my flesh and his expression changed again, the intensity turning to fierceness, and he repeated, "Yeah."

"We need to ask your parents to come out and arrange to go visit your brother and his family. I don't want to meet them at the wedding."

"I'll give them calls after lunch."

"I want Pat to give me away," I carried on.

"That's your call, honey, but I think he'll be over the moon if you ask."

He would.

Pat would love that.

"But at the father-daughter dance, I'm going to dance with all three of them. I don't know how I'll manage that, but I'm going to do it."

"That's good, baby. It's important not to leave Mike and Daly out."

I held fast to his wrist, like I was hanging over the side of a building and Coert was saving me from falling to the ground.

It trembled when I repeated, "We're planning our wedding."

"Yeah, Cady."

"We're pregnant and we're planning our wedding."

Coert said nothing, just held on and stared into my eyes.

"Beer from a keg," I whispered.

He grinned. It was gentle as were his eyes.

"Perfect," he whispered back.

"Love you," I said.

"Love you most," he said.

"Yeah," I replied, and there was a wealth of meaning in that word.

Because he absolutely didn't.

But he also completely did.

So…

Yeah.

COERT

AFTER HE FINISHED with the phone call, Coert moved from his beer and ballgame toward the kitchen.

But he stopped in the doorway.

He leaned against the jamb and took in the mess before him, doing it needing a second because he felt his throat close and he had to concentrate on clearing the blockage so he could breathe.

The place was a mess.

Cady was at the island and had her back to him. It looked like she was beating something in a bowl.

Janie was on her knees on one of the stools, a pastry bag in her hands, her tongue sticking out, and she was (poorly) piping brightly colored icing on top of a cupcake.

Midnight was lounged flat out on the floor at the foot of Janie's stool. And their pup was so in her zone, she didn't even lift her head when Coert came into the vicinity.

In fact, they were all so in the zone neither of his two girls knew he was there.

"It's time to tint," Cady declared. "What color next, Janie?"

Janie looked from her cupcake to Cady and shouted, "Green!"

From what Coert could tell, they'd run the gamut. There were pink, yellow, blue and purple topped cupcakes all over every surface. Surfaces that were also coated in flour, smeared with icing, dotted with sprinkles and littered with unused cupcake papers.

"You want to add the color or do you trust me with it?" Cady asked.

"I trust you with it, Cady," Janie answered, turning back to piping her cupcake only to blow out an air bubble that sent a messy glob of icing all over the cupcake.

This did not cause distress.

This caused both his girls to burst out laughing.

Right here, watching my girls making cupcakes, Coert thought.

Another version of paradise.

"Daddy!" Janie cried and he looked from her ruined cupcake to her. "Look!" She picked up a cupcake with a wodge of purple icing swirled on top and falling down the side. "Cady taught me how to pipe!"

"Gorgeous, baby," he murmured his lie, sliding his gaze to Cady who had turned to the side to give her attention to him.

She was showing now, barely, just a little baby bump. She was late into her fourth month.

And just last night, they'd felt the first kick.

She smiled at him. He returned it. And then he walked in, moving to his daughter first to give her a kiss on the side of the head then moving behind Cady to wrap an arm around her, hand to her bump, and he kissed the side of her neck.

"Tell me again what this thing is we're doing tonight," he ordered.

"It's a spread-out party!" Janie exclaimed excitedly.

"Progressive," Cady told him. "We start at Amy and Mickey's and they're doing appetizers. Then we go to Jake and Josie's, and they're doing dinner. And then they all come here."

"For cupcakes!" Janie declared.

"Yeah, I got at least that part," Coert told his girl with a grin.

"Ethan's making dinner and he makes yummy food," Janie proclaimed. "And Con and Sofie are home. And Miss Amy says *all* her kids will be there. It's gonna be *great*!"

"I'll drive," Cady told him quietly. "That way you can drink."

"I'll drive," he replied. "I don't need to drink."

And he didn't.

He didn't get why they needed to eat a meal in three different places.

What he did get was that the best buzz he could have was the one he was experiencing right there.

"And Cady and Miss Josie and Miss Amy say we're gonna do this *once a month*! So when the baby comes, *everyone can play with him*!"

At Janie's words, Cady settled back into him but did it still squirting green color into the icing she was beating.

Janie had no problem with a little brother or sister.

No.

Janie could not wait.

"Miss Alyssa says when she's not on vacation, she and Mr. Junior are gonna be in charge of booze when we have our spread-out parties," Janie stated authoritatively. "'Cause she says she's gotta cook for a hundred people every day, so she's just gonna be about the bevahraige when she's around."

"Beverage, baby," Coert corrected gently.

"Bevahraige," Janie replied.

He shot her another smile.

She grinned back and returned to her piping.

"Can I talk to you a second?" Coert murmured in Cady's ear.

She twisted her neck and looked up at him.

After she caught his eyes, she nodded and turned to Janie. "You good for a second, honey?"

"Yeah, Cady," Janie told her.

She let go of the spoon, grabbed a towel, wiped her hands and then they moved out into the hall.

"Is everything okay?" she asked.

"Just got a call. The entire Board of Governors for unincorporated Derby County have resigned in lieu of criminal charges being lodged for public corruption."

Coert watched her eyes grow wide. "Really?"

"Yup."

"All of them?"

"Yup."

"So this is the super-secret thing you said I'd like a whole lot when it all fell out," she remarked.

He grinned and repeated, "Yup."

"They pushed it and Sheriff Coert nailed them," she whispered, eyes shining.

"And that's another yup," he replied, putting his hands to her hips. "They tried to throw Baginski under the bus so she rolled on them. No 'they said, she said.' She knew who she was working with and didn't take chances. So she recorded meetings without their knowledge. They started setting her up as the fall guy, she brought them all tumbling down."

"So, it's done?" Cady asked.

"Yup," he said again. "The injunction stands and the referendum will be back on the ballot for reinstatement of zoning the parkland into Magdalene with the oversight of the City Council come November."

A huge smile spread on her face. "That's fabulous."

"I know you're up to your ears in icing but you want more?"

The glee remained on her face as she replied, "You can never have enough icing."

Coert preferred the cake.

Actually, Coert preferred pie.

But with this, he didn't mind an additional dose of sweet.

"Stone's house is on the market. Word is that he's retiring early. Word also is he's closing on a home in Malibu."

"Wow," she whispered.

"Saw the writing on the wall and to top that, he's *persona non grata*, not feelin' the love of Magdalene, but more, not getting the money because no one wants to work with him. So he's done. And he's practically Baginski's only client so word going around is that she took some job at a firm in Florida. In other words, it's not just done, it's *done*. And they're not just gone, they're gonna be *gone*."

"In other words, we didn't just win, we *won*."

Coert nodded.

Cady started giggling.

Right now, watching and hearing Cady giggle, Coert thought.

She leaned into him and he felt her hand on his chest, their child in her belly resting against him.

No. Right now, with her close, Coert thought.

"I wish I could drink champagne," she told him.

"We'll save it up for when she gets here," he told her.

"I feel it, Coert, and he's a he," she replied.

He wrapped his arms around her and pressed her closer. "I feel it, baby, and she's a she."

"We'll see," she murmured.

They had the ultrasound scheduled for next week and then they would.

She rolled up on her toes and kissed his throat before rolling back and saying, "I better get back to cupcakes."

"Yeah," he whispered.

She lifted both hands to give the sides of his neck a squeeze then she pulled away.

He let her go and watched her walk back into the kitchen.

"My bag's empty, Cady!" Janie exclaimed.

"I've got you covered, honey," Cady replied.

Coert wanted to go watch. In fact he knew he could stand in the doorway for hours and take in the beauty his two girls gave him.

But he needed to give them time together. They hadn't had much and soon there'd be another girl in the mix.

Or a boy.

He really didn't care.

As long as he got his green.

So he moved back to the living room and his beer and ballgame.

And in the background, he heard chatter over cupcakes and icing.

Coert folded into the couch, lifted his feet to the coffee table, and settled back into paradise.

CADY

I WALKED DOWN the aisle carrying the huge bouquet of flowers in front of my very pregnant belly.

I looked to the front and saw Coert standing there smiling at me.

I smiled back and kept going, wanting to run to him, like I always wanted to run to him, but not wanting to ruin the proceedings.

I got close to the first row and it was then I turned my head when I heard, "*Mama!*"

I looked down and to my left to see Kath sitting in the front row, smiling at me, my baby boy, Dean, in her lap, fidgeting and fussing and trying to get free.

I blew him a kiss, gave Kath a lingering, soft smile, beside myself to see the glow in her face, and turned back to the front where I walked, my eyes now on Elijah, who was standing front and center, also fidgeting, but not fussing, and not paying a lick of attention to me.

His eyes were behind me, looking over a sea of people in white chairs to a sea of tulips toward the lighthouse, a place I just left to take my trek with four other girls trailing me.

The place Verity would be walking out of shortly.

A place where he now lived with my niece, taking care of the lighthouse, taking care of his girl.

"*Daddy!*" Dean shrieked as I turned to walk across the flower-festooned arch to take my place at the front and await the rest of the wedding party.

My eyes moved to my son and then toward my husband.

Under a tent beyond the male half of the bridal party were two men, one at a shiny grand piano and another behind a cello.

They were playing a musical version of "A Thousand Years."

It had been the song Coert and I had danced to at our wedding, though that one had words.

The perfect words.

I saw the grin playing at Coert's mouth and I felt the same happening to mine.

I'd surprised him with the song. He'd never heard it before we'd danced to it. He wasn't exactly a *Twilight* fan whereas I had years of *Twilight* girls on my hands.

But as he'd danced with me, his eyes looking into mine, I knew he'd liked it.

I felt the girls start lining up beside me as I turned and saw Melanie and Ellie, with Janie trailing, walking down the aisle together, junior bridesmaids and the flower girl.

Janie was now a practiced hand at this. And of course she was doing beautifully tossing the creamy petals, most of which floated away on the sea breeze.

My eyes slid from Janie through the crowd and I saw Kim with her boyfriend Josh. They were both smiling at Janie, with Kim waving.

In front of them were Alyssa and Junior. Their brood was taking up a whole row. But Alyssa had her attention focused on her man, her head turned, her lips at his ear. Junior was facing forward but the expression on his face shared he was trying very hard not to laugh.

Junior, I'd learned, wore that expression often.

But most of the time, he just let himself laugh.

My gaze drifted, and a row in front of Alyssa and Junior sat Jake and Josie. Ethan sat next to his mom. He looked like he was doing something on his phone. Connor, Jake's son, was next to Jake and staring down at his fiancée, Sofie's lap, where their clasped hands were. Their wedding was scheduled for June, at Lavender House, where Jake had married Josie.

Amber couldn't come that day. She was at school in Paris.

But she'd be there for her brother's wedding.

Josie had her head on Jake's shoulder, and I couldn't see her full face because his chin was dipped down, hiding her, and with the way his head was turned, I could only catch his profile.

Even so, I could see her lips turned up in a soft smile at whatever Jake was saying.

My gaze drifted again and I caught Amy and Mickey two rows behind Alyssa and Junior's brood. Mick's son, Cillian, sat next to Amy, but the rest of their kids were away at school. To Amy's chagrin, but understanding considering they were California kids really just going back home, her son Auden was at USC and her daughter Pippa was at Stanford. Mickey's eldest, Aisling, had joined Verity at Yale.

For various reasons, including the festivities today, Verity had worked hard to graduate a semester early.

Mostly, she'd wanted tulips.

Amy was twisted almost fully to Mickey, her hand resting on his suit jacket under his shoulder. I only saw the back of her head but I had Mick full face, looking down at her with a gentle expression even if a huge smile was on his mouth.

I felt my hand taken and looked down to see Janie there, her eyes shining up at me almost as brilliant as her smile.

"You did good, baby," I whispered.

"Thanks, Cady," she whispered back.

Then she leaned into my legs and turned her attention to the aisle in order to catch Verity.

My eyes moved too, and I saw Walt and Amanda. Rob and Trish. Jackie. Paige. Mike, Pam and Riley, Daly, Shannon and Corbin (Bea was in line in front of the arch beside me).

And of course, the mother of the bride, Kath, sitting at the front (Dexter was amongst the men in Elijah's line, and yes, as suspected, he too had joined his sister at Yale).

Finally, I looked toward the back, not wanting to miss Verity walking from the lighthouse.

And the time was getting close.

Doing so, my gaze caught on my brother in the last row.

His eyes were on me.

I smiled at him.

His face got soft.

Then Camilla stood up excitedly at his side, Orson popped up on his other side, and Caylen gave me a wry smile before he stood too.

The wry was self-deprecating.

His children appreciated having a huge family, aunts and uncles and cousins.

And even if it came in a delayed fashion, they'd learned the hard way the important things about life, so they appreciated their father more for giving it to them.

I just appreciated having Caylen in my life.

We still weren't close.

But we were now, finally, a family.

All of them standing could mean only one thing and my attention darted to the lighthouse.

The lace of her gown floating in the breeze, a huge bouquet of flowers in front of her little baby-bump belly (we were wedding twins in more than just using "A Thousand Years," Verity was five and a half months pregnant), Verity walked next to her dad, a radiant smile beaming from her lips, her veil lifted high with the wind, her focus riveted in the direction of where her feet were carrying her down the path toward her future.

Her forever.

Her Elijah.

The strains of the cello drifted on the breeze, punctuated by the chords of the piano, as the sea crashed against the rocks behind us and the lighthouse stood tall and strong before us.

Verity finally made the first row and my son shouted, "*Verry!*"

He loved his cousin Verry.

Then again, Dean was as sweet and social as his older sister so he just loved everybody.

Verity's body shook with a little giggle.

She loved her cousin Dean too.

But she didn't tear her eyes from Elijah.

Tears hovered in my own.

And it was then I watched something play out that seemed to happen to me forever ago at the same time it was just yesterday, when Patrick Moreland, Jr. gave away a woman he adored to a man he trusted and loved.

I felt the wispy tulle of my strapless taupe dress glide along my legs, the breeze kissing my bare shoulders along with a cool spring sun, the gentle wind making Verity's veil take flight and the tulips around us wave and bob like they were doing a dance.

And finally my eyes moved back to my husband.

That moment wasn't lost on him and I knew it by the way he was gazing at me.

"Love you," I mouthed.

He lifted his chin and mouthed back, "Most."

Reverend Fletcher started speaking and Coert and I turned our attention to the happy couple.

My mind was on them.

But my mind was also on something else.

Patrick got his wish.

My husband, family and friends, happy and healthy, *all* of them, Caylen and his children right there, at the lighthouse, with me.

My version of a happy ending.

And I got my wish.

Verity and Elijah happy, getting married, making a family.

And I got my little boy.

Coert also got his wish.

Our Dean had my green eyes.

But Coert was getting another wish too.

The baby I carried was a girl.

I just hoped she had his hazel.

But I wouldn't care either way.

The End

77958774R00333

Made in the USA
Middletown, DE
28 June 2018